THE EXORCIST AND THE DEMON HUNTER

BY AMY KUIVALAINEN

THE MAGICIANS OF VENICE
The Immortal City
The Sea of the Dead
The King's Seal

THE FIREBIRD FAERIE TALES
Cry of the Firebird
Ashes of the Firebird
Rise of the Firebird

AMY KUIVALAINEN

THE EXORCIST

AND THE DEMON HUNTER

A NOVEL

bhc press™

Livonia, Michigan

THE EXORCIST AND THE DEMON HUNTER

Published by BHC Press

Library of Congress Control Number: 2022941260

ISBN: 978-1-64397-352-4 (Hardcover)
ISBN: 978-1-64397-353-1 (Softcover)
ISBN: 978-1-64397-354-8 (Ebook)

For information, write:
BHC Press
885 Penniman #5505
Plymouth, MI 48170

Visit the publisher:
www.bhcpress.com

For my mother, because it's her favorite.

THE EXORCIST AND THE DEMON HUNTER

In the beginning, there was a girl who walked with angels…
The devils were never far behind her.

PART ONE
THE EXORCIST
OF ESSENDON SQUARE

1

THE HOUSE WAS A redbrick, Victorian-era cottage in North Melbourne lit up prettily from the inside. It had a well-trimmed hedge, and a wrought iron fence painted dark green. If it weren't for the waves of menace radiating from its civilized front yard, I would've doubted that anything evil or malicious was going down inside. I rang the doorbell, wondering if I was about to make an idiotic mistake.

The woman who answered was in her late fifties and plump. She was the sister of the pastor of my dad's church, and I knew looking at her worried expression that she was *way* out of her Pentecostal comfort zone.

Yep, this was feeling more and more like a mistake.

"Jael, thank you for coming," Linda said, going in for a hug as I stepped back, but she grabbed me anyway. She had rung my mobile an hour beforehand, claiming her son was possessed by a demon. I had done my usual exorcist duty and asked her the standard questions: how had his behavior changed, did he have a history of mental illness, and had he been to a doctor or a shrink.

Some people will blame anything peculiar on demons or curses, but sometimes mental illness is just mental illness. If it weren't for my nagging intuition, I would've hung up on her. Right now it wasn't so much intuition as a psychic slap in the face that demanded I go away, that I had no business being here, that I should walk away.

"How is he?" I asked.

"He's been irritable and abusive. The language, Jael. My Maxy would never speak in such a way," she insisted. "Will you please just talk to him? I know I sound crazy, but he's so different, so angry."

"It's okay, Linda. I'm comfortable with crazy," I said, trying to reassure her, "but I'm going to need you to leave the house."

"What? Why? I need to be here for him…"

"Right now you're going to be more of a hindrance than a help. If you are right and we are dealing with demonic activity, it's best that you aren't around." She was hesitating for too long, so I added, "You are putting yourself and me in danger. I can't do what I need to do if I'm concerned about your safety. You don't want to see this, Linda. Trust me, trust in God, and go get a coffee somewhere. I'll call you when it's over."

"If you think it's best…"

"If you think I'm going to take a step inside with you still here, you're wrong," I said, my patience vanishing. "Either you go, or I do."

"Okay, Jael. Okay. I'll go to Sally's house around the corner, we can go for coffee and pray for you," Linda said, caving in.

"Pray for Max," I said, stepping through the front door. "I'm going to be just fine."

The inside of the house was as neat and restored as the outside, with warm cream walls and tasteful furniture. Linda said her adult son lived alone, but I couldn't imagine a man keeping the place so neat and clean. I trod down the hallway to the kitchen at the back of the house, the tightening in my gut leading the way.

A man with curly brown hair sat on the tiled floor in front of the pantry eating flour from a tub. *Okay. So it's going to be a weird one.*

"Hey, Max, you hungry or something?" I asked. He looked up from the tub and growled. "Oh, don't worry. I've already eaten tonight."

"What are you doing in my house?" he asked threateningly.

"Linda invited me over to hang out with you for a bit," I said, sitting down on a barstool. "She thought you might need the company."

"I do not want the company."

"I'm not that bad! But I can see you are struggling a bit. Don't worry. I'm not going to judge; I get moody and want to be left alone when I have an existential crisis as well."

Watching Max eat his flour made me want to call my dad, to convince him once and for all that I wasn't a nutjob. Like many good Christians, he held the misguided belief that they couldn't get possessed. For if God was in us, how could the two tolerate each other in a human body? While it was true that demons couldn't live within our spirits, they could definitely hang on to our emotions, body, and will. The mystery of why it was tolerated was just that. A mystery. It was my opinion that Christians had become lazy when it came to this particularly messy side of the belief business.

"Jael, murderer, murderer," Max said with unexpected malice.

"That's me," I replied calmly. "What's your name? Your *real* name."

"I am Chashak, the darkness that lingers in the corners of your mind, where fear dwells." He crawled slowly across the floor and up to the kitchen counter where I was sitting. His face started to change, and I saw the beast that was riding him.

"Hello, ugly." I smiled viciously, feeling the old rage come back and work its way through me.

"Little exorcist, you don't have the strength to take us on. You've never been strong enough. Are you going to tie us up? He might like that, not a lot of experience with girls this one." It chuckled. "His flesh is so well-maintained. So soft, so sweet."

I rolled my eyes. "Dull." I whispered the prayer in my mind, feeling a calmness come over me. "I command you to be still in that body." The hands that reached out for me stalled in midair.

"Tricks have you." It chuckled. "I have those too."

Before I could speak, I was picked up by an invisible hand and tossed against the wall.

"Telekinetic. Great," I muttered, my side burning.

"Come out and face me, exorcist! Release me, or I'll make it worse for you. So, so much worse. I'll peel skin from bone and drink your blood."

The windows around the room smashed one by one as I crawled flat along the floor, hidden behind couches and furniture. Before it could spot me, I was behind it, hands gripping Max's head.

"Lord, release your fire and burn up the works of the darkness." I held on as it squealed and hissed. "This man doesn't belong to you, so stop tormenting the poor bastard."

"The master has found them, and they are waking, Jael Quinlan," it said, snarling. "They will remake the world, and we will feast on your bones. Your precious Uriel and his angels will burn."

"Have a nice trip down," I said sweetly, and then it was gone with a departing shriek of profanity. I caught Max as he collapsed, coughing up chunks of floury saliva.

"It's okay, Max. Breathe buddy, just breathe." I got some paper towels and wet them, placing one on the back of his neck and passing him the other to wipe his face.

"Who are you?" he asked, his big chocolate-brown eyes wide with shock.

"My name is Jael and you, Max, are going to be just fine. Have a shower, get some rest. Get Linda to make you a few healthy meals to set you right again. Possession takes a toll on the body."

"Possession?" His voice was so small that I knelt down beside him. I try not to coddle, but there was something so vulnerable about him I couldn't help it.

"Yeah, a big one had you, but that's not what you need to focus on right now." I put my hand on his shoulder. "You were strong enough to beat it; you're free. That's the only thing that matters."

Those beautiful puppy eyes filled with tears. "Thank you, Jael."

"No worries, Max. You take it easy."

I got up and messaged Linda, making sure she was back before I left. Coming out of possession can really mess a person up, and Max was going to need his mom to fuss over him a bit.

Linda wanted to hug me again, but I held up a warning hand. "Don't...I'm hurt." My side was going to bruise from ankle to neck, and it was already killing me.

"Are you going to be okay getting home?"

"I'm fine. Go take care of Max. Make sure he has a lot of water in the next few hours."

"Are you sure? I bumped into your dad when I was down the café strip with Sally. He was having some dinner. I can call him I'm sure—"

"Back off, Linda," I said, a little too sharp. "I said I'm fine. Go and see your son."

I was down the path and out the gate before she could say another word. Or before I could. To say that I had a complicated relationship with my father, Lewis, was only the tip of an angry iceberg. I should've known better than to answer the phone when it rang, but the demon's warning was already getting to me, and I was itching for a fight.

"Father." I answered the phone as calmly as I could.

"Jael? Where are you?" he asked instead of saying hello.

"I'm almost home," I lied, shuffling along the street to the nearest tram stop.

"I just saw Linda in the café, and she told me that you were doing an exorcism on her son. Tell me this isn't true, Jael."

"Linda wouldn't lie. You know that."

"How could you embarrass me like this? Did you take money from her? Because if you did, I demand you pay it back."

"I don't take money for exorcisms," I replied coldly.

"You are still tricking people, Jael! Didn't you put your mother and me through enough of this as a child? You're over thirty. It's time you—"

I hung up.

Three days later I was still hurting and fuming about the whole encounter. It was a quiet Saturday night as I sat on the concrete railing of my building's roof, sipping tequila, and watching the lights of Essendon Square flash beneath me. I lived in the upper half of a weirdly triangular building situated on a roundabout and tram stop that's dangerously busy. Most people would hate the noise at all hours of the day and night, but I found it grounding, something I sorely need-ed some days. Mr. Wu, the landlord, only charged me $150 a week on account of the demon I chased out of the building for him. The huge, busted clock face on my balcony still refused to work, leaving its hands stubbornly fixed at one o'clock. Mr. Wu thought it was a small price to pay to keep his restaurant and his wife's massage parlor free from the power shenanigans they had going on be-fore they called me. I'm positive he still thinks I've trapped a demon inside of it.

A cold breeze crept up under my jacket and tickled my hair, bringing mist into the square from the city. If I shut my eyes and cleared my mind, I could hear whispers on the wind…

"Nope! Not listening," I shouted. The crow on the power line looked at me, sharpened its beak threateningly, and flew to the other side of the square. I'm a bit of a loner for a reason, mainly because I can't handle too much of the every-day drama that comes with people.

As I sipped my drink, I felt a fleeting moment of contentment before the phone in my pocket started buzzing. I pulled it out, glanced at the screen, and winced. My mom, Heather, had her meditation group tonight, and without fail, she'd call me to tell me about it. I didn't mind so much, but I was trying to re-lax. Mom and her "Crystal Cassandras" tended to rev me up far more than they should.

"Hey, Mom, what's up?" I asked before taking a large mouthful of my drink. Something told me I'd need it.

"Jael? I've just had a vision. Billie and Joanne are here too, and they both felt the power of it. There's a dark energy building up in the city." Heather's voice was high and excited, and I couldn't help but wonder if she'd finished her session with a few wines.

"Sounds intense," I replied, chewing on my thumbnail.

"Darling, please take this seriously. It was terrifying."

"I am, I am."

"What's wrong? You sound tired."

"I *am* tired. It's ten o'clock, and I'm beat from my last job. I need some days off." Understatement. I needed a month off at least after dealing with that. Exorcisms, like magic, always came with a price. Wanting to crawl into a hole and cry was my current price for helping Max.

"Was it…difficult?" she asked tactfully. A New Ager mother with an exorcist daughter wasn't always an easy situation to deal with, but we tried to support each other's spiritual growth the best we could even when we thought the other was cracked.

"You could say that. I stupidly took a gig with a person from Dad's church, and he didn't take it well. At least he's stopped carrying on about his thirty-two-year-old daughter still being single." I laughed bitterly.

"Jesus, that *was* stupid of you. Your father is such a misogynistic jerk sometimes. You don't need a man; you're an enlightened, empowered woman," she said saucily, and I could almost see her snapping her fingers. "And you know how he feels about your abilities."

"Abilities" was their safe word for what I did. They had been divorced twenty years, and they were still creepily alike at times.

"I don't want to talk about it." I shut her down, knowing if I tried to explain it would end in yet another passive-aggressive argument.

"Okay, so we won't talk about it. You don't think whatever problem you had with it was because of the dark aura over the city?" she asked, clearly still talking about it.

"I dunno, maybe? My psychic shields are up pretty tight right now because I'm not feeling so great. I'll check it out when I'm feeling more stable."

"I understand, but please watch yourself, Jael." She sighed the long-suffering sigh of a mother who hadn't understood her daughter in years. "I know you don't always listen to me about this kind of thing because you prefer your patriarchal Hebrew God, but this darkness I saw…it was circling you like you were the eye of the storm."

I fought the urge to groan. "I'll be fine, Heather. I always am."

"Well then, let's hope your guardian angel is wrapping you under his wings and covering you with his healing white light to keep the darkness off you. I love you, honey."

"Love you too. Bye Mom." I hung up quickly as I struggled not to snort tequila up my nose while laughing. If she only *knew* who my guardian angel was. There was no way in hell he'd wrap me in his white light. I grinned stupidly at the silent night, just trying to imagine it.

I woke the following morning to a buzzing phone and dog breath. I picked the phone up without looking at the screen and tossed it at the dirty clothes basket on the other side of my room before giving the owner of the dog breath a haphazard pat.

"Go back to sleep, Meta. It's not wake-up time yet," I muttered into my pillow. Despite my flippancy, Heather's warning the night before had gotten under my skin, and with the week I'd had…let's say it was enough to keep me awake and restless a lot longer than I would've liked.

Before I could doze off again, a wet nose was pushed into my face. I cracked an eye and saw the innocently hopeful expression on my German Shepherd's face.

"You think it's breakfast time already? It's barely morning." Meta's paw landed on the bed as a warning, and I knew I was one leap away from a forty-kilo ball of dog fur on top of me.

"You're such a shit," I muttered, pulling myself out of bed and stumbling to the kitchen. The big idiot could barely contain his excitement as I tipped a cup full of kibble into a stainless-steel bowl engraved with METATRON.

As you could probably guess, my guardian archangel approved of that as much as he would of Heather's suggestion of bathing me in his white light.

"I'm going to pretend to be normal for the next week, Meta," I told him as I made myself a coffee. "What do normal people do on a Sunday morning before ten?"

My dad's offer of attending church hung about my head like an annoying mozzie. Yeah, no way that was going to happen after my last call.

He had always been reluctant to show support for my choice of work. He hated that I refused to let myself be locked into any one church and that I wasn't married with a bunch of kids. I thought about the call. His words dug their hooks into me, whispering that I was a fraud in his voice. Voices of doubt are common, but mine always sounded like him. I told them to shut up.

It's a common misconception that all exorcisms are violent, wall climbing, and spit worthy in nature. But every now and again if a demon or spirit is particularly stubborn, it will fight back. I'd been telekinetically pushed backward into a wall for the first time, but that wasn't what had me so shaken.

It was when it started calling me by name. *The master has found them, and they are waking, Jael Quinlan. They will remake the world, and we will feast on your bones. Your precious Uriel and his angels will burn.*

Three days later I could still hear its voice in my head, my bruised hip and aching shoulder a constant reminder of the threat. It wasn't like demons hadn't talked to me before, and clearly, it didn't know Uriel if they thought he was "my precious" or in any way flammable.

Metatron's warm, soft muzzle bumped into my hand, bringing me out of my head. Animals are good like that, and he was the most sensitive pet I'd ever had. Often I didn't even realize how upset I was until he tried to comfort me.

I opened my fridge and groaned. "Looks like normal people do grocery shopping on Sunday, dog."

As it turned out, only stupid people went grocery shopping on a Sunday. Standing outside of Queen Victoria Market, I wondered what compelled me to bother. Oh right, trying to be normal. Normal day, doing normal things. I'd turned my phone off and refused to check for any messages.

"How're things, Clair?" I asked the homeless woman who was sitting outside with her little dog. Clair had been a regular at the market for years, and being a sucker for anything four-legged, I had gotten to know her and Champ the Jack Russell.

"Bad vibes around," Clair said, accepting the handful of coins I gave her. "You know Crazy Bill who usually hangs about outside the Maccas? He started screaming about the voices in the mist last night and walked straight into traffic."

"*Shit.* Poor Crazy Bill." I shook my head in sympathy. The guy hadn't had any demons, I'd checked. He just found playing crazy got him more sympathy. That he'd heard voices for real wasn't a good sign. Maybe I should've paid more attention to Heather's warnings.

"You make sure you take care of yourself and Champ, okay? Maybe try and get yourself into one of the shelters a few nights a week until things settle down."

"Hear a new one is opening soon. Might check it out," she answered non-committally. She tried her best to stay away from others. She wanted to be left alone more than anything. "You watch your back too, Jael. The bad vibe will find you."

"Will do."

I carried my bags over to the tram stop and managed to get a spot in the shade. Even in the middle of autumn, my fair skin tended to burn without the slightest encouragement.

"They are all going to die," a voice said beside me.

"What?"

A teenage girl with springy brown hair and olive skin was looking at me intensely. She had a sheen of sweat on her skin, and she smiled manically.

"You won't be able to stop what's coming, Jael Quinlan. You should do the world a favor and just kill yourself." She laughed as she backed up to the edge of the platform. I dropped my psychic shields and tried to see what was controlling her, but it was a strange blur, unlike anything I'd seen before. Usually, I could see and feel the shape of a demon under someone's skin, but this was something…new.

"How about you let the girl go, and we can talk about this like big kids?" I asked as I stepped toward her, my hands already burning. *I just need to get close enough to touch her.*

"You are already too late, little exorcist."

I lunged for her just as she turned and jumped in front of the number 19 tram. Screams erupted around me, and I stared in horror at the red smearing the concrete platform. I fumbled for my phone and switched it on. I had seven missed calls and twelve messages from Hunt. I swore viciously and hit the redial button.

"Jael! Where the fuck have you been? I've been trying to reach you since last night."

"We can argue about it later," I said numbly. "I need you to get your ass down to Queen Vic. A girl has just suicided."

Sergeant James Hunt was the product of a white German father and an Indigenous Australian mother which had left him genetically blessed with pale green eyes, brown skin, and curly dark hair. If I was drunk enough, I could admit he was a hottie but never to his face.

The first time I'd seen him, he'd been filled with the terror of the Kurdaitcha man whose spirit had been haunting him. The curse was a present from his mother's tribe in Queensland who hadn't approved of the Elder's daughter running off with a white guy. I helped him get rid of it, and we've been mates ever since. James sometimes called me if something seemed supernaturally off about a case.

"Hey J, how's your mom?" he asked as he joined me where I stood in front of the gift shop, away from the press of coppers and guys from emergency services. He pushed his sunglasses on top of his head and fixed me with those big green eyes.

"She's still wanting to know when you are going to come around so she can align your chakras," I answered suggestively.

"It's been a while. I might just take her up on it."

"That's just gross, dude."

"Why? With all that yoga she does your mom is fit," he said just to annoy me before he got serious. "Are you okay?"

"Hell no. This is messed up. I tried to stop her," I folded my arms so I didn't hug myself. "I couldn't reach her in time."

"It's not your fault, J." He looked back to where they were putting what remained of the body into an ambulance. "This is the second jumper in twelve hours. That's why I've been trying to call."

"I'm sorry. My phone was off. I've been trying to have a few days of peace and quiet. Who was the first jumper?"

"A professor jumped in front of a train at Alma Street. If the dead girl's learner license is right, then she was his daughter."

I groaned. "Damn it. You better get someone over to their house to check on the mother if there is one. I hope it's not some weird family suicide thing."

"You think it might be *your* kind of thing?" he asked tactfully.

I thought about the demon riding the dead girl, the threats and the way it had called me by name. When I looked up to answer, I saw a flash of pale gray and platinum. A pissed off angel was standing near the steps to the men's toilets staring at me. I fought to keep my face neutral.

"Yeah, I'm definite it is. I don't know what it means, that's all."

"I'm going to go and talk to some of the people the professor worked with. Maybe go check out the synagogue in Coburg to see if anyone knows something. I know you're friends with Rabbi Josef, so you can come if you want."

Friends was a great big stretch, and James knew it. The rabbi and I butted heads almost as much as I did with every other man in religious authority.

"Nice try, Hunt, but I'll pass."

"I know that look," he said soft enough for no one around us to overhear. "What are you seeing, Jael?"

"It's nothing. I've got to go home. Meta is probably pissing on my bed as we speak."

"Or humping your pillows."

"Or that. Watch yourself, okay? Something…something weird is happening in the city."

2

I MANAGED TO CAB it home while keeping myself together. The strain and weight of my shopping bags kept my mind focused as I walked up the back stairs and opened the door. Metatron was waiting, tail wagging and purposely stopping in front of me as I tried to walk.

"Get out of the way, you fat idiot." I cursed as I dumped my bags on the small counter of my kitchenette and tried to breathe. Meta's head cocked questioningly at me as I sunk to the timber floorboards and burst into tears.

I'd seen some messed up things in my thirty-two years. I've pulled addicts out of crack houses, seen the results of the most violent domestic abuses, visited murder scenes with James…but today had taken the cake. No one had ever suicided right in front of me before. Despite the words coming out of the girl's mouth, I'd seen a flicker of panic and defeat in her eyes before whatever was riding her threw her into the tram.

It didn't make sense! Demons *wanted* bodies of their own; they wouldn't willingly destroy one. *Unless it wasn't a demon,* a small, unwelcome voice said in the back of my mind.

I rested my head on my knees and sobbed. If I could have only reached her quicker…Meta lay down next to me, his warm body pressing in to comfort me, and I dropped a hand to pet him. A crushing weight squeezed in my chest, and I pushed my other hand into my sternum to try and relieve it.

"Elyon," I whispered. *"Elyon."* I focused on the name, repeating it, trying to use it to clear my mind.

Elyon, Most High, was one of the many names of the Hebrew God, and it was the one name that resonated with me. I found "God" to be too small of a word, the same way I preferred the Hebrew name Yeshua to Jesus. "Jesus" evoked too many images of the skinny, crucified white boy that the Catholics favored in all of their artwork, not the brawny, brown, Jewish carpenter that he would've been.

I was big on centering prayer and meditation and had picked Elyon as the word to use as my anchor, so when my emotions were really messed up, it would calm me down.

"Elyon," I repeated, fighting hard not to groan in pain and frustration. *What is the point of having this gift if I can't save people?*

My phone buzzed, and I reached for it, answering without looking at the screen.

"Hey, you are coming over tonight," an insistent female voice said on the other end of the line. My mate Star rarely used her "mom voice" on me.

"Heather or James?" I asked, trying to make my voice sound as normal as possible.

"Both."

"Shitty loudmouths."

"Yep. Heather rang me this morning about her vision, and James messaged me a few minutes ago to check in on you. I'm so sorry, J. That's totally messed up," Star said, her voice breaking just a little. The empath in her churned with sadness and pity.

"Yeah, it is. It's been a really rubbish week."

"I figured, so I'm cooking lasagna, and you are coming over. Bring Meta."

"Okay, I'll see you soon."

The unfortunately named Starbreeze Lucille Fitzgerald-Mason lived four blocks from my place in a restored brick house with her control-freak older sister Violet Dewdrop. Offspring of two hippies, they had both ended up being curiously straitlaced and stable. Violet especially had turned her back against her parents' "tree-loving ways" and had opened a chain of real estate agencies that she ran with almost military precision.

Star was a touch more artistic and had studied to become an accomplished hairstylist before deciding she wanted to be able to deal with women's insecurities in another way and had gone back to uni to study psychology. As someone who could only handle being an office temp on and off, I was ridiculously impressed with both of them.

Metatron and I had dawdled our way to Star's place, enjoying the afternoon sunlight, and I let him have free rein to sniff and piss to his heart's content. As I opened the cream-painted gate, we were greeted by the excited woofs of a fat Staffordshire bull terrier. Meta's ears went up, and his tail started wagging excitedly. I shut the gate, and the front door opened. Jung barreled down the steps, crashing into Metatron, and they bolted around the yard chasing each other. Star came outside and went to hug me, but I held up a warning hand.

"Don't, or I'll start crying again," I said, and she stopped. She was the only person to ever respect my boundaries.

"Come on then," she replied, heading back to the front door.

Inside smelled like warm melting cheese and the fancy vanilla-and-rose scented candles Violet liked. Star had poured us both glasses of red wine, and we sat down at the kitchen table.

"So, you want to talk about today?"

"In a bit," I mumbled, sipping my wine and wishing I could turn it into tequila. That was a miracle I could really get behind.

"How about you fill me in on your regrowth situation?" Star frowned at my hair, ever the hairdresser. Her hair was a brilliant wave of purples, greens, and blues. With her dark Mediterranean skin, I couldn't help teasing her about her sexy mermaid aesthetic. She was the only person I'd seen who could pull the look off. Star was kind of like that; she could wear pretty much what she wanted and look amazing. I stuck to jeans, Doc Martens, and T-shirts unless I was working in an office.

"Dude, really? You're gonna have a crack at my hair? I've been run off my feet lately."

"It's okay, Jael. You can sit there, and I'll sort it." She got back to her feet and kissed my head on her way past. "A cut and color will help you feel better."

I knew there was no point in arguing, so I sat there listening to her studying woes as she mixed color and arranged the scissors and combs. I had been a few different colors, but the gingery red that she put in the last time had faded weeks ago. I tended to just sit there and let her surprise me with whatever color she chose.

As she knew I would, I started telling Star about puppy-eyed Max, the demon who had thrown me against the wall, and Lewis's reaction.

"You would think he would be all 'Praise Jesus!' for your mad demon-banishing skills," Star muttered as she started to section and clip my hair.

"He doesn't get that sort of spiritual side of things. I think it freaks him out. He likes to go to church, talk to people, and try to be a good person, but anything beyond that...I dunno."

"The way he reacted sounds like he was more embarrassed that you would maybe fail. It's like he doesn't know you at all."

"He was worried that I would make people look at him differently. I don't know why it upset me, to be honest. I stopped trying to get his approval on anything a long time ago. I can't have a conversation with him without it resulting in questions of why I won't pick a church or a husband."

Star snorted. "As if a regular dude could handle everything you are. It would take someone like you to even try to understand your life."

She was right, but I still felt the sharp pang of past failures. I had sought to have a normal boyfriend twice. I hadn't told them what I could do and even turned my back on my abilities a few times to attempt to have a normal life, but both relationships had been epic disasters. I was better off on my own, and if I was honest, I was happiest that way. I couldn't be the girlfriend and the exorcist. I could barely be the friend and the exorcist most days.

James knew I was legit because he'd experienced it. Star knew I was legit because she was spiritual and had experiences of her own. I'd met her at Heather's store when Star was there to pick up her mom, Billie, and we'd become mates after exchanging mutually embarrassing stories about our hippie parents. Star accessed the divine in a very different way than mine, but we could find enough common ground to share dreams and meditations. She was empathic and intuitive to the point of being creepy.

I ended up telling her about the tram stop as she washed the dye out of my hair, so she couldn't discern my tears from the water.

"That's proper messed up," she said as she wrapped my hair in a towel and led me back to the kitchen table. She refilled our glasses of wine and took a big drink before asking, "Was *he* there?" *He* being Uriel.

"Yeah, he was. He was so clear I'm surprised everyone around us didn't see him," I admitted. Star had been the only person who I'd told about the angel that had taught me to fight demons.

"You said you had your shields up tight."

"This was different. It wasn't like a Behinds thing," I said as I dried my hair.

"Behinds" was our mutual slang for the spiritual realm, the world that sat behind this one. Some people describe it as seeing with their Third Eye. For me it was like seeing through my spirit eyes, my eyes behind my eyes.

As I said, not the easiest thing to explain unless you experience it yourself. I could shut my Behind eyes, lift the shields so nothing could batter me, and I could be present. But if I was tired or emotional, both sets of eyes tended to overwhelm me if I wasn't careful.

"Maybe he was worried about you," Star said thoughtfully as she combed my hair and picked up her scissors.

I sighed. "Maybe something big is going on. I doubt Uriel would've been there just for me."

"He's your guardian for a reason. I can feel my guides sometimes when I'm upset."

"You know we don't have that kind of relationship," I said. Guides and their interference were something we didn't fully see eye to eye on, so I changed the subject. "Mom told me that she hopes he's surrounding me with his white light."

"Why does that sound dirty coming out of your mouth?"

"I think it's your brain that's dirty and not my mouth, Starshine," I said with a grin. "I thought it was hilarious because Mom thinks all angels are the placid, winged white dudes in Jesus robes."

"Be patient with her. She's on her own path," Star reminded me. Some days I think I needed to write that on a sticky note and place it on my fridge. Or tattoo it on my arm.

"We should see what the unicorns have to say," Star said, a few hours later. I groaned loudly as she shuffled a deck of cards. They weren't tarot cards, instead they were cards with lovely illustrations of dubious advice given by extinct mythical creatures. I closed my eyes and readied myself for abuse as I pulled a card and handed it to her.

"Pay attention to your dreams," Star read out loud. "Dreams can show us truths that we can't face during the day so look for hidden messages."

"Great. Thanks for nothing, horn heads." I glared at the smug white animal in the picture. "With advice like that it's no wonder you're extinct."

"At least you didn't pull the daddy issues card," Star said with a smirk.

"You and your unicorns can go bite my ass."

I ended up leaving Star's several hours later with a sleek silver-gray bob cut that I'd never make look as good again and a stomach full of wine and lasagna. Meta was exhausted from playing with Jung, and I was ready for a shower and a night of sleep. Some people would be nervous walking through the backstreets of Essendon in the middle of the night, but I found a jet-black German Shepherd tended to dissuade any people I met.

I let Meta into the flat and was about to switch on a light when I saw the figure standing on my balcony underneath the clock face. He had his back to me, but I'd recognize that broad silhouette and sheen of snowy hair anywhere. Uriel was here.

3

Fifteen Years Earlier

MY MOUTH TASTED OF cotton balls and dead things as I tongued the air. *Damn, what did I do last night?*

"What the…" I muttered as I opened my eyes and groaned loudly. That's when I realized I was in a cell of white painted blocks. The furniture was bolted to the ground, and the toilet had no seat. I wasn't going to enjoy that.

"Shit," I hissed between my teeth, as pain shot down my back.

"Miss Quinlan? You might want to go easy," a voice said, and I spotted brown eyes looking at me through the wire-shot window in the door.

"Where the hell am I?" I demanded. "What is this place?"

"You don't remember?" There was a high-pitched beep, and the door swung open, revealing a short woman in a doctor's coat.

"My name is Sara," she said in the calm tone parents use on hysterical toddlers. "What's the last thing you remember?"

Instead of a smart-ass reply, I shut my eyes and tried to think. *How did I end up in the hospital?*

Light, sweat, pain, laughter. A cacophony of dark whispers.

"I had a bad day at school. It was career day. I found it stupid," I said slowly. "What did you do to my back?"

Sara's eyebrows shot up. "You cut up your back, Jael. Your mother called the police because you locked yourself in the bathroom with a box cutter."

I shut my eyes again. *Blood, lights, pain.*

"Your mother said that you were screaming about getting the demon out," Sara said as a cold stillness built in me.

"You don't say." I grimaced as I reached under the back of my shirt and felt the patches.

"There are stitches, so be careful," Sara warned. "Do you have any questions?"

I looked up at her with the briefest flicker of hope. "Did I get it out? Is it gone?"

School had been shit, and I could feel my hitchhiker inside of me. If I shut my eyes, I could touch the back of my shoulders and feel its ghostly spines. I had tried to grab the tricky bastard to pull it out, but it hung on like a bloody cattle tick. That's when I'd lost it and got the box cutter.

They wouldn't tell me how long I needed to stay at the hospital. I paced and itched and muttered to myself, the walls heaving in around me.

They had asked if I wanted to see my mother before visiting hours closed. I didn't. She wouldn't come to the hospital and have her psychic vibes disturbed anyway. Hell, I had to bully her to go for a Pap smear every two years. She believed in herbs and crystals and natural healing now. My dad would leave me here. He'd always thought I was mad.

I sat back down on my bed in the dark and did the one thing that I'd been too afraid to do. With my eyes closed and my hand trembling, I reached behind me. For a second I wished with all of my might that I had simply imagined everything, but then I felt the ghostly curve of a sticky spine and shuddering laughter echoing through me.

If I dropped my guard and focused, sometimes I could see a projection of myself in my mind's eye. Mom called it an out-of-body experience or OBE. I called it a mind screw. When I did it, I could see the disgusting thing that had latched onto me.

The box cutter hadn't worked. I had scarred myself for life for nothing. Now I was locked up.

I brought my knees to my chest and sobbed. "Please, please go away. Leave me alone." The claws dug deeper. A song from childhood came into my head, a tune left over from before my religious father left and Mom had gone crazy.

"Jesus loves me..." I whispered through my frightened tears. We hadn't been back to church in five years. Heather found her new religion with the New Agers. No matter how hard she tried to crystal-cleanse the church out of me, some of it had stuck. I'd always felt *something* was out there, watching over me. I never had that moment of questioning if God was real, I just always believed he was. As a kid, it had been hard to explain, but my faith had always been like a second heartbeat. I definitely couldn't have told Heather, who had turned her back on anything to do with "that Hebrew God."

I kept singing the same line over and over in the dark, unable to remember the next one. Surprisingly the thing inside of me stopped laughing. The third time I sang it a pulse shot through me, and I gasped at the pain.

"It doesn't like that name," a deep voice said from the other side of my cell.

"Who are you?" I demanded. "How did you get in here?" I felt the thing inside of me shift as the man drew himself up to his full height. I spotted a shadow on the wall with the ghost of two wings stretching out behind him.

"Oh shit, I am going crazy," I whimpered, clutching my head.

"Possibly, but that's not the real problem here." The angel frowned, and he reminded me of a painting by William Blake I saw in art class. He was sharp angles, silver-haired, and glacier-eyed. Looking at him was like looking at an ice storm, a terrifying force of nature. Not even remotely human. I fought the urge to piss myself.

"You want to get rid of that thing?" he asked, his tone remarkably frustrated.

"Yes," I managed to say. As I said it, fear rushed through me, paralyzing me and pulling the air out of my lungs. It was fighting like hell to stay exactly where it was.

The angel placed a calloused hand on my head and whispered in a strange tongue that a part of me kind of understood.

When I was little, from around two years old, I used to talk to my imaginary friends in a secret language. Heather, a hard-core Bible-basher at that stage, thought I had been speaking in tongues. Dad had taken me to a shrink who told them it was natural.

For some reason, that was the memory that came rushing back to me when the big freaking angel spoke to me. It wasn't until later that I learned my imaginary friends hadn't been so imaginary. It's one of those strange things that I can't really explain. It's kind of like a language only my spirit knows, and even though my ears hear gibberish, my heart knows what's being said. And now this make-believe language that I was told to forget was being spoken aloud. He told me later it was the Language of Angels.

Whatever he said had an effect because I felt something rip from me like a pus-soaked Band-Aid, and a filthy imp of a creature with long talons flopped off the bed. There was a shimmer of steel as the angel cleaved it in two, the sticky remains disintegrating. For the first time in months, my shoulders weren't aching, and my head was clear.

"You have the gift of True Sight," the angel said thoughtfully. His face remained unchanged as if he hadn't just killed a demon.

"Some freaking gift," I grumbled. "Who're you anyway?"

"My name is Uriel."

"Piss off," I retorted before I could check myself. "Seriously like *the* Uriel? Angel of the North?"

"I have many names."

"Okay." I exhaled slowly. "I'm Jael."

"Yes, I know." He smiled as we shook hands, but it wasn't what I would consider a warm smile. Warm smiles had to be earned. "Would you like to learn how to kill demons, Jael?"

My back twitched, and I thought about the months the little bastard had been tormenting me, whispering to me, keeping me awake, and slowly but surely driving me mad. How many others were out there, unsure of what was happening to them?

I grinned. "I'd like that a lot."

"Good. Because I've been charged with teaching you," he replied, and I could tell he had mixed feelings about it. *Same here, buddy. Unfortunately, it looks like we are stuck with each other.*

Exorcist wasn't on the guidance counselor's career form, but somehow I knew I was going to enjoy it.

4

I WAS SEVENTEEN WHEN I began this strange path of mine, and fifteen years later I had only seen Uriel manifest this robust and human a handful of times. Usually, when I met him, it was in the Behinds through prayer or meditation. But the most common way I met him was by sensation; I felt him there even if I couldn't see him. Seeing him like this, I realized the initial fear and awe and urge to piss myself hadn't faded with time.

He had no wings or armor, but there was no mistaking what he was by his presence alone. He was dressed in a gray split tunic, kind of like a samurai, with a plain, creamy undershirt, gray trousers, and boots. With his silvery, platinum braid, he looked like he could've been an Elvish God from Tolkien's imagination. If his elves were freaking scary and not elegantly aloof that is.

Despite how beautiful and ethereal he might seem, Uriel had an undeniable brawny warrior vibe about him. It was as if Elyon had made him the epitome of what a warrior might be. Crisscrossing scars covered the skin on his hands, and the V in his shirt revealed faint blue tattoos or markings. *What are they?*

I'm on the side of angels, true enough, but these angels aren't like the angels people typically think of. God wouldn't make brainless, slave-minded ninnies with white robes and fluffy wings. William Blake was closer to the truth. They are beautiful like cut glass, so sharp you don't feel the edge until you're bleeding.

Let me get one thing straight. Angels aren't happy, cuddly beings. They aren't perfect. They get angry. They know the kind of righteous fury that could burn worlds. And for all their powers, they still do the one thing that humans constantly fail to do—they obey. They surrender to their purpose, which is the hardest damn thing to do of all.

My tongue stuck to the roof of my mouth, but I forced myself to open the security door and join Uriel outside. Metatron instantly went to Uriel's side and lay dutifully at his feet without so much as a tail wag. Instinct overpowered him; he knew to submit to the dominant alpha in the room. I knew the feeling. My knees were having a tough time keeping me upright too, like my body knew it should be kneeling or bowing.

Instead, I forced a lazy smile on my face as I leaned against the concrete wall to keep myself from falling over.

"Hey boss," I said, managing to unstick my tongue. "I saw you at the market today, plain as day. I'm surprised everyone else didn't see you to be honest."

"I'm only seen by people who need to see me," he answered in his deep voice and recognition rolled through me. That voice I'd heard as a feral teenager, the one I knew almost as well as my own. "You have had a difficult week." He was watching me carefully, so I felt I had to say something.

"I have." I had a feeling this conversation was going far worse than either of us wanted.

The truth was I was relieved to see him like this, so real and solid. I wanted to run to him and let him hold me if only to feel safe for one freaking minute.

Uriel was not that kind of angel.

A few times, when I was a raging teen, he'd held my hand to comfort me. As an adult, I'd only felt his arms around me once, after my drink had been spiked and I was lying on my bathroom floor feeling like I was going to die. I knew how safe he could make me feel, and it was a weakness to want it after a bad day. Even if it was a *really* bad day.

"Why are you here?" I asked as I tried to hold his gray-blue eyes.

"You seemed…upset today. I needed to check that you are clearheaded and focused again. There is darkness settling in the city, but the source can shield itself from the angels."

"And you need me to figure it out because I'm your human agent, right?"

"Correct."

"I don't know whether to feel insulted or flattered."

"Why should you feel either?" he questioned. "This is what you have been trained for."

Damn. I'd forgotten what it was like to try to have a conversation with Uriel, although today he seemed put out and moody even for him.

"That girl today didn't have a demon in her," I said, the unsettled feeling growing in my stomach. "If it was a demon, it's like none I have ever seen before. I couldn't get any kind of read on it. It had no face or form."

"You might not have recognized it because you purposely cut yourself off from the spiritual world," Uriel replied in a tone that radiated disapproval. "If you hadn't, I might not have needed to be so obvious to get your attention."

"Back off," I snapped before I could stop myself. "I deserve a break from all of this sometimes."

"'All of this' is your destiny and your purpose."

"And that's all well and good, but what about all the *life* stuff that gets pushed aside while I'm on this mission? I still have to be human, pay bills and… and function."

"Cutting yourself off spiritually and emotionally isn't the answer."

"You know what? Sometimes it really, really is. I am *tired*, Uriel! I have a human body and a human mind, and I feel like both have been through a meat grinder right now."

I sounded like a petulant teenager, but I couldn't stop myself. All the frustration and anger of the week rushed back into me, breaking the temporary dam that Star had helped erect.

You were never strong enough, Jael Quinlan. I replayed in my mind what the girl had said, followed by the meaty thump and spray of gore flashing brightly in the sun. The memory overwhelmed me, and I couldn't breathe. Uriel caught me as I started to slip down the wall. We ended up on the concrete floor with me curled up in a knee-hugging ball with his arms about me. Knowing that I was a big enough mess for him to actually try to comfort me made me cry even harder.

"It was a horrible thing to see and experience, *yadid*," he said, pronouncing the strange Hebrew sounding word *yah-deed*. A part of me wondered if it meant "dumb shit," but I doubted it. "We need to find out why this happened, so the young one's death wasn't in vain."

When I didn't reply, he started speaking softly in the Language of Angels, and I shut my eyes and let the warmth of it roll through my body and comfort me. I don't know how long we sat there, but I was in a haze when Uriel lifted me up and carried me inside. A blanket came up over me, and calloused fingers brushed the hair from my face.

"Rest, Jael. Tomorrow is a new day, and it will need you," Uriel murmured.

That night, in my half-asleep, half-awake state, I had a vision of a mighty battle. Uriel and three others stood on a desert plain, and before them stretched an army of giants. Amongst the giants there were other angels, terrifyingly beautiful, but something about them seemed…wrong.

Uriel stood next to a black-haired warrior who I instinctively recognized as Michael, the General of Heaven. Beside him stood the golden-haired Gabriel, silver shofar in hand, and the flame-haired Rafael. I wanted to rush to help them, to tell them to get out of the way of the trampling giants. But Gabriel's horn sounded, and terror paralyzed me, forcing me to my knees. The archangels unsheathed their weapons and became justice itself.

I'd never seen Uriel fight before, and I gripped the dirt as I watched him cut through the attacking enemy like they were stalks of dead wheat. The silver sword in his hand ran with gore, his armor and white hair smeared with red. *Uri'el*, literally, meant the Light of God. He was lightning, a blaze of white heat and death.

There are so many descriptions of fighting being like dancing. Whoever coined that phrase had never seen the raw, beautiful, murdersome rage of four pissed off archangels. They were…elemental. Wholesale destruction and death. It had only taken one of them to lay waste to the city of Sodom; the four of them fighting together as a single unit decimated the army before them.

I was crying, unable to look away from Uriel. This was who he was, who he *really* was, not the construct I had made of him in my own head. My pet guardian angel who made sure I didn't overdose on a spiked drink. It was too hard to fathom, to reconcile one with the other.

A hand rested on top of my head, and I was terrified to move to see who it was.

"Remember," a voice commanded from behind me. There was something about it that was so commanding and ethereal it was impossible. The vision faded, letting my mind run on to other dreams.

The important thing to remember when it comes to visions is that they don't always make sense at first, and it can take years to understand them. Any man who sees God will always have to face the reality of his own nothingness.

When I woke the next morning, I knew without a doubt I was being told to check my shit because bigger things were coming into play. Shit. Checked. It also was a strong reminder that Uriel was not just my special buddy, he was a freaking terrifying warrior of Elyon. Double check.

But as visions are prone to do, it also left me with a thousand burning questions. Was the battle I had seen past or future? Why was it being shown to me now? And what the hell was so important about me that I had one of the scariest archangels watching over me?

I sat down in the shower, thinking it over as I let the emotional hangover of yesterday wash off me. I wondered if I should text James and see if he had any luck trying to figure out why the family was suddenly possessed. I've seen that kind of thing happen before—generational curses and ancestral demons could be a real bitch to get rid of if they weren't appropriately dealt with, but I didn't think that was the problem. It was weird that both had decided to off themselves within twenty-four hours of each other. As I said, demons wouldn't cast off their shells so quickly. James said the guy had been a professor but in what field?

I thought about Uriel, trying to balance the killing machine with the one who had been so gentle with me the night before. He could be a rude, grumpy bastard but he'd always been patient with me, even when I'd run from my path during my early twenties.

There had been years that I hadn't seen him or been open enough to feel his presence. When I was twenty-five, I fell to my knees in surrender, weeping my apology to a God I'd turned my back on. Uriel had appeared and never held my rebellion against me. I'd been angry last night and said some stuff I hadn't really meant. No matter how bad the day was, I would never stop being an exorcist. I knew too much to give up and let the demons win.

The water ran cold, so I climbed out, pulled on a shirt and jeans, and ran a comb through my cropped hair. It was probably best that Star had cut it so short if I was going to be running about trying to figure out what the hell was going on in my city. I had just picked up my phone when there was a knock on my screen door.

"Good morning, Starshine!" I said in my best Wonka voice as I answered the door.

"One day I'm going to throat punch you, and you'll have no one to blame but yourself," Star replied as she came inside, her hands full of white paper bags. She dumped them on the bench and turned the jug on. "I figured you wouldn't have had breakfast yet."

"What time is it?"

"Lunchtime. James said he was trying to message you and then called me. I swear that guy is such a worrier sometimes."

"Or he was looking for an excuse to give you a call," I argued. They would be so good together and were so clearly into each other it was sickening, but both of them were holding back for some unknown reason.

"Or his friend saw a girl kill herself yesterday and he was worried like good friends should be," Star said, before putting tea bags in the cups and adding sugar to my *Constantine* mug. It had been her idea of a joke last Christmas, but I loved it like I'd loved the *Preacher* print she'd given me the year before that. "Although I have to admit, you are looking surprisingly better. Almost chipper."

"Must've been all that lasagna I ate last night."

"I don't think so." She pulled a face at me. "Out with it, Quinlan. What happened?"

Damn. She was good. I decided to be honest because Star was a human lie detector.

"Uriel was here when I got home. Like not a vision…he was *here* here. I could touch him and everything."

"You touched him!" she exclaimed, eyes wide. "Fuck, this is so *City of Angels* right now. Did he watch you take a bath or something?"

"It was *not* like *City of Angels*. Keep your Nicolas Cage fantasies out of it," I warned as my stupid face turned red. I took the cup from her. "If you had seen Uriel, you wouldn't even joke about that."

"I would probably joke more. Tell me everything."

"I yelled at him."

"Badass," she said, suitably impressed as she emptied the paper bags onto a dinner plate. She had brought croissants and Danishes. I could've kissed her with happiness as I tore one apart with my teeth, the sugary pastry goodness exploding in my mouth.

"It was yell at him or run away. He pitched me the same thing as Heather: darkness is in the city, and whatever it is, angel radar can't find it."

"So it's going to be a prizefight round." Star sighed and sat down at my small dining room table.

"It would seem so. I don't know how I'm meant to get to the bottom of it while keeping demons from jumping me." I fed the corner of a croissant to Meta. "I tried to tell Uriel I need to be able to pay my bills while on his super mission. I swear my recruiter is at her wit's end with me."

I had finished up a one-month contract with a small superannuation company on the previous Friday. I organized their filing system and stopped a secretary from killing her boss before leaving. I liked to keep contracts as short as possible; it meant that they never caught on to what was so strange about the new girl.

"A job is why I am here," Star said, pulling her phone from her pocket. "Well, apart from checking on you. Vi has a gig for you."

I took the phone from her and looked at the gorgeous two-story mansion in the photo. It was Victorian, brick, and badly in need of restoration. A prize house for a wealthy developer who could recover its former glory and sell it to some yuppies for a high price. I let out a low whistle. "Nice digs."

"Vi is trying to sell it but is having a hard time. It should be a piece of cake. The owners only bought it six months ago. They started repairs and then decided a sleek new apartment in the city would be a better option," Star explained. "They won't even go back to get the gear they left in the house."

"And Vi thinks it's my kind of thing? It sounds like they have too much money and couldn't be bothered to put the work in."

"Vi seems to think it's a haunting thing. The couple says they kept hearing old jazz records and seeing a dead woman in the main entrance. She's going to meet us there in two hours."

"Your sister is one of the least spiritual people I know. What if she's wrong?"

Star took the phone and flicked through it before passing it back. "She's not."

The pastry caught in my throat. There was a room scattered with the torn-up corpses of animals, and someone had been finger painting on the walls. The writing was messy, almost childish, but what it said was crystal clear. *JAEL QUINLAN, WE ARE COMING FOR YOU.*

5

STAR DROVE US THROUGH North Melbourne traffic in her dubiously sound Toyota Corolla. I was pissed. Demons had never liked me, but now they were calling me by name and leaving love notes like some bad slasher movie. The worst part about it was I was starting to feel like the dumb girl that walks outside in her pj's to see what the noise was and ends up eaten by zombies.

The front yard of the Victorian mansion was overgrown with dead rose-bushes, long grass, and a large gum tree that covered everything in sap and sticks. Violet was already waiting for us in the driveway looking like a cleaned-up, corporate version of Star. She wore a tan skirt and jacket that would've looked horrible on anyone else, but with her flawless olive skin and her hair in glossy GHD-styled ringlets, she somehow pulled it off. Her red lips barely cracked a smile when she saw us.

Violet was ambitious, driven in a way I couldn't imagine, and was incredibly successful for someone who had only just turned thirty-five. Unsurprisingly, Violet didn't like me. Oh, I was fine when she needed a house to be cleansed, but she didn't like me on account of me having a vague job description and seemingly no ambition or tangible future plans. Apparently "following my higher calling" didn't count as a career path. She loved Star more than anyone else in the world, which is why I was always respectful to her. She'd been more than happy to pay for her sister's ongoing education and allowed her to live rent-free with the condition she got good marks and cleaned up the house. We kept it professional on account of our mutual love of Star.

"You're late," Violet said, not looking up as she tapped an email out on her phone, her heavy gold bracelets clinking against each other.

"A tram broke down, and we had to wait for it to be shifted," Star replied as an apology. She had a frowning contest with Violet, who eventually sighed with defeat.

"Well, you could've called. How long are you going to need, Quinlan?" she asked briskly. "I want to get a house cleaner in at three to sort out the animals, and I want to show a couple through at five."

"Cancel all of it," I said, looking up at the crumbling stone facade. I could already feel the heaviness in the air; the cruelty rolled over me and my intuition started sending up red flags.

"But—"

"Just do it, Vi," Star snapped, obviously picking up on the seriousness in my voice. "Make it tomorrow morning. You can't rush what Jael does. It's craftsmanship. It takes time. You want to sell this dump or not?"

Good old Star. I could always count on her to step in.

"Do you want me to come with you?" she asked me, her frown deepening.

I shook my head. "Hell no. Stay here and keep Violet from breaking her heel when she starts stamping her foot impatiently."

"Be nice," Star whispered. "Shout if you need me or you are like…being murdered."

"I got this." I tried to reassure her with a fake smile and walked up the steps to the front door.

It creaked loudly on its hinges, and my nose was instantly assaulted with the aroma of cold, still house and small, rotting animals. I shut the door quietly behind me; I preferred not to work where Violet could criticize. She had been scathing about both Star's and my beliefs in the past, but without fail, she would call when she needed me.

I reached into my leather satchel and brought out a small vial of oil. It had come from Jerusalem and was proper myrrh anointing oil. There was nothing particularly special about it; I'd cleared a house with olive oil and once in an emergency with Chanel N°5, but the smell of myrrh calmed me and helped me concentrate. I dabbed some on my fingers before touching my forehead, my heart, the top of my feet, and palms of my hands.

My process of performing exorcisms is different from everything I've ever read about it, and it's pretty standard that each exorcist has a unique way of doing it. In the simplest terms, I tend to meditate, pop my spirit out of my body, and fight demons on the spiritual plane. That's if it doesn't go all haywire like Max's exorcism did. I don't like doing them on the fly like that because the hangover always sucks.

Everyone also has their own way of putting up spiritual shields, but I found the Armor of God mentioned in Ephesians 6:10 to be the best for me. Each piece of armor cited within the verse added to the spirit Jael before I would walk on the spiritual plane. I could already sense that this job wasn't going to be simple. I was going to need all the protection I could get, and metaphysical armor that would manifest as real armor on the spiritual plane always made me feel better.

I whispered my prayers quickly and the buzzing in my head cleared a little. I took a deep breath, shutting my eyes and sending out my psychic feelers.

Uriel had been the one who had taught me how to do house protections. He had recounted the night he and Michael had checked the doors for lamb's blood in Egypt for the first Passover while he had stepped me through it. Sometimes Uriel would join me on such outings, but I couldn't sense him nearby. Apparently, he thought I could handle it myself. It was flattering because, at that moment, I felt grossly underprepared.

It's hard to explain how to feel out demons and unclean spirits and the difference between them. Unless you've felt them before, it's hit-and-miss at best. When houses are possessed, I can usually feel a strange tickle behind my eyes and pressure in my head. Demons were like a sensation of a sticky, hot tongue running over my skin. Each time I become furiously angry. It's almost instantaneous—like I've been violated on a fundamental level, and I need to destroy whatever it is. My hands get hot, going from a pleasant tingle until they feel like I could melt whatever I touch. My heart rate goes up and adrenaline pumps.

"Teach my hand to war and my fingers to fight," I prayed, and something in the house shifted. It felt like a great cat's ears had pricked up in annoyance.

I walked through the house anointing the tops of the doors and windows with oil, whispering prayers and protections as I went. The presence was stalking me so closely I could almost feel its hot breath on the back of my neck. I wondered, as I always do, what could have happened in the house that would cause such a thing to take up residence.

There is a big difference between the generalized unclean spirits and a full-on demon. Forget everything you've heard about demons being fallen angels. Angels already have bodies. But demons? They *want* living bodies whether it be animal or human. Unclean spirits inhabit stationary things like houses and objects as well as hang on to a person. Could an unclean spirit write on the walls with animal blood? No. Could it manipulate some poor sap to do it for them? Absolutely. I've seen unclean spirits cause mothers to try and drown their kids in the bath and mentally sane people to cut themselves to pieces with kitchen knives, laughing every second. Sometimes it is as subtle as your finances crashing over and over or increased arguments with your spouse. When the Bible talks about cleaning your house, it doesn't just mean the cobwebs but the metaphysical spiders as well.

Unclean spirits get let in; they get permission whether you realize you're doing it or not. For something as sinister as what I was walking through, it had to have been a doozy of an incident or years and years of continuous violence and abuse. If I had the inclination, I could stay there for a while and feel it all out, study it and discern what it was. All hidden things will come to light if you take the time to turn over the right stones.

But I was shaky enough without doing that, and it always left an unpleasant taste in my brain. If the unclean spirit were stubborn, I'd have no choice but to dig deeper.

I saved the animal massacre room until last. The photos hadn't done it justice, and it smelled and looked like a slaughterhouse. I studied the mangled furry bodies and the scrawled message. That my name was written in such an evil room made my skin crawl. Someone had used their own hands to write it. James could've lifted a fingerprint if I called, but sometimes things were beyond the cops, even ones sympathetic to my occupation.

I started to feel the anger and frustration in the room like my chest was being consumed with pissed off rage. I walked around the room anointing the windows, the last doorways in or out of the house. I got out of the stink and walked back to a large room in the center of the house and sat on a tattered velvet lounge chair. There was a makeshift worktable covered in pots of paint, fabric swatches, color charts, and other neglected flotsam of the current DIY owners. Whatever happened in this place, they had been scared enough to never want to step foot in the house again.

Not knowing what I was up against, I got comfortable on the old lounge chair and started working through some scripture I knew would poke the agitated bastard.

"Let your anger be released against the powers of darkness," I prayed, and the hair rose to static snaps all over my body. "I break every contract that gave demons or unclean spirits permission to enter here."

In my lucid meditative state, I opened my Behind eyes and saw the sticky, black, heaving mess that climbed up the walls and the corners of the room. In the spiritual realm, I got off the chair and saw the metaphysical armor that now adorned me. My physical body stayed in the chair, but I could still feel the heat moving through me, hear the prayers whispered from my lips that would keep me focused in this deep state. I took a closer look at the spikey mess, and I could feel the violence radiating from it.

Memories that weren't mine dropped in my head unexpectedly. I felt the angry words hovering around me, the hurling of abuse, the sharp smack of a backhand across my cheek, diamonds and silks being torn away, and the press of a blade against my thigh as a mark was cut into it to teach me a lesson. To remind me that I was his forever, and I would never escape.

Hot tears in a bathroom as the cut is being cleaned. Neat scar lines on pale legs. Powerless. Despair. Trapped. Then a voice, whispering, promising the strength to never have to deal with her abuser again. If she let it help her, she would never have to feel the touch of her husband's knife again.

Yes. Yes, help me, whatever you are. I'll do whatever you want. Her voice was small and desperate. Triumph and anger.

A knife was taken from the kitchen, hidden in the folds of a silk robe. The feel of release, of joy, as the blade sunk deep into her husband's side, into his neck, into his chest, all the while the chant of freedom resonating around her. She would now be the queen of her kingdom, beholden to no man...

I shook the recollections away, trying to focus and not get caught up in them again. At least I now knew how it was invited in. I hovered my hand over the darkness, my prayers becoming commanding as I felt a ball of heat and white light explode out of me. It poured from my hands and body, burning until anything that remained was dust. The light moved up through the house, annihilating any unclean residue and leaving only streaks of luminescence in its place.

There was a movement behind me, and I turned to face a hissing black creature standing in the doorway. It had six spindly legs covered in a leathery black skin with a teardrop shaped head. It screeched at me, baring its sharp, pointed teeth and weirdly reminding me of a bastard love child of Gollum and Shelob.

"There you are, you little shit," I said with a growl as I pulled the short sword from the scabbard on my back. Some people would be frightened to see such a monster, but all it did was piss me off. Based on the sludge it left, it had been here feeding off people for decades. I took off after it, finally cornering it in the kitchen between a busted fridge and the backdoor, the glowing holy oil around the doorframe stopping its escape. The sword hummed in my hand as I raised it.

"Go back to your master, you piece of garbage," I commanded, and as it leaped for my throat, I drove the blade of my sword up through its chest. Hot breath seared my face as it died. "Jael. They are awake."

I shoved it off me in disgust, the wound I had made glowing with white fire until it was entirely consumed. Gripping my sword, I moved through the house and back to where my physical body was still on the chair.

I went through my grounding exercise as I wriggled my toes and felt my spirit return to my body. My eyes were heavy when I opened them, and I was disoriented, wondering how long I had been out.

"Jael Quinlan," a masculine voice said, growling, and hands grabbed me by the throat from behind. Self-defense training kicked in as I brought my arms up to break his hold and slipped off the lounge chair and back to my feet. I turned to see Crazy Bill sneering at me, his eyes wide and mad. I reached into my boot and pulled out my baton, flicking it out to its full length.

"I heard you were dead, Bill," I said as he edged around the couch. "I don't want to hurt you, but keep your damn distance." My inner eye snapped open, and I saw the demon inside of him, using his body like its own personal meat suit.

Bill ran at me, bloody hands and arms flailing like he didn't know how to use them properly. I used my baton to block him, feeling the bones of his wrist crack as he stumbled. The smell coming from him was worse than roadkill. He should've been screaming, but he climbed back on his feet.

"Stop, Bill, let me help you," I said as he turned on me again.

"I don't need your help, murderer," he said, spit flying through his broken teeth. "Once you're dead I'll get a new body to serve…to serve…" He didn't finish his sentence as he ran for me. He was ready for my baton this time, dodging the blow and grabbing me sideways to hold my right arm down.

"You're going to taste delicious." He laughed in my ear. My left hand came up to hit him in the face, and as our skin made contact, burning white fire left my hand and rushed into him. Crazy Bill screamed and thrashed, but I hung onto him until he let me go and collapsed onto the floorboards. His body twitched once and was still.

"What on earth was that?" I panted, looking down at the decrepit body. That had never happened before in any exorcism I had performed. I fought back the shock and tried to focus on the body.

Blood seeped out of his eyes and nose, some unseen wound beneath his shirt opened, and red bloomed over his chest. I found a pair of latex gloves in my bag and put them on before I lifted the sides of his jacket.

Clair had seen him get hit by a car, and looking at Bill's mashed up right side, I could easily believe it. I couldn't figure out why he wasn't bleeding earlier. Trying not to look at the broken ribs sticking out of his shirt, I searched through his pockets and found a half-eaten sausage roll, a handful of cigarette butts, four dollars in change, and a glossy, white brochure advertising Heart of the Homeless, a new homeless shelter that had opened near the old Meat Market on Blackwood Street. It advertised free accommodation, food, counseling, rehab, and back-to-work training. The pictures made it look like a hotel health spa with the benefit of free education.

I whistled softly. "Damn, Billy. I want to move in here." On the back were some contact details and social media sites, as well as the silver-and-white HeosCorp logo. I pocketed the brochure and took off my gloves, stuffed them into a sandwich bag, and put them back into my satchel. Nothing was right about any of it. There had been no soul left in the body, only a demon. In my experience, that just wasn't possible.

Outside, Star and Violet were arguing loudly until they spotted me stumbling out the front door.

"Are you okay?" Star asked, looking me over, ever the watchful best friend.

"Yep," I said, downing half the bottle of water she handed me. I was already feeling exhausted and in need of food.

"And?" Violet asked pointedly.

"*And* it's done. It's gone," I replied. Violet's smile looked a bit too smug, so I added, "But I found a dead body in there as well as the animals."

"What? Where did that come from? There was nobody in there before you went in there, Jael," she said with a snarl, her voice rising in panic.

"Dude, it's in the middle of the living room floor. I don't know how you could've missed it unless someone came back after you left last time."

Star raised an eyebrow at me as if to say, *You think she's dumb enough to believe that?*

My smile widened. *She watches* The Bachelor*, of course she is.*

"Call James, he'll get to the bottom of it," I told Violet. "He'd probably enjoy catching up with you at the same time."

Despite how pissed off she was, the James Effect worked on Violet almost as well as it did on Star.

"I'll call him," Star insisted before her sister could reach for her phone.

James turned up half an hour later, happy to assist and to not report anything until he had the time to check it out himself.

"Second crime scene in two days, Jael? You are spoiling me, girl," he said as he got out of his car.

"I like to treat all of my special ladies," I said, adding under my breath, "Be careful of Vi. Maybe use your snake charming skills on her, because she's on the warpath."

"I'll gird my loins," he replied solemnly.

"Do that. I swear Vi's acting like I killed the guy just to spoil her day."

"Did you?" he asked, the teasing tone gone.

"He was already dead, I swear," I said innocently. "His name was Crazy Bill, and he usually begs around Queen Victoria Market and the Jasper Hotel. Clair said she saw him get hit by a car."

"So how did he get all the way out here? Dead guys don't just get up and walk."

"You're the copper, not me. You figure it out."

Violet came out of the house looking like she was about to call down thunder and lightning and send plagues and exploding volcanos until virgins and goats were sacrificed to appease her.

"You had better start girding," I warned James.

Violet's bitchy, death goddess face vanished when she spotted James, and she hurried down the stairs and straight into his arms.

"Oh, James, it's just so awful! That poor man," she said into his chest, the bruised damsel ready for comfort. I wanted to vomit on her ugly beige shoes.

"Steady on, Vi. It's going to be okay. Don't worry. I'll get it all sorted," James said, going into full masculine protector mode. I rolled my eyes at him, and he winked over the top of her head.

"Gaia save us," Star said, complaining loudly from the patio. "Let the man go, Violet, so that he can do his job." Violet shot her a glare as James untangled himself from her and headed up the stairs, his face softening at the sight of Star.

"How are you, Starbreeze?" he asked gently, the macho act replaced with genuine concern.

"I'm okay," she said, a small smile lingering at the corners of her mouth.

"Show me the way to the dead guy?" he asked, his hand resting lightly on her back as he followed her inside. It was so adorable that I wanted to throw something at them.

"Come on, J! This is your shit show," he called from inside, and I hurried after them, happy to get away from Violet's scowl.

"Damn, he's all kinds of messed up," James said as he studied the remains of Crazy Bill's chest and the ribs poking from his side.

"Considering he got hit by a car a week ago, he was still quite spry an hour ago," I replied. "The guy was ready to stomp my head."

"I wonder what happened to his face?" Star said, pointing to where the skin was burnt and blistered. Any idiot could make out the shape of a hand. I only hoped that I'd successfully wiped all my prints off his skin.

"Care to fill me in, J?" asked James with a raised eyebrow.

"I don't know what you're implying, officer," I said sweetly.

The truth was I didn't know what had happened and I was fighting to not let it freak me out. My exorcisms had never, ever been like that before. I wondered if Uriel knew or if he'd even tell me what it was. I never had power like that outside the spiritual world, but if it had been granted to me, I knew it was for a reason.

The brochure I lifted from Bill burned in my bag, but until I had something solid to go on, I wasn't going to tell James and have him risk his career over one of my dodgy leads.

"Okay, I'm going to call this in. Take Jael home, Star, and keep your head down for the next few days. I'll get Violet on record saying she found the body on her own."

Neither of us questioned his ability to get Violet to agree to anything he suggested.

"Sounds like a good plan, but what's going to happen when they find my fingerprints all over the doors and windows?" I asked.

"If they find them, I'll get Violet to confirm that she hired you to perform a cleansing. I'm positive the police will see it as someone getting rid of an inconvenient body like all the other little furry critters."

"You guys seem to be forgetting the love letter smeared in animal blood all over the other room," Star said.

James swore when he saw it and rounded on me. "You don't think you should've called me about this?"

"You aren't my real mom," I retorted.

He groaned. "Goddamn it, Jael. You are a pain in my ass sometimes. Who the hell wrote it?"

We argued for another hour until we all had a story straight about Crazy Bill stalking me, then James called it in on the official channels.

"Expect a call in the next day or so. They might make you come down for an interview," he said as I climbed into the front seat of Star's Corolla.

"Fine, I'll play the good girl. Thanks for the help."

"And for fuck's sake try and stay out of the shit for one day."

"Yes, big brother." I smiled pleasantly at him. He gave Star one last look, and it was so hot I was surprised she didn't melt in her seat.

"You guys are so gross. You should just make out already," I said as we pulled out into traffic. "Like with tongue and sloppy, drunk white girl groping."

"You should shut up about James and me and start telling me what really happened in that house," Star said angrily. "I know when you are lying, Jael Quinlan."

Sometimes, I hated how well she knew me.

6

I EXPLAINED WHAT HAD happened in the house as best as I could, Star's own built-in bullshit detector making sure I told her the truth.

"Maybe you need to go into a meditation tonight and ask Uriel about your Hand of Power," she suggested, trying—and failing—to seem unconcerned.

"I'm already feeling the spiritual hangover, so I should sleep first and figure out a plan tomorrow when I'm clearer."

I sank farther into the car seat and shut my eyes to block out the cars driving past. Sometimes, when I had exorcised something powerful, I'd be exhausted mentally and physically for days afterward. If I had realized the size of what was in the house today, or if I knew I was going to have to wrestle with a dead guy, I probably would've put Violet off for a few days.

"I'll make sure Vi pays you extra, even if she's going to be pissed that she now has to tell clients someone died in there."

"The house is over a hundred years old; lots of people would've died in there." I thought of the abusive husband being stabbed over and over. Did they ever find traces of him?

"She'll be able to reassure them that she had the place exorcised and cleansed, so they never need to worry about ghosts," Star said.

"Crazy Bill died after I was done, but they still won't have to worry about his ghost."

I didn't tell her the demon that was riding Bill had either taken over his spirit completely or had killed him, sending him to whatever existence came next.

That was the other thing that was bothering me; I'd never seen a possession so complete before. Usually, I could see the real person in there being influenced. There had been nothing left of Bill but his meat and bones.

There were too many *firsts* happening this week, and it was making me feel like I was a rookie exorcist caught with her pants down.

Star pulled up in the service alley down the side of my building.

"Are you sure you don't want me to come and hang out?" she asked and then frowned. "Who is Lawyer Edward Cullen?"

I followed her gaze and saw a guy in a suit and glasses standing on the steps leading up to my apartment. He held a bunch of flowers and waved at me nervously.

"That would be Max." I groaned in frustration. "Damn it."

"That's the bastard that threw you last week? Do you want me to go kick him in the nuts to even the odds?" Her eyes were filled with a dark, vengeful glee.

"I don't think he could handle your Star Power right now. Besides, look at him! You think he'd be capable of violence without a demon in him?" I got out of the car and grabbed my bag from the back seat.

"You tell Bible-basher Edward to keep his hands to himself, or he'll answer to me." Star gave him a long once over. "Although I got to admit, he's an upgrade from the traditional Glitter Edward with the added bonus of not having to share him with a pouty wife."

"*Goodbye*, Star," I said, shutting the door loudly.

"Have a nice date!" she called after me, and I didn't think Max could've turned any redder. I gave her the one-fingered salute as she drove away laughing.

"Your friend has some impressive hair," Max said by way of a hello.

"What are you doing here, Max?" I asked, thinking about how nice a bath would be instead of being forced to have this conversation.

He rallied, pushing the flowers toward me. "These are for you."

"Uh, thanks," I said awkwardly, taking them with my spare hand and pushing past him so I could climb the stairs to my door. I could already hear Meta whining to get out.

"I wanted…to um…thank you for the other day." He followed me until Meta's great black body came out the door, fully alert and sizing up the stranger behind me.

"Get out of the way, Metamucil. He's okay." I shoved his furry butt until he moved.

"Did you really call your dog Metamucil?" Max asked as I dumped my bag on my small table and hunted for a vase. I couldn't remember the last time I'd had flowers. I found a pasta sauce jar under the sink, rinsed it out, and filled it with water.

"No, it's just what I call him sometimes." I popped the bunch of flowers into the jar. "His real name is Metatron."

"Metatron! As in…the angel who acts as the voice of God?" he asked. I could see him weighing it up on the scales of blasphemy in his mind.

"Well done, Sunday school. Looks like they taught you something after all."

"Why did you call him that?"

Meta sniffed at the blood on my shirt, and I answered deadpan, "When he was a pup, he used to have this high-pitched whine that could explode your brain. It was like the voice of Dog. So, Metatron he became." Max's upbringing was good enough that he didn't say aloud whatever horror passed through his head.

"What are you doing here, Max?"

"I wanted to come and say sorry for hurting you," Max admitted. "I'd never hurt anyone, let alone a woman trying to help me."

"Don't worry about it. These things happen." I tried to brush it off. The last thing Max needed was to feel guilty over something he had no control over.

"Your dad thinks you're a fraud," Max blurted, and my hand stilled on Meta's ears.

"And?" I looked up at him knowing there was a threat written on my face.

"He might think that, but I know that you aren't."

"That's great. I'll sleep so much better tonight." I straightened up, getting ready to kick him out, when I felt Uriel's presence in the room with me.

Just looking at Max's awkward, twitchy demeanor, I knew what he was really there for, and that I was the only one who could give it to him.

I groaned. "Let me change my shirt. I'm going to need food if we are going to talk about it."

"What?" he asked, and I realized I had answered the question he'd been too nervous to ask. Whoops.

"You want to know what happened, yeah? So, give me a second." I walked into my room, pulled off my dirty T-shirt, struggled into a clean one, and only realized when I turned that I'd forgotten to shut my door. Poor Max was looking intently at my bookshelf, the red tips of his ears the only indication that he'd copped an eyeful of my blue bra. I could already hear Star's laughter in the back of my head.

"You have a lot of interesting books," he said as he scanned my extensive collection where *Hellblazer*, *Lucifer*, and *Preacher* sat comfortably beside books like *The Dead Sea Scrolls*, *The Rite of Exorcism*, and *The Book of Enoch*. The shelf filled with my favorite Christian mystics and mythology had caught his attention.

"Okay, let's go before you get stuck," I said, clipping on Meta's lead as he danced impatiently.

"Where to?"

"Don't look so worried, it isn't far."

Outside Meta peed on posts and the patch of grass at the tram stop. Max didn't protest as we strolled around the block and back to the café bar next to my building.

"They don't mind you having a dog here?" Max asked, looking down at the menu.

"We come here a lot. As long as Meta doesn't try to eat or hump the other customers' froufrou dogs, Jimmy doesn't mind us hanging out."

Jimmy, the owner, was what I affectionately called a hipster greaser. He was the only man I'd ever seen who could pull off suspenders, a manicured beard, and tattooed, pinup Betties on his muscular forearms. The bar itself was full of memorabilia that should have been lame but turned out kitsch.

"Hey, J, who's your friend?" Jimmy asked when he came outside.

"This is Max." I winked at Jimmy from behind a menu.

Jimmy's bearded mouth broke into a smile as he said, "He looks like demon bait."

"He *was* until I turned up," I replied, accepting the big guy's fist bump of victory.

"Welcome back, Max."

"Uh, thank you." Max shifted in his chair, and I could see his mind trying to determine if we were making fun of him or not.

"You want the usual, J?"

"Yes, please."

"Too easy. What about you, Max?"

"Just an iced coffee, thanks."

"I'll find something for you too, mutt face," Jimmy told Meta, roughly patting the big idiot's head. Meta loved Jimmy which is why I always came to eat here.

"What do you want to know?" I asked Max as he poured us both water.

"Is the demon gone?"

"Yeah, for now." I drained my cup, and he refilled it without hesitation.

"What do you mean 'for now'?" He looked like he was going to spew, and I could hardly blame him.

"Demons and unclean spirits are tricky as well as stupid. Sometimes if you aren't careful, if you don't put a guard up to protect your heart and mind, there are beings that will return. You permitted them to come aboard once, who's to say you're not tempted to let them do it again? Man, what do they teach in that church of yours?" I shook my head, but my despair was short-lived. "Beer! My hero," I said as Jimmy placed a Corona on the table in front of me.

"Jeez, girl, must've been a shit day," he said, popping the lid for me.

"So epically shit." I took a mouthful and let the cold fizzy goodness go down to my empty stomach. My whole body was starting to ache like I'd run a marathon; a sure sign that the night was going to be a long one.

"How can you act so normal right now?" Max demanded, his voice rising. Jimmy all but vanished, sensing the fight.

"Because this *is* normal for me," I said, trying to keep the anger out of my voice. "I deal with this sort of thing every day. You have one brush against the spirit world, and you fall apart. Get a grip, you whiner. God gave us power over demons, so stop pissing your pants with fear. It's like fertilizing a field for unclean things to grow."

Max didn't get up and leave, so I took it as a good sign. I offered him my Corona, and to my surprise, he had a mouthful.

"All that stuff is true then, the head turning and wall climbing." A troubled look passed over his face. "Was I like that?"

"First, everyone is different. I haven't seen any wall climbing yet, but you never know. It worries me that your church isn't teaching you about this."

"I was in a church once where someone said depression was a demon," he answered thoughtfully, and I tried not to roll my eyes.

"Okay, let me get a few things straight here. Don't get me wrong, sometimes depression can be a demon, but it's rare. Most of the time it really is a mental illness." I took my beer back, had a sip, and added, "You can't go about blaming the Devil for stuff for two reasons. One, he doesn't operate that way, and two, man has enough evil in his own heart to destroy the world three times over. Demons can influence and attach themselves to a human, but they are only feeding off what's already there. You think about something like screwing another man's wife, and if you meditate on that thing long enough, you are basically tossing out breadcrumbs into the spiritual world for these things to come find you."

Jimmy came back with a large plate of sweet potato fries with cheese and hot sauce and an iced coffee for Max. It was good timing. I could feel the demon theology tirade getting the better of me.

"You better bring out another two of these." I waggled an almost empty beer at Jimmy. "Young Max is going to be in need of something a little stronger."

"I'm not that young," Max argued. "You're only two years older than me. I…I remember you coming to our church for a bit before, you know…before you got sick."

He had a damn good memory. Heather and I would've only attended a handful of times before she broke up with Dad and I ended up in a mental hospital.

"I wasn't sick. I was possessed," I said, correcting him. "You can talk about me getting thrown in a padded cell, I'm not going to be offended."

"You had a demon too?"

"Yep," I said between a mouthful of fries. "Big one."

"How did you get rid of it?"

"I became an exorcist."

"Sounds hectic."

"It was."

"Is that why you stopped coming to church?"

"Amongst other things."

"Such as?"

"Do you know who Ammianus Marcellinus is? Roman historical writer and a pagan to boot. Well, he had a quotable saying that sums up my feelings on churches: 'No wild beasts are such enemies to mankind as are most of the Christians in their deadly hatred of one another.'"

That shut him up. Max's lips pressed into a thin line. I swallowed slowly, wondering what he was driving at until the metaphysical penny dropped. "You are wondering how a heathen like me can banish demons," I said, taking a guess.

"I wouldn't call you a heathen, but I have to admit I'm curious to know how a pretty, non-Christian woman, who claims no allegiance to a church or any other religious body, can work as a full-time exorcist."

I don't know what surprised me more: that he'd managed to talk to me in full sentences, or that he had the balls to say to me what he did.

"You think I'm pretty?" I asked, only because I knew he would turn fire-engine red. He was far too old to blush like that, and I had to grudgingly agree with Star that he was nerd hot.

"Do you always dodge this many questions?" he replied, and I grinned, knowing that I was pushing his buttons. I loved messing with white-bread Christians to see how far their manners would take them.

"The best way I can describe it is that I have a Christ-centered spiritual practice. I follow the teachings of Yeshua to the best of my ability," I told him truthfully.

"So, you are one of those people who doesn't go to church but claims they live by the Sermon on the Mount, and that's it?" said Max.

I couldn't stop the laughter from bubbling out of me. "Dude. *No one* can keep to the Sermon on the Mount. That's the whole freaking point of it. If you can read through that whole thing and not realize your own inability to do what it says without God helping your worthless ass every step of the way, then your arrogance knows no bounds."

"Okay, so help me understand how you see it," Max argued.

"Fine! I'll give you the *Reader's Digest* version of the complex beast that is Jael Quinlan, Exorcist Extraordinaire," I said, my exhaustion killing what remained of my manners. "You imply that I'm not a Christian, because I don't attend an institutional congregation. I never will because I don't agree with church politics or dogma. I don't like hypocrites. I don't like the way they blow smoke up each other's butts about how good of a Christian they are and then walk past a homeless person without a second glance. I don't like the additional rules and regulations that they like to bolt onto the Word of God. I don't like how much hate they show toward each other and their fellow man. I don't like the shit they like to do in God's name. Yeshua taught love and compassion, yet I don't see them making friends with prostitutes and eating with tax collectors."

I stabbed my fork angrily into my fries. "I was commanded to cast out demons when I was just a kid, and all I'm trying to do is fulfill that command. I wasn't told to only help the Pentecostals or Catholics or Muslims or Jews but to help *everyone*. I'm a free-agent exorcist of God, and I'm not going to spend a single second losing sleep over how I don't fit into the perfect little box other people like you think I should fit into."

I took a deep shuddering breath. I hadn't realized how loud I was ranting until I saw other patrons staring at us. Max's face was pale, but he wasn't angry; he looked ashamed he had pushed me so far.

"I'm sorry if I upset you," he said sincerely.

"Be sorry for asking such a stupid question and for thinking it actually matters what church I go to. If everyone stopped being concerned about the state of each other's souls and focused on their own, the world would be a better place."

Max fiddled with a napkin, tearing it methodically into confetti, and looked like a pretty puppy I'd just kicked. *Damn it, Jael. You've hurt his feelings.*

"And that's another reason I don't go to church," I added gently. "I'm a jerk. I have no patience for people. I can't even work a full-time job for longer than a month or so before I have to move on. Look at your nice suit. I bet you do something really cool and important."

"I'm a lawyer. When I'm not possessed that is."

"How fortuitous. I'm probably going to be needing a lawyer after today." I fed a few fries to Meta and wondered how things had gone with James at the house.

"Can I ask what happened?" Max looked genuinely interested behind his square, black frames.

Going against my better judgment, I decided to tell him about my last few days. I left out a few details though, like the way I had picked through Crazy Bill's pockets. I hadn't forgotten for a second that he was a lawyer.

Max took it surprisingly well, and even more surprising, he didn't think I was lying to him. Apart from Star and James, I couldn't really talk to anyone about my bad days. Unlike Star and James, Max had enough biblical teaching to wrap his head around a lot of what I was saying.

"If you think something is happening in the city, shouldn't you maybe tell people?" Max asked, twisting one of his brown curls thoughtfully.

"Like who?"

"Well, the Churches for a start, so they can be vigilant."

I nearly fell off my chair laughing. "That's so precious. If you think my dad is disapproving of what I do, you should see the other religious bodies in the city."

"Still, you need to warn them even if they don't listen. Don't Catholics still get into the exorcism thing? Pretty sure I saw the pope do one on TV the other day."

"The last time I stepped into Saint Patrick's for a friendly chat, the archbishop had a bunch of baby priests kick me out. I don't think they would let me back in even to warn them."

"You don't strike me as someone who would take no for an answer." He smiled then, and it lit up his face and crinkled the lines around his eyes. Yep, definitely nerd hot.

"I should let you get home," I said, getting up. I gave Jimmy a wave, letting him know I was going. He had my credit card details on file so I could come and go without having to bring Meta into the restaurant.

Max walked me to my steps without questioning my abruptness and gave Meta a pat. "Thank you for letting me ask questions."

"Thanks for the flowers. I don't think I've ever received flowers for an exorcism."

He reached into his wallet and handed me a business card. "I owe you, Jael. If there's anything I can do for you, please give me a call."

I pocketed the card without looking at it. "Thanks, Sunday school. Good chat. Take care of yourself."

"You too, Jael. Watch your back," he said sincerely, and with a parting smile, he headed for the tram stop.

I hadn't realized I was staring until Meta pawed at my leg. "What? I can totally make friends when I need to." At least other people could see this one.

Which reminded me, I really needed to talk to Uriel about what happened today. My hands had stopped burning hours ago, but they still had an unfamiliar ache which unnerved me even more than making a new friend.

7

THE NEXT DAY PASSED in a blur of anti-inflammatory tablets and sleep. It wasn't uncommon for me to ache a bit after an exorcism, but this pain was on another level. My whole body felt like I'd been thrown in a sack and beaten with sticks. The hand that the white fire had come from was fine, but it still felt the imprint of something alien, like the ghost memory of a lover's kiss. My dreams were stranger than usual with talking demons, arguments between angels, and a thick choking darkness. I woke sweating and burning every time.

"Sounds like you're getting the flu," Star said when she called to check in.

"I don't have the time to get sick," I mumbled half into my pillow.

"Your current work contract is up, and Vi should've paid you by now so take it easy while you can afford to. How was your date with Max? I told James that he turned up, and he threatened to pay Max a visit if he gets too stalkerish."

"Max isn't a stalker, he's a lawyer. And he needed someone to talk to about crazy shit." I rolled over and found Meta sleeping beside me. He looked so cute that I didn't have the heart to yell at him for being on the bed. "And it wasn't a date either. We went to Jimmy's and drank some beers. He's okay."

"Flowers and some drinks? Sure sounds like a date to me."

"Oh yeah? What were you doing talking to James in the middle of the night?" I said, countering. "Were you whispering all the weird hippie names you are going to call your babies someday? Like Neo Spock Moonlight and Ariadne Flame Bringer."

"Actually, dumbass, he wanted to give me an update on Crazy Bill," she replied defensively.

"Sure he did. What was the verdict?"

"So far they are buying the story that it was a hit-and-run and someone dumped the body in the house. James is having problems locating your friend Clair. He wanted to talk to her about Crazy Bill's alleged hit-and-run and the Jewish girl."

"Clair rarely leaves the Queen Vic. district." My eyes snapped open. "Shit, I hope she is okay. She might be hiding from James because he's police. His good looks might not be enough to convince her."

"I doubt it. She's probably freaked out after seeing two people get killed in front of her."

"Maybe."

"Speaking of which…how is your crazy head this afternoon?"

I thought about the dead girl talking to me in the dream. She'd been shouting, but not a sound had come out of her as she waved her arms to try and warn me. I had been listening to old jazz all day, trying to dispel the dead woman's memories from my head.

"I'm surprisingly good," I lied. "Just a bit of spiritual hangover from yesterday."

"Talk to Uriel about the Hand of Power yet?"

"Keep calling it that and I'll give you the Finger of Destiny."

"That's a no." Star laughed. "Stop being chicken because he turned up and looked after you the other night. Go into a meditation and *talk* to him about it."

"Yeah, maybe later," I answered vaguely. "Max seems to think I have a responsibility to tell the Churches what's going on."

"Wow." Star let out a low whistle. "What great big balls that kid must have to even suggest that to you. What are you going to do?"

"Today I'm going to go back to sleep. Tomorrow? I might make some calls. Maybe drop by Saint Patrick's."

"Double wow. Max must've gotten under your skin to convince you to go to the Catholics."

"He's a lawyer; of course he made a decent argument."

"Did you get his number?"

"Yeah, why?"

"Because if you show your face at Saint Patrick's, you'll probably need a lawyer by the end of the day."

"Very funny. But you don't have to worry. I plan on being all sweetness and light to Archbishop Bob."

"Be careful he doesn't crucify your ass," Star said before hanging up.

Despite my bravado, I wasn't looking forward to seeing the Catholics. They had seriously strong views when it came to exorcisms and women, so I was a double threat.

I stretched out in bed and tried not to wince at the pain shooting through my muscles. Being this tired after a house clearing and an exorcism was uncalled for, and only one person could give me answers. With a sigh of resignation, I put in my headphones and turned on my classical playlist.

Technically I didn't need the music to go into a centering prayer meditation, but it helped block out the constant stream of trams and traffic outside of my bedroom window. I steadied my breathing, whispering my grounding over and over until a deep calm settled over me.

Sometimes Uriel shows, other times he doesn't. When I go deep enough, it's like stepping in the Behinds but on a completely different world. There were certain places I always seemed to end up: beside a lake, at a cabin, in a forest, or in a valley surrounded by mountains. This time it was the lake. A part of me knew my body was back in my bed, but the larger part of me was walking along the shoreline, enjoying the wet, earthy smell rising from the forest beside me.

"You look tired," Uriel said as he walked beside me.

"That's what happens when you exorcise a dead man," I replied. He stopped me and took my hand, turning it over in his.

"I can feel it," he said as he studied my skin, his rough fingers tracing over the lines of my palm. "You used the power of Heaven."

"Huh?" I said, distracted by the sensation.

"You were a conduit for the power of Heaven, and through you, it destroyed the abomination. The vessel was already dead, you say?"

"Crazy Bill had been hit by car. When his hitchhiker was burnt out of him, he went back to being dead. I've never seen a zombie demon before. It scared the shit out of me," I admitted without any feeling of embarrassment or weakness.

Uriel was the only one I could be truly honest with, and even if I tried to lie, he would know anyway.

"You have nothing to be frightened of. You instinctively knew what to do."

"And what if it doesn't work next time?"

"It will," he said simply. "You seem to forget that you are never alone. Even if you are unable to wield this power, you'll always have protection."

I took a deep breath. "Why are the demons coming after me like this? What's going on?"

"You are a threat to them. They are becoming more aggressive because your abilities are growing. As for the darkness in the city, it is up to you to find the source of it."

"Can't you just use angel power and track it?"

Uriel pulled a face. "The angels are not omniscient, Jael. We have our limitations the same as you. You are cleverer than most humans. Use your instincts, find the pattern. You can do this."

"Whatever you say." I folded my hand up in his, and he squeezed it gently. "I promise to check in, Mr. I'm Not Omniscient."

"Please make sure you do. I still haven't been able to find what's hiding behind the shields all over the city and has the power to block the angels." He frowned, and the warmth vanished from his eyes. "Although, I have my suspicions."

Something in his face told me not to question him further, so we continued to walk and enjoy the silence in each other's company, still holding hands.

It's hard to explain what I felt move through Uriel's palm and into mine. He was all light and heat and sharp edges of strength. He gave me the courage to get out of bed and keep going, even though I was scared shitless of what could happen next. I knew that I wasn't alone, even though sometimes I forgot that.

In school I remember getting teased. The other kids decided the best thing to bully me about was church and the way I used to hide in the gardens and talk to my invisible friends. No matter how hard they threw the rocks or how hurtful their insults, I knew that I could take it. I wasn't alone, they just couldn't see what I could see.

I woke up to find my face wet with tears and feeling as if my insides were too big and wide to cram back into my body. Let the demons throw their taunts like the childish beasts that they were. I'd spent a lifetime rolling with the punches. People could call me crazy, but there was no denying the feeling coursing through me. I could only describe it as love, though even that seemed too small of a word. I wasn't the perfect kind of white-bread believer, but I would never deny this.

When I could move again, I climbed out of bed and made a cup of tea as my laptop booted up. I hadn't checked my emails in over a week, but it was good to see that Violet had put money into my account. It seemed like a lot of money, but I had stopped arguing with Star over what her sister paid me a long time ago. I'd always do exorcisms on people for free no matter how difficult they were.

Star knew the personal cost of what I did, so she made sure that her sister paid me for the trouble. It meant I would have rent and food covered for another week, so I could hold off a little bit longer before calling my recruiter to hook me up with a day job.

I had a whole bunch of emails demanding my attention, including ones from Max before he had arrived on my doorstep—*I was hoping I could speak to you*—and after—*We should catch up again. How did talking to the Churches go? Are you feeling better?* I sent him one back reminding him that stalking was illegal, and no, I hadn't called anyone, and yeah, I was fine.

I flicked through my contacts list on my phone and made two calls, one to the synagogue where I left a message and another one to the Anglicans who hung up as soon as I said my name. I was about to call the Greek Orthodox Church when a call came through.

"James? What are you doing calling me on the formal landline?" I asked as I deleted all the emails that were offering to enhance my penis size.

"Calling on official business, Miss Quinlan. I'm going to need you to come down and make a statement."

"Right now? I only just woke up."

"Yeah, right now. The sooner you get here, the less guilty you'll look. Don't worry. They'll go easy on you. I think Vi might have tenderized them."

"Vi does that."

"I've always found her rather sweet."

"That's because she wants you to play Kinky Copper with her."

"All cops are kinky. Now get your ass moving." He hung up without saying goodbye, and I got into the shower.

✦

Despite having to sit in a dull interview room with cloud-blue walls, I could've done a lot worse than giving my statement to Janice. She was one of the only police officers that James worked with who wasn't a total douche.

As she wrote down my account of what happened in the North Melbourne mansion, I couldn't help but wonder why I had said yes to a coffee when I knew it was going to be International Roast. Why did government institutions buy the powdered sadness to make your visit even more miserable? Was it only Australia or would I end up in a jail in the Middle East one day with another cup of freaking International Roast—

"Jael?" A small crease appeared between Janice's eyebrows.

"Huh?"

"You said that you only noticed the body after you had finished…cleansing the house?" The only problem with Janice is that she can't believe what I do for a living. Not that I could blame her. I only gave her the vaguest sort of details when it came to what happened in the house.

"I didn't notice him. I had been in the other rooms mostly. And I was distracted by the room of dead animals."

"Where someone had written your name in blood?" asked Janice.

"Yeah, that's pretty distracting if you ask me. Look, I don't know who did it or who I pissed off to make them want to do it. I have a bit of a reputation in the city. Maybe a bunch of kids thought this was a good joke. It's not the first time something like this has happened. Two months ago, I had a dismembered crow left on my doorstep."

"Do you think you are being targeted by a particular person or group?"

"Like the incidents are linked? Nah."

Janice sighed. "You don't seem too concerned."

"Why should I be? There are some weird people out there." *And in here.* "That house has been left empty for years because everyone thinks it's haunted. Maybe someone thought it would be a laugh to write my name in there. I have a website offering services to cleanse haunted houses; that's probably where they got my name from."

"It's possible."

"Are we done? I kind of have things I need to do today."

Janice put her pen down. "Yes, we're done, but keep your phone handy in case we need to talk again."

"Thanks, Janice."

⋆✦⋆

James was waiting outside the architectural train wreck that was the North Melbourne Police Station. The designers or architects in charge clearly didn't think putting massive stone bars over the front of the building was going to look like the police were locked in a prison of their own.

"How did you do?" he asked.

"They let me go, didn't they?"

"For now." He looked around him, shifting his weight from one foot to the other.

"What now? You have too much caffeine?" I asked.

"Some people think that you're responsible for the animals and the note."

I snorted with laughter. "Why would I do that?"

"To enhance your reputation. To get publicity. You're a Satanist. The list goes on."

"You should've told them I'm a lesbian vampire killer."

"It's not a joke, Jael. It's suspicious. The whole business."

"You don't have to remind me. It was my name they finger painted after all." I punched his arm. "Don't worry. I have a lawyer if things go downhill."

"Oh, that's right. Star told me about your date with…*Max*," he said breathily. Teasing me was a good sign.

"Star tell you how hot he was? I swear she was just about ready to swoop in she was so sweaty and bothered for him."

"She neglected to mention that." The mischief in his eyes vanished.

"Max is a nice guy. I'm thinking of setting them up on a blind date."

"He's not her type."

"And how would you know?"

He shrugged. "She can do better."

"No one can do better than a hot lawyer who's also insanely polite. You should've seen her checking out his ass in that tight pinstripe suit."

"Whatever. Just so you know, I'm not allowed to work this case even though you called me in," he said, changing the subject.

"Conflict of interest?"

"Yeah, you know how they are about these things. Any closer to finding out what made the zombie demon?"

"Nope." I wasn't about to tell him about the Hand of Power. I didn't even know how I was going to tell Star the truth about that one. "I'll let you get back to work."

"Where you off to now?"

"Going to piss off some Catholics."

"Good luck with that. Thanks for stopping by."

"Thanks for the crappiest coffee in Melbourne."

"It's because I put crap in it," he called after me as I headed toward the Royal Melbourne Hospital to catch a tram.

8

MY SENSE OF PURPOSE left me as I jumped off the tram at Fitzroy Gardens. I wandered about, keeping the towers of Saint Patrick's Cathedral in the corner of my eye. I'd had an unsteady peace with the Catholics for six months now, and I didn't know if pushing that was the best idea.

I grabbed an almond milk latte from the information center café and smiled at the people dressed in period clothing at Captain Cook's Cottage before retreating into the greenhouse to find a free bench to sit on.

Like most of my encounters with humans, the last time I had a conversation with Archbishop Robert hadn't gone down well. One of the parishioners had come to me for help after she had been denied an exorcism.

It had been a messy and exhausting night which ended with the lady freed of three demons and me accusing the priests of neglect and arrogance. I should've calmed down before I had the conversation with them, but it was as if they denied demons existed. From what I'd seen of the new pope, it seemed like the overall attitude of the Catholics was changing. I had to hope that the archbishop would get on board.

My word meant nothing to them, but they wouldn't be able to turn around and say I hadn't warned them. Damn Max for getting in my head! Two beers and he was like my own personal Jiminy Cricket telling me to grow a conscience.

I hardened my resolve and left the greenhouse. Cutting through the park and walking down Albert Street, I reached the sleek water feature with the underground offices that seemed at odds with the Gothic Revival style cathedral. A priest I recognized but didn't know the name of saw me and shut the blinds at my feet before I could bend and wave. I tapped on the window until he gave up and pulled them back again. I held up my phone. *NEED TO TALK TO ROBBO—URGENT.* He gesticulated angrily, *No way.* I typed another message. *GOING TO JUMP THE FENCE AND TRAMPLE THE ROSES. MEET YOU THERE.*

Before he could react, I turned my back on him and walked away. I stood waiting patiently near the fountain on the Pilgrim's Path, when the priest raced through the gardens looking for a raging exorcist.

"You! How *dare* you jump the church fence like some criminal—"

"Hi, I'm Jael. I don't think we've formally met," I said, giving him my most friendly smile. "I never would've trampled the Lord's flowers. I just needed you to come out."

"The archbishop is in an important meeting and has no time in his day to meet with you."

"Right. Well, can you pass on a message?" I asked, my patience thinning faster than I would've liked. "Can you tell him that I know we haven't seen eye to eye, but this warning is genuine. There is some serious demonic activity happening in the city. I'll clean it up, as usual, but I wanted him to give the heads up—"

"It's already being dealt with, Miss Quinlan," he said dismissively, a smug look on his face.

"Dealt with by *who* exactly?"

"That's not your concern. Now please allow me to escort you off the premises." He reached to take my arm, but I dodged him.

"Thanks, but I'll see myself out." He followed me anyway and opened the gate.

"Have a pleasant day, Miss Quinlan, and may God go with you."

"Whatever," I muttered.

I was almost at the corner of Lansdowne Street when a group of men walked out of the underground offices, dressed in neat black suits. The tallest stopped and stared at me, and I felt my intuition flare. He had olive skin and curly brown hair. He would've been good-looking except for the displeased look in his dark eyes. He wasn't wearing a collar, but he held himself like a priest and had a long string of silver rosary beads hanging from his neck. He made a small gesture, and the two other men snapped to attention like they were soldiers and blocked my path.

"You mind getting out of the way?" I asked, not moving.

"You must be the exorcist I keep hearing so much about," the tall one said, his voice carrying a glossy Italian accent.

"Jael Quinlan. I don't think we've been introduced."

"Alessandro Abbadelli." He inclined his head. "The archbishop spoke of you."

"And why would I come up in your conversation I wonder?"

"You might call it…professional courtesy."

The penny dropped. It was no wonder my intuition was losing it.

"You are the International Association of Exorcists…all of you?" I looked at the muscle behind him. They were strong looking in a brawny way. *What are they doing here?*

"*Si*, the Holy Father has assigned us to investigate the ongoing problems in the city," he said. "The Devil has been left unchallenged here for far too long. The archbishop should have sent for *professional* exorcists months ago."

"Professional exorcists. What does that mean exactly?" I demanded. Alessandro looked at my *Supernatural* T-shirt pointedly and then back to my face.

"By professional I mean one who has studied and is qualified to perform the rite. Not a"—he made a small dismissive gesture with his hand—"hobbyist."

"And by hobbyist, you mean one who has been performing successful exorcisms since they were seventeen and not stuck at a desk reading *The Rite of Exorcism* over and over."

"My dear, I studied under Gabriele Amorth himself. I was his finest pupil. I was not sitting at a desk as you say."

"I hope your wise father taught you about the animated undead, because that's what you are up against, sport." There was a snort from one of the other exorcists.

"You have been watching too much American TV I think," Alessandro said, a small smile tugging at his lips.

I lifted the corner of my shirt and flashed the fresh bruises from Crazy Bill and the older yellowing ones. "Oh yeah, these are totally pretend as well," I retorted, taking guilty pleasure at how uncomfortable Mr. Hotshot Exorcist looked until I dropped my shirt. "Good luck, *Alessandro*." I gave his rosary a flick as I passed by. "You had best iron your purple stole; you are going to need it, exorcist."

I kept my face neutral as I moved around the other exorcists and stormed up Albert Street, while the urge to kick every tree with my Doc Martens on the way almost overwhelmed me.

Calm your heart. I heard Uriel's voice whisper through me. *You may need their help before this is over.* I tried not to let my pride feel too affronted as I jumped on the first tram home.

One thing I was sure of was that I had a lot of research to do. Star was on my couch patting Metatron when I got home, which put a damper on that idea.

"What's up, Starbreeze?" I asked as I dumped my bag on the kitchen table.

"I had to get away from Violet for a while," she said, looking up from her iPad. "Have you seen the news today?"

"Nope. I've been playing twenty questions with the cops and had an unpleasant encounter with the Catholics."

"Someone leaked the story of Crazy Bill's body being found. It's all over the internet, and people are already calling it the Melbourne Murder House." She passed over the iPad where *The Age* had splashed an article complete with pictures of the cops in the yard.

"Satanic rituals." I snorted as I read the spin. "Bloody hack reporters. James is going to be pissed and won't be able to do anything about it."

"He got booted off the case?"

"Yep. How did Violet take it? She must be going through the journos right now."

"She is, and she loves it. It will make the price go way up."

"Rich people are so weird. At least if James is off the case, he can focus on my suicides."

"They managed to keep the details vague in the news," Star said. "I can't imagine it would be good for the museum if people knew their ultra-orthodox professor jumped in front of a train."

"I forgot James said he was a professor. What museum was he at?"

"Jewish Museum of Australia. He's famous, J. I'm surprised you haven't heard of him. He's a guest lecturer at La Trobe on Ancient Near Eastern History sometimes when they have a special series running. He's famous in Israel, one of their leading professors."

"He left something like that to come to Melbourne? Why?"

"His wife's family was over here, and they thought it would be a good change for their daughter. Professor Smyth, who teaches philosophy and is a sworn atheist, has had some epic debates with Professor Ben-Ezra."

"I can imagine." My mind was ticking over and over.

"Wait. Shut up. I just realized you said you saw the Catholics today?"

"Yeah, and I met this supposedly shit hot exorcist Alessandro Abbadelli who has been sent to piss all over my turf." I told Star about the encounter as she tapped away on her iPad screen.

"Sweet baby Jesus, I think Signore Abbadelli could definitely be classed as shit hot," she said. "You know the Elsa Perea Flores school incident?"

"Peru. Mass demonic possession of about eighty to a hundred kids," I recounted. "I was following the story, and then it just disappeared. No explanations or anything."

"He was there, Jael." Star held up the screen to show a blurry photo of priests entering the school grounds and at their head was Alessandro.

"Holy pope on a bicycle." I scanned the article. "He's the leader of their black ops by the looks of that." The article didn't say anything extra about him, but it did mention the pope had personally picked the priests sent to the site. Alessandro couldn't have been much older than me. To have the pope on his side already, he had to be something special.

"He exorcised eighty kids. That's beyond hard-core, J. Maybe you need to play nice with this one."

"Maybe he should play nice with me." I paced my small living room, tapping my phone against the palm of my hand. "If he's been sent by the pope to Melbourne, it would mean that this situation is a lot worse than what I thought it was. I had five exorcisms last month, Max's being the last and most difficult. That's a lot to have had actual possession and not just in need of mental health services. If I saw that many, then I wonder how many demoniacs went to the Catholics for help."

"You know you really should talk to your mom. She saw this in her meditation," Star said, stopping me dead in my tracks. "Billie said she saw it too."

I groaned. "Come on, Star. Don't make me deal with both the Catholics and our mothers on the same day."

9

HEATHER LIVED IN A renovated Kensington town house inherited from Grandma Julienne. Violet had been trying to convince Heather to sell it for years, but my mother had put her foot down and refused to budge. After the divorce from Dad, she'd turned the bottom floor into a shop with a meditation and yoga haven in the backyard.

"I don't see how this is a good idea," I said to Star. With her prodding, I showered and changed into fresh jeans and my favorite Doctor Strange T-shirt. By the time I'd gotten out, Star had called Heather, who had called Billie, who was now cooking dinner. Star was intelligent enough to put in place a contingency plan like food, so I would be forced to go without feeling like I'm inconveniencing people.

"My girls!" Heather exclaimed when she opened the door. She was wearing purple jeans and a spangly aqua singlet, and her graying red hair was piled on top of her head. She gathered me into a vanilla-and-rose-scented embrace.

"Hey Mom," I murmured through a mouthful of hair.

"Darling, you look exhausted," she said, holding me at arm's length. "I see you're still wearing boys' T-shirts instead of real clothes."

"Hey, don't mess with the T-shirts. Besides, this is the Sorcerer Supreme, so I thought you'd approve."

"You're a grown woman; you don't need my approval," she insisted, though her frequent criticism of my clothes suggested otherwise. "And look at you, my beautiful Starbreeze. Your hair almost matches your aura—"

I tuned out as they chatted over each other's clothes and jewelry before I escaped upstairs to hunt for wine or whatever Heather was drinking. I walked slowly through her little shop with my shields down, making sure that nothing malicious was hanging about with the chakra charts and More Dharma, Less Drama T-shirts. I knew Heather was careful about what she sold, but she couldn't account for the people who came to buy stuff from her or to do a meditation. Sometimes people drag their bad juju wherever they go, and the last thing I needed was some dark user opening a Hell portal in the middle of my mom's meditation session.

As a child, it had been more than difficult to not only live through my parents' divorce but have one parent switch religions entirely. New Age wasn't the first thing she tried either. We had to work through all the remotely Christian sects and cults like Scientology and Mormonism before she'd met Billie and found the New Agers. I had to hide the little silver cross that I had received for my eighth birthday to make sure she didn't get rid of it when she started insisting on making me wear amethyst and hematite. Instead of saying I had guardian angels, she insisted I had guides to help protect me and soothe my always angry aura.

Looking back, it was surprising that I didn't end up in the loony bin years earlier than I did. And I don't even know if Heather ever actually found what she was looking for. She was happy and content, and that was more than I expected after all this time. She had stopped trying to impose her ways on me and didn't have a crack at my "Patriarchal Hebrew God" unless she was feeling particularly pissed off or vicious.

I'd learned long ago that I couldn't win with either of my parents.

Star's mom, Billie, was already pouring something red into large wine glasses. Looking at Billie, you would never think that she'd have a daughter as straight as Violet. She wore a pair of leather leggings with a tight black dress and a golden dragon claw necklace. Her black hair had been given a Ruby Rose buzz cut, with the longer top styled into a teased mohawk. With her gold eye shadow, liquid-eyeliner cat eyes, and bronzed skin she looked like a Cleopatra rocker goddess.

"Hey, Jael. How's the demon hunting business?" she asked, her smile warm but her eyes uncommonly serious.

"Busy, Lady B," I replied as I hugged her.

"Well, I'm sure this will help." She passed me a glass of wine and turned to kiss Star's cheek.

"Leave Vi at home, did you?" Billie asked, and Star groaned.

"She's too busy taking calls from rich crackpots who want the Murder House. She is in her element."

"I don't know how I ended up with such a consumerist child."

"Some accountant must've pissed in the gene pool," I said, teasing her.

"I love her, but I don't think she's on the right path. She's completely cut herself off spiritually, so she will never be fulfilled." Billie shook her head. A part of me wanted to point out that most parents would see Violet as the stable and successful one in the family.

We all ended up on the back patio with bowls of Moroccan salad. It was a warm night, so we wanted to take advantage of it before Melbourne's weather turned on us. Letting the others talk, I felt the tight ball of anxiety inside me ease a little. As much as we were different, sometimes the familiarity of being around Heather and Billie helped. I wanted to know what the other exorcists were up to, what they were finding out. How much did the Catholics know about what was going on? Had there been more suicides?

"I want you guys to tell me what you saw the other night during your meditation. The darkness over the city," I said when we had moved on to a dark chocolate tart. Billie and Heather shared a look, silently swapping messages only years of friendship could decipher.

"It might work better if we show you." Heather stroked my cropped hair. "We'll do a meditation. It's been too long since we did one together." I hadn't been ready for that offer, but the smiles Star and Billie wore said they had. I really, really hated when they all ganged up on me. I sighed dramatically. Sometimes it was easier to roll with it.

We headed back downstairs and out into the garden where Heather had built a shady pergola and meditation space. We sat on large flat cushions, and I kicked off my boots to get comfortable.

After Dad left, meditation was the only thing that grounded Heather, and she had been determined to make me a balanced teenager by teaching it to me. It was a shame that my demon wouldn't allow me any kind of peace or concentration until Uriel beheaded the bastard. After I got out of the hospital, Heather had tried again with better success.

Going into a meditation was like engaging in a different level of the spiritual world that's distinct from the Behinds. It's like going into the most real dream you can ever imagine.

It was a good way for me to bounce ideas off Uriel when I couldn't feel him close by, but most of the time I found a nice tree in my meditation space to sit against and check out for a while. Praying is talking to God, but when I meditated, I just patiently waited to see if God wanted to talk back. I felt like I needed guidance, so I took a few deep, clearing breaths and tried to block out the world around me.

Out of habit, Heather guided us through the relaxation of our muscles, but after a few seconds, I was already under.

I was on a hill, walking beside a stream that cut through a valley surrounded by mountains. I had been to this spot many times before, and it never failed to astound me with its beauty. I was supposed to be with the others as Heather guided us toward the darkness in the city, but I couldn't help breathing a sigh of relief that I had broken away and found myself on my own.

It was one of the only places I ever felt truly at peace. I looked around, and suddenly Uriel was there, leaning against a massive tree. He was dressed casually again without his armor, and his long hair was loose around his shoulders.

"I didn't think you were going to turn up," I said with a smile.

"Were you expecting someone else?"

I recalled the man with the impossible voice who had shown me the battle, but I wasn't ready to talk to Uriel about it.

I merely shrugged. "You never know who will turn up for a chat."

"Are you tired of my company already?" he asked as I joined him. I fought the urge to hug him, but scary Heaven Battle Uriel was too fresh in my mind to want to risk it.

"Who would ever get tired of talking to a surly archangel?" I joked. "I don't suppose you feel like showing me this darkness in the city I keep hearing about. The new black ops exorcists in town have me worried."

"Don't be. I have a feeling they will be your allies." He offered me his hand. "I will show you, but I don't know what insight it can provide you that you don't already know."

"You never know. Human eyes might see something different." I slipped my hand into his and instantly felt safe. Whatever happened in the future, if I had Uriel with me, I somehow knew I was going to be okay.

He drew me to him, and for the first time, I felt a little awkward being so close to him. Maybe it was because he'd tucked me into bed the other night or the fact I had yelled at him. I didn't have time to think about it though because we moved, and I was standing on the roof of the historic ANZ Building on Collins Street. The city was a network of lights beneath me.

"This is how you see it with your normal eyes. And this"—Uriel brushed my eyelids closed—"is what it looks like in the spirit world."

When I opened my eyes again, the city was choking in a thick miasma of darkness. I tried not to throw up the Moroccan salad from earlier. It was so much worse than what I'd thought. I tried not to stare at it or to listen to the susurrus of whispers that seemed to emanate from it.

"It seems to be thicker on the north side," I commented as I moved to the other side of the roof.

"Is it thicker or a different kind of darkness?" he asked, making me pause. He hadn't used his teacher voice on me in a while, so I doubled my concentration and turned back to the south. There was a movement to it, like water that has a deep current underneath it. The one in the north was sort of choppy.

I let down my final shields and stumbled back at the intensity of the evil. Whatever the south was, it was deeply angry, its whispering reaching across to me in a language I felt I should understand. It was pleading, but there was a discourse to it that was unmistakably malicious. As it started to become too much, Uriel came behind me and his wings came around us, shielding me from the barrage of noise. I wrapped my arms around him, shaking at the intensity of it all and not caring about the terrifying vision I had of him in battle. He was a scary warrior, and I needed to feel protected.

"What did your human eyes see?" he asked, gently stroking my shaking head.

"It wasn't what I saw. It was what I heard."

His hand stilled. "What did you hear, *yadid*?"

"Whispers. But I didn't understand the language. It doesn't sound demonic, more like…ancient and angry." I wanted to repeat what I had heard, but the words were gone, vanishing like smoke.

Uriel didn't give me any warning, but I blinked and we were back in the valley, far away from the city lights and the surging evil.

"Do you know who the speaker was?" I pressed him.

"No, I heard no voices," he admitted. There was a concerned look in his blue-gray eyes that I hadn't seen before. "I have to go," Uriel added by way of a goodbye and vanished.

I thought I would wake up then, but instead I took a step and found myself in a dark alley. Rain fell heavily, but none of it touched me. A window smashed overhead, and two wrestling figures plummeted to the ground, landing in front of me with a shower of glass. There was a flash of silver and a choked gargle of profanity as one man killed the other.

No, it wasn't a man he was killing; it was a demon. I stepped closer as the flesh of the creature putrefied and washed away in the rain. Faster than any man could move, the attacker was on his feet, and the tip of a long silver spear pressed to my throat. He had to have been at least six foot four in height with curly black hair and black eyes that cut straight through me.

"Who are you?" he demanded angrily through a thick accent.

"Jael," I blurted, hands up in surrender.

"A spy?"

"An exorcist," I said, and his eyes sheened gold in the darkness like a cat's. "What are you?"

He looked like he was going to reply to me when the ground opened up and swallowed me whole.

I cried out as I was pulled farther and farther down, finally landing in a hollowed-out cavern. The darkness was absolute, and I stretched my arms out blindly, searching the floor beneath me. As my hand touched a foot and shackles, I jerked myself backward. Eyes shone in the darkness, and as a cracked voice started to speak, I screamed and screamed.

I jerked out of my meditation with Star's hands on my feet and Heather's hands on my shoulders trying to ground me.

"What's happening?" I asked through numb lips. I was trembling violently as the terror of the cavernous darkness and the cold voice still clung to me.

"Are you okay? You were gone for like two hours," Star said, rubbing my shins. "Literally gone. We couldn't rouse you."

"And then you almost gave me a heart attack by speaking some crazy language," Heather added. "I've heard people speaking in tongues, but that wasn't it. It sounded…"

"Ancient and angry," I replied, shaking myself.

"You were channeling something dark, girl." Billie handed me a glass of water, and I gulped it down. I wasn't channeling, only repeating what I had heard, but I didn't want to fight them about it.

My mobile started ringing as soon as I stepped through the back door. My ringtones were personalized, and it was a rare night that I heard a shofar horn blowing. I emptied my bag upside down on the couch in my hurry to find it.

"Hello?" I answered.

"Jael? I'm sorry to call you at this hour." Rabbi Josef's voice sounded strained and breathless.

"It's fine. What's happened? Where are you?" I asked, shoving everything back into my bag haphazardly.

"I need you to come to the synagogue. There's—" His voice was drowned out by a woman's high-pitched wail. Before he could say anything else, her voice changed, and she started speaking in a deep voice. My body broke out in goose bumps as I recognized the language, ancient and angry.

"Stay put. I'll be there as soon as I can," I promised.

I was in an Uber fifteen minutes later, when I realized my neck was bleeding from the cut made by the demon hunter's spear.

10

THE SYNAGOGUE IN COBURG was relatively new but less grand and imposing than the ones in Toorak. There was still something regal about its white columns and the varnished, olive wood doors that made me wish I'd dressed in something nicer. The best I could do was to take my scarf from out of my bag and cover my head with it. It wasn't a proper *tallit*, simply a maroon-colored scarf. It wasn't strictly needed to enter the synagogue, but a part of me felt better for it. Josef pulled the side entrance door open as soon as I knocked.

"Come in quickly," he said urgently and locked the door behind us.

"You look like death warmed over," I said, my uneasiness spiking uncomfortably. He smelled of sweat and myrrh and was more flustered than I had ever seen him. "What's going on?"

"Do you know of the man that suicided off the Alma Street platform?" he demanded.

"Professor Ben-Ezra. Yes, I know. His daughter threw herself in front of a tram while I watched."

"What? Why didn't you tell me? The police never mentioned you were involved in the incident."

"I told them not to. I was just another witness. What has that got to do with anything?"

"The girl was seeking you out. She knew something was wrong. Sweet Rebecca, how I failed her." He pulled at his graying hair, and I wanted to reach out and give him a comforting pat on the shoulder. He was super Orthodox though, so I resisted.

"Who was it that was screaming on the phone?" I asked as he started shuffling down the hallway.

"It was Rebecca's mother, Esther," he said, unlocking another door for me.

"The police have been trying to find her for questioning," I replied. "Have you been hiding her here the whole time?"

"I told them she was here," Josef said defensively. "She was too distraught to speak with them."

"More like too possessed to speak with them. That's why I am here right?"

Josef nodded fractionally as if it pained him to do so. "We've been trying to help her for days. I have completed successful Jewish exorcisms before, but nothing we do seems to have any effect on this creature. It's a hard thing for a rabbi to admit he's out of his depth. I didn't…I didn't know what else to do. I feel like I failed…"

"It's okay, Josef. I might not have any better luck than you, but I'll try. Take me to her, and we'll see."

"The others won't like that I called you so don't expect a warm welcome," he warned.

"Do I ever?"

Another scream echoed through the building, and I mentally locked every psychic shield I had down tight. A tremor ran under my skin as the strange language I'd heard in my meditation reached me.

I didn't recognize the ten men of the traditional *minyan*, the witnesses that made up the ritual quorum, but they recognized me. There were loud protestations in Hebrew and English, mostly along the lines of allowing a Christian in on Jewish business.

I tuned them out, focusing my attention entirely on the woman tied to a chair in the middle of the room. Her hair hung in a long sweaty mess about her face, and she'd been thrashing about until she saw me and went dead still. Her dark eyes stared at me like a hunting hawk.

The room stank of the sulfur and myrrh that they had used to try and fumigate the demon within her. Like her daughter, when I tried to see the demon controlling her, I saw a strange sort of shimmering blur. *What the hell is it?*

"All of you get out," I said coldly. Josef hustled the others, snapping at them until they gave up and left me be. I dropped my bag on a chair and took a step closer. "Hello, Esther."

"Jael, Jael," she said. Her voice had the same manic tone her daughter's had had.

I smiled. "No tram for you to jump in front of this time is there?"

Quicker than I thought possible the leather strap holding one of her wrists snapped, and she grabbed me by the front of my shirt. I tried to stay calm as she sniffed at me.

"You stink of the angels, exorcist," Esther hissed, and her tongue shot out to lick the cut at my throat. *"Michael."* I made a quick movement with my arm, bringing it across and around to break Esther's hold on me. She collapsed back in the chair smacking her lips.

I wiped her spit from my neck. "Gross."

The creature started speaking in the same complex tongue I heard in my vision. I managed to catch the word "Duda'el" and the desert and the Hebrew word for treasure a few times, but otherwise it was gibberish.

"Why do you keep speaking of the desert? What desert?" I demanded.

"Sleeping. Resting. Hidden. Dark, dark, dark," Esther said. "There will be a battle, little exorcist. Oh yes, I see them now: those haughty archangels shining so brightly, full of self-righteousness. They cut us down with impunity because we rose higher than them. They couldn't stand our glorious freedom; they slave under a master who tried to cut us away like we were a rotting limb. Down in the darkness they placed us with our dead sons. Our beautiful wives. They threw down our temples and our palaces, but we will have vengeance in this life and the next. We will tear them down, we will break their bodies…"

It fell out of English into its original tongue as the rant continued, full of malice and self-pity. Whatever the being was, it was closely tied to Israel. *What had the professor been working on?*

The only Jewish exorcisms I knew, I was positive Rabbi Josef and the others would have tried. Days of work had only pissed the creature off and worn Josef out.

I was aware of the arguing voices outside the door, but I tried not to let it throw my concentration. I always tried to be careful and respectful with Elyon's chosen people; they didn't have to believe in my Messiah for me to believe in their God.

"What makes you think you'll have better luck where the others failed, Jael? Do you think yourself a killer of generals like your Uriel?"

"Are you a general?" I asked as I searched through the mess in my bag.

"I am not what you think I am, exorcist."

"You know what? I really don't care what you are. I just want you gone."

I anointed my hands and head with myrrh oil before rubbing some on Esther's forehead. Pulling up a chair in front of her I took a deep breath and started to recite one of the "Songs of Exorcism" found in the collection of *The Dead Sea Scrolls*, and whatever was inside Esther hissed threateningly.

"It doesn't matter what Psalms you sing to me. I'm not a demon that you have authority to command. But I am tired of this old flesh."

"You might not be a demon, but I'm still going to send you to Hell so Esther can be free of you," I promised.

"Do you want to know a secret, exorcist?" A demented smile spread across her face.

"Sure."

"I'm already dead." Esther shuddered, convulsing violently, and the presence left her. I unstrapped her arms and lowered her to the floor.

"Josef! Call an ambulance!" I shouted when I realized she wasn't breathing. I felt around in her mouth to see if there was anything blocking her airway before I started doing CPR. In this line of business, it paid to know first aid.

Josef came in with his mobile phone already to his ear, and by the time the paramedics arrived, I was just about fainting. They moved me out of the way, but they didn't have any luck reviving her.

"I don't understand what happened," I told him as we watched Esther's body being loaded into the back of the ambulance.

"I'll go over the tapes and see if there is something we missed."

"You *filmed* me?"

"I film all the exorcisms we do in case something like this happens," he replied before letting out a tired sigh. "We need to in case of legal action. So much can go wrong. You know that."

I felt violated, but it would stop the other witnesses from thinking I had killed her just to spite them.

Josef was kind enough to drop me off at home, and I went over my conversation with Esther before she died.

"I don't know what we are dealing with, Rabbi, but I want you to know I'm going to find out," I told him as I got out of his sedan.

"I'll look through my books and see if I can find any references to such a creature," he said.

I waved him goodbye as I stood alone on the footpath, feeling like I'd just killed another woman.

11

"THANKS FOR DOING THIS for me, James," I said and took a sip of the coffee he brought me. To say that my night had been rough was an understatement. It had been a terrifying fever dream. I had refused to call on Uriel because I was so gutted by my failure. Nothing about Esther's exorcism had been right. Nothing made sense.

"It's cool, Jael. I wanted to double check the museum anyway. I don't think Bobbie and Chris would've done it right." Bobbie Saunders and Chris Anderson were two of the biggest douchebag police officers I'd ever met and were about as culturally sensitive as a brick.

"Did they have any luck tracking Clair down as a witness?" I asked.

"Nope. Wherever she's gone to hide, she's doing an excellent bloody job of it. None of the shelters have seen her, not even the new one you gave me the curiously random tip about."

"It wasn't random at all. She said she was thinking of checking it out." The fact Crazy Bill had a brochure for it made me even more curious. Bill and Clair talked a lot, so if one was thinking of checking into the fancy place, the other was likely to follow.

My phone buzzed with an unknown number, and I opened the message.

> It's Max. Are you okay? Gonna sound weird, but I had a crazy dream about you and wanted to check in.

I groaned. Another sensitive little empath. Exactly what I needed.

> You had a dream about me? If you weren't so guileless, I'd say you were being a creeper right now. How did you get this number, you amateur stalker?

> My mom had it from that time you pulled a demon out of me.

> Oh yeah. Good times.

I hesitated a moment.

> Rough night but I will be fine. On the case.

> You got my number if you get arrested.

"And who has you smiling all of a sudden?" James asked, nudging me with his elbow.

"Max has decided to ask Star out. I'm encouraging him to go for it."

"You're a pretty big liar for such a little exorcist," he said, though I noticed his hands tighten on the steering wheel.

"You clearly haven't met many of us then. Max was checking in on me actually. He had a dream. Little bastard could be a bit psychic, so I'll have to watch out for that. I don't need anyone looking too far into my future. It could be why the demon fought so hard to stay with him. They do love people with unusual gifts."

I realized I was talking aloud and shut my mouth. James was a good sort and tolerant, but I didn't want to dump too much of my crazy on him. Even if he thought he could handle it, James's big brother and protector cop instincts would kick in, and it would be a concerned lecture or three for me.

"It's good to see you are making friends, J. I'm starting to think you are going to need them before all this is over," James said as he turned off Queens Way. "Especially one that's got a bit of legal background. There seems to be a lot of bodies around you lately."

"It's not as if I want there to be. You should've seen this chick last night. I don't know what was riding her, but it killed her for the fun of it." I shook my head.

"According to the coroner, her heart exploded," he admitted.

"What? I thought they weren't going to let you in on the case."

"The coroner owed me a favor, so she told me after a bit of persuasion."

"Persuasion, was it? Your magic charm strikes again," I teased, and he smiled. Oh yeah, I bet it would have been *real* hard to convince her to spill her guts.

"She said it was as if all the blood in Esther's body went straight to her heart, and it popped under pressure. It freaked the hell out of her. She's a good Catholic girl, and it sure put the fear of the Devil in her. She was muttering something about leaving early so she could go to confession." James laughed, but I didn't. If he had seen what I had, then he would probably be doing the same thing.

I got an unexpected visual of Alessandro giving me a confession, and I quickly wiped it before my ears started burning. The previous night of terror had also made me want to ring Mr. Black Ops Exorcist for advice since he was the only other exorcist in town. But I couldn't bring myself to admit how badly I'd screwed up. My pride hurt.

I was saved from more uncomfortable thoughts as James pulled into a car park in front of the solemn gray block building of the museum. Brightly colored posters advertised exhibits as we pushed open the polished glass doors and walked into the cold foyer.

"Are you sure they are expecting us?" I asked nervously.

"Yep, I called ahead," he told me as a lady with gray hair and dressed in a neat suit approached us.

"Mr. Hunt?" she said, smiling. I politely smiled back, trying not to look like someone he should've been arresting. They exchanged pleasantries as I experimentally dropped a shield. Instantly a flutter of anxiety spread across my ribs. Something was going on. Dianne led us past the gift shop and swiped her access card over a panel, opening the doors that led out to the offices, storage, and preservation areas.

"This was the professor's office," Dianne said, opening another door. The room was packed with overflowing bookshelves, a large desk, and a double-screened desktop computer. "Take as long as you need. He was an incredibly honest man."

"Thank you. It's much appreciated. You don't mind if I talk to a few of the other staff members?" James asked, smiling wide.

"Not at all. They would be more than happy to chat with you, I'm sure."

I fought the urge to roll my eyes as James said, "My assistant, Jael, will look over the office if you would like to lead me to the others." Smooth. He was trying to give me as much private time in the office as he could, and I made a mental note to buy him a beer.

Professor Ben-Ezra was almost too clean for an academic. I studied the contents of his tidy desk and the framed pictures on his shelves. There was one of the family, not looking demonic but happy, in front of the Sydney Opera House and another older photo of Esther on their wedding day. There was a newer shot of him standing next to a young woman with a distinctive Lara Croft vibe about her. They were standing on the dusty, white ground, and the wind was blowing her long brown hair out. She wore aviators and a khaki singlet and smiled easily.

"And who is this babe you're hanging out with, professor?" I asked their smiling faces before I undid the back of the frame. On the back of the photo, someone had scribbled in blue ink: *Nazirah and Aaron. 2014.* I clipped the frame back on and put it in its place on the desk. A small tray of mail sat beside it, and I flicked through the pile of junk until I stumbled on a picture postcard of some ancient ruins.

My Teacher,

They are going to let me do it! More days of scratching about in desert sand, but the dig is going ahead.

Wish you would reconsider and join me.

Nazirah, your greatest student

I took a photo of the ruins with my phone, and my eyes drifted to his over-flowing recycle bin. There was a wrapper from a small parcel dropped beside it, and I knelt to pick it up. It was covered in stamps, and from the smeared postage ink, I could make out that it had been posted in Be'er Sheva, Israel. Under the word "From" was written: *Your Greatest Student.*

I dropped the packaging and hurried to find James. He was looking through a large magnifying glass at some antique jewelry and laughing with one of the young female assistants.

"Do you know of any parcels that the professor received before he died?" I asked her, breaking up their conversation.

"The professor received a lot of mail," she said, confused.

"Did he mention anything about an old student of his? Nazirah?"

"Nazirah, the shining star," a sarcastic voice said behind me, and I turned to face the newcomer. He looked about my age and had the vibe of a disgruntled PhD student.

"So, he mentioned her," I said.

"Of course, he did. She was ten feet high to him. None of his other students could live up to her, especially not here in Australia. He was always talking about her achievements. Apparently, she'd just gotten approval to dig in some site based off some goat bones a Bedouin found," he replied.

"Did he say anything about her sending him something from Be'er Sheva?" I asked.

"He didn't say who it was from, but the day he died he got something that he could barely contain his excitement over," the girl said. "He was worked up about it and was muttering some lines from *The Dead Sea Scrolls* over and over. He was always so obsessed with them; I don't understand why he left Israel."

"What lines?" I demanded.

"They were names, I think," PhD said. "He kept saying them over and over like he was stuck in a loop. Pretty sure Azazel was one of them."

The girl butted in. "He was saying something about chiefs of ten who took wives, and something about teaching men things like sorcery—"

"And magic. And the women becoming pregnant?" I asked. They nodded and my latte rose in my throat. "Where is your bathroom?"

"Down the corridor to the left." PhD pointed.

I hurried past them and pushed myself into a stall before I dry heaved. Nothing came up, so I sat down on the lid and tried to breathe. My heart was racing and sweat pricked my skin. *What the hell did Nazirah send him?*

"Jael?" a voice asked on the other side of the door. Just what I needed.

"What are you doing hanging out in the ladies' toilets, Uriel?" I took some toilet paper and wiped the tears from my eyes. "What if I was peeing?"

"But you aren't. Come out of there."

I fumbled with the lock and stepped out. He was leaning against the bay of sinks, his arms folded and his face like an ice storm.

I shuffled past him and turned the cold tap on. "What's up?"

"You tell me," he said. "You blocked me out last night. I don't recall the last time you did that, and now you are crying in the toilets."

I splashed cold water on my face and was fumbling for a paper towel when one was pushed into my hand. "Thanks. I messed up, and I couldn't handle seeing your disapproval on top of that."

The ice storm in his eyes melted a little, and I struggled not to burst into tears again. Uriel didn't touch me, but I felt comforted just by seeing him. "A woman died, and I think it was my fault. I'm meant to protect people from demons." I sniffed. "I don't know what's happening or how to stop it. And now I have a dead family and some cryptic lines from *The Book of Enoch*, and I don't know what to *do*—"

"Breathe," he said gently, his hand moving to rest over mine on the sink. "I'm not omniscient or a mind reader, Jael. Tell me what happened from the beginning."

I told him what had gone wrong the night before, including Esther's heart exploding in her chest.

"I'm going to have to seek advice on this," Uriel said when I finished. "It seems extreme for a demon to do such a thing. You will follow up on what the professor received in the mail?"

"Of course. Although if I don't get out there soon, they are going to think I have fallen in the toilet."

"Calm your heart, Jael. The woman's death was not your fault, and there was nothing you could have done differently." Uriel let go of my hand. "And don't shut me out again. You are my charge. I am here for you." His serious expression didn't change, but I felt like crying again knowing I was never really alone even though sometimes it felt that way.

"Damn, J. Are you okay in there?" James asked from the corridor outside, and I felt Uriel's presence leave me.

"Yeah, I'm coming," I called back and dropped my snotty tissues into the bin before I opened the door. James had a bottle of water ready, and he handed it over.

"What was that about?" he asked.

"Nothing, I think that leftover Thai food I ate for breakfast was too old," I lied quickly. Too many lies. "Did you learn anything else from the nerds?"

"Only that the professor had a big argument with his rabbi the night he died."

"Damn, I knew Josef was holding out on me," I said before taking a long drink of water.

"It doesn't mean anything. He could have been talking about a point in theology for all you know."

"He still should've said something to me about it. Esther ended up at the synagogue too. He definitely knows something."

We said our goodbyes to the museum staff and headed back to the car. My head was starting to pound, and I knew I was going to have to do some serious studying when I got home.

"What was that quote the professor was saying? You turned white as a sheet as soon as she started saying it," James said as we climbed in.

"It's from a copy of *The Book of Enoch* they found at Qumran. The professor probably studied them in Israel. It was probably just stuck in his head."

James sighed. "Jael, you really are a shit liar."

12

WHEN I GOT HOME later that afternoon, I hit the research books hard. Meta stuck to me like Blu-Tack, which made me think I wasn't hiding my churned-up emotions as well as I thought.

As a rule, I always journal each exorcism I perform to try and learn where I went wrong or if I did something right. Yeshua hadn't given a precise handbook on casting out evil spirits to the disciples but told them to experiment. I took this to heart pretty early on, and you'd be surprised at some of the things that had happened. I used to have a recurring nightmare that someone would start to read my journals one day, and I'd be locked up. Now I know I could just tell them I was working on a book series, and they'd probably let me off. After my first trip to an asylum, I wasn't eager to return. I still had recurring nightmares about being surrounded by those white concrete blocks when I was stressed.

I found space in the newest notebook and started jotting down everything I knew about what was settling over the city, the deaths, the Murder House, and the details of the day's visit to the museum. I pulled out my copy of *The Book of Enoch*, reread the passages, and wrote extra notes.

When I had exhausted my book collection, I ordered some takeaway from downstairs and booted up my laptop. I had no last name for Nazirah, and when I looked up digs around Be'er Sheva I drew a blank. It wasn't until I was looking at Google Maps that I paused. Be'er Sheva was on the fringes of the Negev Desert.

"A dig in the Negev..." I murmured aloud. It barely took two clicks of my mouse to find the image of the ruins that matched the professor's postcard. I had the whisper of the answer on the edge of my mind, when my phone rang, scaring the hell out of me.

"What?" I demanded, my mind still half-buried in the desert.

"*Buona sera, signorina,*" replied an accented voice as smooth as melted dark chocolate. "Do you always answer the phone in such a manner?"

"Is that you, *Padre*?" I asked, trying to keep my voice steady as my stomach clenched anxiously. "How did you get my number, Alessandro?"

"A strange thing happened today," he continued, ignoring my question. "A little bird flew to me and spoke of a strange murder that occurred in a synagogue."

"A little bird, you say? What type of bird?" I tried to dodge. "And why would you want to ask me about it? I am only a *hobbyist* after all." It was childish, but I couldn't resist throwing his words back at him.

"Sometimes those on the outside can see different things, helpful things." He sighed on the other end. "I would like it if we could call a professional truce, Jael."

"That's a big opinion change to have in the last two days," I replied, barely containing my shock. Mr. Hotshot Exorcist wanted to work with me?

"It has been an illuminating forty-eight hours, to say the least." He sounded tired, and I wondered how much he'd slept. If he was anything like me, I knew it wouldn't have been much.

"It sounds as if you are finally realizing how much the archbishop and the others have ignored my warnings over the years where demons are concerned," I said. Meta pawed my leg impatiently, and I got up. I needed to walk if I was going to have this conversation tonight. I clipped on his lead and headed outside.

"The archbishop is like many priests who have misguided views when it comes to exorcism. Things have been left alone here for far too long." He must have felt my silent disapproval because he added, "You are only one person, Jael. You couldn't have known or stopped the tide on your own."

"It's not like I'm someone's first choice, even if they do eventually find me," I admitted as Meta smelled a bare patch of ground excitedly. "They usually try the Catholics first and are turned away."

"Exactly, and that shouldn't have happened. I'm thinking you and me, we started…wrong. I apologize if I offended you at our first meeting. I've never met an exorcist like you before, and from the stories the archbishop had told me, I imagined you to be something that you obviously aren't. It was a shock to me to meet this terrifying, rebellious woman that the others spoke of. You were not what I expected."

"I rarely am," I replied, wondering where this conversation was going. "Vows don't make you an exorcist." He didn't sound like the arrogant priest I'd met on the street. "Were you serious when you said you wanted a professional truce?"

"*Si.*"

"And what would that entail?"

"A mutual sharing of information and experienced backup, should it be needed. We need to be allies."

I took a moment to think about the sheer number of exorcisms I'd been to in the past month and the extreme weirdness of the last few days. The dead professor's family weighed heavily on me, and I had the feeling I was going to hit a wall with my research pretty soon.

Never in my wildest dreams did I think I'd ever be willing to work with a Catholic priest, but my stubbornness had been swayed the moment I had seen him in the grainy photo of the school in Peru. Oh boy, did I want to know what had happened in that school. *Damn my curiosity.*

"Okay, *Padre*, let's be friends. You show me yours, and I'll show you mine," I said finally. "You can go first as a show of good faith."

"Very well. I have performed twenty-seven exorcisms in the past two days."

I stopped dead. "Come again? Twenty-seven? By yourself?"

"My companions Paulo and Gregory have performed at least ten each as well," Alessandro added. Black ops exorcists indeed.

"That's *incredible*," I said in a daze. "How are you even still awake right now?"

"Lots of espressos." He laughed softly, and I smiled at the sound. Good to know he could still laugh after all of that. I'd hate to think what kind of state I'd be in.

"I can't believe that many people have come to you, and they have all been legitimate possessions. It's going to sound crazy, but it's almost like a…"

"Like a plague? *Si*, my thoughts too. The demons are all telling lies, but there's a thread of similarity to them. Lots of chatter about something being found and some kind of war coming. They also have a lot to say about you."

"About me? Let me guess. Something about me not being strong enough and how they want to kill me. I've heard that a lot lately."

"They seem somewhat fixated on you. Any idea why?"

"None whatsoever. I thought it might be because I was an exorcist, but if that was the case then they'd be getting excited about you too."

"These things have a way of escalating so be careful, *esorcista*."

"Always. Okay, your turn. What do you want to know?"

"What happened at the synagogue last night? I had a look at the body and the heart…"

"Was exploded? Let me guess. Your 'little bird' was the pretty coroner who worked on Esther?" There was a knowing silence at the end of the line.

"She went to her priest as a concerned woman of the faith, and he placed the call," he admitted finally, surprising me with his transparency. "What happened to her?"

I looked about to make sure the street I was on was empty before I started telling him about the professor and his family, *The Book of Enoch* he was obsessively quoting, and finally, about Nazirah.

"We are dealing with two separate problems here," I said. "The demons I have seen lately have been completely different from what was inhabiting the family."

"It doesn't sound like anything we have seen either. The Negev Desert, on the other hand, used to be named the Duda'el, the Cauldron of God. It was where Michael and the other archangels bound the Watchers before the Flood," Alessandro said thoughtfully.

"Damn, I'm so thick sometimes! That was why the professor was quoting passages from *The Book of Enoch*. It recounts that battle and the times when the Nephilim walked."

"Perhaps the student shipped something from one of the cult sites they have found there. I know a few have been uncovered in recent years."

"I might have a lead on whatever was in the packaging," I said, thinking of the rabbi. "But I will have to tackle it alone."

"I look forward to hearing about what you find," Alessandro replied. "Are you home yet?"

"Just unlocking my door now. Why?" I asked as I juggled my keys and Meta's lead to get back inside.

"The house you cleansed. You said the possessed man came looking for you, and that your name had been written in blood."

"And?"

"And the girl, she came searching for you before she leaped to her death," he added seriously.

"What's your point, priest?"

"My point is you know these demons are looking for you specifically. Actively seeking you out, going as far as baiting you, to try to stop you. You shouldn't be making it easy for them by walking by yourself at night, Jael."

"Are you my big brother now? I can take care of myself."

"I have no doubt, *signorina*, but aren't you wondering why it's you they are hunting?"

"I told you it's probably because I'm an exorcist, and the human side of them wants help."

"You know a fully possessed person won't seek the help of an exorcist to get rid of a demon. It wouldn't allow it. What makes you different then?"

"Absolutely nothing. I'm not special; trust me."

"You are special to God, otherwise you would not be an exorcist. If I know one thing about being an exorcist, it's that it isn't something you wake up and decide it would be a good idea to become. You were given a choice, yes?"

"Yes," I answered, knowing that there was no way I would tell him about Uriel. At least not yet.

"You chose to be an exorcist, to look the demonic in the face every day, and that makes you special. The fact you have no formal training and refuse to be under the protection of a church either makes you very strong or very vulnerable."

"I don't answer to doctrine; I answer to God alone," I replied sharply, my hackles rising unexpectedly.

"So you have made clear. Thank you for your conversation tonight. It has been interesting." He sounded sincere enough that my temper vanished.

"It really has," I agreed and meant it. "I don't remember the last time I talked to someone about this kind of thing. I've never known another exorcist before."

"It's a lonely path we walk, full of danger. Be mindful of your safety, *signorina*. You might not think there's anything different or of interest about you, but the fallen ones do. My offer of backup is available to you while I'm in the city. The archbishop might warn me against getting involved with you, but I believe the situation too precarious to have lone wolves."

"I will take it under advisement. I'll let you know if anything else happens that is important." I hesitated before I asked, "One day will you tell me what happened at the school in Peru?"

"How did you know about that?" he asked, faintly amused. "Are you checking up on me?"

"Maybe."

"One day I will tell you." His laughter was light on the other end. "Good night, Jael."

"Good night, Alessandro. Let me know if you want to howl at the moon sometime." I placed my phone on the kitchen bench and stared at Meta. "Well, that was weird."

A second later his mobile number and email address were messaged to me. Uriel's warning about me needing the exorcists came back to me, and I carefully stored the number under A-Team. I really hoped I wasn't going to have to use it.

I slept late the next day; my body seemed determined to rest up after the stressful couple of days I'd had. My dreams were a blur of talking demons, ancient ruins, and a blood-splattered woman in the desert sun. The dark demon hunter I had seen in my meditation also made an appearance, and this time he had no idea of my presence. The guy was next-level scary. Was it just a dream? Or was it a warning?

I tried to continue studying after talking with Alessandro, but my concentration had been too scattered. A part of me hated how much I'd liked talking to someone about the demonic activity in the city without censoring myself. Star was awesome, but she'd never understand everything I saw and experienced. We had made peace with that early on. She didn't need to know the exact ins and outs of what I did, only that they were effective and had a cost. I had never known another exorcist before and making friends with one seemed like an intimidating prospect.

I checked the messages on my phone, but the one from James stood out from the rest. They still hadn't found Clair. Most people would be inclined to let it go because of how many homeless are already listed as missing. But it was a thorn in my mind, and I knew I wasn't going to be able to concentrate on the books without going to look for her myself.

It was one of those ridiculously perfect days that Melbourne would occasionally produce with a warm breeze and a cloudless sky. My fried mind and emotions started to clear despite myself as I rode the tram into the city. At Flemington Bridge, a man got on and sat a few seats in front of me. He looked as if he'd been living rough, his face placidly happy until his eyes locked on mine. The bliss vanished, and he stared me down. Alessandro's warnings came back to me too late as the man rushed toward me, breathing rapidly through his teeth.

"Who are you?" he demanded, gripping the chair in front of me. I could hear voices raise behind me, but I didn't take my eyes off him. This wasn't just normal crazy tram guy antics. I made to get up, but he moved in front of me, grabbed me by the shoulders, and pinned me to the wall of the tram. "Why do they want you so badly?"

"You got five seconds to let me go, buddy," I warned. "I don't want to hurt you."

"But they want you, and they won't shut up about it!" He wheezed desperately, letting go of me so he could clutch the sides of his matted head. "In here."

"Settle down before someone calls the cops on you," I said and sat back down. I pointed to the chair opposite me, and he slumped into it and started weeping. Great. I hated criers.

"They keep telling me that I need to kill you. I don't want to kill you, lady. Why do they want to kill you?"

"They usually do, mate. I can help shut them up if you'll let me. I can get rid—"

He started thrashing about in his chair as if his arms and legs were fighting each other to get away.

"I command you to be still," I said firmly but softly, knowing that the demons would hear me. The arms and legs stopped moving at once.

"It's hurting, it's hurting."

"To the demon inside this man, I command you to stop your attack at once. Come on out. We need to talk."

"Slut," he hissed in a chorus of voices.

"There you are." I leaned back in my chair. "Why do you keep insisting that this man kills me?"

"Orders are orders. They want you dead. The bosses. Jael, Jael, the light one with the powerful guardian. You are going to be dead."

"I'm afraid that won't be happening today. Go away, so I can talk to the human."

He shuddered, face going from snide to terrified in a moment. "What are you doing to them?"

"Getting them to behave, so we can talk. What's your name, mate?"

"F-Freddie."

"Excellent! You are doing really well, Freddie. Any idea how these hitchhikers came to be riding along with you?"

"There…there was a fight. I called out for someone to help me, to stop these other guys from kicking my head in. Heard these voices. Said they'd give me the power to make it stop. I said okay."

"What happened to the guys you were fighting, Freddie?"

He looked down at his hands, helplessly clenching and unclenching them. "I d-don't know. The voices won't leave me alone. They won't shut up even in my sleep. I hear them in my dreams."

"It's going to be okay," I said, trying to soothe him. I prayed for angels to uphold and protect us, and a deadly calm washed over me. I hadn't even prayed it aloud, but Freddie gasped, pushing himself back in his chair. I felt the presence of angels around us but didn't dare take my eyes off him.

"Are you seeing this?" he asked, eyes bugging out of his head. "Are they really angels?"

"They are. They are going to help us with your little problem."

"The voices don't like them."

I couldn't help the small smile that twisted my lips. "No, I don't suppose they would."

"Who is that?" Freddie whispered, and I stilled. Warmth spread down from the top of my head and down my back and shoulders. My heart started to pound, and I didn't dare turn around as words reverberated through me. *Touch him.* As if by command, my palms started to burn, heat spreading up my arms. I started to shake, and my teeth chattered. I leaned forward and took his mud-slicked face in my hands. There was static and fire in my veins. It was lightning. And then it was gone from my hands and into him, and I collapsed backward in my seat. The presence of the demons inside the man vanished.

Freddie leaned forward to clutch his knees, sobbing his eyes out. Around us, voices started to rise and filter back through. I looked at the other commuters, but none of them were looking at us. They were oblivious to what had happened right next to them as they were checking their phones. Freddie was near hysterical, and no one batted an eye. Just another crazy homeless guy on the tram.

"What do I do now?" he asked, through his hands.

"Go to Saint Patrick's. Tell them Jael sent you and exactly what happened here. They'll take care of you." At least I hoped they would. Alessandro said if I ever needed help, I should go to him. I figured that extended to some of my new friends.

I got off at Queen Victoria Market, leaving poor Freddie a mess. I tried not to look at the platform, or where I had talked to the professor's daughter. My legs were starting to shake, so I sat down at the vegetarian café and ordered a coffee and some sweet potato fries. I needed carbs and sugar in a hurry. I wasn't expecting to do an exorcism on the fly this morning, or I would've had breakfast.

The caffeine and starch did their work as I went through the exorcism in my mind. Demons were usually a little subtler in their approach; if I didn't prod them, they'd leave me alone. Everything I knew was slowly going out of the window. I stared at my hands looking for any redness or bruising, but there was nothing, just a faint itch beneath the surface.

"You okay?" the waitress asked me as she cleared the table next to me.

"For now," I said, failing to keep the worry out of my voice. "Hey, this is going to seem like a random question, but you haven't seen a homeless woman with a Jack Russell by any chance?"

"Clair and Champ? Not for a few days now. I usually save them some food at the end of the day, but they've been a no-show all week. Why are you after them? They aren't in any trouble, are they?"

"No, nothing like that. I usually give her a few dollars while I'm here, that's all."

"She might be staying at the new shelter on Blackwood Street. I hear a lot of good things about it."

"Thanks for the tip."

It wasn't hard to find the building on Blackwood Street. Heart of the Homeless had bought out a whole block and created a silver, glass, and white haven. I felt dirty standing on the opposite side of the street, let alone considering the idea of stepping into it. I wondered what it would look like in five years' time, when the kids had had a chance to graffiti the walls and enough drunks from the pub down the road had puked in front of it. If I felt too worthless to enter, I wondered how the homeless felt about it.

The glass doors opened revealing a wide white desk, lounge chairs in the waiting area, and huge vases of flowers. A well-groomed lady with black-framed glasses smiled as she approached me.

"Welcome to Heart of the Homeless. How can I help you? Are you in need?"

"Uh…no. At least not in the way you are thinking. I'm looking for someone," I explained, the urge to pat my hair smooth almost overwhelming me. "She's one of the homeless. I was told she might have come here."

"We see many homeless people here. Do you have a name?" She moved behind the desk and started tapping at the keyboard.

"Her name is Clair. She never gave me a last name," I said, leaning against the cool counter. I hoped I didn't leave a smudge.

"Clair, Clair, Clair," the woman repeated, her eyes scanning the screen. "Are you sure that is her real name?"

"I have no idea, but it's the one she goes by."

"I'm sorry, but we have no Clairs checked in with us."

"She would've had a little dog with her called Champ. Brown-and-white Jack Russell," I said, pressing her. "You do let them keep their animals, right?"

"Of course we do. Most of the time they are the only companions these poor people have. Let me have a look." She typed in something else. "How do you know Clair?"

"I've talked to her a bunch of times. Gave her some money. Fed Champ some treats. She's well-known around the market. People have noticed that she's not hanging about." I looked at the elaborate flower arrangement in the vase beside me and tried to control the urge to purposely tip it over. The place was too pristine, too perfect. The Stepford secretary in front of me made it even eerier.

"It's nice of you to want to check in on her. Many of these unfortunates wouldn't be noticed or missed even if they did disappear." She looked up from the screen. "I'm sorry there's been no Jack Russells either. Do you have a photo of them?"

"No, I don't have a photo. Look, can I just go for a walk around and see if I can spot them or talk to some of the other homeless here who might have seen her? There was an accident, and I need to talk to her about it."

"I'm sorry. We don't allow anyone just to walk about the shelter. These people are going through rehabilitation. They don't need strangers coming in to gawk at them and judge them when they are at their lowest."

"I'd never judge them! That's not what this is about. I just want to see if they know her—"

"I can take your name and number, and if anyone turns up here matching the description, I can give you a call."

"Jael bloody Quinlan," a voice said behind me. "I'd recognize that argumentative tone anywhere."

I turned to see a man coming down some stairs on the other side of the room. Wearing a suit with a deep blue shirt that matched his eyes, the stranger looked like a walking version of a *GQ* model.

"Do I know you?" I asked, wondering if I had cut him off in traffic or helped one of his relatives with a demon problem.

"Seriously? You don't recognize me?" He laughed. "Tom Warner. High school math buddy." A gawkily tall kid with wild black hair and glasses flashed in my mind. Talk about changing from a nerdy duckling to a disturbingly hot swan.

"Tom! I'm so sorry. Yes, of course I remember you," I said, rallying and taking the hand that he stretched toward me. "What are you doing here?"

"I opened this place a few months ago."

"What? That's incredible. It's...nice."

"I couldn't help overhearing that you are looking for someone?" Tom looked at the Stepford secretary. "Any luck, Gemma?"

"No, Mr. Warner. I was going to take Ms. Quinlan's number and—"

"It's okay, Gemma, I'll take her for a walk around."

"But—"

"She's an old friend, Gem. I want to show her about. The rules can be relaxed this one time." Tom smiled at her, and she flushed.

"Of course, I'll just need you to sign in, Ms. Quinlan, and I'll give you a swipe card."

"She's a stickler for security and procedure which is why I hired her," Tom said as we left the foyer and went through a set of double doors.

"It's fair enough too. I imagine you get some pretty interesting people through here." There were wide hallways and rows of doors which reminded me uncomfortably of a posh hospital.

"Everyone deserves a second chance. You know what's funny? I was thinking about you the other day," he admitted. "I've been living in London the past two years and only got back to Melbourne last month. It's nice to be home. I was wondering if you were still about. What have you been up to?"

"Oh, this and that. I do a bit of consulting work and contract myself out when I feel the need to," I replied. I couldn't tell him I was an exorcist. Not yet anyway. He would probably try and lock me in there for treatment.

"You always did dance to the beat of your own drum, Quinlan," he said as we came to a large dining area with a cafeteria. "It's what I used to love the most about you. Coffee? I swear it's a decent brew."

"Uh, sure."

He surprised me by going behind the counter to the fancy coffee machine. "How do you have it?"

"Black with two sugars."

"Here I was thinking you were going to challenge me." He laughed.

"Do I really look like the non-fat, caramel, hazelnut Frappuccino sort of girl?" I asked, leaning over the counter so I could watch him deftly grind some beans.

"Absolutely not," he said and winked at me. "You'll love this blend. I came across it when I was hiking through Guatemala. The farmers were thinking of closing the farm due to debt and small crop production compared to competing farms. I bought them out and left them as well-paid tenants. Everything that is beautiful or delicious needs to be protected. There is already too much ugliness, and I couldn't let something this magical leave the world."

"Tom Warner, the great beautifier," I teased.

He poured a small amount into a cup and stirred in my sugar until it dissolved, before filling the rest. "It is best strong, black, and sweet, so you are in luck. I should warn you though; it packs a punch."

I took the cup and sipped. I couldn't stop the smile that spread across my face. "Damn, Warner, you missed your calling in life as a barista."

"I told you it was worth buying the farm." He finished fixing his own cup. "Come on, I think everyone is going to be out at the park at this time."

"You have a park?"

"Of course. Nature is an important part of rehabilitation."

"I don't mean to be nosy, but how do you afford all of this? The government isn't exactly handing out benefits for helping homeless people," I asked as we stepped out a set of glass doors and onto the thick turf.

"Private investors and philanthropists mostly. I've had a good run with the businesses I've managed and felt the need to spread that good fortune around."

"Businesses like HeosCorp?" I asked, remembering the silver logo on the back of the brochure.

"HeosCorp is one of our biggest stakeholders. There isn't much they don't have their hands in, so when I pitched them the idea for this place, they were keen to give it a shot. If it works out, we'll set them up like a chain."

As we walked, I spotted people in blue-and-gray tracksuits doing yoga or talking in groups. There were teachers scattered throughout the groups giving instruction about painting or simply reading out loud.

"Everyone learns differently, so we try to cater to that as best we can," Tom explained when he noticed me staring. He gave me a playful nudge. "I remember someone wasn't very good at sitting still for too long looking at a whiteboard."

"Someone still isn't very good at it," I admitted, smiling at his easiness. Everywhere we went people waved and called out to him, and when they approached to say hello, he knew every single one of them by name.

"I'm sorry your friend is missing," he said when we went back inside and out to the foyer. He passed me his phone. "You should put your number in here."

"I appreciate you keeping an eye out for me. Clair is a nice lady," I said, taking it and punching in my mobile number. "Call me if you find her."

"I have no doubt she is, but that's not the only reason I want your number."

My fingers stopped entering my name. "Why else would you want it?"

"Oh, I don't know. So I can call you, and we can catch up sometime? I forgot how much I enjoyed hanging out with you. I'm pretty sure I owe you a drink for when you kicked Jim Hicks's ass for pushing me over that one time."

"I had forgotten all about that! Jim Hicks. I wonder if he's still an asshole."

"Probably," Tom said as I passed back his phone. "So, would it be okay if I called you sometime?"

"Yeah, that'd be nice," I found myself saying. We were smiling awkwardly at each other when Gemma cleared her throat.

"Excuse me, sir. I have the Meat Market people on the phone wanting your clearance on a few of tonight's details," she said primly.

"The Meat Market people?" he asked vaguely. "The gala. *Right*. Actually, that's perfect. Jael, come to the gala tonight!"

"What?" I asked.

"We are having our official opening tonight at the Meat Market. You know, shaking hands and drinking too much with the other stakeholders and whatnot."

"You make it sound so exciting," I replied unenthusiastically.

"It's going to be annoying, and that's why I want you to come. I need someone *real* to talk to. While I can't say the conversation is going to be invigorating, the food will be amazing."

"Well, I guess if the food is going to be good," I said thoughtfully.

"Excellent. Party starts at 8:00 p.m., Cinderella. I'll see you then." He took the phone from Gemma and walked off, chatting with the organizers.

"It's black tie," Gemma said, giving me a meaningful once over. "I hope you have something other than Doc Martens to wear. Mr. Warner is flippant about tonight, but it's important to make a good impression on the investors." I didn't know much about dates, but I knew a threat when I heard one.

"Don't worry, Gem. I have just the frock," I replied with a sickly sweet smile. I walked out the glass doors and pulled out my phone. "Star, I'm in need of a dress."

13

"THIS IS THE DUMBEST thing I have ever done," I said as I stood up in a pair of too-high heels.

"That's not true, and you know it," Star said as she arranged a part of my hair she had curled. "You need a night off before you go more mental than usual. Think of it as a self-care night. You'll have some drinks and a flirt with a hot guy, and you will be clearer tomorrow for it."

"That logic doesn't make any sense."

"What doesn't make sense is how you've gotten two dates in a week." She laughed, shaking her head.

"Max wasn't a date, and I'm 86 percent sure that this isn't either. Tom just wants to catch up about school days. We used to hang out a lot because we were both bullied. You should see him now, damn—"

"I have. I stalked him on LinkedIn. Not to put you under any pressure, but he's a total babe. I'd climb that like a tree." Star let out a low whistle. "Seriously, I'm jealous that I'm not invited to a fancy party with a fancy man."

"He's not that fancy," I lied and readjusted the strap on my black dress. She had tried to talk me into something red, but my confidence hadn't been up to it. I was uncomfortable about showing so much cleavage. But the back of the dress covered my scars, so I couldn't complain too much.

"Stop twitching," Star said, chastising me as she straightened my shoulders. "Your Uber is going to be here any second. Do you need help getting down the stairs?"

"Of course I do. This dress is made for your Amazon legs, and I'm worried I'm gonna fall tits up." She grabbed my clutch purse and scooped up the skirt of the dress.

"Just take it one step at a time," she said as she shut the door so Meta wouldn't follow us. He was disgruntled that I hadn't been able to pat him in the hour Star had been doing my hair and makeup. I didn't need to turn up to a gala with dog hair all over me.

"How are those psychic shields of yours?" Star asked as we waited for my driver.

"Up and super tight."

"Good. You're on a night off," she said firmly. "I still can't believe you exorcised someone on a tram today."

"It surprised me too. But a girl's got to do what a girl's got to do."

"That includes having fun tonight. You remember what fun is, don't you?"

I was saved from having to answer when my Uber driver arrived. Star helped me into the car, carefully tucking my skirt in so it didn't catch in the door. "Now remember, Quinlan; have a good night and no glovey, no lovey."

"I hate you," I said as she shut the door laughing her ass off.

Cars were lined up and blocking traffic on Flemington Road as they tried to drop people off in front of the Meat Market. I struggled not to fall over as I climbed out of the car and hurried across the road. The pair of bouncers at the door had clipboards and were taking invitations and marking off names at the entrance. I swore under my breath.

"Invitation," one asked me, and I smiled sweetly.

"Uh, I don't have one. I got a verbal invite," I said nicely.

"Name."

"Jael with a *J*, not a *Y*."

"Look, lady, if you're not on the list—"

"She's with me, boys." Tom appeared like magic, dressed in a tux. I was suddenly very grateful that I had Star in my life to make sure I looked good. He was all dark-haired deliciousness, and I suddenly had no idea how to act around him.

"Apologies, Miss," the bouncer said and moved out of the way.

"And don't you clean up pretty as ever." Tom offered me his arm, and I took it, hoping he wouldn't be able to notice the nervous tremble in my hands.

"I could say the same for you in that fancy suit."

"I feel like a damn penguin, but it's all part of the game. Drink?"

"Yes. Lots of drinks," I said as people pressed in around us.

I hated crowds and tightened my shields even more. Tom was like a magnet, and wherever we walked, we were stopped for introductions and congratulations. Everyone seemed to love him, from the white-haired old ladies dipped in diamonds to the waitstaff who offered me cocktails made of crushed strawberries and tequila. My social awkwardness eased as he took the lead.

"I think we need to tell each person a different story about who you are and let the rumor mill churn," Tom said playfully when we were on our third set of drinks. "It's killing them that they don't know who you are."

"Okay, but I want to be a rich European heiress at least once." I laughed as he spun me straight into a familiar face. "Max! What are you doing here?"

"It's a work thing. My company is owned by HeosCorp," he replied automatically. His eyes were so big they looked like they were going to fall out of his head. "Gosh, Jael, I didn't even recognize you for a second there. What are you doing here?"

"I went to school with Tom, and he invited me along," I said as Tom's arm draped around my shoulders.

"She's my date, Max. God knows I let her cheat off enough of my math homework to earn it," said Tom. "How do you know my lawyer?"

"Max's family is friends with mine," I said, giving Max a meaningful stare.

"My mom and her dad have been friends for donkey's years. Jael and I go way, *way* back. You could say we are like family, and I'm her big, overprotective brother," Max replied smoothly but with a definite tone. "Small world, isn't it?"

"Indeed, it is," Tom replied with an amused smile. "You two catch up; there is an investor over there that I have to suck up to for a moment. Don't wander too far, Miss Quinlan." He disappeared into the crowd, and I turned back to Max.

"He doesn't know that I'm an exorcist, and you can't tell him," I blurted out.

"Are you really on a date with Tom Warner?" Max asked incredulously. "I think I have more trouble believing *that* than the fact you're an exorcist."

"Will you keep your voice down?" I said, looking around. "Tom and I went to school together, and I bumped into him today when I was looking for a friend at the homeless shelter. He invited me. It's definitely *not* a date."

Max's smile was as infuriating as Star's had been. "Does he know that? I don't know you that well, but he doesn't seem your type."

"Oh really? Hot, rich, nice guys are everyone's type," I said irritably.

"You won't tell him what you are," Max said. "Anyone who makes you feel embarrassed about being yourself shouldn't be your type, Jael." It was so sincere and honest that I felt like punching him. Hard.

"Here; hold this. I need to go to the ladies' room." I pushed my empty cocktail glass into his hand and walked away before he could stop me. I locked myself in a cubicle, taking a few steadying breaths. My intuition started to pull at me, but I pushed it away. It was my night, and I was going to have fun.

"Stupid Max," I murmured under my breath as I struggled to keep the long skirt from falling into the back of the toilet when I stood up. It wasn't like I *wouldn't* tell Tom I was an exorcist, but it was something I eased people into.

I made sure none of my dark eye shadow had run before I headed back out. Max and Tom were talking together at the bar, and I hoped Max wasn't outing me.

"Shh, she's back. We need to stop talking about her," said Tom cheekily.

"You remember that time I kicked Jim Hicks's ass? I'm still capable of doing it to you, Warner." I poked him in the side, and he laughed.

"Isn't her fierce face adorable, Maxy?" he said as he pushed a fresh drink toward me.

"I've seen her fierce face, and trust me, that's not it," Max replied, and I took a deep drink. The night was going to hell a lot faster than anticipated.

A strange murmuring hush settled over the room, and I tried to spot what everyone was looking at. A man had entered the room. He towered above everyone, and the crowd cut a path for him. His Nordic silver hair was pushed back from his high cheekbones, the ends brushing against his wide shoulders. He was dressed plainly in a dark gray suit and a pale silver button-up shirt, cutting a striking figure in a room full of dark tuxes.

I dropped my glass to the bar as his slate blue eyes rested on me. *Ohmygod! Ohmygod!*

The way the other people in the room were staring told me that my favorite archangel was being seen by everyone and was not just a figment of my jaded imagination. He was *here*. The band started back up to fill in the strange moment, and the noise rose around us again.

I tried not to run away as I watched Uriel move easily through the dancers and other guests, all of them instinctively moving out of his way. My pulse was racing a thousand miles a minute as he approached us.

"Another friend of yours?" Max asked beside me. "Because the way you are staring at each other makes me think he's definitely your type." I'd forgotten how to speak; I was only capable of acting like a deer caught in headlights.

Tom stepped away from the bar and held out a hand to Uriel. "Tom Warner. Pleasure to meet you Mr.—"

"Uriel North," he replied as he took Tom's hand and shook it.

"And what is it you do, Mr. North?" asked Tom, sizing him up.

"Uriel is in charge of a software design company from Scandinavia," I said, making sure to speak before anyone else could. "Nice to see you again, Uriel." I stepped up on my tiptoes to give him a welcoming kiss on the cheek.

"What are you doing?" I whispered in his ear. He chuckled softly in response, and I felt it slide over me.

"You two know each other?" Tom asked skeptically. "Why am I not surprised? Jael knows just about everyone here tonight."

I went to move, but Uriel's hand casually rested on my lower back, and I stilled, my skin breaking out in goose bumps.

"Jael works for me from time to time," Uriel said smoothly. "She's one of the finest women I've ever known, and she owes me a dance. If you will excuse us." Without waiting for any kind of reply, Uriel led me out amongst the dancers.

"I don't dance," I said, feeling my face go red.

"Something slow then," Uriel replied and the music changed, the musicians not missing a beat as they performed a waltz.

"What's going on? Why are you even here like this?" I made a feeble gesture at the suit and his general humanness. His hand came up to my waist and brought me closer to him. My poor human heart went into overdrive being pressed up against so much angelic muscle. It was throwing my brain and emotions to see him so real and solid. *Don't think about it. No good can come of it.*

"I'm here to warn you," Uriel whispered into my ear. "You have foolishly ignored all of your training and raised your shields so tightly you don't know the danger you are in." His hand tightened over mine. "I couldn't get your attention any other way, and I couldn't leave you here to become demon food."

"So you revealed yourself to come to my rescue?" I asked, the alcohol making me brave. I risked looking up at his face, and the worry I saw in his eyes made me feel ashamed. The last time I'd shut down, the professor's daughter had jumped in front of a tram. Was I never going to learn?

"I'll always come to your rescue, Jael," he replied gently, and something burned inside of me. We waltzed slowly together, and there seemed an infinite rightness to it; an exorcist and her angel fighting the good fight together. I took advantage of the moment and placed my head against him, ignoring the looks of the other dancers as I felt his calm, unshakable steadfastness flow over me. *I could really get used to this.*

"Jael, we need to leave before they decide to attack," Uriel said, breaking the stolen moment.

"Before what decides to attack?"

"Open your eyes and see what you have walked into."

I dropped my shields, and if it weren't for Uriel's hands steadying me, I probably would have collapsed. Nearly half of the people in the room were possessed. I could see past their smiles and curious glances to the beasts inside of them, the monsters that watched every move we made. If one guy could throw me across the room like a doll, a room full of demons could turn me to mincemeat.

I leaned into Uriel, my hand gripping his shirt and feeling his strength beneath it.

"Please," I begged, tears of panic filling my eyes. "Get me out of here. I've been drinking, and I don't think I could fight them off like this."

"Breathe, Jael. Pretend like you can't see them." He lifted my face with his hand. "Look at me, *yadid*. I need you to focus. No time for exorcisms. Right now I need you to pretend that you've fainted and let me do the rest."

I didn't have to pretend as I slumped in his arms, and he scooped me up, carrying me easily across the dance floor.

"What's wrong with her? Is she okay?" Max appeared through my hazy expression.

"A little too much alcohol, I think. It makes me wonder how much the bartender was putting in them," Uriel replied accusingly.

"Here. Put her on a barstool," suggested Tom. "I'll get her some water."

"She needs air," Uriel said in a voice that made the two other men pause.

"I need to go home," I said and looked up at Uriel. "Can you give me a ride?"

"An excellent idea. If you will excuse us, gentlemen."

Before any goodbyes could be said, Uriel carried me through a pair of double doors and out through a fire escape.

"Close your eyes and hold tight," he instructed. I felt a rush of air, and then he was lowering me to my feet on the street in front of my house.

"Oh God." I doubled over trying to breathe, to process what had happened. "I need to warn Max." I pulled my phone out of my purse and tapped out a message, hoping he would get it.

    Get out of the party Max. No questions. Ex-
    plain later. J.

"You know the demons are aggressive at the moment. Why would you be crazy enough to risk yourself like that?" Uriel demanded. I straightened up, not wanting him to see how scared I still was that I'd walked into a demon party. "You could've been attacked, and not a single one of those humans would've lifted a finger to stop it! I trained you better than that."

"Why are you acting like this?" I asked, feeling like he was kicking me when I was down.

"Why are *you*? You turned your back on your instincts tonight, and nearly got yourself killed again. What for? What could be worth it? Some party with people who have no idea how important you are? People who you don't even like?"

"To be a typical adult for once! To go out and just forget about everything for one damn night. To go on a date with a guy...to be normal like everyone else!"

"But you aren't like everyone else, Jael, and you never will be!" Under his anger, I saw how worried Uriel had been for me. His rough hands were gentle when they clutched my face. "You're too special to throw your heart away."

"Elyon made us all special, so what makes me so different? Get specific for once."

The anger on his face melted, the sharp planes softening as he brushed my cheeks with his thumbs. "Let's say that Elyon was feeling particularly *creative* when he made you. You're human, but you are more like the angels than them. Stop trying to be like everyone else. You're better than that. You were made for different things."

"Made to be lonely? To never belong anywhere? That's what you're saying right now." I squeezed my eyes tightly to stop the tears welling in them. "I'm human, and I'm doomed to be alone forever."

"You are *never* alone, Jael." Uriel surprised me by holding my shaking body to him. "Even if you can't see us or feel us, we are always here. *I* am always going to be here for you, *yadid*."

Standing drunk on the sidewalk, held by an archangel in a human form, I became even more aware of how nice it felt to be able to physically touch him. I let my hands gently slide over his back, copping a feel of all the heat and muscle that made my heart go into overdrive. Then my common sense caught up. *He's an angel, not your date, Jael. No matter how much you wish it were otherwise.*

"We should get off the street," I said awkwardly as I stumbled my way upstairs. Uriel followed, making sure I didn't tumble backward in my ridiculous heels. Meta eyed him curiously but then rubbed himself all over him like an overgrown cat.

"Maybe it's a good thing you arrived when you did; these things were killing me," I said as I kicked off my shoes and breathed a sigh of relief.

"Better the shoes than the demons. Do you have any idea why there were so many in that place?" Uriel asked as he sat on the couch. Meta rested his head in Uriel's lap affectionately, and Uriel cuddled him. I felt a pang of love seeing them together. *Why couldn't looking at Max or Tom make me feel this way? Why does it have to be the impossible one that you want?*

"There's something I'm missing, and just when I think I see it, it's gone," I admitted, trying to focus. "I don't understand why the demons are so interested in me either."

"Isn't it obvious? You're a threat to whatever they are doing. You are making them nervous, so they are lashing out. It is why you can't risk not being on your guard."

"I know. It just hurts that I can't be normal sometimes. Thank you for stepping in. I never thought you would do something like that. That you even could. I mean, it's going to raise a whole lot of questions. I could see it bothered Tom that he had no idea who you were, and Max is going to be on my case about it as well."

"Let them ask. They won't find any answers unless one of the possessed shares that information with them. It's not like I exist on any human systems," Uriel said as I sat on the couch beside him, our knees touching.

"Well, I kind of like seeing you as a human. It makes you less intimidating," I lied. *Such* a big lie. Everyone in the room had been staring at him and for good reason; he was big and gorgeous, and I felt stupidly overprotective about other people getting to see him. He was *my* angel after all. *But he's not just yours. You know that.* It was unnerving me to see him like this, patting my dog affectionately like he was an average guy that had come home with me.

I needed to change the subject and get my brain back on track. "Just when I think I've got things pegged about demons and exorcisms, I realize I know nothing."

"I know it's frustrating, but sometimes not knowing everything is a blessing. You can never unknow. Knowledge will always change you." He seemed to hesitate before he said, "I'm sorry you couldn't enjoy your night. You look particularly lovely, though I don't like how that Tom was staring at you. It made me have violent thoughts."

I laughed to keep from dying of embarrassment. "Tom isn't hard up for a date. He needed someone different to talk to for the night, and his old high school buddy fit the bill. Besides, you aren't my father; you don't need to be concerned with the men I date."

"I most definitely do," he said protectively, and Meta huffed in agreement.

"You two can go judge someone else for the night," I said, bopping Meta's nose. "I have to come up with a plan to stop being attacked on the street. Maybe I need to ask Alessandro how to do mass exorcisms."

I spun out drunken theories to Uriel before passing out, shamelessly curled up against him with my head on his chest. When I woke later in the night, he was gone, making me wonder if it had been a dream after all.

14

"LET ME GET THIS straight," Star said as we walked through Flagstaff Gardens the following day. "You're at the party, having a grand time at the open bar, and then Uriel, the actual freaking archangel himself, arrives to bail your drunk ass out where everyone could see him."

"Pretty much," I replied, feeling like I should have stayed in bed. Star had taken me into the city for a greasy brunch that was sitting uneasily in my stomach.

"Wow. Uriel as a human. What was that like?"

"Like Aleksander Skarsgård's Tarzan, but a bigger, hotter version," I admitted. "In a suit."

Star's eyes went wide. "Jesus, no wonder they were all looking at him."

"Yep," I said, feeling more awkward by the minute.

"And he carried you out like a distressed damsel? That's kind of hot."

"Says the girl with a serious Kylo Ren carrying off Rey fetish. It wasn't hot. It was embarrassing, and he was right. I shouldn't have been dumb enough to walk in unprepared like that." I clutched my throbbing head. "I feel like such an amateur."

"Hey, lay off my friend, Jael," she said, chastising me. "There's no crime in what you did. You didn't exactly think you were walking into a room full of rich, white-guy demons."

"True, but with everything happening you'd think I wouldn't be that dumb. Uriel had to pretend to be human, because I cut myself off completely from the spiritual world. Stupid." I kicked a McDonald's cup someone had left on the grass and Coke splattered up the side of my Doc Martens.

"Well, that was mature," Star said dryly. "You can go pick it up and put it in the bin now." She had used her "mom voice," so I did as she asked. As I was putting the lid down on the bin, I saw a woman walking toward me in a neat, black suit. Her graying hair was pulled into a tight bun.

"Clair?" I hurried over to her, and she clutched her bag tighter. "Clair, what happened? I've had people out looking for you. The cops want to talk to you about the tram accident. Where's Champ?"

"I'm sorry, Miss. I think you have me confused with someone else. My name is not Clair, and I don't know who Champ is either," she said primly, pulling away from me. I stood speechless, watching her walk away in her sensible black shoes.

"What was that about?" Star asked as she caught up with me. I pulled my phone out and took a photo of Clair's retreating back.

"That was Clair! She looked straight through me. She didn't even know who poor little Champ was."

"Wow, that's a huge change to go through in under a fortnight," Star said and then rested a hand on my shoulder. "You're right. We definitely need to follow her," she added, reading my mind.

"Come on then, Nancy Drew," I said, and we headed after Clair. We followed her easily down William Street using the crowds to stay hidden.

"Her aura is strange," Star said with a frown. "Huh. She doesn't even have one."

"Make sure I don't bump into anything," I said, taking her hand and dropping my shields. Star's grip tightened as I swore. "The reason she has no aura is because she has no spirit. She's like Crazy Bill but more in control." I shook my head to clear it, and Star let me go.

"Even more of a reason to see where she goes," she said as we passed the Law Courts.

As we headed down King Street, I felt a chill settle over me, and I pulled Star behind a parked van.

"What is it?"

"I know where she's going." I pointed to the huge silver-and-white logo illuminated on the side of a building a hundred meters from us. "HeosCorp. Again. They are the ones that help fund Tom's rehab center."

Clair walked through the revolving doors, disappearing from view.

"You think we should follow her?" Star asked. "We'd be on camera, but it might be worth it. The problem is that we don't have a legitimate reason to be there if we are stopped."

I thought for a moment and then smiled. "Actually, we do. But we are going to need some sandwiches."

Hogren and Allan was a stretch of open-plan offices on the fifth floor. Clutching bags of food, we approached the receptionist with winning smiles.

"Can I help you ladies?" she asked, looking up at us over her glasses.

"We are here to visit Max for lunch," I said confidently. "Give him a call; he's expecting us." She eyed me skeptically and Star with downright disapproval before placing the call.

"He says to go on through. First door on the right," she said and buzzed the door open.

"Told you," I said, unable to resist pointing out to Star that I'd been right as we went through the door.

Max had a nice corner office complete with a window view of the building next door. I had expected creative chaos, but everything seemed neat and had a place.

"What did you bring me, ladies?" he said loud enough for other people to hear. He shut the door and added, "You have to be the strangest woman I've ever met, Jael Quinlan. First, you bail out of a party, then leave cryptic messages on my phone, and now you deliver me lunch."

"We were in the area," Star said with a smile. "Nice to finally meet you properly, Max."

"And you. Is Jael always this sporadic?" he asked as he accepted a piece of focaccia from her.

"Always."

"You both love it. I inject excitement into your life," I said, taking a seat on his plush leather desk chair. I dropped my shields for half a second to check he wasn't possessed again before laying food out on his desk like a picnic.

"Not that I don't enjoy the break in monotony, but what's this all about?" Max asked. I caught him up on bumping into Clair and following her to his doorstep.

"There are twenty floors to this building, Jael. She could be anywhere," he said. "And what was the deal with last night?"

"Demons at the ball," Star said.

"I couldn't let you stay in the middle of it," I said and smiled at him. "Thanks for trusting me."

"Easy to do. Tom was a bit sad-faced watching you leave with another man though," he said.

"He wasn't a man; he was an angel," Star said, and I glared at her.

Max laughed brightly. "I'm sure you think he looked like one. It's probably the first time Tom Warner hasn't gotten what he wanted."

"That's not true. He was a massive reject at school just like me."

"Well, it was still good for him to know that there's someone that's not impressed with him. Although if you have men like Uriel North willing to carry you away, then I can see why."

Star and I shared a look, and I shook my head. I didn't want Max to know any more than he needed to.

"How easy would it be for you to do some snooping, Maxy? Find out some more about the odd stuff happening here at HeosCorp?" I asked sweetly.

"Depends on what it is I'm sticking my nose into. You think there's something bad going on just because of one possessed woman?" He frowned and picked the onion out of his sandwich.

"Don't forget you were possessed too," Star said, and Max's expression clouded. "Do you remember how it happened? Or what changed?"

"I don't know. I've been over it again and again. One moment I was fine... working on something...I don't know what. And then it was like I was a stranger inside my body," he admitted in a quiet voice. "I suppose you have a point. It could've happened here at work."

"At least you could come back," I said. "Clair is dead. I want to find who is responsible for that too. See what you can find but only enough that you don't arouse any suspicion. I don't want anything happening to you because of me."

"Any idea what I'm looking for?"

I got to my feet. "Anything weird."

"Nothing more concrete?" he asked. "Corporate people are all kinds of weird already."

"Don't go behind any closed doors if you can avoid it," I added. I didn't know how they were choosing people, and I didn't want to risk him. "Now, we are going to get out of your hair. Message me if you notice anything."

"Will do. Thanks for lunch, ladies. It's been random as always," he said.

"Hey, Max?" I paused at the door. "Thanks for believing me."

"Anytime, Quinlan. Watch your back. We need all of our exorcists."

When we got into the lift, Star smiled sideways at me. "He's a good guy. I like him."

"Yeah, me too. Probably a good thing to have a lawyer as well as a cop in our crew."

"Knowing you...yeah, it probably is."

The lift doors opened, and as we were heading for the revolving foyer door, I spotted three security guards in black. One saw us and lifted his walkie-talkie to his mouth. I didn't need to drop my shields to see the same wild rage that Crazy Bill had back at the house.

"Star, when we get out of this building, we are going to make a run for it. Head toward Bourke Street."

"Jael—"

"Don't ask questions; just do it. And don't let them separate us."

There was a shout behind us, and we bolted for the doors and into the street. As we hit Bourke Street, I checked over my shoulder and saw five guards chasing after us.

"Go, Star! Don't stop," I said as I took her hand.

"Where are we going?"

"Not far. Don't look back." We pushed past a group of tourists, and I pulled Star into the churchyard of Saint Augustine's. The green wooden doors were open, and we almost slipped ass-up on the polished floors in our haste to get in.

"Stay out of sight," I told Star, and I peeked outside. "Damn it, they are multiplying." The five guards paced outside the gates but were being joined by other people in plain clothes.

"Why aren't they coming in?" Star whispered beside me as she looked over my shoulder.

"Blessed ground."

"Can I help you, ladies?" a voice asked, and we both jumped. The priest was elderly with an almost-bald pate.

"What's your name?" I asked.

"Father Stephen."

"Excellent! Father Stephen, I'm going to need you to relax and not leave the church grounds," I instructed. "Understand?"

"Not at all. Who are you?" he asked.

"Jael Quinlan. You've heard of me, right?"

"Not pleasant things," he replied, taking a step back. "Apparently, you're an exorcist."

"There's no 'apparently' about it," snapped Star, but I rested a hand on her arm.

"Look outside, Father Stephen. You see that crowd? They are all possessed, so go and sit in a pew."

"I should call—" he said, crossing himself as he looked at the shouting mob outside.

"I'm on it," I replied, shutting the doors and pulling out my phone. I opened my contacts and scrolled through them.

"You called him 'A-Team'? That's adorable." Star smirked as she looked over my shoulder.

"Shut up," I said, and on the third ring someone answered. "*Padre!* How do you feel about coming to bail me out of trouble?"

"Who is this?" Alessandro asked uncertainly before chuckling. "*Signorina* Quinlan, where are you?"

"Jerk. I'm cornered at Saint Augustine's on Bourke Street. Lovely group of possessed office workers hanging around out front if you want to come do your thing."

"Have you found the priest?" he asked, all business.

"I'm with Father Stephen now."

"Put him on the phone."

I handed it over, and Father Stephen held it to his ear. "Yes?"

There was some rapid-fire instruction from Alessandro's end, which made Father Stephen turn red, before he answered, "Yes, father. I'll do that now." He gave me my phone back.

"Jael? I'll be there soon," Alessandro said.

"Wait! Do you want me to do anything before you get here?" I asked. "Throw some holy water at them? Start quoting saints?"

"Don't blaspheme while you are standing in a church," he said, chastising me. "I will be there shortly." He hung up, and I pulled a face at the phone before turning to the priest. "What did he tell you?"

"He said I was to do exactly as you said and not to argue," he replied. "Also, to go and lock myself in my office."

"Well, you better go do it. He's Rome's Top Exorcist after all." He hurried away, and I turned back to Star. She looked at me, head cocked to one side. "What?"

"Your face changed when you talked to Mr. Hotshot," she said. "It's kind of cute."

"He's a priest, you perv." I flicked her in the temple as she batted my hand away. "Stuck like Quasimodo in a church surrounded by demons, and you still are trying to set me up with every boy that I talk to."

"I have to take advantage while there are so many around." Star opened the door a crack. "What are you going to do? You're not seriously going to wait for someone else to turn up and sort it out, are you?"

"I was thinking about it." I folded my arms. "What? I want to see how good he is."

Star stared hard at me until I caved.

"Fine! I'll have a look," I grumbled before sitting down on the front steps outside. Star made to follow me out, but I stopped her. "Stay put, Starshine. I don't want to be worrying about you while I do this." She did as she was told, propping herself up on a pew where she could watch me through the doors.

The crowd had swelled to twenty people outside the square-wired fence. Commuters heading to and from Southern Cross Station didn't seem to notice anything odd; they simply detoured around them.

I closed my eyes and focused on shutting out the noise around me, before praying silently. I steadied my beating heart and let my spirit jump in the Behinds.

Looking at the spiritual world is like adding an extra vivid layer to the real one. I could see the grounds and the people just like before, except now I could also see the slimy gits that were leeching off the humans. The five guards in the crowd were already dead like Clair, but the rest could be brought back, even if they were going to be severely traumatized. Instead of their eyes staring at my physical body, they now followed my spiritual one as I pulled a wispy sword from the scabbard at my side and approached the fence.

"Come out, little girl," a woman in a business suit hissed at me. "Come and play with us."

A man reached out to me, his mouth foaming. "You're dead! You're so fucking dead you whore of—" I held up my hand, and his tirade stopped.

"Elyon, give me the strength to push this usurper from this body."

"Stop! I'm sorry, I'm sorry. It's burning me," he whimpered in his human voice.

I didn't stop.

The demon shrieked as it pulled itself free, ejected from its stolen flesh temple. When it came loose, the sword in my hand came down, slicing off its corporeal head. As it vanished, the man slumped to the ground in a dead faint. One down.

The dead ones, the five security guards from HeosCorp, backed away and disappeared, satisfied to leave the possessed humans to do their dirty work.

I had exorcised three more demoniacs by the time a black van pulled up. Alessandro stepped out, and the other two exorcists flanked him.

"*Kyrie, eleison. Christe, eleison. Christe, audi nos...*" they began to chant in Latin as Alessandro let the crowd press in around him. The effect was instantaneous. Angels appeared in the churchyard and surrounded the crowd, hedging them in. They were as varied in skin color and features as humans are, and if people saw the powerful, towering soldiers around me, they would have checked their manners and opinions of serene white dudes with fluffy wings.

Alessandro glowed with righteous anger as he held his rosary out to the crowd and started *The Rite of Exorcism* from memory. With one voice, the demons shrieked as they drew back from him before surging forward to attack. Alessandro and the others stretched their arms out through the flailing crowd. I heard his voice cry out over the din, switching back to a Latin prayer that I couldn't follow.

The bodies dropped like paper soldiers around them, and Alessandro stood clear of them. I snapped my spirit back into my body and got up on shaking feet, hurrying to help those that were still alive.

"Are you okay?" I asked as Alessandro checked one woman's pulse. "I've never seen the Catholic rite be so effective before." There were scratches down his arms and one bleeding on his neck from where they had attacked him.

"I'm fine, help me move these bodies before anyone sees," he said, insistently, and with the help of the other exorcists, we lifted the unconscious people into the van. Alessandro gave them instructions in Italian before they got in and drove off down the street. We were walking up the path to the church when he stumbled, and I took him by the arm to steady him.

"You two are freaking insane, you know that?" Star demanded, standing with her hands on her hips and looking like a vengeful mermaid with her aqua and purple hair.

"*Si*, we know," Alessandro said with a grin. "You must be *la Stella*...uh... the Star."

"Just Star," she said, the faintest of reds blooming under her brown cheeks. "Now what?"

"Now you run down to Southern Cross and get your perky butt on a train home," I said, letting Alessandro's arm go. I hugged her, and I could feel the fear under her bravado. I didn't blame her. "Starshine, I'm fine."

"Then why are you shaking?"

"*Because.* That's why. They are after me, not you. So please get home or go to James's, yeah? I'll call you later," I promised.

"What are you going to do?" she demanded, looking inside to where Alessandro had sat down on a pew, his head in his hands.

"I'm going to go and get something to eat, and probably take the priest with me before he collapses."

"Coffee date with a priest? Now is not the time to indulge that fantasy," she teased lamely, and I knew she was going to be okay.

"Now is not the time to crack that kind of joke, you dork. Go home, so I don't need to worry about you."

She hugged me tightly. "I love you. Be safe."

"I love you too. I'm going to be okay. I even got my priest sidekick in case I get into trouble."

"I hope so. After seeing that, he kinda scares me."

"Yeah, me too. Lucky he's on our side, right?" I gave her a final squeeze before watching her walk down the street and into Southern Cross Station.

"She is going to be fine," Alessandro said from behind me. "I checked on the priest, and he gave me a blessing. I told him to consecrate the grounds again in case anything comes back."

Alessandro's color was coming back even though he was still holding a handkerchief to his bleeding neck. His purple stole was folded neatly in his other hand.

I looked at him for a long moment before giving in. "Want some food?"

15

WE ENDED UP AT a busy bistro and managed to get a table in the back where we wouldn't be overheard. Alessandro got a few appreciative glances from ladies who seemed unperturbed by the fact he was wearing a priest's collar. I was doing my best to forget about it as well but for entirely different reasons.

I ordered hot fries and a Coke from the kids' menu and ignored the amused look on Alessandro's face before he ordered a pumpkin ravioli.

Cleary, all exorcists craved carbs after a big day.

"Tell me what happened, Jael. I honestly never thought you would use my phone number," he said as he placed a napkin down on his lap.

"I saw the lady I was with the other day when the professor's daughter jumped in front of the tram. Clair has been homeless for as long as I've known her. The police are after her to get a witness statement, and I spotted her walking through Flagstaff Gardens about two hours ago. She was completely changed. Dressed up in a suit and had no idea who I was or memory of her dog, Champ. I might believe she'd forget me, but she would never forget Champ. That little dog was her entire world."

"She was possessed?"

"Not just possessed; she was dead. No Clair left."

"You have seen this before?"

"Would you say I was crazy if I did?"

"I would say that you've been holding out on me." Alessandro wagged his finger at me but then stopped. "You are many things, Jael Quinlan, but crazy isn't one of them."

"Okay, then. You know how I told you about Crazy Bill?"

"The possessed man that attacked you at the house?"

"Yep. He was possessed, but he was also dead."

"You didn't mention that when we talked a few nights ago."

"I didn't know how much I could trust you with. Possession, sure. You'd understand that. Zombie demons are more of a stretch."

Alessandro leaned back in his chair. "You did warn me that was what we were up against the day we met."

"Tried to." I dropped the sugar sachets I'd been playing with.

"When you warned me, I thought you were being dramatic."

"And now?"

"Now I've been to the house where the demons wrote your name on the wall."

"Violet let you into the Murder House?"

"She didn't let us in; we bought it from her."

"Of course you did." I huffed. I was about to make some smart-ass comment about it being bought with Templar money, but the food arrived just in time. I'm always a bitch when I'm hungry. Alessandro was playing nice, and I wanted to keep it that way. I was trying hard not to show him how freaking impressed I was as well.

"The Church didn't want the house to fall into anyone's hands that could bring back the evil that was there. I don't know if it matters to you, but the blood message has been washed away and the animal room blessed," Alessandro said, poking the creamy ravioli with a fork.

"Thanks," I said after swallowing my mouthful of fries. "I didn't dig too deep into what had happened in that place over the years, but it was nothing good. What are you doing with it now?"

"The other exorcists, Paulo and Gregory, and I are using it as a base. What we do…it makes other priests uncomfortable, so it's better we are away from the church."

"I guess no matter where you are, everyone hates an exorcist."

"They don't hate us. They fear us," Alessandro replied. The combination of pasta and coffee was bringing color back to his face, but he still looked a lot less cocky than a few days ago.

"Are you working on someone…difficult at the house?" I asked tactfully.

"What makes you ask that?"

"You're wrecked. And you are hanging out with me, which means you're completely bloody stumped. Caught one of the dead ones, did you?"

Alessandro sat back in his chair. "Yes. There's no point in lying about it. I've never seen anything like it. We didn't even know it was dead entirely, which begs the question…how did you?"

I took a long sip of my Coke, weighing up how much I could trust him. He had just saved Star and me, so I decided to take the chance.

"I saw that it was different."

"How it moved?"

"No, I saw that it didn't have a spirit."

"You can see demons?" he asked tentatively.

"If I focus. I try not to unless I am working. It gets to be too much otherwise, like two sets of eyes trying to work at once."

He didn't laugh in my face, so I gave him a basic rundown of how I performed larger exorcisms by projecting my spirit into the Behinds and gave him some examples of different jobs I had done. When I finished, he was quiet and thoughtful.

I fidgeted in my chair. "It's okay if you think I'm cracked. Everyone else does. I won't take it personally."

"It's not that, Jael." He held his hand up to pause my argument. "It's only that I'm starting to see why the conventional religious structures don't interest you. Your faith, your life, it is supernatural. You exorcise demons by moving your spirit into the spiritual realms to fight them on their own grounds. That is…unheard of. The routine of a church is for those who are still crawling in their faith, and you are trying to grow wings. It stifles you, but it makes them feel safe to be a part of something that makes them feel good."

"There's nothing safe about faith. That's what they don't understand. They are too frightened of what it would mean if they started to really *seek* anything," I said far more viciously than I meant to.

"I know, but it's their faith and journey to discover, Jael. You need to respect that they aren't ready to see like you do," Alessandro replied. "Tell me, this calling you have. This ability to see evil. How did it come about? Who taught you how to perform exorcisms this way?"

I finished my Coke and poked at the ice with my straw. "A conversation for another time, *Padre*."

"One I'll have to earn I see." Alessandro nodded. "That is fair."

"Can I ask you something? How did you manage to exorcise all those demons at once? I've tried the words of the *Rite*, and they have never worked for me. I figured it was because I wasn't a priest."

"Where there are faith and conviction, power flows. At least it always has for me. How did you exorcise the dead one last time?"

I thought about the heat in my hand and Crazy Bill's body sagging to the floor.

"It's hard to explain."

"Will you come with me and see if you can do it again?" he asked hopefully.

"Won't your companions get angry about me being there? They turned up today, but I know it wasn't because they are fond of me."

"It doesn't matter what their personal feelings are. I'm in charge of them. They will accept it, or I'll send them back to Rome," he said with the tone of a general. It made me wonder what he'd done before he'd become a priest.

"I'll come with you, but I can't promise that I'll have much more success than you have. I mean, I just watched you drop nearly twenty possessed people like it was nothing. I had only managed four by the time you got there. I'm hungover today, but even at my best, I couldn't do that."

"I saw the body of the homeless man that was a dead one. I saw the handprint. I want to know how it happened."

I wasn't ready for that, and my shock was obvious. *Damn it.* "Well, we'll just have to see what happens when we get there, won't we?"

We had just stepped out of the café when a sleek black car pulled up, and Alessandro opened the door for me.

I made a low whistle. "What excellent timing. Did they put a microchip in your butt cheek that you don't know about?"

"I'm sorry. My English isn't good enough to understand you," he said, but his dark eyes were shining with amusement.

"You shouldn't lie, priest," I replied as I got into the car.

We were gliding through traffic when I got a message from Tom wanting to know if I was okay and offering to catch up again sometime. I didn't answer it, shoving my phone deep into the bottom of my bag.

"You aren't going to answer that?" Alessandro asked.

"It's only the guy I bailed on last night. There were too many demons at the party for me to be comfortable staying there." He made a small, amused sound, and I had the urge to pinch him. "What?"

"It's nothing, I just didn't think you'd be the type to date," he said, trying to articulate.

"You don't know anything about me."

"I know that you're an exorcist. This road isn't one that sits easily with the type of person who needs to be in a relationship."

"And you don't think I'm someone who needs to be in a relationship?"

"No, I think you are someone who sees the darkness in all of humanity. You have a compassionate heart, but deep inside you find people irritating and underwhelming. You are never going to want anything more than you want to be an exorcist. Nothing and no one are ever going to be more important to you than your faith, and no one else is ever going to understand that."

"Don't talk to me like you know me." I tried to hide the choke in my voice.

"I wasn't only talking about you," he said without looking at me.

16

THE MURDER HOUSE HAD been cleaned up since I'd last visited. The yard had been tamed, and the piles of renovation scrap and rubbish had been taken away. I hadn't even reached the front door when I felt a creeping menace reach out to me.

"It knows we are here," I said and walked inside. The interior of the house had gotten the same treatment as the yard, and signs of habitation were littered throughout. I tried not to think about the dead woman's memories as I followed Alessandro to the kitchen. Paulo and Gregory were eating and arguing in Italian.

"What is she doing here?" one asked.

"She was invited, Gregory. She has dealt with this before," Alessandro said firmly. "Is it awake yet?"

"It sleeps?" I asked.

"It *hides* to be more accurate," said Paulo.

"It's messing with you because it knows you can't get rid of it," I replied, earning a glare from Gregory. "Where is it?"

"Upstairs. Come, I'll show you," Alessandro said, and we left them to their lunch. The main bedroom had been cleared, and iron security bars had been drilled over the windows. A large cage now took up half the room with the brackets bolted into the bricks.

"Here I was expecting a chain and a manacle," I said, looking at the setup. "This is intense work for a short time."

"We were worried it would try to chew its foot off if we chained it."

There was a man sitting on the floor of the cell dressed in a filthy tux. He was staring off into space, as vacant as a coma patient.

"Damn, I recognize this guy. He was at the same party as me last night. Introduced himself as Charles something. Where did you pick him up?"

"About a street away from your apartment," Alessandro replied. The horror I was feeling must have been written all over my face because he added, "Of course we have security teams looking in on you. You are a magnet for demons at the moment. Despite how the archbishop feels about you, he didn't hesitate to give the order when I told him."

"After we are done here, we are going to have a very serious conversation about privacy."

"You," the man on the floor hissed softly. It got to its feet and approached the bars of its cage. "I should've stuck a knife in your throat last night when I had the chance."

"If only I had a dollar for every time someone said that to me." I laughed. "What did I do to piss you off, I wonder?"

"You have been noticed, Jael Quinlan, and it's only a matter of time before someone feasts on your flesh." It looked me over and started rubbing its crotch on the bars. "Oh, the things I'd do to that flesh to make you scream—"

"Silence, demon!" Alessandro commanded.

"It's okay. I don't think it has enough blood in its body to make its dick work." I chuckled.

"You think you are so untouchable with your big archangel protecting you, but one day, slut, one day he's not going to be quick enough to save you. There are stronger beings in this world than him, and very soon we are going to get revenge on him and his kind." It gripped the bars in front of me. "We will have our time. We will."

"I thought you said that this thing wasn't talkative. A better trick would be to get it to shut up," I said to Alessandro. "Sounds like waffling demon lies to me. I don't think it's important enough to know anything of value. It's not high enough in the food chain."

"I'm high enough," it said with a roar, its voice turning feral as it reached out to try and get at me. "Our beautiful army is growing, and we'll take this city. Our seeds are planted..." It rattled the bars, shouting in a mishmash language of guttural sounds. Plaster dust fell from the roof as it climbed the cell bars and started beating against the ceiling.

"If you are going to do something, Jael, I'd suggest you do it soon," Alessandro said. "I'll uphold you."

"Thanks, *Padre*."

I prayed silently for protection before turning back to the cursing creature in front of me. Alessandro started whispering in Latin, and I cleared my head. My Behind eyes opened, and I saw the shuddering, twisting thing jammed inside the body turn its burning eyes on me.

"Elyon, release your fire and burn up the works of the darkness," I whispered. As I stepped closer to the bars, the world slowed, and my hands started to burn.

On the other side of the cage, the demon turned its head toward me. It moved so fast, it was a blur. Strong hands grabbed my shoulders and pulled me close.

"You stupid bitch," it said, spitting the words at me.

"Got you." I grinned and grabbed it by the head. White heat left me in a rush, and the demon pulled itself backward. It screamed as the light moved under its skin, swelling it up. I didn't have a chance to duck as it exploded like a wet bomb, splattering me and the rest of the room in red, fleshy half-burnt chunks.

I turned to say something to Alessandro, but I couldn't look past the gore that covered me. My knees wobbled, and I collapsed in a dead faint.

✦

I came around to the feeling of a warm, damp cloth and the sound of soft Italian words sung under Alessandro's breath. It was a simple little tune that sounded almost like a lullaby, and I pretended to still be knocked out so I could enjoy it. I couldn't remember the last time anyone had sung to me. I let it slide for a few more minutes before I cracked an eye open. I had been placed on a couch with a rolled-up towel underneath my head.

"Some brave *esorcista* you are," Alessandro said, wringing the cloth into a large bowl of pink-tinged water. "It is like you haven't seen blood before."

"I don't know how your exorcisms usually go down, but mine don't involve the demoniac's bodily fluids."

"I used your phone to call your Star. She is on her way to get you," he said, straightening up. "She was not happy to hear that you had passed out. She blamed me for it."

"That sounds like her." I smiled and slowly sat up. I looked down at my dirty shirt and gagged. "Gross."

"There is a clean shirt there if you want it." Alessandro pointed to the back of the couch. "I'll be out front when you are ready."

I waited until he had gone and pulled the ruined shirt off, rolled it into a sticky ball, and put it on the floor. I pulled on the neatly pressed black men's dress shirt, wondering what the other exorcists would think of me taking their boss's clothes. I didn't let it worry me too much. I was just grateful that I was clean, and that he hadn't left me lying in the filth upstairs. I found Alessandro sitting on the steps, singing the same song under his breath.

"That's a nice tune. What is it?" I asked as I sat down beside him.

He looked a little embarrassed at being caught out as he admitted, "It is a song that the children used to sing in the part of Tuscany where I grew up. In the summertime, they sing it to attract fireflies to catch. It always seems to get stuck in my head after an exorcism."

"Why is that?" I asked.

His expression shut down. "Perhaps one day I will tell you."

"You know, Alessandro, you aren't nearly as scary as you like to pretend," I teased. "Did you sing it to the children at Elsa Perea Flores?"

"Why do you want to know?"

"Call it curiosity. I'm not the one that has people following you," I said defensively. "That is proper spying."

"Do you want me to apologize for it? I won't. We still don't know why they are so determined to end you. Although if what that creature upstairs said was true, it might be because of who your 'archangel' is. Something you want to share? Because archangels don't get involved with something unless it's world threatening."

"One day, *Padre*, I'll give you my confession, but I don't have it in me today," I replied.

Star's car pulled sharply into the driveway, and she got out, looking like she was ready to tear us both apart.

"Jael, what the actual fuck?" she demanded.

"Such language in front of a man of God," I said, getting up in case I needed to make a run for it.

"I thought you two were going out for some coffee, not to the Murder House to do another exorcism. Can't you hang out with regular people?" Star turned on Alessandro. "And you! You are a priest; you should've been looking after her better."

"Stella, Jael doesn't need your protection, and she certainly doesn't need mine," Alessandro said, climbing to his feet. "We can control her as much as we could control a thunderstorm."

"Don't get all poetic with me, priest. Jael can't find her way around a grocery store without getting lost half the time! I'm not pissed off because I want to control her. I want to protect her, so she doesn't lose her mind to this crazy shit because she's overdoing it to impress you," Star hissed.

Underneath all her anger, I saw the fear in her eyes. It was finally getting too weird for her. I gave her a hug, careful not to touch her with my blood-splattered jeans.

"It's okay, Star. I'm fine. Alessandro looked after me when I fainted. It's all good."

"No, it's not fine. What happened? Why are you wearing that, and whose blood is on you?" she demanded, unshed tears in her eyes.

"I'm going to make some coffee." Alessandro sighed and went back into the house.

"I need to know what's going on with you," Star demanded. "I know you are lying to me about stuff, and after today...being at that church and seeing you guys… I'm *worried*, Jael. Like not usual level of Jael worry but the deep and serious kind."

"Sit down," I said, pointing at the step. "You know more than you think you do, so I'm not lying so much as not telling you things. But if you think you are ready for it, then here it is."

I spilled everything, not caring how wild it sounded. I included popping the demon upstairs and what Uriel said about my hands unleashing the power of Heaven. As I said, she knew most of it, but if she was going to start crying at me, I was going to tell her straight and not care about any of her spiritual sensibilities.

"That's everything. Zombie demons, hearts exploding, the works. I swear," I said, folding my arms stubbornly in a protective gesture I could never seem to kick.

"So, your Hand of Power…that's real…"—she seemed to physically struggle to say it—"that's God's power."

"Yeah, I guess. I mean, that's what Uriel said."

"And you're not only exorcising demons when you use it but killing them?"

"I'm pretty sure I am."

Star got to her feet and paced, mulling over what I had said. She was probably contemplating calling James to take me in to get my head checked. Alessandro saved the awkward silence by returning with three cups of hot coffee.

Star turned on him. "You're an exorcist. Have you seen anything like this before?"

"I've seen many things, but no, nothing like Jael's gift," he admitted, handing us both cups we hadn't asked for. "She's disturbingly unique, wouldn't you say?"

"That's one way to describe it," Star grumbled. "If these zombie demons are after you, what are we going to do about it?"

"Jael could stay here under our protection, but I doubt she will," said Alessandro.

"Stay with a bunch of grumpy Catholic exorcists?" I snorted. "Yeah, not in this lifetime. The only place I'm going is home to my dog, who is probably desperate for a pee and cuddle right now."

I took a too-large mouthful of coffee, but the heat in my stomach felt oddly comforting. I tried not to think how bad I must look if Alessandro the Badass was making me cuppas.

"I could come and stay with you," Star said.

"No offense, but I don't want you any more involved in this than you already are. Besides, I need some space to work some of this out in my head," I said, looking over at Alessandro. "Exorcists need some alone time occasionally."

"Don't worry. We have people making sure no one gets too close to her," said Alessandro.

"And how does your pope feel about you using the papal money to buy private security for a secular, female exorcist?" Star asked, unable to keep the cynical tone out of her voice.

Billie had once put her in a Catholic private school because there was too much violence in the state school near them. It had lasted a month, and Star had hated it and fought it every step of the way. I had never asked what the nuns had said to rile her up so much, and she'd never brought it up. It had been better to let sleeping dogs lie, but now her dislike of Catholics was awake and snapping.

Alessandro didn't seem phased as he smiled at her. "His Holiness trusts what I do when I'm working. If that means looking after Jael, then it's not going to be an issue. She's an exorcist, and that's all any of them need to know."

"Lying to the pope, that's pretty gnarly," I said with newfound respect.

"It's not lying. If the Church asks, I'll tell them my exact reasoning behind it. She's going to be protected, Stella," Alessandro said before turning to me. "But for now you need rest more than anything."

I finished my coffee and handed the cup back to him. "If you have a big enough discretionary budget, you might want to hire some professionals to look into HeosCorp and Heart of the Homeless. I don't think Tom is dodgy, but the guy that's in chunks upstairs was one of his investors. If zombie demons are investing in a homeless shelter, it can't be from the goodness in their hearts."

17

DESPITE ALESSANDRO'S REASSURANCES, STAR wouldn't go home. She stubbornly followed me up the stairs and walked Meta, while I took a long shower. I wasn't shaking like last time, so that was a start. I was dismissive in front of Alessandro, but the whole Hand of Power thing was still worrying me.

"Pizza or pasta?" Star asked when I finally resurfaced. She'd tidied up while she waited and poured me a shot of tequila. Star in care mode was a weirdly intense thing that you kind of had to roll with at times.

"Pasta. Gnocchi if they have it." I slumped down at the kitchen table and took a small sip.

I rarely got drunk—my head was crazy enough sober—but I did enjoy a nip. If I ever had a day where I felt I had earned it, it was this one. Dressed in old pajama pants and a hole-riddled *Constantine* T-shirt, I began to feel normal again.

"Do you ever think about just giving it up?" Star asked quietly.

"Giving what up?"

"All this crazy exorcism crap. Don't misunderstand me. I love you, J, and that's why I'm asking. I get that you've had to live with it, but now it's getting insane. I mean, zombie demons, suicidal teens, and don't get me started on the fact that you're all chummy with a Catholic priest all of a sudden. I don't care how hot he is. I could understand you having a bit of a *Thorn Bird's* moment with him, but you seem to genuinely like him."

"I'm not having a *Thorn Bird's* moment." I sighed, not wanting to continue the conversation. "Alessandro is easy for me to get along with because he gets it, Star."

"I get—"

"No, you don't." I interrupted her. "I know you try to, but you don't understand what it's like. If you did, you would never ask if I could give it up. Look at me, Starbreeze; *really* look at me."

We stared at each other until the anger in her eyes faded away, and she faced the truth. She was scared of seeing what I did and facing the reality of demons for herself. But more than anything else, she was scared of *me*. I don't know much about people, but I know my best friend. She always acts angry to hide her fear.

"There is nothing I can do to help you," Star said finally.

"I don't know about that. You should study hard, because I'll probably need a good shrink when this is all done with."

"You need one now, who is a lot more qualified than me." Star sipped her drink before looking back at me. "What are you going to do?"

"What I usually do. Wing it until it sorts itself out. Hopefully, Max and Alessandro can find out some inside information into HeosCorp, and I'll focus on whatever was happening with the professor's family."

"What about Uriel? Couldn't he wing about and bring something up?"

"He's already had to bail me out once. This is my mission, not his. You can't expect Heaven to help because you don't feel like doing it for yourself. It doesn't work like that. They aren't into the instant gratification business," I said with a tired sigh. "I'll work it out. I just need some time."

Meta cuddled against me, and I gave his goofy ears a pat. I had to keep it together, to be safe, if for no other reason than Meta needing food and belly rubs.

"I don't know how I'm going to sit back and let you do this on your own," Star admitted. "I hate this feeling."

"If you want to do something, believe in me. The job has gotten more intense in recent weeks, but it's still the same fight. I've been doing this since I was seventeen, Star. If I weren't used to it by now, I wouldn't be much of an exorcist."

Despite my reassurances, Star stayed over that night. She and Meta piled in next to me in my bed. It was weirdly comforting and normal to have them with me. Their soft snores echoed around me as the sound of a lullaby about fireflies sent me off to sleep.

Star left for classes the next day after multiple promises and assurances that I'd call her if anything happened. My shoulders were bruised from being slammed into the cell bars the day before, and I struggled to remember what my body used to look like without all the purple and yellow.

I rearranged all of my research on the professor's family and tried not to look at my phone every few minutes to see if Max or Alessandro had found anything about HeosCorp.

My search on the internet had only revealed some basic company information and the larger industries they were involved in. Nothing of note or suspicious. I tried searching for various archaeological digs in the Negev, and when that failed, I searched the professor. There were multiple pictures of him at lectures, glossy shots of him studying fragments of ancient texts, and one of him with Nazirah at his last major dig in Jerusalem. He looked happy in every single photo. Not like a guy who would jump in front of train unless pushed by something malevolent.

The last picture I found was of him and Rabbi Josef at the opening of the last exhibit less than three weeks ago. If Professor Ben-Ezra had problems of a spiritual or mental nature, surely he would have confided in his good friend and rabbi. When Esther had been troubled, she'd gone straight to the synagogue. But Josef had claimed that he didn't know anything about what his friend was working on.

"Something seriously isn't adding up, Meta," I said to him. He tilted his head, walked around in a circle, and went back to sleep. I thought about calling Star and asking for a lift to the synagogue, but I suspected she needed a break from my crazy life. I was saved from having to mull over the decision for too long when my phone rang.

"Hello?" I answered, still looking at the papers.

"I have been waiting for days for you to give me a call. I swear to God you like to make a man squirm, Quinlan," Tom said cheerily from the other end of the line.

"Tom! Shoot, sorry. I was going to get back to you, but I've been up to my eyeballs in…well, in drama. I haven't gotten to it yet," I said apologetically.

"Drama called Uriel North?" he asked. "I must say I've never had someone swoop in and steal my date so effectively. Damn, that man was huge though. Makes me wonder if steroids are legal in Scandinavia."

"It wasn't a date," I said too quickly. "Was it?"

"You cut me to the quick, Quinlan. Of course, it was a date. Why do you think I was so nervous all night? Do you know how many years it has been since I was nervous around a girl?"

"Well…I…I didn't realize."

"I was going to make it more obvious, but the enigmatic Mr. North stepped in. What is the story there? He's not your boss, is he?"

"Yeah, he is," I said stubbornly. "There is nothing going on other than work and a bit of concern because I foolishly drank too much."

"I saw how he danced with you, and he didn't exactly look at you like an employee either. You are delightfully clueless about all this, aren't you?" He laughed. "You were a kooky, cute girl who grew up to be a gorgeous, mysterious woman, and you haven't the slightest idea about it. I'd be showering you with flowers and gifts right now if I thought it'd work on you."

"Look, Warner, I know you're a big CEO, but it's poor form to be drunk this early in the day," I replied, glowing so vibrantly red that I thought I was going to combust.

"I'm not drunk! I'm jealous and frustrated," he admitted. "I also think I went about this whole thing backward, and I've blown it completely. Can we start over and just get a beer and catch up sometime? I'm surrounded by people who want things from me all the time, and it's nice to hang out with someone who sees through all the bullshit."

"Yours included?"

He made an amused groan. "Mine above all. Jesus, you're a tough nut to crack."

"I'll take that as a compliment."

"Good to know you'll take some compliments. I was starting to worry you weren't human." He laughed. "I want to convince you to go on a proper date in the future. Please just call me for a beer sometime? Like really soon? Not a proper date just yet, only mates for a beer."

"I can do that." I looked down at my pile of research, so far removed from the conversation I was having. "I have some things I need to sort out in the next week or so, but I'll text you, yeah?"

"You'll text me. You're such a dag, Jael. Call me, leave a message with a receptionist, send a goddamn carrier pigeon for all I care. Just do it."

"Now who's the dag? I'll talk to you soon, loser."

"You'd better, or I'll run away with some bimbo supermodel that I can't stand."

"Do it; see if I care."

"You're still a pain in the ass."

"You're still full of yourself. Now bugger off, I'm busy."

I hung up on him and cracked up laughing for the first time in days. We had always argued and flirted and being over ten years out of high school hadn't changed that. My phone rang again, insistently.

"You really can't stay away, can you?" I demanded.

"Well, Jael, I would stop calling you every day if you stopped leaving bodies everywhere you went," said James.

"My favorite boy in blue," I answered feeling like a total idiot. "What can I do for you?"

"You can tell me what you did to get Star so upset for a start," he replied sharply.

Great. It was going to be *that* kind of conversation.

"I didn't do anything to her. She's probably having to reconcile her New Age belief system with the epic biblical smackdown she saw yesterday. She's going to be fine," I added, because upsetting James was the last thing I wanted to do. "She could probably do with a big, strong man hug though. It was a rough day."

"She said you are getting chummy with a scary Catholic priest. That's a bit unlike you."

"Yeah, it is, but he's okay. What else can I do for you?"

"I thought you might want to know that I got a call from the cute research girl at the museum. She didn't want to mention it in front of her other colleagues. The professor not only argued with the rabbi the day he died, but insisted on delivering something to the synagogue to keep it safe so 'the evil wouldn't fall into anyone else's hands.' She thought he was cracked," James said.

"Damn Josef! I knew he was hiding something from me the other night." I groaned, my mind going into overdrive. "Esther's heart freaking exploded, and he still didn't give it up."

"I figured as much. I'm heading over now to get you," he replied.

James looked at the research sprawled over my dining table with a mix of amusement and interest. "Jeez, Jael. This thing has gotten under your skin, hasn't it?"

"A girl threatened me and splattered herself on a tram in front of me. Of course it's gotten under my skin," I muttered as I pulled on my boots. "A whole freaking family is dead now, and Josef said nothing. What is he playing at?"

"I'm more concerned with how much the object was worth."

"Josef doesn't strike me as the type who would have antiquities contacts, especially ones in the black market." I shook my head. "This isn't about money."

"What if it's something else? Like a secret he's trying to protect? The guy is pretty orthodox from what I can tell. If it's something sacred to Judaism, he's not going to hand it over to a bunch of cops where it could be damaged or sit in evidence for the next however many years," said James.

"You're not just a pretty face are you, Hunt?"

"I do have moments of sheer awesomeness," he admitted, humble as always.

"How do you want to approach this?" I asked James on our way to Coburg. I didn't want to admit that I wasn't fit to fight. But I'd seen the creature in Esther's eyes, and I couldn't risk it possessing anyone else.

"I know my manliness shouldn't be willing to admit this, but I think I'm going to sit this one out until I'm needed. Sometimes ignorance is bliss when it comes to your job."

"Maybe for you. Right now, ignorance is kicking my ass," I said, complaining and rubbing my sore shoulders. "I'm in so much bloody pain I should be in bed."

"There's some Panadeine in the glove box if you want it, you whiner," James teased.

"No, I'll have some after we are done. Drugs will hinder me and make me groggy. The pain will make me sharper."

"Sadist."

"If there was any other way, I would be drinking tequila and popping pain-killers right now."

The car park was empty when we pulled into the synagogue. I hadn't wanted to phone ahead to see if Josef was here, in case he tried to dodge me.

"Are you sure you don't want me to come with you?" James asked.

"Unless you want to end up in a mood like Star's, I wouldn't recommend it," I said. And because it came out harsher than I expected, I added, "I don't want to see anyone else get hurt."

"Then I'll wait here for twenty minutes, and if you're not out, I'll stick my head in. How about that?"

"You big softy."

"Death Star would kill me if I let anything else happen to you. I need to stay on her good side."

"So when you grow a pair and ask her out, she'll say yes? You should just skip all the awkward stuff and kiss her. Like with tongue."

"Don't you have a rabbi to roughhouse?" said James, the tips of his brown ears turning a dusky pink.

"I'm going, I'm going," I said and tried to get out of the car without moving my shoulders too much.

Stepping inside the cool interior of the synagogue was like entering a bubble of hushed, reverent silence. I walked softly through the foyer, and with each step my intuition screamed to back away.

"Rabbi Josef?" I called out, and the thick cloud of sickening dread grew heavier. Oh yeah, this was definitely where the damned thing was hanging out.

I found him in his office, pouring over paperwork. When he looked up, he didn't seem surprised to see me.

"Jael, I didn't hear you come in," he said with a strained smile. "As you can see, I've had a lot to catch up on with the police wanting statements every other day." He seemed okay enough, but a film of sweat was starting to cover him.

"Tell me about it! I was interviewed for hours the other day. How has it been here since Esther?" I asked, sitting down in the guest chair in front of him. There was a slight tremor in his hand as he ran it over his neck.

"There were many people who were upset. The family was well-liked, and it was a horrible thing to happen. We told everyone it was a heart attack, because who would believe the truth any more than they'd believe powerful beings are living amongst us that we can't see? But you didn't come here today to talk about the synagogue, Jael. Why are you really here?" Josef asked, setting aside his pen.

"I want to ask you some questions about Genesis." I shrugged. "I came across something that confused me."

"A Torah lesson then." He smiled indulgently. "What's troubling you?"

"In Genesis 6:4, it talks about the Nephilim. Who were they? Why aren't they around now, and why is there no archaeological evidence to prove they existed?" Something flickered behind his glasses, but it was gone again almost instantly.

"They were the beloved children of the Watcher angels, those sent to guide mankind, and the human women they took as wives. The archangels were jealous that the Watchers could take wives and make these powerful, strong children. The archangels left *Shamayim*, the Heavens, and slaughtered the Nephilim like the merciless soldiers they are." Josef's voice had changed while he talked, the ancient anger seeping through and his eyes becoming unnaturally bright.

"The archangels answer to Elyon only. If they killed the Nephilim and the Watchers, then it must have been divine will," I said matter-of-factly. "Huh, I thought it was pretty interesting anyway."

"Is there anything else I can help you with? If not, there's a lot I need to finish today," he said, dismissing me.

"One last thing, what did the professor give to you before he died?" I asked. His eyes flicked to a polished box on top of the fireplace mantel and then back to me, but he said nothing. "You don't need to deny it. There was a witness. What was so important that you felt you had to lie to the cops about it? I mean we are all a little guilty of not telling them everything, but you're a rabbi; you should know better."

"What does it matter if Aaron gave me anything? It was a gift, and it has nothing to do with a disrespectful Gentile exorcist."

"Nothing to do with me? His daughter splattered herself like a pancake in front of me! What if this object had something to do with it? Think Josef!"

Before he could stop me, I leaped out of my chair and snapped up the polished box. "Oh, what's this? It looks new and fancy—"

"Don't touch that!" Josef was on his feet and hissing his indignation in an instant.

I opened the box and inside, resting on a bed of velvet, was a clay idol. It looked like a strange mix of Babylonian and Egyptian art and was unmistakably a powerful man with outstretched wings like a griffon. It thrummed with menace, and my Behind eyes snapped open; its aura was unmistakably the same as Esther's before she died.

"Put it down, you filthy whore of Gehenna!" Josef shouted, his hands like claws stretching out toward me.

"Old school cursing; I like it." I faced him, gripping the box tightly. "Jumped into the good rabbi after Esther, did you? I must say, you had me fooled. What is this? Is it meant to be you?"

"In the time I walked on Eretz, men worshipped us like the gods we were, and they will do so again."

I did my best to keep space and office furniture between us as he stalked me.

"When you walked the earth? So, you're a ghost and not a demon?" I turned the box in my hand. "Let me guess…you tied yourself to this little trinket, and now you are body-hopping as it changes hands. Clever, if messy. What's the point?"

"The world is changing, little exorcist." Josef heaved. "Better for you to be dead now than when the tide rises. Humans are going to learn that their dominion is—" He faltered as I tipped a vial of myrrh oil onto the idol. Before it could stop me, I threw the idol to the ground, breaking it to pieces. A high-pitched scream tore from Josef's throat as it flailed at unseen enemies.

"Get away from me, brothers of betrayal," the spirit hissed with its ancient voice. Through my Behind eyes, I saw angels fill the room, pressing into it as it tried helplessly to fight them off. Another stepped from the crowd, and I looked away, unable to stand the intensity of its light. Josef fell to his knees in front of it, sobbing.

And then they were gone, leaving the real Josef shaking on the floor but wholly himself once more.

I knelt down and gathered the three broken pieces of clay. Despite how hard I had thrown it against the ground, it hadn't shattered. I wrapped them in a tissue and clutched them tightly. I'd show it to Uriel and then grind it to dust.

"Jael," Josef whispered, and I knelt down beside him. "Jael, I'm sorry."

"It's going to be okay. It's gone," I said, helping him sit up. He gripped my hands tightly, tears running down his face.

"Tell me you saw that, Jael," he begged. "Tell me you saw…"

"The angels? Yeah, I saw them. You aren't going crazy."

"And the other one?"

"I saw, but only for a moment, then I couldn't look anymore."

"I saw…I saw…" Josef trailed off and cried harder. "What am I going to do now?"

"You are going to go home, have a shower, eat something, and go to sleep. That's all you can do, rabbi. You will feel better when you wake up."

"My mind is so clouded. I can't remember. Eyes like fire…" He shook his head. "If there is anything I can ever do to thank you, please name it and it will be yours."

There was one thing that had been bugging me. I asked, "Do you know what *yadid* means? It sounds Hebrew, but I haven't come across it before."

"*Yadid*? It means 'beloved,'" Josef said, giving me a confused look. "Why?"

"It's nothing, just something I heard," I replied as my tired heart swelled a little in my chest.

James was pacing the parking lot when I finally emerged into the milky sunlight. I smiled, trying to hide how wrecked I was.

"How did it go? I was getting ready to come in after you when I heard shouting," he said. My eyes welled up for no reason, and he hugged me. "Oh shoot, do I need to call an ambulance?"

"No, he's okay. He's not hurt physically." I sniffled, grateful to have him there. "It's over, I exorcised the spirit finally."

"Then why are you crying?"

"Just tired. That's all. It killed a whole family before I got it." I let him go and wiped the tears from my cheeks.

"But you *did* get it, Jael. It could've gone through hundreds of people if you weren't here. Stop kicking your ass because you don't know everything." He opened my car door, and I collapsed in the seat.

He was right; I knew it, but it didn't make me feel any better.

18

J AMES DROPPED ME OFF, and I crawled into bed and didn't move until the next morning. The week's exhaustion had finally caught up with me, and apart from taking Meta upstairs to pee on the rooftop garden, I didn't leave the apartment.

The next day I finally got up. I cleaned up the messy research about the Watchers and the professor, and I spread out the information about the zombie demons. I found websites and books ranging from voodoo to botched resurrections to a badly translated article from a Russian paper talking about farmers who swore they had seen walking demons in the forests within the last six months. Half of it was crazy, and half of it wasn't what I was after.

I thought about ringing Alessandro, but I fought the urge. If he had found something important, I'm sure he would have gotten ahold of me. He had two other exorcists with him to watch his back, but a small, annoying worry was twisting its way into my heart. I hated to admit it, but I liked the guy. I wanted him to be okay.

On my second night of hiding, there was a knock at the door that set Meta barking. I had expected it to be Star, but it was two pizza boxes.

"I have a delivery for a cranky exorcist. Does one live here?" Max said from behind them.

"Smart-ass." I laughed as he lowered the boxes, revealing glasses and a smile. "What are you doing here?"

"Well, I figured I'd stop in and tell you about all the interesting things I've found out," he said as he came inside. "But knowing you, I thought I had better bring food to soften you up."

"You already know me far too well." He was dressed casually in jeans and a T-shirt which made him look younger and less serious. He put the boxes down on my kitchen bench and smiled at me. Suddenly I was really glad I'd decided to shower and change out of my pajamas today.

"Bit of light study?" he asked, looking from me to the dining table I'd pushed against a wall. It was now covered in pictures, articles, and other bits of research. "It's starting to have a bit of *A Beautiful Mind* vibe in here."

"I've been digging about," I said around half a mouthful of pizza.

"Zombie demons? You found some?" Max pushed his glasses up his nose as he leaned to read some of my notes.

"Found stuff that's close, but nothing that really fits. How did the sneaking around at work go?"

"Tricky," Max said as he took out a piece of pepperoni pizza. "They have so many passwords on everything that I could only look so far digitally. HeosCorp has so many companies that it would take years to find any corporate corruption."

"What about their investments in Heart of the Homeless?"

"That I did find. They've given Tom at least $8 million in the last quarter alone. His is not the only shelter they give to either. There's at least a hundred spread out worldwide. Similar setups, aimed at rehabilitation. I found out about most of them because of the complaints."

"What complaints?" I asked as I hunted for beers in the fridge. "Who would complain about free food and education?"

"The relatives of the people mostly," Max replied. "The ones that actually found their lost ones claim they have been brainwashed. They think it's some cult, because they come out of the place different from when they went in. The claims never went anywhere because HeosCorp Legal dropped on them like a ton of bricks. The ones that did make it to court were dismissed, because there was no real evidence that the changes weren't the result of them wanting to start their life over."

"Start their life over as demons maybe, if they were anything like Clair."

"That's not all," Max said with a frown. "I've done this research on them before."

"What do you mean?"

"I mean I found some stuff at home, a whole archive box of copies of files and statements about HeosCorp. I don't have any memory of doing it," Max replied, lowering his beer. "I asked Mom about it, and she said right before I…I changed…I became paranoid and secretive. I told her I was working on a case, and I couldn't talk to her about it."

"And you remember nothing about it? I've seen cases where demoniacs have lost whole swaths of memory before and during their possession. What is the last thing you remember before there's nothing?"

"I remember being at work. I was nervous, because we had performance reviews." He picked at the bottle label. "I shook my boss's hand, and then there is darkness until…until I woke up and saw your face. You were smiling at me, because it was gone."

"Always a reason to celebrate." I smiled. "Even if I get my ass kicked in the process."

"I really hurt you, didn't I?" His voice was tiny with the horror of it.

"It was nothing I couldn't handle. It comes with the territory, unfortunately. Stop freaking out." I squeezed his arm gently. "Maxy, seriously, it wasn't you. I know that."

"I'm sorry for it anyway." He blinked a few times rapidly and added, "I don't know if I like people calling me Maxy."

"Get used to it. A nickname is my way of showing how much I like you," I said, getting myself another piece of pizza. The last thing I wanted was him freaking out about what a demon made him do. The pizza fell from my hand.

"Jael? Are you okay?"

"What…what if someone put the demon into you?" I asked, my mind reeling.

"Why would they do that?"

"Because you were on to them! Your box of files at home proves it. If they thought you were going to report them to IBAC or something, they would have wanted to shut you up. You're a good Christian boy. There is no way you'd take a bribe, and they couldn't fire you. What if they put a demon in you to make sure you protected their interests?"

"If that's the case, then someone higher up is either controlling possessed people or is one of the possessed themselves," Max said slowly. "It sounds completely crazy."

"Or completely brilliant in an evil mastermind kind of way," I admitted. "Anybody gets too close and *bang*! Another possessed worker bee for the cause."

"That's sick."

"That's a good way to save on legal fees. Sorry, bad joke. I looked into HeosCorp, and you know what I found strange?"

"What's that?"

"There's no picture of the boss. Usually, CEOs or big company founders love to have their faces splattered on everything, so that it becomes almost synonymous with the brand." I pointed at the wall of research. "No pictures. All the board members worldwide have photos but zero of Lucian Heosphoros. There are a few quotes in some *Forbes* articles, a blurry pic with him in sunnies, and that's about it."

"He's famously eccentric and reclusive. Everyone in the company knows that. You know who the richest people in the world are?" Max asked.

"No."

"No one knows, and that's the point. With that kind of money, you wouldn't want people to know who you are. You want to be able to walk down any street in the world and be ignored."

"I suppose it makes a weird kind of sense. It is still a bit strange."

"What is?" a new voice said from the other side of the room, and I almost dropped my beer. Uriel was standing there, plain as day. To Max's credit, he didn't faint or run away screaming. Even though he was visible, Uriel hadn't taken any extra pains to make himself look as human as the night of the gala. He wasn't armored, but he was dressed in angel attire.

"So, Star wasn't lying about him being an angel after all." Max gaped, putting his drink down on the countertop and heading for the front door. "I'm gonna go. Mr. North, a pleasure seeing you again."

"Maximilian," Uriel said coolly. I glared at him as I showed Max out.

"Thanks for all your help," I said and gave Max a quick hug. Uriel's expression was a mix of frustration and annoyance over Max's shoulder. "Do me a favor and call in sick until this is over. I don't want to give them another chance to put a demon in you…I don't know how they managed to do it the first time, and I don't want to have to exorcise you again."

"I will, but only if you'll be careful where you are digging," Max replied. "This world needs its exorcists. I know I do."

"You got it, buddy. Call me if you think of anything else," I said, watching him go down the stairs. I shut the door feeling like a complete jerk. I turned to the surly archangel in my living room. "What gives? I was enjoying his company. You didn't have to turn up and make him leave."

"I didn't ask him to."

"Not with actual words," I grumbled, but he wasn't listening to me. His eyes were suddenly scanning the walls and furniture. "Uriel? What's wrong?"

"I don't know, but something feels…" He didn't finish his sentence as he went out onto the balcony and came back in before searching the bathroom and bedroom.

"Tell me what you are looking for, and I can help."

"It shouldn't be here!" he said, insistent. "What have you brought into the house?"

I rummaged in my bag and brought out the tissues that held the broken pieces of the idol. "Only this. It's strange. I was going to ask you about it be-cause—"

He took it from my hands and hissed as he unwrapped it. "Where did you get this?"

"It was what possessed the professor and his family. There was this strange spirit attached to it that kept ranting about the Watchers and Nephilim."

The pieces in his hands rejoined, and he held it up. "There shouldn't be any of these left."

"It was found in the desert. A student of the professor had a dig somewhere in the Negev. I guess she sent it to her old teacher to get his opinion of it. I've never seen anything like it. Can you tell me what it is?"

"It was an idol to the Watchers from one of the cults that spread in the time before the Flood."

"Are you saying this predates Noah? How could it even survive that long and not turn to dust?" I reached out for it, but he pulled it away.

"Don't touch it. It's a foul thing like the abominations it represents," Uriel said, but there wasn't any anger in his voice, only worry. "They shouldn't be dig-ging anywhere near it…"

"Near what? The Negev? There are digs all over it."

"No, you don't understand."

"Then explain it to me." I took his scarred hand in mine.

"There are parts of that desert that no human, angel, or demon should be able to enter. What's buried in that earth should never be found."

"And you think the statue came from there? If there was a cult worshipping them, these little icons could have traveled with people."

"I need to talk to my brothers and investigate this further." He tucked the statue into his pocket. He looked me over so slowly and carefully that I shifted my feet nervously.

"What?" I demanded.

"Nothing. I wanted to make sure none of its influence was hanging about you."

"The thing that I exorcised out of the rabbi was talking about being a god again and a coming war. It was a mad, ranting thing. Far more than any demon I've ever seen."

"It must have been the spirit of a Nephilim. The Watchers wouldn't be capable of such a thing. As for what it said, there isn't a war coming, because it's already here. There is *always* a war going on. Just because none of the humans can see it, doesn't mean it isn't happening. You know this better than anyone."

I half expected him to disappear then, but instead, he hugged me. Uriel wasn't the hugging type, which told me that despite his words, he was seriously freaking out. I held on to him realizing Alessandro was right; nothing human could compare to how I felt at that moment. Protected, safe, and loved. *God, I love him.*

"Be safe, *yadid*," he murmured, pressing a kiss to the top of my head and then he was gone, leaving me confused and clutching the empty air. Loneliness crashed in on me, so I found my phone and was dialing Star when I heard a knock at the door.

"Back already, Max? I swear you are growing fond—" I was reaching for the handle when the wood was kicked in, and three men dressed in black rushed into the room. I grabbed the baton I kept on a bookshelf and flicked it out. "I don't know who you are, but you decided to rob the wrong house."

The one closest to me pulled a gun, and my baton came up and across his wrist, pushing it away. The shot fired through the apartment. Meta was up on the couch growling and barking, his fur standing up at the intruders. The guy who had dropped the gun rushed toward me, and I dropped my phone as he tackled me to the ground.

"Hello? Hello? Jael?" I heard Star's voice on the other end.

"Star! They've come for me!" I shouted as a heavy fist came down on my ribs. Meta yelped as one of the others kicked him hard against the wall. "META! You bastards!" I started struggling, lashing out at the guy pinning me down.

"For fuck's sake shut her up before someone hears!" a voice demanded, and a bag went over my head followed by the sharp pain of a needle in my neck.

"Get off…you…" I flailed until all went black.

19

I WOKE WITH HIS name on my lips. "Uriel, Uriel."

Intense pain shot through my arms, and I opened my blurry eyes. My arms had been chained above my head, and I was hanging like a cow carcass on a hook. I struggled to get to my feet and relieve the strain on my shoulders. I didn't know what they had shot me up with, but it had been strong. I still couldn't feel half my body; waking up was like a smack in the face. I could smell blood, and looking down at the mess on the front of my shirt, I figured some of it had to be mine.

I was in a bare concrete cell with no window and a drain at my feet. That didn't bode well. There weren't any visible marks on the floor, but my skin crawled, knowing I couldn't have been the only one who had found themselves locked up here. I made sure my shields were locked up tight. I didn't want to see or feel what had happened in the room in the past. *Uriel, help me. Please help me. I'm in real trouble. They have me, Uriel.*

I thought of Meta's squeal and nearly threw up. I hoped he was okay, that Star had called Alessandro, and they had both realized what had happened. I worried my captors had gotten Max when he left my apartment. *Damn it, Max.* I hadn't wanted to bring him further into it. They had already put a demon into him once, and I'd set him free. The next time they'd just kill him and turn him into a zombie demon.

"Uriel, please. Find Max. Please find me," I whispered through my busted lip. He'd come for me. Uriel had always come.

So where is he now, Jael? A small doubtful voice filled me. The statue had sent him to the other side of the world. Could he hear me from that far away?

The door opened with a creaking groan, and a zombie demon goon in black gear leered at me.

"Your pretty little archangel isn't going to save you, exorcist," it said, folding its arms.

"Why are you doing this? What kind of a threat am I to you? This all seems a little extreme and too organized for demons."

"You ask some dumb questions considering how many of us you have killed recently. If it were up to me, I'd be eating strips of you right now." It was beside me in a moment, and I flinched as it sniffed me. I hoped my sweaty BO killed it. "I can *smell* the angels on you. Have you caused Uriel to fall, little exorcist?" It ran its hands down my body, nuzzling against my neck. I struggled in my chains, trying to headbutt it. "Has he touched you so softly? Kissed your little woes away? I saw him dance with you. I think he would like to."

"Shut your filthy mouth," I snapped.

"No, I didn't think he had. Uriel always was the coldest of all those glorified bastards. Angel of the North. Your pathetic human brain can't even comprehend the death you've been courting. He is ice and murder, and he could never care for the likes of you. A pathetic little mud crawler."

I could feel it trying to worm its way into my head, to break me down and mess with me. I started saying an exorcism prayer in my head, and its fist came sharply down on my ribs, sending the breath out of my body. I hung loose, gasping for air.

"Don't think I can't hear you, whore." It tapped its finger on its head. "You can't get me out of this body as easily as the others. As soon as they have what they need from you, I am going to enjoy breaking you apart bit by bit."

"We'll see who's breaking who by the end of this." I smiled despite the pain in my side. Lightning fast, it jabbed another syringe of drugs into me.

I could see the beast beneath the man, and I fought to maintain my glare. It lifted the chain from the hook and tossed me into the corner of the cell.

"The boss wants you breathing for a while longer, exorcist, because he's got a bone to pick with your angels." Its smile distorted in front of me as the drugs kicked in. "But you aren't going to be much of anything when this is over. That I can promise you." It shut the door, its head thrown back in a laugh that scraped up the sides of my mind.

I didn't know how long I was left on the floor of the cell. There was no way of telling night from day. Time was marked by the demon that came to taunt me, slap me about, and give me drugs again. My prayer was always the same. *Uriel, help me.*

When I wasn't getting the shit kicked out of me, I was dreaming about the demon hunter I'd seen in my visions. It was almost always a night scene with this haunted, dynamo of a man slaying demons with his silver spear, dropping them like they were straw men. Was it just a dream? Who *was* he? The fine cut still healing on my throat was proof that his spear was real enough. I didn't know if I was hallucinating or not, but when I watched him fight, I also saw two angels watching over him. They seemed to be waiting for something, but I couldn't determine what. What troubled me most was the fact that most of the creatures he was fighting were fully manifested in the real world. Not a spirit, but there in the flesh. There were zombie demons and what I decided to call half-and-halfs; it was like the body containing them was mutating under the pressure of having such an evil thing inside of it. The demon hunter was a murdering shadow. He didn't exorcise anything, he just cut it down and scattered the pieces to the wind.

Who are you? I called out to him, but he never heard me. Once, he turned, but he didn't see me or the angels standing in the snow. The angels seemed to be talking and arguing with each other. It was the first time that the Language of the Angels wasn't understandable for me. I knew from their tone that they were worried about the demon hunter, and I could see why. The guy was wasting away, already skinnier than the first time I had seen him. And when I caught the look in his eyes, it was like he had the full weight of despair on his broad shoulders.

Then I would wake up. Cold, alone, and in pain.

"Where are you, Uriel? You came when I was at the party, and now you leave me in a cell? Why won't you answer me?" I whispered through my tears.

My spirit recoiled at the thought that he'd abandoned me. Even if he wasn't visible, I could feel him when he was nearby, feel our connection. And now there was nothing but silence. My feeling of safety no longer existed.

He was gone. He'd finally abandoned me, because I was just a pathetic human like the demon said I was.

Why did I think I was special enough to have an angel on my side? There wasn't a special thing about me. I had been a tool, and maybe the job I had been used for was over.

Whatever the demon had done to me so far, it was nothing compared to what I felt in that moment of abandonment. The innermost essence of myself burned with grief. A vital part of the foundation of who I was cracked and broke.

When the demon came next, I welcomed the physical blows. Anything to stop feeling my shattered heart.

I finally stopped crying out for Uriel.

Jael. A gentle, impossible voice reached out through the haze of drugs and pain. A pair of bare feet stood in front of me. *Jael.* I roused but didn't move as a hand brushed my blood-matted hair. I felt something pass through me, and my mind cleared a little.

"Who are you?" I whispered, my eyes too swollen to make him out.

"One who has heard your cries. I need you to get up, Jael. Your fight is not over."

"Yes, it is. Uriel's gone." I sobbed helplessly. "I don't know what to do. The demon was right. I'm not strong enough to fight them on my own."

"Your strength doesn't come from Uriel, or have you forgotten that?" He chastised me gently, and I flinched. "You don't need him for this battle. It belongs to you. Get up and fight back, Jael. If you don't, this city will be theirs."

I struggled to sit up in my chains. "I can't do this alone."

Warm hands clutched my face, wiping my tears away with his thumbs. "You are *never* alone."

Heat and light filled my vision, and I woke up. My mind was clear, supernatural strength filled every muscle in my body, and my spirit was on fire.

"Time to wake up, meat sack," my warden said, kicking me playfully in the ribs. I lay still. "Get up! The boss wants to see you."

It gripped the front of my shirt to haul me to my feet, but I was faster. My chain swung up, smacking it in the face before I kneed it as hard as I could between the legs. It fell backward, and I was on it, smashing my manacles against its head. My hands burned hot as I grabbed it by the face.

"It looks like you won't get to eat me after all," I said, growling.

"You bit—" It screamed as light and power roared into it. The head beneath my hands crushed in on itself until it was nothing more than broken bone and sagging skin.

I snapped the manacles off my hands like they were made of paper, and I walked from the room, ready to find the boss that was so eager to make my acquaintance.

20

THERE WEREN'T ANY OTHER guards in the bare concrete hallway, but there were at least a dozen more cells. I checked the first three, but they were clean and empty. On the fourth try, I found a heavily muscled man hanging up like I had been but suffering worse damage.

He started awake at the sound of me using the winch to lower him to the ground.

"Jael?" he murmured, trying his best to stand straight. His face was busted up, but the accent gave him away.

"Paulo, it's going to be okay," I said as calmly as I could. I could still feel the impossible strength in me, so I snapped his chains off.

"Mother, have mercy." He gasped in fear as I gripped the extra length of chain.

"Paulo, are the others with you?" I demanded. "Where is Alessandro?"

"I don't know where they took him. We were following up on a lead about HeosCorp, when we were ambushed."

I was burning white-hot with rage, and I didn't stop to check if he was following me as I stormed out in search of Alessandro.

The next cell revealed two dead but unpossessed women. I didn't look too closely at their wounds and quickly moved on to the next cell. We found Gregory, but I left Paulo to get him down.

I had almost given up on finding anyone else, when I heard a demon laughing and mocking someone in Italian. My hand gripped the chain tighter. Alessandro's reply was vicious and followed by the sound of spitting. I opened the door just as the demon raised its fist to hit him again.

"Get your filthy hands off my exorcist," I said with a growl. I whipped the chain hard across its face, followed by a kick to the guts. I grabbed it by the head, and the power left my hands, bringing it down.

"*Mia eroina*," Alessandro said, wheezing as I released him from the chair. His back and torso were covered in bruises, cuts, and to my surprise, various tattoos.

"I thought you were meant to be good at this, priest," I teased lamely, slinging his arm over my shoulder and helping him stand. "Paulo is helping Gregory. You need to leave with them while you can."

"And what are you going to do?" Alessandro asked as he straightened. He didn't seem like he was going to fall over, so I let him go.

"I'm going to find out who is responsible for this," I said darkly. "This is going to end tonight."

"I'm coming with you," he replied in a voice that I couldn't argue with. He looked at the body on the floor and back to me. "Let's hope God is still with us."

Paulo and Gregory met us in the hall. Alessandro swapped quick words with them in Italian, and the inevitable argument ensued.

"They are refusing to leave," Alessandro said, huffing and then calling them something that didn't sound very priestly. The other two exorcists simply smiled big, bloody grins.

"The more the merrier," I said. "Let's find a way out of here."

We found a service elevator with the HeosCorp logo, and my rage cooled to an icy calm. Gregory had the foresight to search one of the dead guards and had lifted a set of keys and a swipe card from him.

"We must be underneath the car park," I said, looking at the buttons for the forty floors with the addition of an extra basement and a penthouse.

"Where do we go first, Jael?" Alessandro asked, following my lead. I ran my fingers down the buttons before selecting the penthouse.

"We'll start at the top and work our way down," I said, gripping the bloody chain as I started praying. Beside me, the exorcists started prayers of their own and heat swelled within my chest.

Instinctively the other exorcists gave me space, except for Alessandro who said, "We'll drop them, you touch them. We are with you, Jael." I wanted to thank him for saying something encouraging, but I felt like I was underwater, like what made me Jael was riding shotgun to something infinitely more powerful.

The prayers continued, upholding me as they had Alessandro at Saint Augustine's. The elevator pinged and opened to a foyer full of demons.

"On second thought, perhaps you should go first," Alessandro suggested, but I was already moving.

It should be noted here that those who say they are going to "raise hell" just to be tough have clearly never seen justice rain from Heaven. I had always been angry at demons and the way they slowly destroyed human lives, but I'd never felt the rage that I did when I saw them today. It bubbled up and poured out of me.

As the possessed people rushed at me, I simply touched them, and they fell dead. I was vaguely aware of the exorcists behind me, their prayers rising above the growling screams of demons. Some of the weaker ones I didn't need to touch; merely drawing near to them caused them to fall.

If that was what was guarding the foyer, I couldn't wait to see what was inside. I opened the office doors with an angry jerk. A man standing by a bay of windows turned and smiled.

My world fell out from beneath me.

"Tom?" My voice sounded tiny, a dying thing in the space between us.

"What the hell did you do to my men, Jael?" he asked as if I had merely spilled some water on his nice carpet. I dropped all of my psychic shields, and what I saw horrified me more than anything else I had seen that night.

"You aren't possessed."

"Me?" He laughed brightly. "God, no. That's only for the help."

"Why Tom? Heart of the Homeless was meant to help people."

"No, Jael, it was meant to clean up the shit that pollutes the streets," he said matter-of-factly. He rested against the front of his mahogany desk, calmly picking up the gun that lay on it. "Jesus, Quinlan. You look like I just killed your favorite kitten and not given the dregs of society a purpose. You said it yourself; I'm a great beautifier. Where's a better place to start than my hometown?"

"They were *people*, Tom. You are killing *people* so that demons can possess them!" I shouted. "Why? For what possible—"

"The only thing that's worth anything…power." He shrugged like it was the most obvious thing in the world. "And for a place in the new order. The world is dying, Jael. Overpopulation is killing it, and so many humans are a waste of space. I'm merely taking out the trash. If we don't get organized and make the right allies now, it is going to be too late."

"You complete and utter bastard. How dare you rob people of their free will like this. Demons don't *share*. Once you have completed whatever task they set for you, you are going to be food for crows."

"I'm their partner, and they respect me. *They* wanted you dead, and it's only my affection for you that kept you alive. What we had building between us was real, despite you being an exorcist. Oh, don't look so surprised. Of course I knew what you did." He smiled charmingly. "I always did have such a soft spot for you. Join me in cleaning up this city, creating a real and lasting change, or I'm afraid I'm going to have to kill you. I can't have you and your dogs here frustrating any more of my well-placed plans."

"*Esorcista*, may I break his jaw for you?" Alessandro asked, moving closer to me.

"What a shame." Tom sighed. The gun went off in his hand as I was pushed aside. I clutched at my stomach, but it was Alessandro who fell.

I threw the chain, smashing it into Tom's gun hand and knocking him off-balance. I was on him in a heartbeat, tackling him to the ground. I caught the fist that he swung at me, and I crushed the bones beneath my hand. I walloped him in the face, and he stilled beneath me.

"Alessandro," I said, hurrying to him and pushing Paulo out of the way. "Paulo, chain up Tom so he can't escape." Blood was pouring out the wound in Alessandro's stomach. "You shoved me out of the way."

"Of…of course," he managed to say through a gasping breath.

"Stand back," I warned the exorcists as I felt the heat build in me once more. *Elyon, please save him. What use is this power if it is not to heal… This one holds the darkness at bay; he is worth saving,* I prayed, placing one hand on his head and the other over his wound. He slumped underneath me, his breath leaving in a rush.

"Oh no, you don't," I said threateningly as I took his face between my hands and brought my lips to his, breathing into his body. "Come *on*, Alessandro." *Elyon, please. I need this one.* I breathed into him again, and light left my lips and filled him. Alessandro jolted violently as the windows behind us shattered and furniture went flying backward.

"Get up, Alessandro. You are the only exorcist I know," I said, my voice not quite my own.

Alessandro started to laugh underneath my hands, and I gave him the bloody bullet that rested in my palm. He looked from it to me and laughed all the harder. I helped him wipe some of the blood away. His wound was completely healed.

"You stupid girl, you have no idea who you are dealing with," Tom said, spitting the words out. Paulo tightened the chains around him.

"I know exactly who I'm dealing with," I said, filled with a deep sorrow at the state of his soul. I turned my back to him.

"You might have miraculously saved the priest, but you're too late to save Max," Tom said smugly.

I stilled, and Alessandro met my eye. "Don't, Jael. He's human and you don't need his death on your soul."

"Where is Max?" I demanded, closing in on Tom with my fists clenched.

"He's dog meat. You put the nail in his coffin the day you took his demon out. We couldn't have a big know-it-all like him walking around sticking his nose in everything. Especially one that was so taken with you." His smile fell as my hands closed in around his head.

"Where is he?" I squeezed. I felt the strength in me, felt the burning desire to crush him, and I knew that Elyon wouldn't stop me.

"He's at the shelter, probably getting gassed right now," Tom replied. "Go ahead and kill me. My master will just bring me back again."

My hands shook with the effort not to give in to every murderous desire I had in me. I could taste the fear in his sweat as I kissed his forehead with trembling lips. "I. Forgive. You," I said with a snarl before letting go of him.

"I don't," said Alessandro, and he punched Tom in the face, knocking him out cold. Alessandro put a gentle hand on my arm and led me away. Paulo dragged Tom over to the bathroom and locked him inside. I found a set of car keys and a mobile phone on Tom's desk.

"Come on. We need to get to Blackwood Street."

Thunder roared above us as I drove Tom's BMW through the wet, nighttime streets, paying no attention to the road rules as I used tram lanes and drove through traffic lights. In the back seat, Gregory was making anonymous phone calls to the police to send men to HeosCorp for bodies in the penthouse. The handgun sat ominously between Alessandro and me in the center console. I was glad they had decided to come with me though I was too worried and heartbroken to show it.

Fine. Have it your way, Uriel. I got free without your help. As far as I'm concerned, you can stay away too. I don't need you anymore. Lightning flashed overhead so brightly it was almost like daytime, and I gripped the steering wheel hard as my vision cleared. Alessandro was trying his best not to hold the dashboard too tightly.

"Thank you for coming with me," I said as we cut off two cabs to turn onto William Street. "Even though it's going to be dangerous, and none of you are wearing shirts, and you are all in pain."

"Thank you for bringing me back from the dead," Alessandro replied softly.

"I couldn't let you die. You are meant to be the greatest exorcist in the world," I said, trying not to think about Max. "An exorcist with a lot of tattoos."

He smirked. "I wasn't always a priest, and I don't think I can claim the title of the greatest exorcist in the world now either."

There were no lights burning at Heart of the Homeless as we pulled onto Blackwood Street.

"Can any of you pick locks?" I asked and was met with a resounding silence. "Okay, then I suggest you hang on." I put my foot on the accelerator and plowed into the glass front doors. The sound of alarms going off was instantaneous. Good. Let the cops come and see. I shoved open my busted door and got out, trying to remember the way through the corridors.

"You two try down that way toward the dorms. Alessandro and I will head to the clinic area," I instructed. Alessandro followed me closely as I switched on lights and searched rooms.

"I don't feel any demonic presence," Alessandro said. "Do you?"

"Nothing. I think Tom might have called them before we reached his office, and they scattered."

"I've never seen demons this organized before," Alessandro said as we searched.

"Something has got them all antsy, that's for sure. A few recently mentioned some uprising. I thought it was just boastful, demon bs but after…after Tom, I don't know." The bigger picture, and what I was feeling about Tom, was going to have to wait. My only concern at that moment was finding Max.

"There's a light." Alessandro pointed to the end of the corridor. He had brought the handgun with him, and the way he held it told me more about his previous life than the tats did.

"Be careful; there are demons behind there," I whispered. I didn't feel the same easy strength as I had back at the HeosCorp Tower. He had already been shot once tonight because of me.

"Stand back," Alessandro said and kicked in the door with a practiced maneuver. There were two big zombie demons inside with Gemma, the rude receptionist. The room was set up like a surgery, complete with an operating table and medical equipment. Alessandro dropped the two demons with headshots. I moved behind him, touching the first demon on the chest because even without a face, it was still trying to fight back. The second was swinging wildly at Alessandro to fight him off.

"You have to admire their persistence," I said, grabbing a flailing arm. The body collapsed on the ground in a pile of decomposing meat.

"She's not one of the dead," Alessandro said with a growl, training the gun on Gemma.

"Good." I turned to her. "Where is Max?" She started to smile, and I punched her hard in her perfect nose before I could stop myself.

"There is a door." Alessandro pointed to the other side of the room as I raised my fist again.

"Check it."

He moved around to the small glass pane of a heavy metal door. "Jael, there are people in there."

"Almost dead people. You're too late, you—" I grabbed Gemma by the shoulder, and the demon inside her screamed like an angry cat. I could feel it squirming around in agony inside of her, and I held on to it, refusing to let it leave.

"Open it." I pushed her toward the keypad, and she typed in a number. Ventilation fans went off loudly, and after a moment the light on the panel turned green. Alessandro opened the door and went inside.

"Let me go, exorcist. Please, I'll help you. I'll do whatever you want just don't—" the demon begged, but I was already exorcising it. It screeched once and was gone, leaving only Gemma shaking and bleeding from her busted nose.

"It's okay, Gemma. It's gone. I've—"

"What did you do?" she cried hysterically. "Bring it back, bring it back!"

"You knew you were possessed?" I asked confused.

"It made me strong and powerful, and it was never going to leave me—" She broke down, and I shoved her off me, disgusted by her desperation. I locked her in a supplies cupboard as she hurled abuse at me. Alessandro had started pulling people out of the gas chamber.

I went inside, my flesh crawling at being in the evil thing. It took me but a second to spot Max, glasses crooked, pressed up against a vent as if to slow whatever chemical they had been pumping through.

"Max? Wake up, Max. You're safe now." I crouched down, shaking him. "Alessandro! Help me!"

We carried him out and laid him out next to the others. His pulse was there, but it was so weak I had to swallow a sob. I grabbed the phone off the wall and typed in a number.

"Hello?" a groggy voice answered.

"James! It's Jael. No time to explain. Get guys and come to Heart of the Homeless; the friggin' bastards have been gassing people. I'm going to try and get through to emergency services, but if you have any direct cop lines to the hospitals, call them now," I said urgently, in one long breath. He started to speak, but I interrupted him. "No time; just do it!" I hung up and called 000, hoping that the operators weren't busy. I started to cry, and Alessandro took the phone from me.

"Go and be with your friend," he said, moving me out of the way. I found some clean scrubs and tossed him a shirt before rolling up the rest into a pillow for Max's head. I took off his glasses, popping them on my own messy hair to keep them safe, and placed a pile of wet towels on his forehead.

"Come on, Max. Wake up," I murmured. "Linda will kill me if anything else happens to you because of me."

Elyon, if I can't heal him, please keep him alive until help gets here. Whatever power was still in me was fading, and I was left feeling empty and broken. Alessandro sat down on the floor beside me, whispering soothing prayers. He leaned softly into me, his arm looping around my shoulders while I wept softly, unable to stop.

Sirens wailed in the distance, drawing closer, and I breathed a little easier.

James found us twenty minutes later as the paramedics were loading Max into an ambulance and arguing with me about going with them.

"Jael." James's relief was palpable as he wrapped me up in a hug.

"Hey, buddy, thanks for coming," I said, trying my best not to get weepy again. "They are trying to take me to the hospital, and you know how much I hate those places. I don't suppose you could wield some police power and get me out of it?"

"Absolutely not. Get your ass into that ambulance right now," James said gruffly.

"How's Meta?" I said, more concerned about my dog than myself. Had he been locked up and alone all this time?

"He's been with Star the last three days and has a broken leg, but he is okay," James replied. *Three whole days.* It felt like it had been weeks in my concrete block.

"Does…does she know…"

"I rang her. We are going to meet you at the hospital later. It's a huge mess you left me with again, and from what I hear, there is another at HeosCorp?"

"I'll tell you later."

"You better."

"Oh, don't forget about Gemma in the cupboard. She's a right psycho but don't leave her in there." I climbed into the back of the ambulance with Alessandro.

"You're the worst mate ever just so you know," James called.

"Yeah, but you still love me," I replied as the doors shut him from view.

21

I HAD TWO BROKEN ribs, needed eight stitches, and was suffering from dehydration, but the nurse told me I was going to be okay. I hated the feel of the fake cotton pajama pants and backless shirt, but at least I was clean again. Well, mostly. I hated hospitals with a passion, and I couldn't wait to get home and scrub myself to pieces. My psychic shields were up so tightly I could barely touch my emotions, which was probably the best thing for me at that moment.

When they had escorted me to my room, I had seen Uriel, broken and bloody, at the end of the hallway, despair and failure in his eyes. His relief and sorrow when he saw me cut me so deeply that I wanted to run to him and feel his arms around me and ask him a million questions. But my hurt and sense of abandonment were too fresh. Instead, I closed up, and turned away from him for the first time in my life. I'd let the doctors take me away and give me morphine and anything else that would numb what I was feeling. They talked to me in monotone voices about trauma and debriefing with a shrink, but I ignored them.

After helping me out of the shower and into some clean clothes, the nurse told me I had a guest waiting. I had been expecting Star, but instead, I found my father, Lewis, talking to one of the doctors. He looked the same as the last time I'd seen him ten months ago: graying brown hair, long face, and eyes that were far too much like mine.

"Jael, I see you are still in one piece," he said stiffly. He didn't go to hug me, and I wouldn't have accepted it anyway.

"As always," I replied, wondering if it was the drugs that made me think there was more than the usual dose of disappointment in his eyes. Neither of us knew what he was doing here.

"They called me when they couldn't reach Heather," he said by way of an explanation. "The doctor said you're banged up but should recover. I'm glad you are in here actually. It might give them a chance to find out what's wrong with you."

"They know what's wrong. I was held against my will and had my ribs broken and—"

"I mean they are going to do a proper psych evaluation on you, not like that quack who saw you when you were younger, but someone who can help get you better," he said, reaching out for me.

I stepped backward, so angry and high on painkillers that I could hardly make sense of what I was hearing. I wanted to hit him so badly my hands hurt. "I don't need an evaluation. I know what happened at HeosCorp."

"Do you? Because with the trauma that can come from such an experience and your history, you might be blocking out the real truth. There is something wrong with you, and we need to find out what it is so you can stop all this demon nonsense and get better."

The screaming from my inside was about to become screaming on the outside when a stern voice said, "There is nothing wrong with Jael." Alessandro moved into the room to stand by my side, followed by Paulo and Gregory.

"Who are you to tell me about my daughter?" Lewis demanded.

"We are exorcists," Alessandro replied coldly. "And your daughter is the bravest woman I have ever met."

"You are all completely cracked! There is no such thing as demons! She has gotten into your head and made you believe her bullshit. She was in a psychiatric ward when she was young for this very thing and—"

"You need to leave," Paulo said with a growl, resting a hand on Alessandro's shoulder as a warning not to do something violent.

"Fine! But don't say I didn't warn you when her stories end up being lies." He looked at me; my hands were balled into tight fists. "Don't bother calling me when the hospital bill comes in. I've only ever tried to help you."

"I think you have 'helped' enough," Alessandro hissed. "Now get out before I make you a patient instead of a visitor."

Lewis looked over at me like I should say something—anything—but I just stood there, furious at him for being such a disappointment as a father when I needed him most.

"Get out," I whispered. He made the small, frustrated sound that he always did when he wasn't getting his way and stormed off.

Gregory, the silent one, placed a hand on my shoulder and said, "My father is much the same. Your true Father is in Heaven, *esorcista*, and that is the only one you need approval from."

"Thank you." I sniffed. "All of you. I don't think I could have handled him tonight."

"We might be Catholic, but we are exorcists first," Paulo said, his hand resting on my other shoulder.

"Exorcists protect each other," Alessandro added, taking my hands. "You are not going to have to worry about them keeping you here. No one can make you do what you don't want to. Not anymore." I hugged him, not caring that he was a priest and that there were probably rules about it. In any case, he allowed it; the two other big exorcists brought their arms around us in a massive group hug.

"Am I interrupting something?" Star's voice came from the doorway.

"Yes," I murmured against Alessandro's firm chest and then laughed to keep myself from crying.

"Then move over and let me in on the love. Stop hogging all the big Italians," she said, pushing her way in so she could hug me. She looked tired and emotional but was otherwise whole. I let her fuss over me as the exorcists disappeared back to their rooms, the feral intensity of our friendship taking over.

"I saw Lewis in the hallway. He looked like he'd tried to eat a jellyfish," Star said as she climbed into the hospital bed with me.

"The exorcists scared him away when he tried to tell us we were all losing our minds," I said, cuddling with her.

She stroked my hair gently and said, "When you are ready to talk about it, you know I'm…I'm here for you. No matter how bad it is."

"I know." I hugged her tighter, relieved Tom's goons hadn't hurt her like they had hurt Max. "How's my Meta?"

"High on drugs. I went straight to your apartment to find you after your call. He was bleeding and hiding in the bedroom, so I took him to the twenty-four-hour vet. They reset and plastered his leg, but he's going to be okay," Star said, and my eyes started to fill. My poor Metatron. "It's so funny seeing Jung try to figure out what's wrong with him. Meta is so high he can't fight back, so I have to watch that the little fatty doesn't annoy him too much. Jung's figured out that Meta's hurt though and keeps bringing him tennis balls and rawhide chews to try and cheer him up. Animals are so much nobler than humans."

"Humans are horrible," I said, thinking of Tom. "They are never what they seem."

"Don't be hating too hard, my Jael. You saved a whole bunch of humans tonight including Max."

"They won't tell me how he's doing. They only said he's not awake yet."

"You got him here with a heartbeat, so that's a win. Three other people died in that chamber, but his heart kept going until you got there. That is a freaking miracle, Jael."

"He wouldn't have even been there if it wasn't for me."

"That's not true either. You didn't put Max in there. Those assholes did," Star said firmly. "Don't think about it now. You're alive and are going to be okay. You're safe now."

I thought about crying out for Uriel in that dark cell, the despair I'd felt until the pain in my heart became too much to bear.

"No, Star, I'm never going to feel safe again."

The next night I woke up screaming my lungs out from night terrors. The nurse had shaken me awake, and I punched her in the face on reflex as I fought off demons that were tearing me apart piece by piece. It was only when Alessandro came in and kicked everyone out of my room that I finally calmed down.

"That is a very distinct scream you have," he teased once we had been left alone.

"I'm sorry," I said, sobbing and bringing my knees to my chest. "Usually, I can snap myself out of night terrors, but these drugs that I'm on are messing with me."

He sat down on the edge of my bed. "It's not just the drugs. I'm not sleeping either. These walls are filled with memories and death."

"I hate hospitals too." I sniffed. "I hate that I'm crying in front of you right now."

"It's good for you." Alessandro smiled, his busted face still handsome.

"Will you stay with me a while? You said you weren't sleeping, and I could do with the company," I asked, half expecting him to tell me to toughen up. Exorcists didn't need comfort.

Instead, he made a little gesture with his hand. "Move over." I shuffled and gave him one of my pillows. It felt weird to think that a few weeks ago he was the scary Catholic exorcist, and now we were hospital invalids hanging out together.

"Tell me a story?" I asked.

"A story? Which one?" he asked, eyes half-closed.

"The Elsa Perea Flores School in Peru."

"You pick that story out of all the stories I could tell you?" he said exasperatedly.

"Yep. I want to know. Nearly a hundred kids got possessed, and they called you in. I saw the photo of you going inside the building."

"Sometimes I hate the internet."

"Out with it, Abbadelli," I demanded.

Alessandro sighed dramatically in defeat. "I wasn't called in until a week after the outbreak. They thought it was probably mass hysteria or maybe something in the water. When the priests started getting involved, nearly eighty students were stricken, and by that time they were unsure how to fix them. I got flown over with Paulo and a few others to investigate and to exorcise the children if needed."

"And was it possession?"

"It was. They had built the school on a Mafia burial ground, and that kind of violence lingers and attracts territorial demons. The man in black that the children kept seeing was just such a demon. The children had been playing, trying to call up ghosts of scary mafiosi, and instead, a powerful demon answered. It had possessed only one child, but it was strong enough to produce symptoms in multiple children to try to protect itself and confuse the priests."

"But not you."

"No, not me. I had seen it before. We only had to do one exorcism, and all of the children were released from their afflictions."

"You did a proper cleansing on the site too right?"

"Of course."

"Wow, I have to say I'm a little disappointed," I admitted. "Here I thought you had gone in and mass exorcised eighty kids. I called you to come to Saint Augustine's that day, because I thought you could deal with crowds of possessed."

"Who says I can't?" He smiled smugly. "Memory serves that I dispersed that crowd rather easily."

"You are such a show-off." I poked him, and he winced as he laughed. "You have done mass exorcism before?"

"Yes."

"How many people at once?" I pressed.

"The most was 147."

"What?" I exclaimed, almost falling out of my side of the bed. "Are you lying to me right now?"

"I would *never* lie to you," he answered solemnly.

"Wow, that must have been the worst exorcism ever," I said, settling back down.

"No, it wasn't the worst." His voice was barely more than a whisper.

I rolled onto my side to face him. "What was the worst?"

"My sister."

"I'm sorry," I said, resting my hand against his.

"Most exorcists get into the business because of a family member." He wrapped his fingers around mine. "Who was it for you?"

"Myself," I admitted. "I've got the sexy scars to prove it."

Alessandro swore in Italian. "No wonder you hate them so much. I've never seen such rage. Will you tell me about it sometime? And maybe I'll tell you about my sister."

"Okay." I swallowed the lump in my throat. I'd never told anyone the full version of that story, but there was something about Alessandro that made me think he would understand.

We talked until we fell asleep, hoping the other would protect us should the demons come again.

22

THE HOSPITAL LET ME out two days later. I was so tired of the constant noise that I had barely slept the whole time I had been in there. The police had come and gone, always asking questions under James's watchful eyes. I didn't have any family to step in since Heather was still unable to bring herself to enter a hospital, so James was my proxy guardian to make sure no one tried to screw with me.

There would be more questions later and cross-checking my answers with the other exorcists, but our story was holding up. We were kidnapped when we had started to uncover a criminal ring; we had been tortured and we had escaped. We had found the bodies in the penthouse and locked Tom up to make sure he didn't kill anyone else. James wasn't saying anything about Tom and where they had taken him or what else was going on with the investigation. To the best of his ability, James was keeping me out of it, and I was grateful. Until I could process what I already knew, I didn't want to know any more. Max was steady, but he hadn't woken up yet. I was left feeling helpless.

Going home was the best thing I could do. Star argued with me about me needing rest, saying that she would look after him a little longer, but I wanted Metatron with me. I hugged his warm body gently, and I felt like maybe I was going to be okay, that I could bounce back from everything that had happened. We lay in bed, both heavily sedated with painkillers and not moving much at all.

I was kept well-fed by the Wus and Jimmy. Star was stress baking and bringing her baked goods over regularly when she checked in on me. A week passed, and I barely registered it.

"I'm sorry I didn't come and see you at the hospital," Heather said as she tidied up my kitchen. "I tried… I was outside the Royal, and I started to shake. I couldn't go in."

"It's okay, Mom. I'm fine, as you can see," I replied, not wanting to upset her.

"You are not fine at all!" she said passionately, throwing the dish towel in the sink. "Your face is every color of the rainbow, and you move like a ninety-year-old woman. You were *kidnapped*, Jael, and you are just sitting there like…like it wasn't a big deal. Like you don't even care."

"I'm hurt, and I'm tired. I'll deal with the rest later," I said with a growl. "Stop acting like I need to console you about it when I'm the one that it happened to. I don't have the energy in me to hold your hand and comfort you so you can deal with *my* pain."

I shuffled off to bed and shut the door behind me. I could hear her crying, but I didn't care. I knew I'd feel bad about it later, and I would most likely apologize even though I spoke the truth. Then we would go back to normal.

Whatever that was.

My shields and emotions were shut up so tight that not a lot registered as I drew deep within myself; my soul was raw and curled up in the fetal position.

Once or twice since the hospital, I'd felt Uriel near me, but I'd shoved the feeling away. Locking him out. My faith in him had died on the concrete floor of my cell. I couldn't stop being an exorcist, but I could stop myself from relying on anyone like that again.

My unshakable faith was as broken as the rest of me.

Sitting in the bath one night, I tried counting the bruises on my body and gave up. It still hurt to breathe with my broken ribs, but my cuts had healed enough for me to pick out my stitches with a pair of tweezers.

I was having a lot of baths, nothing healing the ache in my muscles like hot water and Epsom salts. As a child, I'd always sought the bath as a way to quiet the world around me, and since my darkest night, as I had come to call the HeosCorp fiasco, it was one of the few places that still calmed me. There was something about the warm embrace, the stillness, the closeness of my own heartbeat that reminded me I was still alive even if I didn't feel it.

Ever since I'd busted out of the cell, I had felt dirty. Like I wouldn't be clean again no matter how much I scrubbed. Star had said something about it being a side effect in abuse cases. You felt like your body and soul now had a dirty mark on them, that a piece of your innocence had suddenly been violated. I did my best not to dwell on it too much but was careful with how hard I was scrubbing my already damaged skin.

It was in my second week at home when there was a knock at my door late in the afternoon. I hadn't been expecting Alessandro standing on the other side of it.

"You won't answer your phone," he said weakly, as if that explained his sudden appearance. "May I come in, Jael?"

"Of course you can." I moved out of the way. "I must've let my phone battery die. I seem to be forgetting stuff like that since I've come home."

"And who is this handsome man?" Alessandro asked, crouching down and offering a timid Metatron his hand. Since the attack, he had developed a whole new wariness of people. I knew exactly how he felt.

"This is Metatron," I replied, waiting for the rebuke.

"A noble name indeed, *cucciolo*," he said approvingly. Meta, ever the sucker for pats, moved over to lick his fingers tentatively before leaning against him. "I see you are walking wounded like the rest of us, my friend. I miss having a dog."

"He is good company. Beer?" I had been struggling to eat food, but alcohol I seemed to have no problem downing.

"Yes, please," Alessandro said. He took a seat at my kitchen table, his dark eyes taking in my bookshelves of paraphernalia and the random notes I still had up about the Watchers and zombie demons. "This place looks like you."

"It's a good space." I handed him his drink and sat down beside him. "What's on your mind, *Padre*?"

"They are sending me back to Rome." He ran a hand through his black curls. His face was still darkened with bruising on one side, but even under that, I could see how conflicted he was.

"Isn't that a good thing? Demons are under control, Tom's locked up, and—"

"Who told you he was locked up?" Alessandro demanded. "He's not locked up. He's dead, Jael."

"Dead? How do you know?"

"Police reports," he replied, not sharing how he had gotten copies of them. "They got to the penthouse, and when they opened the bathroom, there wasn't much of Tom remaining."

"But that's… We left no demons in the building."

"They must've found him after we had gone. Whoever Tom answered to must not have been impressed with his work. One police officer noted it was the most horrific thing he'd ever seen," Alessandro replied, giving details without the detail. I rested a hand on my chest as my anxiety and grief spiked dangerously.

"Damn it. I thought maybe if he was locked up there might be a chance to help him. I don't think he even knew he was the bad guy, or that he was doing the wrong thing."

"I'm sorry. I know he was a friend of yours. I thought they would have told you," Alessandro said softly.

"It's…it's okay. Why are they making you go to Rome?"

"The Holy Father wants to be briefed on what happened. I sent reports, we all did, but they recall us all the same. I think they want to send us out to one of the remote monasteries for contemplation."

I thought about how nice it would be to be secluded away from the world for a while. To live simply and quietly until the screaming in my head went away.

"Doesn't sound too bad at all. Why are you so upset about it?"

"They think I'm lying to them to protect you. That I am too…fond of you," he said diplomatically. "They want to interrogate us properly, because they don't believe their fearsome *Cuore di Pietra* could possibly speak so highly of a woman. They think you might be trying to get me to break my vows."

I grinned. Alessandro was beautiful, even when he was broken, but I knew how he felt about being an exorcist. I couldn't compete with that. "What does it mean?"

"*Cuore di Pietra*? Heart of Stone," he explained a little bashfully. "Or the Stone Heart, if you prefer."

"It makes you sound very fearsome," I teased. "It's like they don't know you at all."

"Or *you* don't."

"Those with hearts of stone couldn't be as good of an exorcist as you are. You need empathy and compassion to do this job. But, as you told me that day, there is a price to what we do. We are paying it right now, here in this moment," I said and took a mouthful of beer. "I don't know how to come back from this."

"One moment at a time," he suggested. "Gregory and Paulo keep calling you *Angela della Morte* and terrifying the other priests."

"The Angel of Death? I like it." I smiled crookedly. "And the other priests need to be terrified occasionally."

"I agree. I hope these events will make them more aware of demonic activity instead of leaving it all on your small shoulders. No matter how strong they are."

"I'll be okay…at least, I think so. Some days are better than others." Star's message tone went off. "She's checking in on me again. Do I look that bad?"

"She cares for you deeply. I can understand that."

"You know what?" I said, reading the text. "I'm going to take you somewhere."

"Where?" he asked, black eyes glittering in amusement.

"Somewhere neither of us is going to feel particularly comfortable, but it's necessary."

Heather answered the door and then frowned at Alessandro behind me. He wasn't wearing a collar, and yet somehow, she knew. "Of all the unsavory men you could've brought home, I never thought it would be a priest."

"You'll get over it. Alessandro, this is Heather…my mother," I said as he stepped forward to shake Heather's hand.

"*Buona sera.*" He greeted her with a smile, charm itself. "It's so good to meet more family of Jael's." I struggled to contain my grin as Heather flushed.

"I heard you met Lewis," she said, struggling with the words. Yep, that's where I got my smooth moves from.

"Well, let's say I am more eager to make *your* acquaintance. Your ex-husband seemed to inspire only violent tendencies in me," Alessandro replied as she led him inside.

"He does that to the best of us. You know, I like you more and more by the second," Heather said, looping her arm around his. "Let me show you around." Star came to hug me as Billie and Heather flushed and blushed over Alessandro.

"Are you sure that's a good idea? Bringing him here?" Star asked, handing me a glass of wine. "I mean, they are in menopause. What if he says something in that delightful accent of his and what's left of their ovaries spontaneously combusts?"

I laughed harder than I had in weeks, and she hugged me close.

"I'm glad you came out. I worry about you."

"I'm totally fine. Look, I'm even in clean clothes." I gestured to one of my many *Hellblazer* shirts.

"I'm just glad to see you out of the apartment. James should be here any second. I asked Violet to come, but you never know if she'll show," Star said.

"Probably a good thing. If she recognizes Alessandro as the buyer of the Murder House, she'll be all over him."

"All over who?" James came in carrying more wine. He was the only man I knew that could wear a white T-shirt and keep it perfectly clean. With his brown skin he looked great in white, and by the look on Star's face, she knew it too.

We all ended up on the back patio around a table, drinking wine and talking about random things as James and Star cooked a barbecue and stole glances at each other. I felt a pang of loneliness as I watched them and how easy they were together.

It was the first time I had ever felt alone, and I didn't quite know what to do about it. Uriel hadn't appeared again, even in his human form, and I hadn't encouraged him to. There was a pressure of emotions building inside me, and I didn't know when it was going to explode. A warm hand brushed against mine under the table.

"Come back, Jael. You can't leave me alone in this," Alessandro whispered, and I smiled.

"Sorry, sorry. I keep getting a bit lost in my own head," I admitted.

"Well, get out of it," James said across from me. "Shit, girl, you had us all so freaking worried. I swear I've aged a whole year."

"Only one? You are looking a bit old and haggard," I said, and he flipped me off.

"Woman, please. No matter how old I look, it's nothing compared to you," he retorted playfully. "Are you going to get a quiet job for a while? You know, so I can stop finding bodies wherever you go."

"I'm sure my recruiter would love to put me in some mindless data entry job, but I might wait a bit," I said, heart pounding at the thought of doing something in the future.

"You need to heal and not worry about it," Alessandro said beside me.

"We can't all escape to a beautiful monastery somewhere," I replied. "Don't worry, *Padre*, I'll be a good girl and wait until I am all better."

"Holy shit, priest, I've never seen little Jael agree to anything suggested to her," Billie said. "You need to come back again; she seems to listen to you."

"I make very convincing arguments," he said, and they all teased him about that, drawing him into the comfortable circle of banter.

We both needed it, that small dose of normality, to make us forget what we were feeling and to remind ourselves why we did what we did.

"Thank you for taking me there," Alessandro said when we made it back to my apartment. "I can see why you like them so much."

"They are a really good distraction. I thought it might help us out of our emotional funk," I replied, sitting down on the couch beside him with two glasses of tequila.

"They love you. You can see it. But they don't understand you, do they?"

"Not a single one. Star understands most things, but she's probably the closest. It's easy to go there and give them what they need, so I can continue to do what I do without them worrying about me."

"It sounds so sad when you put it like that." He paused for a moment before he asked, "Jael, what is wrong? I know we both went through so much, but there is something else, isn't there? Some pain that's eating its way through you."

I sipped my tequila. "You might think I'm crazy."

"Jael, you pulled a bullet from my body. I'm sure I can handle it."

"Okay." I breathed and swallowed back some of my tears. "Will you take my very first confession, Father Abbadelli?"

"*Si*, tell me what's troubling you." Alessandro crossed himself, failing to hide his smile.

"It's a long one," I warned. "It began when I was about three years old, and I could hear the voices of the angels…"

I told him everything. About my parents dragging me to shrinks, about being a teenager and living with a demon, about the day I took a blade to my skin, and about Uriel. I explained to Alessandro how much I relied on Uriel, and how the feeling of safety he gave me was the only thing that kept me together through the worst times in my life. I spoke of the visions of the battling archangels and of the Nephilim spirit that had been attached to the idol. In a tiny whisper, I told him of the man with the impossible voice, how he came to me in the cell when my spirit had been broken, and about Uriel abandoning me. I spoke out my pain as best as I knew how, the emotional pressure cooker inside of me threatening to explode at any moment.

"And now I feel like everything I knew, those solid truths that made me who I am, is suddenly broken. I have this resentment and anger that was never there before. That night at HeosCorp I was given this incredible gift of power, and while I should be euphoric with victory, all I am is hurt so deeply that I don't know how to recover from it. So many people died, Max is in a coma, and all I can do is sulk, because Uriel didn't come for me," I said finally, pouring myself more tequila. "I think that makes me just the most rubbish, selfish person ever."

"No, it doesn't," Alessandro replied softly, brushing a tear from my cheek. "You can put it down to abandonment or anger or selfishness if you want, but the truth is as simple and as complicated as this… Your heart is broken. You love him, and for whatever reason, he couldn't come to you in your darkest hour. *Amica mia*, you seem to be forgetting that he is an *archangel*; they are the ones that fight the battles no one else can. You have no idea why he couldn't be with you, but from what you tell me it must have been something immense. He made himself look human to save you from possibly being hurt at the gala. You know now that Tom wouldn't have allowed it because of how he felt about you but, Jael, Uriel came for you even then."

"Don't you think I know all this? Why do you think I hate myself so much at the moment? I know what he is, what he *really* is, and I still can't stop feeling this way. At the hospital, he looked as crushed as I did and I…I couldn't…"

"I wish I had an answer for you that would make some sense." Alessandro sighed, taking my hand. "He hasn't tried to appear to you since the hospital, so he knows you are hurt and angry. Perhaps he's waiting for you to call to him, and he is respecting your time."

"Even if I did, how could I trust him again?"

"He would have to earn it I would imagine," he said simply. "Only you will know what to do when the time comes. Talk to God, always. No matter what you feel, never stop. Wait, be patient, listen to his answers. You are favored, no matter what you seem to believe."

"Yeah, but God's favored have the hardest walks."

"And the greatest victories as well."

"I was simply the right tool for the right job at the right moment."

"You are too blinded by your pain to see clearly right now, but you are special." He pulled out a necklace from the inside of his shirt, a bullet attached to it. "I know this with more certainty and gratitude than I can ever express."

"You're keeping it as a good luck charm?" I asked, turning it over in my fingertips.

"As a reminder. I've never met anyone like you and never seen anything like that night. I'll never forget you storming into my cell, brimming with the power of God. You were like a bloody avenging angel, and you were there to save me."

"Well, I couldn't let you be demon fodder, even if you are a Catholic," I said with a smile.

"There is something of the Old Prophets about you, Jael Quinlan," Alessandro said with a shake of his head. "Stubborn. Righteous. Outcast. Flippant about the laws of man. And answerable only to God."

"That's one of the nicest things anyone has ever said to me." I laughed brightly. "I'll take it."

"Here. I want you to have this," he said, pulling his long silver rosary from his pocket and putting it over my head. It was a beautiful piece of jewelry with a plain cross and thankfully, without a sad Anglo-Saxon Jesus crucified on it. "I know you are not Catholic, but this has been with me through some of my darkest times. It will give you something to remember me by."

"I will wear it always, although I don't think you're someone I'm ever going to forget," I said, hugging him. "So what now, Alessandro?"

"Now, I return to Italy for a time and after that? Who knows where I will be sent," he replied as I walked him to the door. "Where I am needed, I suppose."

"Will you call me sometime? I don't know any other exorcists, and if I get stuck, it would be nice to bounce ideas off someone."

"Of course, I will call you. I'd recruit you and take you with me right now if I thought you would come." Alessandro took my hand and held it to his chest.

"Do you feel this heartbeat? It exists because of you. You breathed your life inside of me. You called down God's power to save me. We are always going to be kindred because of that. It is beyond belief or blood. All the interrogations and the disgruntled looks from the other priests will not change how I feel about you."

I leaned into him, wrapping my arm around him. "I'm going to miss you, Alessandro. You are one of the best men I've ever known."

"I'll miss you too, little exorcist," he said gruffly. "We will talk soon. You are going to do mighty things, Jael Quinlan. You have a warrior's heart that was made to protect and to love. Now, I really must go before you convince me to break my vows and stay in Melbourne."

"As if I could convince you to leave the Church," I said, releasing him so he could walk out the door. He paused on the second step and turned so that we were eye to eye. With an elegant gentleness, he took my face in his hands and kissed my bruised cheeks.

"If anyone could convince me," he said with a deep sadness, "it would be you."

I watched Alessandro drive away, crushed with loneliness and confusing emotions about letting the only person who had ever really understood me drive out of my life.

Most of all, I was frightened by the magnitude of my longing for Uriel. I wanted him to hold me and tell me I was going to be okay. To reassure me that Max wasn't going to die, and I would be able to hang out with Alessandro again; that we would be able to stay friends even if his Church disapproved of me. I wanted to feel Uriel's hand stroking my hair as I went to sleep.

And still…I didn't call out for him.

23

AFTER ALESSANDRO AND THE other exorcists left Melbourne, things became worse. The damage done to my body was healing, and I was finally able to breathe without wincing. Investigations into Heart of the Homeless proved that over two hundred people had been gassed since it opened three months ago.

They had found the remains of only five bodies, which left a lot of zombie demons wandering about the world. I knew they were out there, but I didn't know where to start looking for them, or if they still had me on their kill list. I hadn't done an exorcism since that night at HeosCorp, and while I knew I'd have to get back on the horse sometime, I wasn't pushing myself to get out there.

Jimmy hired me on for two days a week to sort out his accounts and office, while I was still recovering. He let me have Meta in the office, which helped with my anxiety and comforted me when I started to feel too overwhelmed.

"It's a part of going through a trauma, Jael," Star said, reassuring me for the hundredth time. "You can't expect to go through all of that and walk away mentally unscathed. It was nearly a month of trauma on top of trauma for you. You need to stop and take it slow."

"I have no choice; my stupid body won't do it. If I am around too many people, I start to freak out. I could barely walk through the train station the other day. I was looking over my shoulder, expecting a zombie demon to push me in front of a train," I admitted to her.

We were sitting in camp chairs on my roof, watching the sunset streak the sky red and blue and purple. Melbourne summer can be a brutal, fleeting thing, and we were in shorts and singlets, sipping a few margaritas to celebrate Star finishing a particularly hard semester. She'd done her best to give me as much space as possible, but I could tell she was starting to worry.

"Do you feel like they would still be hunting you?" asked Star.

"I'm not sure. I haven't seen any, and maybe that's why I'm so twitchy about it. I'm expecting something to happen, and nothing is," I said, thinking about just how messed up that was.

"Something happened," she said, pinking up around the ears. "Not demonic of course but…um…"

"What? Did you finally kiss James?" I asked excitedly.

"I don't know who kissed who, but yeah, the other night at the barbecue we were just talking and cleaning up and suddenly we kind of…kissed."

"You should see your face right now. This is so high school I could cry." I roared with laughter. "Finally! You guys have been driving me crazy, you know that right? Violet is going to be so pissed that you are the one that nabbed him."

"I didn't…I mean I haven't… It was just a kiss! We aren't like picking out curtains or anything." She huffed. "We've talked since then but haven't seen each other."

"You guys are such chicken shits." I leaned back in my chair. "Seriously, Star, something good needs to come out of everything that's happened. Being in that cell, waiting to die, it reminded me of how short life is. I know it sounds stupid and cliché, but if he makes you happy, you need to go for it because you don't get too many moments like that. People you can connect with on a deeper level are so rare. Treasure that. Don't hold back with him."

"Deeper connections like you and Alessandro?"

I choked on my margarita. "Please tell me you are not implying what I think you are. He's a priest!"

"Look, I'm not an idiot. I know it's not romantic with you guys, but there is something there. You two are like different versions of each other; you think and act the same way. It was intense seeing you together casually. Even Billie and Heather commented on it. It was like you found someone who made you feel like you belonged. It's hard to explain from the outside. I can only tell you how I saw it, but it's like you relaxed around him like you don't relax with anyone else. Your auras connected whenever you were in the same room."

"We are both exorcists, and it's how we are. We went through hell together, and you can't not feel something for other people in that kind of situation," I said dismissively. "Shared trauma and all that."

I hadn't told her that I'd pulled a bullet from him. That it had been a miracle in a night of horror. Only the other exorcists knew, and they would probably take it to their graves. "Paulo and Gregory almost fought my dad afterward, because he was a bullying jerk. It must be an unspoken exorcist code to look out for each other."

"Oh really? Because you didn't seem that way around Paulo and Gregory, and you never told me what happened with Alessandro after you guys left the barbecue," she said, her gaze softening. "You aren't talking about him, J. Not even in passing conversation. What happened?"

"Nothing happened. We talked about stuff. I told him about Uriel and how I came to be an exorcist." I brushed over the topic and crossed my arms. "And then he said goodbye." *And I should have asked him to stay longer in Melbourne, so that I wouldn't feel so alone.*

"You miss him, don't you? You only knew each other for a few weeks."

"They were a busy few weeks…and yeah, I miss him," I admitted angrily. "He's the only other exorcist I know."

"And Uriel?"

"I'm not talking about him," I said, shutting down as the anger and hurt rose again.

"But you'll talk about him with Alessandro?" she demanded.

"He's a priest. It's different."

"Jael, Uriel is your angel, and you won't let him anywhere near you. I know that I am different from Alessandro... I'm not Christian, and I don't understand a lot of what you do. But I do know *you*, and I know that you love Uriel more than me, more than *anyone*. This separation is eating you—"

My vision swam with red, and I threw my glass hard at the concrete wall opposite us.

"He abandoned me, Star!" I shouted. I was shaking so badly that I curled over my knees, trying to physically hold my rage and betrayal in. "He left me to *die*, so don't you dare tell me how I need to feel about him."

"Jael...I'm..."

"Please, just go. I'm sorry, but I can't. I just can't," I begged as the anger inside of me threatened to boil over again. I didn't want to say anything that would hurt her, but knew that I would have to, so she'd shut up about him forever. "I don't want you to see me like this. *Please*. I'll call you tomorrow, okay?"

"Okay, Jael," she said softly. Her hand touched my head on her way past me. "I'm sorry I upset you. Take care."

I heard the stairwell door slam, and I gently rocked backward and forward to try and get my emotions under control.

"Just breathe, Jael." I tried to calm my heartbeat. "Elyon...*please stop this*."

I'd completed my special mission, stopped the demons growing in the city, and cast out the body-hopping Nephilim spirit, but I'd lost everything else in the process. Max hadn't woken up, Alessandro was gone forever, and Uriel...

A sound of wild and feral rage ripped out of me, and I stood up, grabbed Star's empty camp chair, and threw it hard across the rooftop.

"What more do you want from me?" I shouted at the twilight sky.

The fire door slammed again, and I whipped around. "Star, I told you to leave—" But it wasn't Star. It was a guy of an average height and the strong, wiry build of someone used to physical labor. He was wearing a deep red shirt and black jeans and looked Middle Eastern or Mediterranean with brown skin, dark brown hair, and a clipped beard. I wondered if I had served him at Jimmy's, and he'd found his way upstairs by mistake. I opened my mouth to give him a piece of my mind, but then my eyes locked on his and I froze. I *knew* those eyes. I knew him like I knew the sound of my heartbeat. I slumped to my knees on the hot concrete roof.

"Hello, Jael," he said, and my ribs tightened. *That voice.* That impossible voice that had found me in my cell and told me to get up. He came and knelt beside me.

"Yeshua?"

"Come now," he said, coaxing me. "Let's talk for a little while." He picked up Star's chair, placed it down next to mine, and sat down to wait for me. I shuffled over and sat down beside him.

"For a woman who survived a terrible situation with impossible odds, you don't seem to be coping very well," he said.

"That's an understatement. I'm trying. I really am. I just can't…"

"You can't forgive Uriel." He finished my words for me and looked across at me. "I saw you in the cell. You looked as if your whole world was destroyed."

"Why are you here…like this?" I asked, hardly breathing.

"Because you aren't going to listen to anyone else right now. I thought this way would make you more comfortable than more angels."

I made a squeaky awkward laugh. "Sure. I'm loads more comfortable."

"I could've turned up all light and brimstone, but I didn't think you would respond well to that. I need you to listen to me, Jael Quinlan, because there are things moving in the world that you're going to be a part of whether you want it or not."

"I don't know if you've noticed, but I'm not exactly fit to fight right now. What is it that you want to tell me?"

"Do you remember the story of Daniel?" he asked unexpectedly.

"Of course, he was a hostage in the Persian court, helped interpret visions, and was thrown to lions and survived," I said, summarizing vaguely. "What about him?"

"Daniel was in mourning and prayer for three weeks. An angel finally came to him and told him that he'd been trying to enter the city, but the Demon Prince of Persia kept him away until the archangel Michael intervened and defeated him," Yeshua continued, ignoring my sarcasm.

"And?"

"You're an exorcist, and you know that demons can be territorial, right?"

"Yes."

"And that each city and country can have a demon prince ruling the demons in it?"

"Yes, though I've never experienced it myself. I know the scripture behind it." I struggled to see past my own broken heart to see what he was getting at.

"The night you were taken," Yeshua said softly. "Uriel was fighting the demon prince of this city. It worked hard to keep you apart, because together you are unstoppable."

"He was fighting a demon prince? Why?"

"For you," he said, like it was the most obvious thing in the world. "He never would have left you if it wasn't against his will. Uriel had to battle him and defeat him on his own, knowing all the while that you were suffering, in pain, and thinking that he had abandoned you."

The image of Uriel at the hospital, bleeding and broken, flashed in my mind, as did his look of agony when I shut him out. I had thought he abandoned me, left me to die after all we had been through. My hurt was so strong that I hadn't even asked why he never came. I hadn't considered what he had been doing that whole time.

Jael, you are a damn fool.

"Is he healed? I mean, he was pretty bashed up. Is he okay?" I asked, guilt twisting its way through me.

"Like you, he's physically fine, but spiritually and emotionally he's broken over what happened to you, and that he failed you so completely. You won't speak to him, and that's hurting him most of all." He reached over and placed a hand on my shoulder. "And it's destroying you. There's a reason why he was given charge over you when you were seventeen, and it was for his benefit as much as yours."

"Why would an archangel need a human?" I asked helplessly. "Especially a messed-up one like me."

"Would you believe it's because he's equally messed up? Uriel listens to you, he cares about you in a way he hasn't cared about anything. He loves you."

"I didn't think angels were allowed to love, you know, like Jedi," I said, my heart hurting painfully.

"Angels love," he answered with a small smile. "And I think we both know Jedi do too."

"Does he know that you are here talking with me?"

"No, but I'm sure you'll tell him sometime soon."

"I don't know about that." I looked out over the night sky. "Maybe we are both too hurt, and we'd just end up yelling at each other. If he spent three days battling a demon, why didn't Michael fly on down and help as he did in Daniel?"

"Because Michael was preoccupied on account of him being human at the moment."

"Uriel would've been pissed about that." I shook my head. *Human? How is that possible?*

"Uriel is furious. So much so that right now in Hungary, he's about to beat Michael to death. I need your help to stop him, because if you don't, there won't be anyone to stop an apocalypse."

"This is insane," I said and got up to pace. "I stopped Tom and the Nephilim spirit! This craziness is over for me. My job is done! If Uriel has beef with Michael, I don't see what that has to do with me. Let alone figuring out how I could get to Hungary."

"You are the only person Uriel will listen to." Yeshua got up from his chair, taking my hands in his. "Jael, this battle is the reason why you were born, so why are you afraid now that the time has come?"

"Because I'm not worthy or capable of doing any of it!" I exclaimed, feeling small and dirty in front of him. "I'm not strong enough—"

"Little one, it's not about worthiness. You are loved, and you are clean and perfect as you are. You were born for this fight." He brought me to him in an embrace. "And you are going to change the world."

I didn't feel us move, but suddenly I was standing in a dark car park with icy sleet pelting down around me. There was a small café ahead of me, and as I took a step toward it, a man was thrown through the wide bay of windows. He sailed through the air, hitting the ground with a shout of pain.

"What the…" I hurried forward as something silver and white came down and hit the man in the face. Uriel's expression was cold and deadly, twisted with rage as he lifted the man by the front of his shirt.

"You spoiled, ungrateful—" Uriel was shouting at him over the rain. *He's going to kill him.* Nothing could live through that abuse.

"Uriel!" I called out and started running toward him. "Uriel, stop!"

He didn't even register my voice, didn't look up from hurling insults at the man on the ground. As Uriel lifted his arm to hit him again, I launched myself into him, wrapping my arms around his neck.

"Uriel, stop! Stop this," I begged him. "Please stop. I'm sorry. I'm sorry for everything." Recognition replaced the rage, and he sank to his knees in front of me. I lifted his face up to mine, pushing the wet, silvery hair from his eyes. He pulled me to him, holding me so tightly I thought my ribs were going to crack again.

"Jael, what are you doing here?" he asked helplessly.

"Apparently I came to keep you from killing someone," I replied.

There was a choking gasp from the ground beside me, and I looked down at the pulpy mess that Uriel had made of the man's face. I did a double take as I recognized him from my visions. The demon hunter with the spear.

"You shouldn't have stopped him." He coughed up blood in a wheezing, bitter laugh. "Exorcist."

In the beginning, an angel made a deal to become human…
It always ended in blood.

PART TWO
THE DEMON HUNTER
WITH THE LONG PAST

24

THE DEMON WAS TWISTED around the bartender's spine like a tar-dipped stripper. It was an oozing, eyeless mass of cancerous tentacles feeding off his fear and anxiety, and it mocked Mychal with its very existence.

Mychal clutched the shot glass in his hand, the words to banish the demon running through his mind in a wave of Hebrew, English, and Hungarian.

He lifted the glass to his lips before he whispered, "Get off him, you piece of trash."

It was not the most elegant or forceful of exorcisms, but Mychal felt the creature hiss with a mouth it didn't have as it dissolved into nothing. The bartender fumbled with the bottle of vodka in his hand before shaking himself.

"I'm sorry, sir. What did you say?" the bartender asked.

"I said keep them coming," Mychal said, rubbing his eyes and wishing that he didn't see demons every moment of the day.

Since the attack that had robbed him of his partner, Aleksandra, his abilities had gone into overdrive. He was worried that they were becoming hallucinations. He had been on a hunt only a few weeks ago, when he saw a ghost woman in an alleyway. He couldn't remember the last time he'd eaten or slept, but he could've sworn she was real.

"Who are you?" he had demanded after he killed the demon he'd been hunting. Then as clear as a bell he'd heard her.

"I'm an exorcist." And then she simply vanished in front of him as if the rain had melted her away.

The vodka warmed in Mychal's chest, alleviating the constant dull ache that sat there, and he wished he could talk to the ghost woman now. He'd ask her how she lived with being an exorcist, and how she could appear out of nowhere.

Exorcisms had never been his specialty. That had always been Father Vadim's area of expertise, because Mychal lacked the delicate touch it took to deal with people. His mentor was now dead, killed by demons like nearly everyone else he knew, so the everyday exorcisms had fallen to him.

The glass door to the bar opened, letting in a sharp gust of cold air and car fumes. The back of Mychal's skull tingled, and his hand moved to the edge of his coat, where one of his knives rested. Mychal had always been able to sense demons; the scars down his back ached if his extra sight failed. He was picking up something new though, not a demon but not human either. He took his drink and sat down at one of the tables close to the fire exit. Only then did he look up at the newcomers.

Two men were buying a round at the bar. One had deep red hair and wore an easy smile. The other's hair was golden, his braid disappearing under the collar of his wool overcoat. Mychal's anger rose high enough to choke him. He recognized them both, but he had never known that they were angels. Now, he could see the gold-and-white aura around them, the faint ghost of wings behind their shoulders. Ásgeirr, the blond, took the lead and approached Mychal's table.

"Mychal…"

"Go away. I don't have time for liars."

"He's moodier than I remember," Galen said as he sat down. Mychal had met him only briefly in New Orleans a few months ago and thought he was an upstart hunter.

Ásgeirr was a different matter. They had met by chance while Mychal was doing research, and they had spent weeks training and exchanging information together. Ásgeirr was an expert with a spear, and the spear Mychal sometimes carried while hunting had been a gift from him.

"I didn't lie to you, Mychal. I just couldn't fully disclose the truth," Ásgeirr said as he sat down.

"I was researching angels, and you *were* one," Mychal hissed. "I suppose our meeting wasn't by chance either?"

"No, it wasn't." Ásgeirr looked at his drink but didn't lift it. Neither of them was drinking, so Mychal reached across and swapped out his empty glass.

"You aren't going to drink, so I might as well. I'm going to need it if you two aren't going to leave."

"I tried to warn you about the demons that were after you," Galen said. "It's not my fault you didn't listen."

"Demons have been hunting me since I was a boy—you weren't telling me anything I didn't already know. Maybe if you would have been specific, I could've been more prepared."

"I am sorry about Aleksandra," Ásgeirr said gently. "She was a good woman."

The fragments of Mychal's mind ground together like broken glass. It had been six months since her death, and he still couldn't handle it when someone said her name.

"Don't talk about her like you knew her." Mychal drank to try and stop his eyes from burning.

"I know you have suffered greatly, Mychal, but we need your help," said Galen.

Mychal stared at them before a sarcastic bark of laughter broke from his lips. "You two are *angels*. Archangels by the look of those wings. What the fuck could you possibly need me for?"

"Have you remembered what you are yet, Mychal? To see angels the way you do is not a gift you possessed when last we met," said Ásgeirr.

"We don't have time to coddle his temper," Galen said insistently. "Just tell him, Gabriel, so that we can go."

"Gabriel? This joke keeps getting funnier." Mychal shook his head before draining his drink.

"This isn't a joking matter. We need you, even in this wretched form you are trapped in," said Galen. "Only together can we stop Hel'el."

Mychal looked blankly at the fiery young man for a few moments before he laughed full in his face.

"Hel'el? You mean Lucifer, right? I know I'm an excellent demon hunter, but you two are on your own."

Mychal got up, and as Galen made to grab his arm, he found Mychal's blade pressed against his neck. Galen flexed, ready for the fight, but Gabriel put a hand on his shoulder.

"Don't, Rafael. Let him go," he commanded.

Mychal removed his knife, stepped sideways, and walked out through the fire door just as water exploded from the sprinklers.

Mychal had returned to Budapest four months ago, deranged and grieving. He had to get far away from the farm in Russia where Aleksandra died, and Budapest was his old stomping ground. If nothing else, he had to get the emergency cache of weapons and money he had left there.

The Mátáyás Templom had finally reopened after the massacre of its priests the year before. Vadim, his mentor, had been one of the priests there, and Mychal had been raised within those stone walls. The priests had refused to give up Mychal, and so the demons had killed them all.

They weren't even given a proper funeral. All the bodies had been shipped off to Rome for purification rites before they could be laid to rest.

Mychal had been raised by them, but he was no priest; he wasn't even Catholic. Vadim had saved him from a demon attack when he was a boy, and Mychal had become his apprentice demon hunter. The other priests hadn't liked it, maintaining that if Hell wanted something that badly, then there would be no way they could protect him. It was the equivalent of leaving an inconvenient child on a mountain to die, and Vadim wouldn't allow it.

Mychal's natural affinity for killing demons soon shut them up. Vadim was getting old, so he handled the exorcisms, but anything that took over a body completely or managed to manifest fully in the natural plane was dealt with by Mychal. Demon hunters didn't have an outstanding shelf life, but Mychal was exceptional by making it past thirty.

Despite his skills, he had been too late to save Aleksandra. Mychal had paid those demons back in a rage of blood-soaked fury. He tried not to think about that day; something had broken in him, and something primal had taken the reins. He had cut through the demons like a hot blade in the brutal mess of a battle. He had tracked and killed every one of the demons that had come after them. Once it was finished, Mychal had nothing left to do but go back to Budapest.

"Come in for a drink, my beautiful," a whore asked Mychal as he trudged through the slums of Józsefváros. He could smell the cheap perfume, alcohol, and sex on her. He ignored her, just like he had every other time she had asked in the past weeks.

He knew Budapest well, and there was no better place for him to hide than a rat's nest hotel in Józsefváros. It was a place where the people knew instinctively whether they could mess with you or not. Mychal had an aura of death that spread wide around him, and none of the gypsies, thugs, or pickpockets had dared to give him a sideways glance.

The hotel was quiet as he climbed the broken staircase and opened his room. There was a woman sitting on his bed. His heart gave an involuntary thump as he spotted the abundance of dark curls and huge blue eyes. His gaze lingered longingly on her full burgundy lips as her mouth opened. "Mychal, I've been so worried."

"Aleki?" Relief and confusion flooded him even as he reached out to her.

"I've missed you," she said as his hand bunched in her soft hair. His scars burned and his chest tightened with fresh heartache. Mychal's grip tightened and her sweet face twisted. "What are you doing? Mychal! You are hurting me!"

Her blue eyes flicked black as Mychal drove his knife into her pale throat. The demon screeched as black blood sprayed on the bedsheets. He let it go with a rough jerk.

"How did you know—" the dying demon said, spluttering. Mychal picked up his sword from the bedside table and took its head off with one strike.

Mychal watched her features dissolve into ash before he stumbled to the grimy bathroom and vomited in the tub.

"Wasn't her," he muttered. "Wasn't her, wasn't her." He sank to the tiles and sobbed in horror and grief. Every minute for the last six months had been agony, and now the archangels wanted to throw him back into the fray.

Mychal was over being the target of demons, and he wasn't about to be a pawn for the angels. He pulled the knife from his belt, and before he could second-guess himself, he ran the blade along the soft insides of his forearms. Bright scarlet poured out of his open veins as the knife dropped from his fingers. He curled up in the warm pool of his blood to wait for the inevitable.

The soft thump of footfalls on the carpet alerted him to someone else's presence in the room. Through murky vision, he saw a pair of feet.

"Oh, my Mychal, what have you done?" said a gentle voice. Through a haze, Mychal's mind itched as it searched for the face of its owner. Warm darkness wrapped its silky cloak around Mychal as he died; his last thought was relief that it would finally be over.

25

MYCHAL WOKE LATE IN the afternoon stinking of sticky iron and sweat. His bathroom was covered in blood, and drunken recollections of the night before came flowing back.

He had died. He was sure of it. The jagged lines of long, fresh scars running up his forearms were proof enough that he'd taken a knife to his flesh.

Panic seized him, and Mychal quickly washed the blood and vomit from the tub before jumping in the shower and scrubbing his tall, scarred body clean. Something, or *someone*, had brought him back to life and placed him in his bed. He wasn't about to stick around to wait for them to come back.

In half an hour, Mychal was on a train out of Budapest. He had left extra money for the landlord and hoped it was enough to stop them from calling the authorities about the carnage he'd left in his room.

The steady rocking of the train failed to calm his rattled nerves. Against his better judgment, he had bought some sandwiches and coffee to try and alleviate his death hangover. It took a lot to spook Mychal, but his own personal resurrection was driving his crazy scale to all new heights. Mostly, he was embarrassed and shaken that he had tried to kill himself. He had never considered suicide before, but the meetings with the archangels and the demon Aleksandra had been enough to finally push him over.

Demons he could handle, but now angels were after him too. If he kept moving, he'd remain hidden.

There was only one other time he had met an angel, and he had been dying then too. He had run away from the tribe he had been born into, and after days spent freezing and starving, he had come to a camp. The man had been kind until he started to offer Mychal fantastic, impossible things like bringing his dead mother back to life. All Mychal had to do was agree to stay and work for him. Mychal hadn't known about demons then, but he had known about evil. He had turned the man down before running once more. That was when the demons had first come after him. He had been struck down, and his back was clawed to ribbons.

Vadim had saved him that night. According to him, an angel had visited the church where they had been staying and had healed Mychal. Mychal couldn't remember anything past his back being ripped apart. He had flashes of dreams, but that was all. The scars still decorated his back, and they hurt whenever demons were close.

Now he was trying to remember anything about what had happened after he'd cut his arms the night before, but there was nothing. Just a feeling of darkness and warmth. A voice.

"Great," Mychal said aloud without realizing it.

"What is?" asked a prim-looking woman over her paperback.

"God isn't going to let me die." The woman frowned before she got up and moved seats.

Mychal caught his reflection in the tinted window of the train and flinched. He had always been lean, but the last few months of nonstop hunting and binge drinking had left him gaunt. The blood loss from the night before had made his skin pale, and it stretched over his high cheekbones. His hair was a messy tangle of black curls. The hood of his long, black trench coat was up, making him look like a grim reaper.

The sun was a smear of yellow on the horizon by the time Mychal got off the train in Szeged, a small town two hours from Budapest. It was enough distance to give him some breathing space and to make a plan while he recovered. By the time the angels and demons realized he had skipped town, he would be long gone from Hungary.

Mychal found a quiet restaurant and collapsed into a chair. He was starving, and his whole body ached. He ordered a bowl of *szejekygulas* with dumplings and a glass of vodka. He'd only taken one hot, delicious mouthful, when Gabriel and Rafael came through the door. Mychal swore under his breath, but he was too hungry to fight.

"Mychal? What did you do?" Rafael's face was twisted with worry. Gabriel grabbed Mychal's arm and pulled his sleeve back. Horror filled his golden eyes as he touched the scars. He dropped Mychal's arm.

"Why would you try to kill yourself?" he hissed as he took the chair next to him. "You're stronger than that, Mychal."

Mychal's embarrassment was back again, but anger overrode it. "It's none of your business."

"You are our *brother*. Of course, it is our business!" Rafael said, his expression momentarily making him look incredibly young. The waitress was staring at them nervously as if expecting a fight, so Mychal waved at his food, gesturing to her to bring two more bowls.

"Keep your voices down," Mychal said with a growl. "You don't need to cause a scene."

"Mychal, I know you think I've wronged you, but I was trying to help you when we first met. You prayed to me in the library, only moments before we met. I came to comfort you, to try to give you some guidance. You weren't ready to know who I was or who you are," Gabriel explained. "I taught you what I could, but that was as far as I was permitted to interfere. Now I'm here to tell you the truth of what you are, and you try to kill yourself."

Their food arrived, and while they smiled politely at the waitress, they made no move to eat it.

"So you two healed me? I should have known." Mychal huffed. He reached for his vodka but changed his mind when his stomach trembled. He drained a glass of water instead.

"We didn't heal you. My skills are exceptional, but even I can't resurrect without permission," said Rafael with a shake of his head.

"Who did it then? God?" Mychal asked sarcastically. Gabriel's mouth tightened, anger seething from him.

"Yes, Mychal. Elyon did give you your life back. You selfish, disrespectful child," Gabriel said with a growl. The hair on Mychal's arms rose at the threat in his voice.

"Now I know you are feeding me bullshit. I am *nothing*. I'm a demon hunter who wants to die. Why would God bother?"

"Because you made a deal, even if you can't remember it," Rafael replied.

"I think I would remember a deal like that."

"Not in this form you wouldn't," Rafael said.

"Enough with the insinuations. Just say what you need to and leave me the fuck alone," Mychal said, scooping the last of the *szejekygulas* into his mouth.

"You are the human incarnation of the archangel Michael, sent to Earth to fight for mankind whenever it's facing an evil that it can't defeat on its own," Gabriel explained calmly. "A war is coming, and only with you will we be strong enough to contain it."

Mychal looked at the sincerity in his eyes for a long moment before something cracked in his mind and maniacal laughter exploded from him.

"We are *serious*, Mychal," Rafael said.

"I know you are, and that's what is so funny about it! You two are on your own. I won't be dragged into another war by you or demons or God himself, so you can go and tell him for me to go and get fuc—" Mychal's rant was cut short as the restaurant started to shake. The staff didn't look worried or alarmed. In fact, they didn't seem to notice at all.

"Oh no," Rafael murmured, looking around him. "Now you have really done it. He's here, Gabriel."

Glass casings fell from the lights above them, smashing to the floor with the cutlery that slid from the tables. The doors to the restaurant blew open, and a tall archangel walked in, bringing a flurry of snow in his wake. He had white hair and the burning eyes of a thunderstorm. Unlike the other two, he didn't try to disguise himself as a human. He wore a long, gray cloak over a leather breastplate, trousers, and high boots. He had a face like a hatchet and wore an expression of pure fury.

The *szejekygulas* moved threateningly in Mychal's stomach when the cold eyes found him. The other two had played nice. This one was nothing short of terrifying.

Gabriel was on his feet and trying to block his way. "Uriel, please don't do this. He doesn't know, and he didn't mean it. You are too angry from other matters and—"

"Get out of my way," Uriel commanded with a frozen, flintlike voice. He pushed past Gabriel. Mychal was already on his feet, pointing a gun at the newcomer.

"Mychal, you are coming with me."

"I'm not going anywhere with you."

The archangel reached for him, and the gun exploded in Mychal's hand. The expression on Uriel's face didn't change as he backhanded Mychal, sending him crashing into a group of tables. Mychal spat out a mouthful of blood as he climbed to his feet and broke a chair across Uriel's shoulders, following it up with a punch to the face that made no impact. Uriel picked him up by his throat. Mychal kicked and flailed to break his grip, but the big hand only tightened.

"Please, brother. Stop this," Rafael begged. "He's human! You are going to kill him."

"Don't interfere, Rafael!" Uriel shouted. "I've had enough of his selfishness."

Mychal swung and punched him hard in the nose. Uriel glared up at him, making Mychal regret that last punch. Uriel bellowed with rage and threw Mychal out of the restaurant windows. He landed hard in a rain of glass, his bones cracking on the icy road. Mychal barely shifted when Uriel crouched over him, punching him in the face.

"You spoiled, ungrateful—" Uriel shouted at him over the rain.

I am about to die again, Mychal thought distantly just as someone plowed into the archangel.

"Uriel, stop! Stop this, please," a woman begged. "Please stop. I'm sorry. I'm sorry for everything."

"Jael, what are you doing here?" he asked her, the sight of her defusing his anger.

"Apparently I came to keep you from killing someone," she replied. She looked down at Mychal, and he recognized her. It was the woman he thought he'd hallucinated in the alleyway. She was real. Mychal laughed; it came out as a choking gasp.

"You shouldn't have stopped him." He coughed up blood in a wheezing, bitter laugh. "Exorcist."

26

Zin Valley, Negev Desert, Israel.

NAZIRAH WIPED THE SWEAT and stifling, incessant dust from her forehead. The fine sable brush in her hand quivered as she lightly brushed the white dirt from the carefully pegged area around her. She lay on her belly and was trying to ignore a cramp that was building between her shoulder blades. She chewed slowly on a half-dissolved fig, the seedy sweetness rolling in her mouth.

It had been six weeks since the dig began, and they still hadn't found anything. At least nothing she'd been willing to report. Mumbles of discontent hummed around the camp. Whispers of words like "dead end" and "Bedouin's hoax" reached her ears, but Nazirah stoically ignored them. She had believed the nomad. He had brought a piece of bone and a small clay idol to her at the Jacob Blaustein Institute for Desert Research nearly four months ago. The idol, though strange, could've come from anywhere, but the bone was what had fascinated her. She had fought hard for her chance to find the rest of the skeleton the bone belonged to.

Nazirah had discovered bone fragments in the last few days, but they were still waiting for the rest of their analyzing equipment to arrive. A dig in the desert could be a logistical nightmare, and if it wasn't for the interest of their private backer, the project wouldn't have gotten off the ground at all.

Nazirah blew softly at the loose dirt to try to get a better idea of what she was looking at. An hour ago she thought it was just another fragment, but now the length of a full bone was beginning to reveal itself. She tried not to squeal with enthusiasm as she got up to stretch her back and have a drink from her water bottle. The white-and-gray logo of HeosCorp stared at her as the stale water washed the last of the dried fig from her mouth.

HeosCorp, their investor, had provided Nazirah and her team with everything they needed without question.

Nazirah had been wary when she had been approached by the lawyers of Mr. Heosphoros, a Greek tycoon. She had thought it was too good to be true, but her investigation into HeosCorp had checked out. Mr. Heosphoros was barely seen in public, but the business was a large network of companies and conglomerates that dealt with everything from oil mining to baby toys. Nazirah had taken the lawyers at their word that Mr. Heosphoros was a collector and was passionate about Near Eastern artifacts. He was more than happy to provide her with anything that she needed.

So far they had stuck to that promise, and that's what wasn't sitting well with Nazirah. She had worked on privately funded digs before, and the investors had fought against her every step of the way. Every piece of paper had to be accounted for in the budget, because they cared about results and the bottom line.

Just be grateful a rich man is interested in your hobby, she thought, hearing her mother's voice in her head. To her mother, Nazirah's career was just a nice hobby until she married a nice Jewish boy. Nazirah pushed her mother's criticizing voice to the back of her mind, though she grudgingly agreed that she should be grateful. An archaeologist's dream gig was to be able to pick their team and run their site without the hindrance of governmental red tape or pushy investors.

"Found anything?" asked Noah, one of her assistants.

"It looks like a finger bone, but I should have reached the end of it by now," Nazirah said as she lay back down in the dirt.

"If we find a hand, how amazing would that be?" he said eagerly as he positioned himself a few meters from her. She liked his enthusiasm; she didn't want to get his hopes up too high, but she didn't want to discourage him either. She knew what it was like to work under negative dream killers and was determined not to be that kind of boss.

"I think I have an elbow joint," Noah said an hour later. Nazirah barely looked up. She had uncovered four fingers, but they were the largest and longest fingers she had ever seen. The middle finger was almost thirty centimeters. She needed her equipment to arrive, so she could test it. She refused to get too excited about something that could have been planted.

"Do you think these two were buried side by side?" asked Noah as the space between their bones grew closer together.

"It looks likely. We are going to run over each other soon," Nazirah said jokingly as her heart hammered. She didn't think they were working on two different bodies. Her suspicions were confirmed as the bones they were working on met, revealing that they came from the same arm. They stood up and looked at the size and shape of the bones. The four other archaeologists had moved from their fruitless sites to observe the find.

"This has to be a fake," Frank said with a shake of his balding head. He had been working in the Egyptology Department of the British Museum, when Nazirah had convinced him to take leave and come to the site. She had wanted her mentor, Aaron Ben-Ezra, to come from Australia to help her, but he declined. His family needed him in Melbourne more than she needed him in the desert. She'd sent him the idol as a tease but so far hadn't heard anything from him.

The sound of engines broke through their excitement. A silver-and-white helicopter was moving toward them. Every two days HeosCorp had been sending a helicopter from Jerusalem, loaded with equipment and food.

"It's not a fake, Frank," Nazirah said determinedly. "Can't you feel it? This is real, and that helicopter will have everything I need to prove it."

"I'm not going to believe anything until it's dated," he said stubbornly. "In the meantime, let's have the assistants continue to uncover the rest of it. We have five good hours of daylight left."

"Get them to help unpack the helicopter when it lands," Nazirah said as she pulled her coppery-brown hair back into a tight ponytail. "I'm staying right here."

The helicopter landed, kicking up clouds of dust all over the camp. Nazirah hoped they had brought more figs. It was going to be a long day.

Floodlights were set up around the site as night fell. They were all working feverishly and had uncovered the full arm and a skull that was three times the size of a normal person's. That alone confirmed what Nazirah already expected. The body was male and a giant.

"Is the carbon dating machine set up?" Nazirah asked Frank as she made another strong coffee in the mess tent.

"I still can't believe they gave you one, but yes, it is. It's calibrating. I will get some samples in it tonight. I'm not going to get excited until I have some data in front of me," Frank replied. "If it is real, we could be making one of the most significant finds of the century. I fear it will raise more questions than answers though."

Nazirah fiddled with the star on her necklace. "I know. We have to keep this quiet until we know something solid. The Torah mentions giants more than once, Frank. Maybe they weren't just stories."

"Goliath out there is either an anomaly, a freak of nature, or we will find more bodies. Best to take it one step at a time, my girl." Frank sipped thoughtfully on his Earl Grey. "We should alert our benevolent benefactor too. Mr. Heosphoros doesn't seem to be the kind of person you wait to share significant information with. I am sure one of the helicopter pilots would have already told the higher-ups."

"I will send him an email," Nazirah said, uneasiness spiking in her stomach like it always did when she had to report to him.

Be grateful, the voice said again, and she hurried back to her giant.

27

TEN MINUTES AGO, I was standing on a roof in Melbourne screaming out to a God who I thought had abandoned me. Now I was in the freezing rain trying to convince angels to stop killing each other.

"We need to get him off the road and to a hospital," I said, crouching down next to the unconscious stranger. I had seen him in meditations and dreams a lot in the last month, and now he was bleeding and broken in front of me.

"How did you get here?" Uriel asked beside me.

"Yeshua sent me," I replied and glared at him. "I had to stop you from killing this poor guy." I was still dressed for a Melbourne summer and was shivering violently. Uriel took off his cloak and draped it around me, the big hood coming over my head to keep the rain from my eyes.

"I wasn't going to kill him," he said gruffly. He didn't sound convincing.

"You could've fooled me," said the man with flaming red hair. He knelt down beside me and checked that the demon hunter was still breathing. "Can you hear me?"

The golden-haired man simply smiled at me. "I'm glad you are here, Jael Quinlan." It took me a long moment to recognize them in everyday clothes, but my vision from the previous months came back to me. There had been four archangels fighting in the middle of a desert. Gabriel and Rafael lifted the unconscious demon hunter. *Holy shit, I'm with the archangels!*

"We need to get Mychal out of here," Gabriel said.

"Mychal!" I exclaimed. "But...but he's human."

Uriel let out a tired sigh. "It's a very long story."

"Where are you taking him?"

"Somewhere safe," Gabriel replied. "Bring her, Uriel. She's needed." They seemed to vanish in front of me, taking Mychal with them.

Uriel held his hand out to me, and I took a step back. We hadn't spoken for over a month.

"I can't go with you. I need to go home to my dog and my life."

"You were brought here to help us."

I couldn't stop the bitter laugh that bubbled up inside of me. "Like you were there to help me when I needed you?"

A growl of frustration rumbled through him. "This isn't the place to have this conversation," he said. Before I could struggle, he scooped me up in his arms, and we were gone from the car park. The air charged around us and reality tore. I clung to Uriel as everything blurred and we reappeared outside of a wooden hunting cabin. My stomach churned and fought to keep down the drinks I'd had with Star.

"Where are we now?" I asked, climbing out of his arms and putting space between us before I started yelling or crying.

"Somewhere safe," Uriel replied. He looked about to say something else when the phone in my pocket buzzed.

```
Came back to see u and u are gone? Where are
u? Meta's freaking out. I'm freaking out.
```

Damn, Star was going to be pissed. I took a deep breath before typing back.

```
In Hungary with Uriel. I promise you I'm safe.
Please look after Meta. I'm okay. I love you.
Talk when I can.
```

"I wish you guys would have prepared me for this extra mission," I said angrily to Uriel. "I can't keep disappearing on Star. I don't even have clean clothes with me!"

"There will be clothes for you inside. I didn't know you were going to be pulled into this," Uriel replied. "If I had, I would've tried to prevent it."

"Like you tried to prevent me from getting kidnapped by a bunch of demons?" I snapped, the wound deep inside of me bleeding fresh. My faith in him had been broken, and now all I had was my pissed off, shattered heart. I'd said it to him to provoke him, but instead of being angry, Uriel looked like I had hit him.

"I would've stopped that from happening if I could. I would've done anything to prevent you from getting hurt," he said under his breath. "Jael—"

"Later." I stopped him abruptly. "Right now, we have a half-dead guy inside that needs to be looked after, because apparently, he's the archangel Michael." I trudged up the wooden stairs and went inside. Rafael and Gabriel had placed Mychal on a couch and were watching him carefully.

"I know it's not my business, but you shouldn't be so hard on Uriel. You need to hear him out," Gabriel said to me.

"You know, you're right. It *is* none of your business," I replied sharply. There was a throaty gurgle from the man on the couch.

"I like you, exorcist," Mychal said through his heavy accent and busted lips. I ignored Gabriel's golden eyes.

I found a small kitchen in the back of the cabin and boiled a pot of hot water and found some clean towels. By the time I returned, Rafael had taken off Mychal's coat and shirt and was checking his wounds.

Like my own healing body, Mychal's was discolored from old and new bruises, cuts, and scrapes. My eyes flickered over the black outline of the large, tattooed cross on his chest. It brought to mind the tattoos I'd seen on Alessandro's body, and I locked the thought down. He should've been the one called into a mission like this, not me.

Mychal was covered in scars, but the ones that drew my attention were the raised pink lines on the inside of his forearms. I ran my fingers down them and was bombarded by images of a woman. There was deep pain and despair and finally a blinding light as the self-made cuts were healed. Mychal's hand was quick as a cobra as it darted out and gripped my wrist.

"Easy there, demon hunter," I said, my pulse racing as his black eyes studied me. "I only wanted to clean you up and make sure you aren't going to bleed to death." He looked at the bloody towel in my hand.

"Let her go or I'll break your hand too," Uriel said from somewhere behind me. Mychal released me; his dark gaze fixed hard on Uriel.

"Go and glower at the other angels," I said over my shoulder. I dropped the towel into the bowl of dirty red water.

"They are gone," Uriel said, looking like he wanted to hit Mychal all over again.

"Already?"

"They have other things to do, and it's my turn."

"Your turn to do what?"

Uriel frowned at Mychal, who had drifted back to sleep. "My turn to help him as he remembers who he is."

"He doesn't know? Like, at all?" I asked, shocked.

"Not fully." Uriel touched Mychal on the forehead. "It's starting. As he gathers his memories together again, he'll suffer. We have to make sure he doesn't hurt himself or die as he goes through it."

Mychal shuddered as Uriel removed his hand from his head. The guy looked half-dead, and if the memories I'd seen were true, then he was the most broken person I'd ever met, including me. I dreaded what would make him suffer worse than what he was already going through.

"Considering you almost killed him yourself, I don't know if you are the one that should be left with him."

"I had my reasons for attacking him," Uriel replied cryptically. "He'll dream about them now."

"Sleep sounds like a good idea."

I found an empty room with a double bed, and I shut the door on Uriel and all the things still unsaid between us.

28

MICHAEL...MICHAEL... A VOICE called out to him in the empty void. *Michael...Michael.*

That sound, that voice, called him out of the darkness. Shaped him. Gave him form and purpose.

Rolling in an eternity of stars, Michael saw the first earth being formed from gas and dust, gathered together and formed into shape. Michael watched life spring up, crawling from the oceans. Great scaled beasts now dwell on Eretz, the earth.

Praises rise up from the ones Elyon calls *man*. The praises are brought to the third Heaven by Hel'el, Elyon's only anointed angel blessed with two offices. He's an archangel with the office of a Cherubim, and he is beautiful. Those in Heaven gather to hear him when he returns from the earth. They listen to the song of Elyon's wonderful creations, the simple joy and love that everything on the earth has for their Creator.

Over time the song on the earth changes.

Deep within Hel'el's music are notes of discord, a distortion. The archangels approach the throne, bringing their concerns to Elyon, the Most High.

This time when Hel'el returns, he has changed yet again. Elyon demands he stop amidst the song. The angels draw together as Elyon questions Hel'el. He has betrayed the earth, his most holy office. The messages from Elyon to the earth have been changed; Hel'el in his vanity kept the praise intended for Elyon for himself, sharing only a version of it in the throne room of Heaven. Michael falls to the ground, covering his head with his wings as Elyon's rage shakes the Heavens.

"You've betrayed me, Hel'el, and stolen my glory. For this, you are banished to the earth that you have manipulated for your own desires. You are cut off from my grace and Heaven forever."

Hel'el's excuses fall on deaf ears as Elyon picks up the betrayer and casts him down. The angels watch him hurtle through the second and the first Heaven, a burning star surrounded by darkness. Hel'el hits the earth with such a force that it breaks apart.

So mighty is the wrath of Elyon that the earth is shut up in darkness, leaving it without form in the void. The angels mourn for their fallen brother Hel'el, alone in the torment of his own pride, far away from the love of Elyon.

For thousands of years, they lament until Elyon's anger subsides, and he sends his spirit down over the waters of the earth.

"*Yehi 'or!*" he commands, permitting the light to shine once more. He calls the light *Yom*, the darkness *Lailah*, and separates them forever.

The angels marvel and worship as Elyon recreates the first heavens, lighting the night with a million stars and a moon and the day with a burning sun to warm the Earth. The dry land appears once more, bringing forth vegetation. Out of the waters come the living creatures and the fowl of the air. Elyon blesses them, commanding them to be fruitful and multiply.

Then Elyon does something that surprises all of the angels. He declares that he will create humankind in his own image. Forming the first man in primordial clay, Elyon breathes his own life and spirit into him, making the man an extension of himself.

Hidden deep within Elyon's new creation lives Hel'el and the restless, deformed creatures that had been birthed in the darkness. Elyon tells Adam and his consort, Eve, that as extensions of himself, they can wield the power of Heaven on Earth. They have the power to protect themselves from Hel'el and all of the dark ones. Now the praises of creation lift to the Heavens in an unhindered song, no longer needing a messenger to bring it to them.

The pride and anger of Hel'el grows every day against this new man, this one that is made like Elyon. Created more powerful than all of his other creatures. Elyon has given them what Hel'el sought and was so severely punished for. Hel'el's twisted mind turns to hate and revenge. He vows to do everything he can to rob this creation of Elyon's power and make the earth his own.

Every day he transforms himself into a snake and enters their dwelling places. He follows them closely, watching as they name all things as Elyon has commanded. With more power than the angels will ever possess, there is none to guard them; they are left to do their sacred work in peace and freedom.

In the center of the garden grows the most magnificent tree of all, the one that Elyon called the Tree of the Knowledge of Good and Evil. He warned them not to eat of it, for if they did, they would die.

Michael watches in horror as Hel'el takes on a snake's form and starts to talk to Eve. He rushes to Elyon to tell him the news. They must intervene and stop what is about to happen.

"We can't, Michael. They must be able to choose, otherwise there is no point."

Michael knows the wisdom in this, but he can't contain his anger and distress when they give up their birthright, their immortality, and the ability to use the power of Heaven.

Outside Eden, Hel'el watches the clouds of Elyon's judgment cover the land. He has taken the power of Adam, and now all of Elyon's creation is under his rule. His victorious laughter shakes the earth, and in Heaven the angels scream.

Mychal woke with a start, a piercing, unnatural scream emanating from his mouth. His heart was crushed inside of him, his chest bones cracking in agony. He fell off the couch and onto the ground, gasping for air. Uriel was beside him in seconds, a gentle hand on his back. Air streamed back into Mychal's lungs, and he took great breaths to try and ease the pain.

"It's okay," Uriel said. "Tell me what you were dreaming about."

"I saw…I saw…" Mychal stammered. Tremors wracked his body, and he fought to control them. "I saw the fall of man. I saw Hel'el being thrown down by God. I sp-spoke to Elyon." Tears flowed from his eyes, and he clutched his head to try to slow the images that were burning through him.

"Then you have finally started to remember. This is a good sign."

"How can this be good? I can't function like this," said Mychal.

"It won't be forever," Uriel said, assuring him before rising quickly, as if to attention.

Mychal looked up and saw the exorcist watching them from the doorway of her room, her eyes wary.

"I'll put the coffee on," she said, as if finally making up her mind about something. She pointed to a pack. "There are clothes in there if you want them."

Mychal grumbled something, struggled to his feet, and stumbled to the small bathroom. His body was stiff, but he didn't have a bruise on him despite the beating Uriel had given him.

What is happening to me? Mychal scrubbed himself, tucking his tall frame under the low showerhead.

There was a smell lingering in the little room of something floral and undeniably female. The exorcist. He needed to know how she fit into the situation. She obviously knew Uriel, though he couldn't guess at their relationship. She was also pissed off at Uriel, though once again, Mychal couldn't figure out why.

By the time Mychal made it to the kitchen, bowls of hot vegetable soup and cups of black coffee had been set on a table. The exorcist was sitting on the far side, her back leaning against the wall.

"Apparently the soup is the only thing you can stomach when the memories start coming back," she said. Her sharp face watched him carefully over the rim of her mug. "You should sit your ass down before you fall down."

Mychal slumped into a chair across from her, picked up his spoon, hesitated, and put it down again. He drank a mouthful of hot coffee instead.

"So, what's your name, exorcist?" he asked.

"Jael Quinlan."

"Australian?"

"Yep. Melbournian."

"How did you get dragged into this?"

"I'm assuming it's because you are going to need an exorcist in the immediate future," she said.

"And Uriel?"

Her eyes narrowed. "What about him?"

"You kept him from killing me," Mychal said with a small shrug. "It looks like he listened to you over Gabriel and Rafael. That's impressive for a human."

"And?"

"And now you look like you want to stab him with something."

Her grin was a flash of mischievous malice. "Can you blame me?"

"All depends. What did he do to you?" Mychal replied. It was awkward talking to someone again. He couldn't remember the last full conversation he'd had. From his visions of her, he figured Jael could handle the strange situation better than he could.

"It's a long story," Jael mumbled, sipping her coffee. She was wearing the same clothes as he was: a long-sleeve hooded shirt, fitted black pants, and boots. She had slashed the pants across her knees in a curious act of individuality or defiance; Mychal could only guess.

"We are going to have some time together, exorcist. I'm wary of sleeping under the same roof with someone I don't know," said Mychal.

"Me too. And considering I have this thanks to you." Jael pointed to the fine white scar on her neck. "I think you can go first."

"I cut you?" The first vision he had of her, he had pointed the tip of his spear to her throat, but he had thought she was a ghost. "How is that possible?"

"I don't know. I snapped out of my meditation, and it was bleeding. It was a tiny cut, but it took weeks to heal. That's an incredible weapon you have."

"Gabriel gave it to me, though I didn't know it was him at the time," Mychal said. His spoon scraped the bottom of his bowl, and he looked at it, surprised the soup had disappeared as they circled each other.

"Here," she said and pushed her still-full bowl toward him. "I'm not hungry."

"You have to eat," Uriel said from the doorway. His wide shoulders filled it almost entirely.

Jael pushed the bowl even closer to Mychal. "You can't force me."

"I can," Uriel replied, his tone icy.

Jael got to her feet. "Try it. I fucking *dare* you, Feathers." Uriel didn't stop her as she pushed past him and out of the tiny kitchen.

"You had best apologize to her for whatever you did," Mychal said, taking her bowl of soup.

"I've tried. She won't let me." Uriel sat down beside him, and Mychal could feel his sadness.

"Try harder. How do you know her anyway?" asked Mychal. It wasn't in his nature to pry or to even care enough to ask, but somewhere deep down he knew that he and Uriel had been brothers once. Even if he couldn't remember it.

"I trained her to be an exorcist," said Uriel.

"And that's why she's angry at you?"

"No, she was captured and tortured by demons a month ago." Uriel's eyes darkened with sorrow and anger. "And I couldn't save her."

"How many times have you done this?" Mychal asked, sensing it was safer to change the subject. "Waited until I got my memories back?"

"I've lost count. You've been particularly difficult this time."

"So why bother?"

"We need you, and you're my brother, even if you don't remember. Something is changing within the fabric of the earth. It's like the calm before the storm. If you had stepped away from your grief for a minute, then you would've felt it too."

"I felt it before Aleksandra was murdered," admitted Mychal, his tongue still struggling with her name. "If I had listened to my instincts, maybe I would've been more vigilant, and I could have kept Aleksandra alive." Just saying her name made a lump form in his chest.

"Let go of your guilt, Mychal. It serves no purpose now. Don't torture yourself for things that weren't in your control."

Mychal scowled. "You didn't come to lecture me on my emotional state and feed me soup, Uriel. What do we do now? Wait until my memories return, while Jael sulks?"

"We train. I can't take this malnourished creature before me into battle." His lip curled in mock disgust.

"And the exorcist?"

Uriel's gray eyes flicked toward the door. "Jael can join in. If she likes."

"You don't know why she's here do you?" Mychal couldn't help pressing him.

"She's here because it's her job, like it's ours. If it were my decision, Jael would be back in Australia. I don't want her here. She shouldn't be involved in this." That was when Mychal saw it. The terrifying archangel, who had almost beaten him to death in anger, was worried about a human girl.

"If you care about her, send her away. Don't be selfish like I was. If I had been a better man, I would've let Aleksandra be, and the demons would have never gone after her."

Uriel glared at him. "Don't you think I have tried to send her back? I can't. She has a part to play in what's coming."

"Then you had better train her too, because wherever I go, there's a fight," Mychal said. "I won't be the one protecting her."

"She's mine to protect, not yours," Uriel said with a growl. "She's probably not going to let me train her."

"You never know. Jael looks like she wants to hit you a lot right now."

"Finish your food," Uriel instructed, his patience vanishing. "Meet me down at the shore of the lake, and we'll begin."

Mychal searched the bag of gear that had been left for him and found his spear and guns. *Least they didn't leave everything behind.* He stretched his back, trying to relieve the ache in his muscles. Maybe training would be a good thing. Anything to take his mind off the dream.

Mist rolled through the forest outside of the cabin as Mychal pulled up his hood and followed a small track that led down to a silvery-gray lake. *Where are they?*

On the shoreline, Uriel had stripped down to a pair of loose, gray training pants. His arms and torso were a wall of pale, heavy muscle, covered in blue runic script. His white hair had been braided back, and he stood ready, sword in hand.

"Because that's not intimidating at all," Mychal muttered. Ásgeirr, the man he now knew as Gabriel, was lean and lithe. Uriel looked pure berserker, all muscles and power, and for the first time in a very long time, Mychal felt a flicker of nerves.

He groaned. "This is going to hurt."

"Only if you move too slowly," the angel replied.

"I always thought I did okay against Ásgeirr...Gabriel...whatever he chooses to go as." Mychal flicked the bar of silver metal in his hand, and it stretched out, growing into a spear.

"Gabriel was holding back on you. You're adequate against a human, but angels? No."

"I know a few demons who would—"

"Demons possessing humans are bound to a human shape."

"Well, I am human too."

"You are *more* than human, Mychal. The moment you accept that, the easier it will be for all of us. Now, defend yourself!" Mychal had barely started trying to follow the white blur, when he was on his back, pain lacing through his body.

"You bastard…" he said, wheezing as he climbed back to his feet. He gripped his spear and attacked. Uriel blocked him with his sword and dodged the kick Mychal aimed at him.

"You taught *me* how to fight," Uriel said as their weapons clashed again. "Your mind might not remember who you are, but your body does. Stop holding yourself back."

Resigning himself to getting his ass kicked again, Mychal took a deep breath and lunged.

29

I GRABBED A JACKET from my room and headed outside and into the forest. Seeing Uriel's eyes full of concern for me made me want to scream.

Oh God, what were you thinking when you brought me here? I wanted my dog and the Melbourne heat. I didn't want to be stuck in the woods with a surly angel and a demon hunter.

Whatever Mychal was, he set all of my psychic shields humming. Even underfed and haunted, there was no denying he was the sexy kind of trouble. He was as tall as Uriel with curly, black hair and dark, dark eyes. He was damaged, even more so than me, and that was really saying something.

I pulled out my phone and checked the reception. Nothing. Great. I was stuck God knows where, and I couldn't call for help or advice.

The trees around me thinned, and I found a lake, still as glass. It wasn't a huge lake, so I decided the best thing to do was continue walking. There was nothing I could do, and the thought of sitting in a cabin with Uriel wasn't my idea of a good time. Not when I couldn't decide if I wanted to kiss him or strangle him. Both were dumb ideas. My momentary relief at seeing him had faded in the face of a half-dead demon hunter.

You're going to have to talk to Uriel at some point. I shoved the thought away. And say what to him? That he hurt me? He knew that.

I walked, trying to sort my head out. My thoughts turned to Max, the Nephilim statue Uriel took, Tom's death by demons, and Alessandro. What would he do in a situation like this? Why couldn't he have this mission instead of me? He was the better exorcist. He probably would have had a great time.

I checked my phone again, the desire to call the priest overwhelming me. He was probably kicked back in a beautiful monastery, drinking Italian wines and making nuns second-guess their vows.

I had almost completed the circuit of the lake, when I stilled at the sound of clashing steel and loud male voices arguing. The trees and mist cleared, and I stopped dead in my tracks.

Holy God above.

Uriel and Mychal were half-naked, armed, and clearly out to hurt each other. I groaned. I didn't want to have to break up another fight between them. I opened my mouth to yell at them and paused. If they were really fighting, Uriel would be pummeling Mychal as he had the night before. I had seen Uriel fight in my vision, and that was terrifying; this seemed to be training. Mychal turned his back to me, and I saw that long scars from demon claws covered his muscled back.

"Holy shit," I muttered. *How had he survived that?*

Uriel knocked him on his ass in a swift move that made my breath catch. I had never seen Uriel without a shirt on. I knew from the few times he had hugged me that he was ripped, but he was massive in height and muscle. The blue lines I'd only ever glimpsed at his collar were now on full display on his scarred and creamy skin. They looked like some kind of runes that circled around his collarbones to his shoulders and down his back. His long silvery hair was pulled back in a messy braid that whipped around him as he fought.

I was still far enough away that they hadn't seen me, and all I could do was stand there like an idiot with my mouth hanging open. *What use am I going to be in this fight, if they can do that?* I sure as shit couldn't move like that. I thought they were getting along until Mychal said something, and Uriel's face changed to anger. He grabbed the demon hunter and tossed him into the water.

"Hey! What the hell!" I shouted at Uriel. He looked up in surprise like he had only just realized I was there.

Mychal had been half-dead the night before, and I searched the water, waiting for him to resurface. I hurried down to the water's edge, but still there was nothing. *He can't swim.* I pulled off my jacket and shoes and plunged into the freezing water. I made for the spot where he had landed, searching the dark water.

"Mychal! Oh shit, oh shit…" I ignored Uriel as he shouted something from the shore. I took a deep breath and dove, arms flailing about. Through blurry vision, I spotted something glowing in the water and swam toward it. My hands brushed against hair, and I reached out, catching the curve of Mychal's shoulder and hauling him toward me. I kicked hard through the water, breaking the surface and sucking in cold air in deep gasps.

"Mychal!" I shook him as I tried to keep his head above the water. I kicked backward and crashed into Uriel. He pulled me to him with one hand and grabbed Mychal with the other.

"It's okay, Jael. I've got you," he said, but I struggled out of his grip.

"Help Mychal. I can swim back myself," I snapped. "What is your problem? This is the second time you have tried to kill him in the last twelve hours."

"I didn't know he couldn't swim!" Uriel replied as he pulled Mychal through the water. "Useless human."

"Yeah. Well, I guess we all are to you," I said as I climbed up the pebbled beach. Uriel placed Mychal on the ground and bent over him.

"He's still breathing." I rolled Mychal over onto his side, opening his mouth to let any water out.

"He'll be fine, Jael," Uriel replied.

"Carry him back to the cabin before he dies of the cold," I said through chattering teeth. I walked down to get my coat and boots, and by the time I got back to the cabin, the adrenaline of the moment was gone, and I was shivering hard.

Uriel dumped Mychal on a rug on the floor and built up the fire in the fireplace. He pulled a blanket off the couch and placed it over the unconscious demon hunter.

"Go and get changed before you get sick," Uriel said without looking at me. I clenched my hands into fists but headed for my room. I peeled off my wet clothes and dried myself with a towel. The last of my bruises stood out against my too-pale skin, and despite their recovery, my ribs were aching where I had broken them. *Just perfect.*

I pulled on some more of the clothes from my new bag and ran a comb through my knotty wet hair. When I opened the door, Uriel was on the other side. He was dressed in new clothes, his hair out of its braid and already miraculously dried. Before I could say a word, he gathered me up in his arms.

"Hey! What gives? Let me go!" I said, but he held me tighter.

"No, not until you listen to me, *yadid*," Uriel said with a growl. He carried me back into the room; the door closed behind us. I felt the fight leaking out of me as his body heat warmed me. The ball of pressure that had been building in my chest since that night at HeosCorp grew so big I started to shake.

"Please," Uriel said, his tone gentler. "Please, just listen to me, Jael. I don't want to fight you, and I can't handle—" He broke off. My shaking grew until I couldn't hold in the tears that poured out of me.

"Where were you, Uriel? I called, and you *never* came… I was going to die, and you never…" I sobbed. He sat down on the bed, and I curled up in his lap, crying against his chest, unable to talk to him.

"I told you that I couldn't get a full scope of the darkness in the city. My 'angel vision,' as you so eloquently described it, had failed completely. The night that you gave me the idol, I went to Gabriel for advice. There's no way that idol should have been pulled from the Negev. That such a thing ended up in your house…"

Uriel's arms tightened fractionally around me as he swallowed the anger building in his voice. "I went to Gabriel. Something's happening in the Negev, and we knew we needed Mychal. Gabriel had been watching over him, waiting for the memories to start returning to him. I felt the moment you were taken. I didn't think. I left Gabriel standing with the idol and a potentially earth-shattering problem, and I returned to Melbourne. But when I got there…I couldn't get back in. The creatures that had been hiding from me finally made their move. They had you. I could hear you, but I had to fight my way to you. I can't describe how it felt, not to be able to reach you. I don't think I've ever been truly afraid, but…I felt it then."

Uriel curled into me, head bowed, as if the confession was costing him something that he would never be able to take back.

"It took me three days to defeat them, and by then you had broken yourself free. I was so proud, so relieved. But then I saw you in the hospital, and I realized how much I had failed you," continued Uriel. "You are *my* exorcist. The one person I'm meant to keep safe, and who I always wanted to protect. Your life is full of people who you can't rely on to be strong enough to be there for you. I was supposed to be that person, and I'm so sorry I failed you. I don't know how to make things right with you. How can I expect you to trust me again? I'm meant to be nursing the greatest of us back to himself, and all I can worry about is *you*. How can I fix this, Jael? Tell me, and I'll do it."

I finally looked up at him and saw the hurt and anguish in his stormy eyes. I realized the brokenness I felt was a shared pain after all.

"I don't know," I admitted, my heart hurting. "I do know that I don't want to fight with you anymore. Maybe my abandonment issues have screwed me up, but I don't feel right when you aren't around. We are stuck together in whatever this"—I waved about at the cabin—"is meant to be. Another impossible mission from a higher power as usual. The trust thing you are going to have to work on, but you aren't all to blame either. I got so used to you always being there that I forgot how to be without you, to fight my own battles. I shouldn't rely on you to have my back every time I mess up."

"Know I will always do my best to protect you, *yadid*." My heart burned at the endearment. *Beloved*. I was all kinds of messed up, but I was still his exorcist and he was my angel.

"I missed you," I said with my hands on his cheeks, studying that face I never thought I'd see again.

"I missed you too. Let's not fight again; I can't handle it," Uriel replied, his grip on me tightening.

"Don't piss me off and we won't."

Uriel smiled then, and it was the most beautiful thing I'd ever seen. *You love him*, Star had said, and in that moment I realized it wasn't in the friend sense. His smile slipped.

"What's wrong?" he asked softly.

"Nothing." *Everything. I can't be in love with you. Anyone but you.*

Uriel didn't get a chance to push me about it, because Mychal's tormented cry echoed through the cabin. We untangled ourselves and hurried out to where Mychal was twisting about on the floor.

"What's happening to him?" I asked as Uriel moved me aside and knelt down beside Mychal. He rested two fingers on Mychal's forehead, and the demon hunter stilled.

Uriel smiled sadly. "He's remembering the first time he fell in love with a human woman, and this whole nightmare began."

"Nightmare? As in, becoming a human? I didn't even know angels could do that."

"We can, but only Elyon can make it happen. This was a special case. Mychal made a deal, and now he has to live with the cost of it." Uriel froze, his head twisting as if listening to a sound I couldn't hear.

"What's wrong?" I asked as he stood up suddenly.

"I'm being summoned by Gabriel. Something has happened." Uriel took me by the shoulders. "I have to leave you to see what is wrong. Will you watch over Mychal for me? Be here for him when he wakes?"

"Of course, though I don't know how much help I will be." I bit my lip nervously, hating the idea of him leaving me again. There seemed to be so much more I wanted to tell him…

Uriel lifted my chin. "This place is protected; nothing will harm you here. I promise I won't be long." He kissed my forehead, and as I reached for him, he vanished, leaving me alone with a demon hunter and my own tormented heart.

30

MYCHAL HAD NO TIME to register what was happening as Uriel threw him out across the still lake. He hit the surface hard; the impact knocked the air out of him. He sank underneath the water, kicking futilely. He was a good swimmer, but he felt something pulling him farther down. Before he could reach the surface, his eyes closed, and he fell into a vision, unable to struggle against it.

Michael was swimming in the lakes of Aravot when he heard a voice crying out over and over.

I beseech you high and holy ones to save us from the death and disease they bring with them… The voice was male and frightened, and Michael didn't recognize it. He stopped swimming and looked around for the source of it. He thought he had imagined it until he heard the name *Semyaza*, and then he realized what he was hearing was a prayer. He turned to head back to the shore and saw Uriel already waiting for him. Uriel was much like his home in the northern mountains of Aravot. He had silver-white hair like the snow and eyes as gray eyes as the winter lakes and as hard as mountain slate.

"Do you hear it too?" he asked as soon as Michael was close. Uriel was distracted and pacing. "Tell me you hear it, Michael. I feel like I'm losing my mind."

"The prayer? I heard it just now," Michael replied as he walked away from the lake and put his clothes back on.

"How's this possible?" Uriel demanded. "There are other angels assigned to the prayers of humans. They shouldn't be able to reach this far into Aravot."

"I don't know, but it troubles me. I heard Semyaza's name mentioned, and he was one of the Watchers on Eretz. The humans aren't meant to be aware that the Watchers even exist, so why are they in their prayers?"

"Something's wrong, Michael. I can *feel* it. Something terrible is happening on Eretz. We should find Gabriel. He has always been far more sensitive to the humans than we are, and if we can hear the prayers, he must be able to as well."

"I don't think we'll have to go looking," Michael said as he felt Gabriel's presence moving toward them. "He's coming with Rafael."

Uriel continued to pace and mutter as they waited. Michael strained his ears to try and hear the voice again.

Elyon, Hashem, Creator, we will all die if they are allowed to keep ruling us. The giants are eating our flesh… The connection to the voice faded as Gabriel and Rafael landed beside them.

"Michael! Please, you must come with me," Gabriel said as he grabbed Michael's forearms. "Eretz is being torn apart."

"By what? Uriel and I heard a voice…"

"It's Enoch; he's *kedoshim*, a favorite of Elyon," Gabriel explained. "I heard him too, so I left *Shamayim* to see what's happening. The Watchers are destroying everything."

"How come we didn't know about this earlier?" Michael asked as they took to the air.

"I don't know. All the angels are connected to the Heavens. We should have felt their betrayal."

"We need to go to the temple and seek an audience," Michael instructed.

As they flew closer to the Great Temple, they could hear the Cherubim singing and the hum of praises in the throne room.

Michael, a voice said, touching his mind, and he halted his descent. *Come to me in the Great Libraries.*

"What is it?" Rafael asked.

"We've been summoned to the libraries. Come, brothers. bar-Elaha wishes to speak with us."

The Great Libraries stood like a jewel in the crown of Aravot. Michael had spent long hours in its wondrous caverned halls reading from the books of the living. The libraries themselves were made of crystal and contained row upon row of shelves. The roof was painted a rich lapis blue, so when the words of the living flowed into the temple, streaming in like wisps of golden smoke, the roof looked like stars in the night sky.

Michael and the others walked silently through the hushed halls until they found bar-Elaha, the Son of God, sitting in one of the small courtyard alcoves. Unlike the others of Aravot, he had the aspect of a human, his eyes the only thing betraying his divinity. As he read from the scroll spread out before him, a seven-tiered fountain bubbled behind him, making a soft musical sound. Unlike the books of the sons of Adam, this scroll's paper was the pale blue of the angels.

"Master," Michael said and bowed deeply. "You wished to speak with us?"

"You were seeking an audience, and now you have one. What's wrong?"

"Prayers from Enoch of Eretz reached us deep in Aravot. Semyaza and a group of Watchers are causing death and chaos on the Earth. We didn't sense it earlier, but the Watchers are all connected to Heaven. We should have sensed a change in them."

"Semyaza and his brothers have separated themselves from Heaven, that's why you weren't aware of the disturbance." He touched the scroll gently, and Michael knew who it belonged to. Even separated from them, Semyaza's deeds would still be recorded.

"We have to stop them," Uriel grumbled beside them. "They'll cause too much damage, and it will confuse the humans to have angels acting like this."

"They already have," the Son said. "They have taught them the Mysteries, but they have been on Eretz for so long that they taught them those that were rejected."

"What are they thinking? The Mysteries are secret knowledge not meant for humans. The rejected ones were cast aside for a reason!" Rafael exclaimed, and then bowed his head apologetically for his outburst.

"You're right, Rafael," the Son said. "The Watchers shared this knowledge and set in motion their own ruin as well as mankind's."

"There's still time," Michael replied. "Send us to Eretz to stop Semyaza and the other Watchers. We can prevent their poison from spreading and corrupting mankind."

"It may be too late for that. The seed has been sown."

"Talk to Enoch. He's *kedoshim* despite the Watchers' influence. There could still be hope," begged Michael. Their master was silent for a long moment, his eyes gazing at the water glittering in the fountain.

"Very well, Michael. I'll allow Enoch a vision of Aravot and all that will befall his people. Those who heed his warnings can still be saved. You and your brothers will bring Semyaza and the fallen brothers to justice. Kill the monstrous Nephilim. The angels that don't die in the conflict will be bound and thrown into a pit under the Duda'el Desert."

"But angels are immortal," Rafael said in a small voice.

"The humans are immortal too, though they like to forget that. Semyaza and the others cut themselves off from Heaven and the grace of their own free will. They can be killed like humans. The rest must be bound in rock, and there they can remain until the end of all things. Go and deal with this," the Son commanded. "Michael, I need a word with you alone." The others bowed respectfully and left their leader to follow after them.

"My Lord?"

"This *kedoshim* Enoch. I need you to protect his family from the violence that's to come," he said, his brown eyes solemn. "It has been revealed to me that they have a great future in front of them."

"As you wish."

"He'll be shown many things that no human has ever been privy to, and he'll witness my naming."

"You have chosen? That is—" Michael dropped his head. "I'm sorry. I didn't mean to interrupt."

"You and the other three archangels won't be here for the ceremony, so I wanted to tell you before you left. El-Elyon has decreed that during my life as a human I will be called 'he who rescues.'"

"He who rescues," Michael whispered, his mind already wondering why that name should be chosen.

"In the land of my birth, it will be said Yeshua," he replied.

"Yeshua." Michael let the word roll on his tongue. "A good name."

"A self-fulfilling one," Yeshua said as he laid a hand on Michael's shoulder. "Go now and stop Semyaza and the others from causing any more chaos."

"I will, although I can't understand why he would do this."

Yeshua smiled, but to Michael, he seemed sad. "You will, Michael. You will."

Michael left the Great Libraries and hurried to catch his brothers who would have already arrived on Eretz. Michael and the archangels would draw Semyaza out, but he needed to choose a space far enough away from humans that they would not become casualties.

Elyon, save me! Elyon! The voice of a woman slammed into Michael's head, full of fear. Michael fell toward the sound and saw a woman being dragged from a river, where she had been swimming and washing clothes. The woman wriggled out of the Watcher's hands and turned to run. Michael landed heavily in front of her, sword drawn.

"How dare you lay a hand on this woman!"

"Michael," the angel said, spitting his name out with obvious disgust. Michael recognized him, a Watcher called Armaros. "How dare *you* get between Semyaza's woman and me, her bodyguard."

"I'm *not* Semyaza's woman!" she shouted angrily, shaking with fury. Cold anger filled Michael when he spotted the bruise on her cheek and saw that her hands were scraped and bloody.

"Semyaza is king of this land now, and he has claimed you as his queen. You are his, woman."

"Stop this, Armaros. Yes, I know who you are. If you surrender to me, I'll be lenient in your punishment. I have been sent by Elyon. Your disobedience is at an end," said Michael.

"You have no authority here, Michael. This world doesn't belong to you or Elyon anymore; it belongs to us," Armaros said. His daggers flashed, his long blades narrowly missing Michael's cheek. He met Armaros's assault with the edge of his sword, the force knocking Armaros back. The Watcher backed out of reach and whistled high and sharp.

A heaving, thumping, crashing sound came in response, but Michael didn't wait to see what was coming. He attacked Armaros while he was caught off guard, and as Michael raised his arm to deliver the killing blow, something heavy knocked him aside. Michael rolled back to his feet as a giant bellowed above him.

"Oh, my brothers, what have you done?" he whispered as the Nephilim closed in on him. Without concern for his monstrous child, Armaros vanished through the air.

"Look out!" the woman cried as the Nephilim picked up a boulder and threw it at him. Michael moved aside and ran at his attacker, his sword swiping at its legs. Michael moved around it and flew into the air behind it. The Nephilim turned as Michael's blade cut through its thick neck, lopping its head off with a single blow. The huge body fell heavily to the ground and rolled in the mud.

Michael dropped back down beside the shaking woman; her bloody hands tried to hold her ripped dress together. Michael unclipped his cloak and draped its heavy folds around her.

"Don't be afraid. I'm not one of them," he said gently. "I won't hurt you. I am…not like them." The woman looked up at him, her dark eyes meeting his for the first time and holding his gaze as she weighed him up.

"No," she said finally. "I can see that." He offered her his hand, and she took it, adjusting his cloak so it would properly cover the tears in her dress.

"I'll escort you home safely. I don't think that Armaros would have gone far, especially if he's under orders. I am Michael; I've been sent to help."

"My father's prayers have been heard," she said and smiled with relief.

"And who is your father?"

"Enoch, son of Jared. I'm his daughter Na'amah."

When they arrived at Enoch's house the old man rushed to his daughter, happy to see her unharmed. She nodded politely to Gabriel, Uriel, and Rafael, who were sitting in Enoch's courtyard. Even though they had disguised their armor and wings under the simple dress of the people of Earth, there was still no mistaking what they were.

"Armaros attacked her, and I killed one of their Nephilim, disgusting brute that it was," Michael explained as Na'amah ducked away quickly. Michael watched her go, his nerves tight with concern. "Semyaza wants her for one of his brides."

"He has since the moment they revealed themselves," said Enoch sadly. "He has approached me many times about it, offered me all sorts of treasure for her. He's become less polite in recent times."

Uriel shook his silver head. "I don't understand what has come over them. What drove them to commit such crimes?"

"I was told that it was Semyaza who made them take human wives even though many didn't want them," explained Enoch as he took a date from the bowl on the table. "He convinced his other brothers somehow. The things that they have told people… There are rumors that there are temples built to them in the north. Effigies and idols and other likenesses being made." Enoch's face screwed up in disgust.

"It's going to be okay, Enoch. We'll stop them and save man from the corruption the Watchers have spread." Michael placed his hand gently on the old man's shoulder. "Don't worry about Na'amah. I promise I'll protect her and the rest of your family. Elyon has decreed it."

"I saw him," whispered Enoch. "I saw him in the great throne room of Aravot. He was given a name in the presence of Elyon and all of the hosts."

The angels looked to Michael who nodded in confirmation that what he said was true. Na'amah stood in the doorway of the house, her eyes glistening with the power of Enoch's vision. She was now in a simple woolen dress, her long, curly hair tied in braids.

"You should write down all that you have seen. Give it to your family, so they can share its knowledge and warnings with others," suggested Gabriel, pulling Michael's attention away from her with a jolt. She had nothing to adorn her, but an unknown emotion moved deep in Michael's chest. He suddenly knew why Semyaza wanted her for a bride.

"We need to find Semyaza and try to reason with him," Michael said later that night by the river. Enoch and Na'amah were sleeping, so the archangels had gone to dispose of the Nephilim body.

"The time has passed for reasoning with him. I wonder if he even knows why he has done this," Rafael said.

"The same reason Hel'el did what he did…because he *wanted* to," replied Uriel.

"No, Hel'el wanted to be like Yeshua. Semyaza wants to be a man," Gabriel said. "Something must have pushed him far enough to dare it."

"He saw that man needed guidance," a new voice said, and Armaros appeared through the trees. He held his hands up to show that he was unarmed.

"I didn't think that you would have left," Michael muttered, his hand resting on the pommel of his sword.

"Lord Semyaza wants the girl. She will be well treated if that's your concern."

"I saw how well you were treating her," Michael said with a snarl.

"Ah, but she is beautiful, isn't she?" Armaros studied him, an infuriating smirk on his face. "Even one as holy and as perfect as you has noticed that. Do you want to know why Semyaza wants to be a man? You only have to look at her dark eyes."

"That explains Semyaza's disobedience and betrayal, but what of you and your brothers?" Gabriel asked. "We don't understand why you would do such a thing."

"Because mankind is weak. They are like stupid children. It pained us to see them in such a state, like animals. They needed our knowledge to evolve."

"The things you taught them have been rejected!" Rafael shouted. "It will only bring chaos and death to mankind. They are worshipping you all like false gods and turning away from Elyon."

"And what? Have you been sent to stop us? How? Send us all home to Aravot to beg and plead like scolded children?" Armaros said mockingly. Michael wasn't fooled; he saw the nervous uncertainty in Armaros's green eyes.

"No, your fate has been decided, and you will never set your filthy feet upon any place in *Shamayim* ever again," said Uriel as he stepped toward him. Michael took him by the arm and stopped him.

"Go and tell Semyaza that this rebellion is over. Elyon has laid his judgment and condemnation on your heads. You won't see another week, and it will be over," Michael said coldly. "Go and beg mercy from Elyon; you're not going to get any from us."

Armaros backed away, his face twisted in disbelief and dread. His wings fanned out, and he lifted into the sky.

"So, they are hiding in the north," Uriel said as Armaros faded from their view.

"Enoch knows where," Michael replied. "Rest tonight, because it will be war tomorrow."

Over the following days, they moved from town to town, pulling down effigies, idols, and temples that had grown like poisonous weeds. Michael sent Rafael to the south, Gabriel to the east, Uriel to the north, and he traveled west. No matter how far they had gone in the day, Michael returned to Enoch's house every night. He wouldn't fail in his duty to protect the old man and his daughter. He found solace in their care and their company after days of destruction. The Nephilim had spread like a disease, but of the Watchers themselves, they saw nothing.

"They must be hiding in their stronghold in the north. I've seen hordes of Nephilim heading back there, being called to their fathers for extra protection," Uriel said.

"Then we'll challenge them and draw them into the desert. Even in their holdings, there will be innocent people. I want the humans spared as much as possible," Michael replied.

"How are Enoch and Na'amah?" Rafael asked. He had taken a great liking to the old man.

"They've been helping the refugees who have fled from the north," Michael answered, a smile coming to his lips. He didn't tell them about his long conversations with Na'amah, her smile, or her lively mind.

From what he had seen and the reports from his brothers, the destruction the Watchers had caused was spread wide in the land. Fear was growing inside of him because destroying the culprits wouldn't be enough. The damage was so wide, so corrupt. Elyon had destroyed Eretz after Hel'el's fall. Would the Most High decide to do it again? What would happen to Enoch and Na'amah?

"Michael?" Gabriel was looking at him expectantly. Rafael and Uriel were gone. "What is it? What's wrong?"

"Does it bother you that mankind has been corrupted because of angels? First with Hel'el's betrayal, then again with Adam, and now with Semyaza and the Watchers."

"Adam's decisions weren't of our making, Michael. Elyon gave them all free will and free choice. Hel'el whispered his lies, but they chose to believe them. They chose a piece of fruit over Elyon. *They chose.* I hate what Hel'el has done, and I don't know why Elyon still suffers him to live."

"The same reason he tolerates us all. Reckless love," Michael answered. "I suppose Yeshua will deal with Hel'el in time."

"You seem…troubled. Different. Has something happened?" Gabriel's golden brow furrowed in concern.

"It's something I feel *will* happen. I must get back to Enoch. Issue the challenge to Semyaza, so we can end this and go home."

When Michael returned to Enoch's house, he found Na'amah walking in the gardens.

"Michael? What's wrong?" she asked, reading his mood far too easily.

"I could ask you the same question. It's late, and you should be asleep," Michael answered with a smile.

"A nightmare woke me up, and I came to look at the stars and calm myself."

"What did you dream? Perhaps I can ease your mind about it."

Na'amah drew her shawl around her. "I dreamt I was in darkness," she began hesitantly. "It was a hot, choking blackness. I wasn't alone. I could smell animals around me, pressed in tightly. Outside there was thunder, but the thunder was made up of screams, booming together. I was weeping in the blackness. Hands clutched around my head to block out the noise. And then there was silence and nothingness, and that seemed so much worse. I woke, and I was afraid, then I wept with relief that it wasn't real."

Michael took her hand. "It was just a dream," he said softly. "Try not to let it trouble you. We have issued a challenge to Semyaza. Soon this nightmare will be over, and your life will return to normal."

"You're going to fight them all by yourselves?" she asked, her hand tightening over his.

"You're worried about us?"

"Of course, I am! Four against an army? Azazel has made them all weapons and armor. Their children have been bred for war."

"Na'amah, we are going to be fine. Elyon would have sent more warriors if we needed them. This is why I was made. We were made to be protectors and soldiers."

"But that is not *all* you are, Michael. You are my friend. I don't care that you're an angel and made for war; I still care for your safety."

"You have a kind heart, and I'm touched by your concern, even though it is unnecessary." Michael looked up at the stars above them and breathed in deeply. "Everything looks so different down here."

"You don't miss Aravot?"

"It's my home, but there are things on Eretz that I will miss more," he said, his heart aching in his chest when he looked at her. She quickly looked back up at the stars, but he saw her smiling in the darkness.

"I'll miss you too," she whispered. "When do you go to face Semyaza?"

"I'll leave tomorrow, meet up with the others, and wait for the Watchers in the desert. Semyaza is proud, so his ego won't keep us waiting long."

"And…and then you will go straight to Aravot?" Na'amah asked.

"I would have fulfilled what I came to do. I'll come back to make sure that you and Enoch are safe and to pay my respects." His thumb brushed the back of her hand lightly.

"To say goodbye you mean."

"I would change that if I could. You know that," Michael said softly and let her hand go. "You should try to get some sleep."

"Yes, you're right," Na'amah replied, and then she softly kissed his cheek. She hurried inside, leaving him touching his face and staring hopelessly after her.

The earth shook under Michael's feet. The last remaining Nephilim protecting the Watchers were approaching in a slow, lumbering march. The tension mounted between his shoulder blades, and he willed his mind to focus on the task in front of him. He would have to kill the Nephilim and imprison the seven Watchers that remained.

"What's wrong? You aren't here," Uriel snapped at him.

"He is worried," Gabriel answered. "He always gets that face when he is worried."

"Enough all of you. Focus on the task at hand and not on my facial expressions," Michael snapped.

"*You* focus on the task at hand and so will we." Uriel grunted.

The first enemy line was made of twenty Nephilim. The sun beat down on them, sending bright sparks off their heavy weapons and armor.

"I want that big one." Uriel pointed to the largest Nephilim, a twelve-foot, sweaty bulk of rage with thick, black hair who carried a battle-ax the size of Rafael.

"In that case, I'll stay close to you," Michael said. "In case you need the extra help."

Uriel rolled his eyes at him and drew his two swords. His wings unfolded, rising up to a complete circle in a defensive challenge. The archangels rarely revealed their wings, but this was a supernatural battle, and there was no need to hide who they really were. Gabriel's long, silver spear shone in his hand like a shard of lightning; Rafael beside him held a sword and shield, his demeanor calm and ready.

"Michael! It isn't too late for you to turn aside from this madness," Semyaza shouted across the battlefield. He looked powerful and majestic in his armor that had been crafted from onyx and gold. Even from a distance, Michael could see that it was Azazel's work. There was no angel better at making weapons of warfare than Azazel. It made his sin of teaching his craft to man so much greater. "Elyon teaches peace, Michael. Where is your justification for all this needless slaughter?" Semyaza continued.

"You speak of slaughter, completely disregarding the destruction you are responsible for. This is your punishment for disobeying your office and the will of Elyon. You have tried to make yourself a god amongst the humans like Hel'el before you. And like Hel'el, you'll be cast down," Michael replied before looking to his left. "Gabriel, now."

Gabriel lifted the shofar to his lips, the silver inlay on the horn flashing in the sunlight. Sound boomed from it, making the rock and earth shake beneath their feet. A few of the Nephilim dropped to the ground, covering their bleeding ears. As the final note faded, the archangels closed the gap between them and the enemy.

Uriel attacked the large Nephilim with a look of joyous fury. It bellowed its rage as Uriel dodged around its swiping arms and clambered up onto its back, taking its head off with a powerful blow of his sword. He dove off the tumbling giant and into the mayhem beneath him, the edges of his wings cutting through their corrupted flesh like adamantine blades.

Michael sliced his way to Uriel's side as Tam'el tried to clumsily block his path. Tam'el was an astrologer, not a warrior, and Michael's blade cut him in half.

"Michael!" Gabriel's shout made him turn just as an ax came down where he had been standing. Michael took off the Nephilim's arm, before it could raise it a second time. It exclaimed inarticulately in shock as Michael drove his sword up under its chin and into its brain. Michael jumped out of the way as the huge body started to topple. Gabriel was beside him in seconds, his spear running red with gore.

"Semyaza is hiding somewhere," he said. "Rafael is battling Azazel."

"Does he need help?" Michael asked.

"No, little brother has it under control."

Together they fought their way through the press of Nephilim bodyguards until they finally found the four remaining Watchers cowering behind Semyaza. Rafael had defeated Azazel, who sat spitting his fury as Rafael bound him tightly in chains.

"I won't be bound and executed like an animal," Semyaza said with a snarl.

"How far you have fallen to think that you are above any animal, Semyaza," said Michael. Michael dodged Semyaza's first spear strike as he charged him, slamming his shield into Semyaza's side. Pushed off-balance, Semyaza hit the dirt and rolled, but Michael tackled him down to the earth and held him there. Semyaza squirmed and said, "Kill me then, Hound of Heaven!"

"That isn't Elyon's will. You and those who swore themselves to you will be imprisoned under the earth. Death is too good for what your pride has led you to do."

"You think these people didn't want to know what we taught them? They begged us for the knowledge that Elyon had denied them. The women desired us, and they wanted us to put our strong children inside of them. Even Enoch's black-eyed daughter. Did you seriously think you could protect her from us, Michael? Did you think you could keep her from *me*? There is want and lust in your heart, brother, the same as ours. She cried out for you when I took her—" Michael drove his fists into Semyaza's face in a blind rage.

"Michael, enough! Don't stoop to his level," Uriel said as he gripped Michael's arms to stop him. "They'll suffer for what they have done."

"Gabriel! Bind these traitors together," Michael commanded as he pushed himself off Semyaza's broken body. He turned his back on the site of their despairing brothers, closing his ears to their pleas for mercy.

Elyon, stretch out your hand and cleave a prison for those who have betrayed you, Michael prayed.

The ground shook, and a pit opened up in the bloody battlefield. Without any ceremony, the screaming Watchers were pushed into the gaping blackness. Azazel swore and spat at Rafael, who shackled him to Semyaza. Michael picked up Semyaza, who was still screaming his curses, and threw him down, dragging Azazel with him. Uriel and Rafael dumped the bodies of the Nephilim in after them.

"Michael, go to Enoch. Make sure his family is safe," Gabriel said. "We can finish this."

Women scattered as Michael landed in front of Enoch's house. He found Enoch under a twisted fig tree in their small courtyard. On his lips were prayers to Elyon, the urgency of them betraying the broken spirit within.

"My lord." He rose quickly when he sensed Michael watching him.

"Where is she?" he asked urgently.

"In the upper room. If she doesn't die from her injuries, she's going to be crippled forever," Enoch said, his face crumpling and tears streaming.

"I'm sorry." Michael touched his shoulder gently before entering the house.

The upper room smelled of the beeswax, herbs, and incense that were burning to cleanse the room. Na'amah lay on a sleeping mat, her body covered with a sheet. Bandages had been wrapped around her wounds, and her face was bruised and broken.

Michael knelt down beside her. "Na'amah?"

"Is it over?" she asked, pain tearing her voice to pieces.

"It is done." Michael hesitantly touched her hand. "Forgive me. I should never have left you alone."

Her fingers slowly curled around his. "The town is talking. I hear the women saying that it would be better if I died, because I won't be able to have children even if a man was willing to marry a scarred and broken woman."

"Don't listen to them. Even like this, you're the most beautiful woman I've ever seen."

"I'm glad that you are here, Michael. I'll never forget the night we watched the stars. I did not want to be alone when I died…" The grip on his hand slackened as her eyes closed.

Fear and panic surged through Michael. "Na'amah?"

Without thought of consequence, Michael scooped her damaged body up into his arms and pulled her close to him, his wings folding in around them. He could feel the damage in her fragile human body, as she fought desperately for life.

Elyon, please, she is innocent, he prayed as his hot tears fell on her. Heat and power rose through him and poured out over her. The enclosure of his wings filled with golden light as the power of Elyon moved through her, healing her body and knitting everything that was broken. Her large, black eyes fluttered open as the bruises and cuts on her face healed.

Michael touched her hair, gently twisting his fingers amongst her curls. His hand cupped the softness of her cheek. She smiled up at him, her countenance glowing. Her lips pressed once inside of his wrist, leaving it burning.

"Thank you, my love," she whispered.

"Michael!" Gabriel gasped from the doorway. "What have you done?"

"Elyon healed her," Michael said as his wings moved back behind him. Na'amah's eyes were fixed on him as he tenderly laid her back down.

"Don't leave," she whispered. His hand stroked her face, knowing it would be for the last time.

"I have to. My task is done, but you will be safe now," he said, reassuring her.

"The Watchers aren't what I'm afraid of."

"Then what? Tell me."

"It doesn't matter," she said and turned her face away from him.

"Michael, we must leave now," Gabriel said.

"I'll join you in a moment. Go and fetch Enoch. He'll want to see his daughter is well," Michael replied without looking at him. He could see tears falling from Na'amah's eyes, and he could not bear it. "What is it?"

"You are leaving," she said, refusing to meet his eyes. "You aren't just an angel; you are an *archangel*, Michael. I'll never see you again, no matter how much I long for it, no matter how much I pray for it."

Michael rested his hand on her shoulder. "I'm sorry that it has to be this way. As I told you once before, if I could change what I am for anyone, it would be you." Michael kissed her brow before letting her go. "Know that I'll *always* watch over you."

His brothers stood outside with Enoch in the courtyard. All looked battle-tired and heartsore.

"Enoch, Na'amah is well again and resting," Michael said as he joined them. The others vanished, and Michael gripped Enoch's shoulders. "Take care of your daughter, son of Jared," he ordered before he launched himself into the sky.

Michael was summoned to the Garden of Shalom, the most beautiful of all the gardens in Heaven. Eden had been created in its image before Hel'el had befouled it. Michael sensed Elyon's presence, but it was the Son who came to him.

"Greetings, Yeshua." Michael bowed deeply.

"Lift your head and walk with me, Michael," he said, in the same voice that called him out of the infinite darkness. "Tell me about Earth."

"The influence of the Watchers has spread all over, Yeshua. We've killed the Nephilim, and the remaining Watchers are in their prison, but I fear the damage has been too great. There are still *kodesh* ones there like Enoch, but they are few. The forbidden knowledge has corrupted them."

"Tell me about Na'amah."

Michael's mouth went dry as he searched for the words. "She is a courageous woman. Semyaza did terrible things to her because she helped me. She has a beautiful spirit that shines on everyone around her."

"Semyaza didn't do that to her just because she helped you, but because she loves you. Do you love her, Michael?"

"I love all of Elyon's creations," Michael answered automatically.

Yeshua laid a hand on his arm. "Speak your heart."

"I would never become like Semyaza to be with her, but yes, I love her. I am an angel, so it will never be."

"What if you weren't an angel? Would you still serve Elyon faithfully in the path laid out for you?"

"I'll always serve you. I don't understand why you are asking such questions."

"I'm asking because I want to know the measure of your heart, Michael. Na'amah is a beautiful daughter of Eve, but I wanted to see if it's love and not lust that drives you. Unlike the Watchers, you let her go, and you didn't cut yourself away to be with her. Because of this, I have interceded on your behalf with Elyon. If you are willing, Elyon wishes to make a covenant with you. You will be granted a human life when the earth needs your wisdom and strength. During this time, Na'amah will also be reborn. If you can find her, you can be with her as man and woman. But know this, Michael, those times won't be easy. The task you'll be sent to perform will need to be carried out whether or not you find each other. You'll have no memories of your angelic life, but when the time comes and you need to remember, I'll send your brothers to guide you on your path."

Michael shook at the honor, the chance to be with her, to be human. "When would I become human? The lives of men are not infinite. Na'amah is already of marriageable age and—"

"You won't be sent during Na'amah's life. Her destiny is to marry Methuselah's grandson Noah. It must be this way."

"But why?"

"You said yourself that the evil the Watchers let loose on the earth has corrupted it. Only Enoch's family has remained true to Elyon. The earth is going to flood, and through Noah and Na'amah new life will begin again."

Michael sank to the grass beneath him. She had seen her future in her dreams, and he had dismissed them, refusing to acknowledge the truth. "I thought we had done enough. This is the second time that mankind has had to be annihilated because of angelic interference. Elyon should consider destroying us instead. How many times will he do this before he abandons mankind forever?"

"After the Flood he will make a new covenant with mankind and many more after that. He won't destroy the earth again. Next time all hope is gone, it will be me that he sends, Michael. Not you or your avenging brothers. It will be up to me to save them all." Michael looked up at him. That such a burden would be placed upon him made Michael feel ashamed of his own.

"I'll help you in any way that I can. I will accept the covenant you have offered me, this chance to be with her. I won't back down from any task." Yeshua helped him to his feet and embraced him.

"I'm honored to have you by my side, Michael. Be patient in the time to come. Elyon's covenants endure forever, and he won't forget this one he has made with you."

"A covenant is sealed with blood. Does Elyon wish me to go back to Earth to make the sacrifices?"

"There will be bloodshed, Michael. But it will be yours. You will live and you will die as a human. That is to be the seal between you for all time."

Mychal woke to the feel of a cool, damp cloth lightly dabbing at his forehead.

"Oh God, what happened?" he said. His throat felt like he had been screaming for hours. Maybe he had been. He opened his eyes and saw Jael's concerned face hovering over him.

"Uriel almost let you drown," she said and handed him a mug. "Try to drink some of this. Your throat is going to be messed up from all the water you swallowed."

Mychal sat up slowly and sipped the hot water, lemon, and honey concoction. "How long was I out?"

"About eight hours now."

"Where's Uriel?"

"He was summoned," Jael replied ominously, sitting down on the couch with a huff. "You know, bloody secret angel business."

Mychal climbed off the floor and sat down beside her. He placed the cup on the small coffee table and leaned back into the cushions. Unexpectedly, he began to cry.

"Are you okay?" asked Jael.

"No. I don't know what's happening. I don't even know why I'm crying." He wiped his tears away with the back of his hand. "I don't cry."

"Yeah, me neither." Jael's expression softened. "Uriel said you were remembering. Tell me what happened?"

Unable to hold back the emotions bombarding him, Mychal did.

31

IT HAD BEEN WEEKS since Nazirah discovered the first giant skeleton. The name Goliath had stuck, but now they had discovered he wasn't alone. Another seven bodies had been exhumed, and the ground-penetrating radar equipment was picking up dozens more every day.

Nazirah and the others were starting to agree that they had found a mass grave, but as Frank ominously foretold, they had more questions than answers.

"These men and women were huge and strong," Frank said to Nazirah over breakfast. "They would have had a much longer life span than the average human at the time."

"The real question that's splitting my mind to pieces is how they all died at once like this. The wounds were made by blades. The cracks in the bones and the decapitations suggest warfare. What could have been strong enough to make that kind of damage? Even an army of humans would struggle against ten of these giants."

"What if they went to war with one another? The Near East hasn't known peace for any long measure of time."

"I know that, but there still would have been a winning side. Where are the winners?"

"Nazirah! Nazirah!" Noah came running into the tent. "There's a helicopter coming, but it's not HeosCorp or military."

"Does it look like the press? A news leak is the last thing we need!" Nazirah put down her fruit salad and hurried after him.

The only thing HeosCorp had been nonnegotiable on was that all media releases were to be organized and authorized by them. They wouldn't even allow Nazirah to send samples to the universities for analyses or second opinions. It was one of the reasons they were willing to set up a demountable city in the middle of the desert and give her whatever lab equipment she asked for. If there had been a leak, she would be raked over the coals. Noah handed her a small pair of binoculars and pointed into the distance.

"Damn it," Nazirah muttered.

The helicopter was a deep red and had no identifying logos. If they had enough cameras, they could shoot the site from the air.

"Cover it up!" she shouted as she ran toward the dig area. They had been placing tarps over the bodies at night to protect them, and now fifteen people scrambled to stop working and cover them back up. The helicopter circled twice before landing on the makeshift air pad.

"Keep your cool, Nazirah," Frank warned as she strode toward the helicopter, wielding the binoculars like a weapon.

The blades stopped just as a man in a shining white linen shirt and khaki pants stepped out of the door. He was tall and tanned and walked toward her with an easy confidence. Sandy-blond hair curled around the corners of his aviator sunglasses, and he smiled winningly. Nazirah gripped the binoculars harder. Whoever had leaked information to this media scum was going to get their ass kicked.

"Stop where you are!" she shouted as the engines died down. "You're on private property and are trespassing illegally!"

The man stopped and held up his hands in surrender. "I swear I come in peace," he said in English with an accent that had an undefinable world-traveler lilt.

"I don't care if you come in peace. You aren't allowed to be here. If you take one step closer, I swear—"

"Is everything all right here, Mr. Heosphoros?" A big man in a black suit had come to stand behind him, a small, white cardboard box in his hand. The earth dropped out from underneath Nazirah as her rich benefactor lowered his hands.

"I think we are good here, Az. Nazirah just looked so beautiful being angry and protective that I didn't have the heart to stop her." Mr. Heosphoros smiled fondly at her, sending a blush running along her skin from head to toe.

"I'm sorry, Mr. Heosphoros. I've never seen a photo of you, and I assumed you would be old," she blurted out. Frank sniggered behind her.

"If you are going to apologize for anything, apologize for calling me Mr. Heosphoros. No wonder you thought I was ancient, having to wrap your lovely tongue around my name like that. My friends call me Lucian, and I would very much like you to be my friend."

Nazirah fought the urge to look at her feet shyly. Instead, she stuck out her hand.

"It's a pleasure to meet you finally, sir...Lucian." His hand was firm when he took her dusty one and pressed it gently.

"Did you hear that, Az? Now she has knighted me." He laughed, and Nazirah smiled back. "It's my pleasure to meet *you*. I'm so excited to see what you have uncovered! Please escort me; show me everything. Oh, here. I almost forgot." Lucian took the white box from Az and offered it to her. "These came from my estate. I saw all the requests you had placed for them, so I knew they must be a favorite." Nazirah opened the box, releasing the sweet cinnamon, musky smell of dried figs. "Thank you. That's extremely thoughtful. They are just one of my little quirks when I'm on a dig."

"Quirks are a little like unusual vices, brilliant in all their forms. Shall we?" He offered Nazirah his arm, a gesture she had always scoffed at when men tried it on her before. He made it seem easy and natural though, so she took it, ignoring Frank's quizzical stare.

"We have uncovered seven complete bodies now," Nazirah said as they walked. "More are being unearthed every day. To be honest, I've been thinking about requesting some more people. This dig is going to be bigger than any of us imagined."

"I knew you would find it," Lucian said as he watched them move the tarps once more. "There was so much passion in your proposal; there was no doubt in my mind that you would be worth every penny I could lavish upon you."

Nazirah soon found herself enjoying watching Lucian Heosphoros spread enthusiasm wherever he went. His excitement for the smallest, most mundane aspect of the project had everyone from Frank to the sour-faced caterer convinced they were vitally important. No wonder he was such a successful businessman.

"What do you think happened?" he asked curiously. Nazirah brought up the scans of the area onto large monitors. They were in an air-conditioned demountable building that served as Nazirah's lab and office.

"Frank and I were speculating about that just before you arrived," Nazirah said.

Lucian was looking at everything in her office from the stacks of papers and books to the pictures taped to the walls and her lucky Indiana Jones action figure that had been a gift from her older brother when she graduated. Lucian slipped his sunglasses up on the top of his head to reveal sea-green eyes. He was a knockout, and Nazirah suspected he knew it. She focused back on the monitors.

"What theories did you and Frank come up with?" He was studying a pho-to of her at a dig in Thebes.

"I think a war, but I've no idea as to why or who the enemy was. There isn't any explanation."

"Yet," Lucian said confidently. "If it was a war, perhaps we need to look for a bigger bully."

"Humans wouldn't stand a chance."

"I wasn't thinking humans."

"Then what? I can't believe there would be something larger than these gi-ants."

"But six months ago, you wouldn't have believed in giants either."

Nazirah folded her arms. "Are you making fun of me, Mr. Heosphoros?"

A mischievous look flashed through his eyes. "I wouldn't dream of teasing such a formidable woman."

"I'm hardly formidable."

"Trust me. You are definitely formidable. Intimidatingly brilliant too."

"And *you* are flattering me, though I can't quite figure out why."

"Because I'm smitten; I thought that was obvious," he said dramatically, a hand over his heart.

Nazirah started to laugh before she could stop herself. "You are goofy and not what I expected."

"Good! You, however, are exactly what I expected. But I have been stalking you quite aggressively," he admitted bashfully.

"That's illegal even for rich playboys. Can I ask why?"

"Why? Because I'm passionate about archaeology and finding treasure and preserving history. You are one of the most promising new archaeologists in the world, and now you have discovered something truly unique." He sighed with exasperation. "And you are really beautiful on top of it all, and it's distracting. I am your boss. I demand you to be less beautiful, so I can concentrate on all the other amazing things around me."

Nazirah rolled her eyes. "That's right. You *are* my boss. There is a profes-sional line that shouldn't be crossed no matter how charming and flattering the employer may be."

Lucian Heosphoros's smiled widened. "Those professional lines sound fas-cinating! You will be able to tell me all about them over dinner tonight. You can call it a business meeting if it makes you more relaxed. But please bring that blush with you; it is delightful."

"It is sunburn."

"Of course it is."

"Will we be talking about work at this business meeting?"

"We can talk about absolutely anything you wish. Except for pearls and the number three, because they frighten me."

"Like Tesla?"

Genuine pleasure filled his features. "You know that? Just…just marry me right now, Nazirah, and put me out of my misery."

"Sorry, not possible. I'm afraid of commitment."

"My heart breaks." Lucian chuckled, and it rolled through her. The moment was shattered by Az knocking on the office door.

"I am sorry to interrupt, sir, but you have a phone call. It is Mr. Osmo, otherwise I would have taken a message," he said.

"If only all my investors were as charming as you, Nazirah. Have dinner with me tonight. Please. I have no dishonorable intentions, I swear it. I just find your company so refreshingly genuine. It's a rare commodity."

"I'll think about it. I have a lot of work to do." She pointed meaningfully at the monitors.

"You are a real ballbuster." He smiled as he stepped out into the sunlight. The door shut behind him, and Nazirah could finally breathe again.

Nazirah threw herself into work for the rest of the day. She did her best to ignore everyone's gossip about their engaging employer. After working on all the data she had received from the ground-penetrating radar, Nazirah was sure it was a mass grave that was hundreds of feet deep.

It raised even more questions, like how would they have managed to dig such a pit with the tools of the time? Unless it had been a place where they had buried their dead over many, many years. But if they had existed that long, why wasn't there more record of them?

Her stomach rumbled loudly in response. She barricaded herself in her bedroom, spreading sheets of paper out on her bed and tacking them to the walls. Her eyes and head were aching, and the black fonts were jumping.

Walking into the little bathroom, she had a quick, cold shower to scrub off the grime of the day. She hadn't even looked at her email inbox, a task she only liked to tackle in her pajamas. As she shut off the water, she heard a loud knocking on the door. Grabbing her towel, she rushed to answer it.

Az, the ever-formidable bodyguard, was waiting for her. "Mr. Heosphoros sent me to get you. He had some calls from government officials about shutting down the site, and he needs your assistance at once."

"Those damn bastards! Tell him I will be right there. I just need to get changed."

"You had best hurry. He's going to have a video conference in fifteen minutes." Nazirah shut the door and pulled on jeans and a fresh T-shirt, running a comb through her wet, curly hair as she pushed her feet into her boots.

Nazirah had been told by Frank that HeosCorp was erecting a tent for Lucian to work from, but what she found was something that could have been pulled from an *Arabian Nights* film set.

"Rich people." She sighed when she saw it.

"This way," Az instructed.

Inside the billowing orange-and-red monstrosity was a large ebony table with books and papers, steamer trunks, and through sheer walls of fabric, she even glimpsed a four-poster bed.

"I have Nazirah here as you requested, sir," Az said when they found Lucian reclining on large pillows. The sides of the tent had been lifted to show the moon coming up over the desert; the tent seemed to be purposely faced away from the camp. Torches were hammered into the ground, and lanterns were hanging from the cedar tent poles.

"What do you think of my camping spot?" Lucian asked from his cushions.

"I think you have forgotten the meaning of packing light. You are set up like a sultan. When is this video conference? I have work I need to get to tonight."

"What video conference…oh, that! I just told Az that to get you here for our business dinner. Sit down, please. You are making me nervous standing there glowering at me." He gestured to the pillows beside him, but Nazirah positioned herself opposite from him with a low wooden table between them. "You can relax, Nazirah. I am not going to bite you." His face turned thoughtful. "Well, I would bite you, but not until you asked me to."

"You don't handle rejection very well, do you?" she said as her posture eased a little.

"I'm not familiar with this 'rejection' word you are using."

"Something else for me to educate you on."

Lucian laughed. "Educate over food. I'm starving."

As if he were some magical white boy genie, caterers filed in with dishes of fruit, salad, seafood, flatbread, olives, tagines, and spiced couscous. He poured her some wine "from the estate," and the people disappeared once more.

"How is work going?" he asked conversationally, like they were best friends meeting after a hard day.

"Frustrating," Nazirah admitted and sipped the fruity spiced wine. She usually hated wine, but this one was exquisite, the flavor changing the longer it sat in her mouth.

"Still more questions than answers?" Lucian clicked his tongue. "Any idea who they are yet?"

"I have only one theory, but it is very unscientific." Nazirah ate an olive while she watched his long, tanned fingers pull apart steaming bread. He caught her watching and offered her a piece. She took some to cover for being caught watching him, but the bread was as delicious as everything else.

"I find that sometimes scientists like to claim authority on everything they *think* they know about and dismiss all the things they don't. It's like they want to take all the mystery and magic out of the world. Do you ever feel this way? Even as a scientist?" asked Lucian.

"All. The. Time," she admitted.

"I thought so," Lucian said with a wink. He had somehow managed to move closer to her, but Nazirah found she didn't mind. "Tell me about your unscientific theory. Don't leave me hanging."

Nazirah took a deep breath and said, "Angels."

Lucian coughed on his wine. "You did warn me, but really? Angels? I know we found giants, but my mind instantly goes to unicorn after giant, definitely not angel. I'm sure that logical mind of yours didn't come to that conclusion willingly."

"It didn't, trust me. Giants are mentioned a few times in the Torah, Genesis and Numbers mostly. They were the monster children of the Watchers and human women. They were wiped off the face of the earth, and then Hashem flooded the world. I can't stop thinking about it. I'm sure we will get answers the further we dig. It always ends up that way."

Lucian placed a hand on her shoulder. "I have complete faith that you will discover what you are looking for. Unscientific or otherwise." The gesture was meant to be friendly, but Nazirah's skin was on fire.

"T-thank you," she said, drinking a quick mouthful of her wine. His hand moved so he could brush his fingers over her cheek.

"So, you did remember to bring that delightful blush," he whispered.

Nazirah's pulse hammered in her throat. His lips met hers in a soft press, and all thoughts of lines and employers and angels vanished from her mind. Her mouth opened as he kissed her again, his hand dropping from her face to trail down her back.

He stopped and pulled back from her. "I'm so sorry. I don't want you to think I am taking liberties with you, and I don't want you to feel like you are being pressured to reciprocate my advances because of the funding for the dig and—"

"And do you always fluster about this much when you are trying to seduce someone?" Nazirah smiled as she licked his top lip before kissing him again.

Lucian's hands gripped her hips, and he pulled her onto his lap. She could feel his heart racing in her mouth as she kissed the side of his neck. With every taste, she wanted, *needed*, more of him.

His hands moved to unbutton her shirt, and she struggled to get out of it. There was too much fabric between them. Her skin was burning as he pulled off her jeans. Underneath Lucian's clothes was a strong, athletic torso, and she ran her hands down the smooth golden hardness of his flat abs and moved them to grip his shoulders.

"You are like some beautiful golden Achilles," she murmured appreciatively. "Definitely not the body of a businessman."

"And you think I expected to find the Queen of Sheba in the middle of this desert? I think we have both outdone each other's expectations."

She gasped as fingers slid under the edge of her cotton underwear and touched her gently. She hadn't been with a man in over a year, and none of them had had this instant effect on her. Shaking, he moved her back onto the cushions, and his firm weight settled on top of her, his mouth kissing her heavy breasts.

"You are so lovely," he said as he looked down at her.

Nazirah's gasp was caught by his lips as he pushed deep inside of her. Blood roared in her ears as her body tried to contain the sensation. She rolled him onto his back, flicking her long hair out of her face. His hands trembled as he gripped her hips while she rode him. As her orgasm ripped through her, her only conscious thought was that she was determined to be grateful more often.

Lucian waited until Nazirah was asleep before he pulled on his khaki trousers and slipped out into the cool night. Everyone had gone to their quarters for the night. He stepped carefully under the fence of the dig area. Tarps had been laid over the most exposed skeletons, but more bodies had been found that day and still lay open under the night sky.

Lucian crouched down amongst the bodies and placed a hand over a skull. He could feel the power in them still. The part of them that was angel called out to him. Something else was calling to him, stronger than the bones.

Buried deep under the pile of dry death he could feel a spark of life. Angelic life.

So, there are some left, after all. Lucian smirked. He stretched his power through the earth like a subtle stream, searching for a weakness. He found a soft spot in the prison and weakened it further, just enough to cause a crack. As he retracted his power, he sensed the life stir from its slumber. He smiled as he got up and dusted his hands off.

Now all he had to do was wait.

Deep in the earth, Azazel jolted in his chains. Something disturbed his long sleep. He sat up, his muscles screaming from disuse. The chains around his feet clinked loudly as he struggled to stand.

"Semyaza?" he said, his voice wheezing out of him. He reached across the wall until he found the angel he was shackled to. "Semyaza?" He stroked his companion's head, fearing that he had succumbed to death. A shudder passed through Semyaza, and relief flooded Azazel.

"Azazel," a deep voice whispered. "What's wrong?"

"I don't know. I felt…I felt something. It woke me. It was an angel."

"A dream, Azazel. Nothing more. No angel would reach out to us," Semyaza replied, the despair in his voice dampening Azazel's enthusiasm.

"Perhaps it wasn't one of us, but something has changed. Can you not sense it?" Azazel ran his hands over the earthen walls, and Semyaza was forced to climb to his feet. They were chained together, and there would be no stopping Azazel's curiosity.

"It has been too long, Azazel. God and all of his creations have forgotten who we were. The human lives are fragile…"

"You are wrong! I can feel…I can feel…here! Semyaza, here!" Azazel took his leader's hand and put it on the wall.

For the first thousand years, they had searched every possible way to escape the prison. There had been no weakness in its design, and now there suddenly was. Small, but it was enough. Years of frustration surged through Azazel, and he slammed his fists against the wall. Rock and bone showered down onto them.

"I can't believe it," Semyaza said as he placed a hand on Azazel's shoulder.

"Come, brother. Let's climb our way from this tomb and be free once more."

"We are cut off from the Heavens, Azazel. What would be waiting for us up there?"

Azazel gripped Semyaza's shoulders hard. "The *world*. Our power might be lessened, but we have survived throughout all this torment, while our brothers have died. We are the strongest. We have paid for our crimes long enough."

"You're right." Semyaza straightened, the old determination back in his voice.

Together, they turned back to the wall of their dead children and attacked it with all of their strength.

Nazirah woke to the earth shuddering beneath her. The space in the bed beside her was empty.

"Lucian?" she murmured as she sat up. Her head was foggy from sleep and wine. She picked up his discarded shirt and slipped it over her head. It smelled of expensive aftershave and sex. She smiled at the memory of his lips on hers as she walked through the tent searching for him.

A high-pitched scream tore through the still night like razor blades. Nazirah ran from the tent, searching to find the source of it. Alien shrieks and the sounds of metal and equipment crashing followed. People stumbled out of their beds, trying to figure out what was wrong.

"What's going on?" Frank asked when he found her.

"I don't know! Stay inside!" Nazirah ran to the dig site and only just stopped herself from slipping into a massive open hole. She stumbled back from it.

Something had buried its way down through the bones. *Or dug its way out.* Gunfire jolted her, and she turned to follow the sound of the screams. Around the mess tent, she tripped and fell over the body of their sour-faced cook. Half of the body had been ripped clean off and tossed out into the darkness.

Nazirah tried not to throw up as she struggled back to her feet. The engines of the Jeeps were starting up. She saw headlights and ran toward them. Something huge and black landed on the bonnet of the Jeep in a crash of screaming metal and glass.

"My God…" she gasped.

An angel, broad wings stretching out behind it, ripped the car apart with its bare hands. A thick broken chain dragged behind it. It roared in anger, and it was the most terrifying noise Nazirah had ever heard. She clapped her hands over her ears to keep them from bursting.

Its pale, angry eyes turned to her, and she ran. Her only thought was to keep going as fast as her legs could take her. She pushed someone over in the dark and kept going. Cries of rage and death rose up all around her, but she didn't look back. A Jeep came up behind her, and the door opened.

"Nazirah! Get in quickly!" Lucian shouted, and she threw herself inside.

"What the fuck?" she screamed.

"Breathe, just breathe," Lucian said as he floored it. Nazirah looked behind her in the rearview mirror to see a fiery helicopter being thrown. She stuck her head between her knees as she hyperventilated.

"We need to call someone…the IDF or just fucking someone," she said as she straightened once more.

When they got to the top of the first ridge, Lucian stopped the Jeep and they got out. The camp below them was burning. Two huge shapes moved amongst the wreckage, the spine-chilling screeches echoing out of the desert.

"Hashem save us, there are two of them."

"Aren't they just…magnificent?" said Lucian, all traces of warmth gone from his voice.

Nazirah looked at him like he was insane. "They are killing everyone, Lucian!"

"Yes. They are quite angry and frustrated after being locked up for so long." His voice had completely changed now. She stepped back from him, fear making her stomach clench.

"You knew they were down there?" She choked on the words.

"Of course, I *knew*. I just needed a human to finally find them for me. It was one of the things they did when they trapped them. They made sure none of the fallen ones could ever find the grave. I just had to wait."

"What are you?"

Lucian laughed, and a cold shudder ran through her. He looked wild, his eyes turning feral as he stared her down.

"I'm just like them. Abandoned and furious and out for blood." A shimmer passed over him, and his physical form started to melt. Nazirah tried to run but something heavy struck her, and she slipped on the rocky ground.

"Where do you think you can go?" He picked her up with taloned hands, and she screamed in pain.

Lucian held her up, so she was forced to look at him. His face was now all sharp angles and furious burning eyes. The side of his face was riddled with burn marks. Wings were outstretched on either side of him, feathers running into sharp-clawed dragon wings.

Despite her fear, Nazirah lashed out at him, trying to gouge out his terrifying eyes. He laughed and tossed her. She slammed into the windscreen of the Jeep.

"Who are you?" she whispered through bleeding lips. He grabbed her leg and pulled her toward him across the bonnet.

"I am Hel'el, the light of God and all the morning. Look upon the ancient enemy of your people, daughter of Abraham!" he hissed viciously.

"Hashem, help me." Nazirah wept, and he laughed cruelly in her face. Nazirah knew there would be no chance of getting away, no hope of surviving. She thought of the night they had spent together, and she almost vomited in revulsion. She kicked out at him in despair.

"What's wrong, Nazirah? You were so accommodating a few hours ago." He mocked her as he grabbed her tightly by the throat. "I bet you are still wet from me being inside of you." His other hand ripped her underwear to shreds.

Nazirah cried out in hopeless fear as clawed hands scratched her skin to ribbons. She tried to struggle, but the grip on her neck squeezed.

"Pray to your God, whore, and when you get into his presence, you can explain to him how you destroyed all of humanity when you spread your legs for Hel'el."

Nazirah no longer had the air left in her to scream as his clawed hand drove inside her, snapping her pelvis and shredding her insides.

Forgive me, Hashem. Forgive me, she thought. The triumphant glare of Hel'el's eyes was the last thing she saw before she died.

32

Long ago in Egypt

MICHAEL WALKED THROUGH THE slave slums of Thebes. He hadn't been to Earth since the Watchers and was now drinking in the sights of humanity, eager to see all that had changed in the brief moments of time that they had. Elyon had commanded his people to paint the doors and lintels with the blood of a sacrificed sheep, to prepare them for what was to happen next. Elyon had told them about the covenant with Abraham, and that his people would endure four hundred years of slavery. But now that time was at an end, and a dazzling future was waiting for them.

Michael remembered the night that Yeshua had summoned him in Aravot. "Come with me, Michael, and see the miracles that Elyon will make with Enoch's kin. This is a moment you wouldn't want to miss." Michael took his hand, and then they were standing on a cliff in the wilderness of Horeb. A man was tending to a flock of sheep and goats, bringing them closer to the shelter of the cliff to protect them from the night.

"Who is he?" Michael asked curiously.

"That's Moses. A great destiny has been set out before him, and tonight it will be revealed to him. Tonight is the beginning."

"Is-is someone there?" Moses called out, gripping his staff defensively.

"Can he hear us?"

"No, but he can sense us watching him. Look!" Yeshua pointed at the dead tree beneath them that blazed with light. Michael watched in awe as Moses removed his shoes with shaking hands and the voice of Elyon filled the canyon. His people, Na'amah's people, wouldn't be subjected to slavery any longer. Elyon was going to fulfill the covenant that he had made with Abraham; their years of oppression under the Egyptians would be over.

"Why are you showing me this?" Michael asked. Yeshua smiled at him.

"To remind you that no matter how much time passes, Elyon honors his covenants and his promises. I know you miss her, but be patient, Michael. Your time is nearer than you would think."

The iron smell of blood and raw flesh brought Michael back to himself as he and Uriel neared the slave dwellings. Moses had come to the people and given them Elyon's instructions. Each household was to cover their doors and lintels with the blood of a lamb as a sign that they were Abraham's people. The *Malach HaMavet*, the Angel of Death, was going to pass through Egypt in a few hours, and Michael and Uriel had been sent to do one final check that they were all protected.

"There's so much fear in this place," Uriel commented as they walked in between the houses.

"There's hope too. They know that Elyon hasn't forgotten them. Tonight is the beginning of a whole new life for them. I wish that I could be amongst them at this time."

"Elyon didn't need you. He has Moses to guide his people," Uriel said. Michael loved his brother, but he wouldn't understand until he could live with humans as one of them. "I saw you looking at the faces of the women today. You're seeking her."

"I know she's not here. Elyon said she would only be reborn when I was. These are her people, descendants of Noah. She may not be amongst them, but I feel her presence," admitted Michael.

"Be patient," Uriel said as he checked the door opposite him. "Your time with her will come again. I like having you with me tonight, brother. This night will always be remembered. In thousands of years, they will still be celebrating it every year. It's one of the greatest blessings of the angels that we can witness such times. Truly Elyon's creation is fascinating."

Michael stopped in front of an unmarked door. He knocked, and an old woman was quick to answer. Michael had made sure they were disguised as humans, but she gaped up at him.

"May I ask why you have not marked your door this night as Moses commanded?"

"I'm old, so I gave my sheep to the other families to protect their little ones. They have more to protect than I."

"For your generosity, I promise you won't be harmed this night. Go back to your bed and rest easy." She kissed his hand and closed the door. Michael ran his hands around the frame, leaving a faint blue shimmer behind that only the angels could see. Uriel was smiling at him.

"It never ceases to amuse me that Elyon made you the strongest and fiercest of us, and yet gave you the most compassionate heart."

"We must be an example to them, Uriel. They go through so much pain in their short lives; the quickest way for them to learn is through the example of others. They will need many teachers before Elyon's promises can be fulfilled."

"It sounds like you have been with the Antecedent of Time, reading the books of the living. You should be careful. If you spend too much time reading and not training, Elyon will be forced to make me the Commander of the Heavenly Host," teased Uriel.

"I could read for the next millennium and still be faster than you, little brother."

A tremor of foreboding washed over Michael, and they both looked up into the first Heaven. A cloud of shadows descended from above and landed in front of them.

"Is it done?" The wings of the *Malach HaMavet* were like molded smoke.

"It is," Michael said.

"So be it." The *Malach HaMavet* melted into the night, and moments later, cries of despair rose into the heavens.

Mychal woke with a dry mouth and a throbbing head. Jael was curled up asleep at the end of the couch. He blinked at the milky sunlight coming through the cabin windows.

How long have I been out? He climbed to his unsteady feet and went to make coffee. He ran his hands through his hair, trying to dislodge the dream from his head.

It had been two days since Uriel left, and he had been in and out of consciousness ever since. Jael had been watching over him, ready with food or water or whatever he needed when he woke. Her easy company reminded him of his friend Hamish, another Australian, who was probably causing mischief on the other side of the world.

"Is Uriel not back yet?" Jael asked sleepily as she stumbled into the kitchen.

"You actually sound worried about him," Mychal replied as he made them both coffee. "You seem to be forgetting he's one of the most powerful beings ever created."

"Yeah. Well, you can't pick who you worry about I guess," Jael said and accepted her cup. "What did you remember this time?"

"Egypt. Uriel and I were there when the Angel of Death came for the first-born." Mychal put his head in his hands.

Jael smiled sadly. "He told me that story a few years ago when he was teaching me how to cleanse buildings."

"It's like it happened yesterday. I remember exactly how I felt. I can still smell the Nile and hear the crackle of food cooking. The fear, the hope, everything. Uriel was there, and I know a part of me cared about him." He pulled at his black curls. "But then there's this other part of me that sees him as a complete stranger."

"Then it's simple. You must choose how you wish to see him now. I mean, he can be a real pain in the ass and a tough teacher, but he's a good guy. You need him, and you need Gabriel."

"I know I do," Mychal admitted. "I just hate that I do."

Jael sighed. "I know that feeling too. It makes me feel weak that I miss the surly bastard so much. Either way, we are in this mess together…if they ever come back."

"He trained you to be an exorcist, right? Did he ever train you in self-defense?" Mychal didn't want to have to worry about Jael in a fight, and if it meant training her himself, he'd suck it up and do it.

"Batons," she said finally. "I'm good with batons and basic self-defense. Nothing like that crazy kung fu you guys were pulling out the other day."

"I could show you some moves," Mychal said, keeping his tone carefully bored. "You know, if you want. We have nothing better to do."

Jael raised an eyebrow. "Right. I'm not great though, so lower your expectations. If I don't do something soon, I'm going to go nuts. I'm not great at sitting still, especially while waiting for an apocalypse."

Despite her misgivings, Mychal found Jael to be a quick student who didn't hold back. They had found a set of batons in Mychal's weapons bag, and she twirled them easily to test their weight.

"How long has Uriel been training you?" Mychal asked as he ducked a blow aimed for his head.

"Since…seventeen…" Jael breathed heavily. She was still recovering from injuries, but Mychal wasn't going to use it as an excuse to go easy on her.

"You've been doing exorcisms that long too? That's impressive," Mychal said. "My mentor was a good exorcist, but he didn't begin training until his thirties."

"Priests!" Jael grinned wickedly as if remembering something. "Not all of them are bad."

"Firm up your stance," Mychal instructed, and she sank fractionally, her legs strengthening. "You're short so aim for the points you can reach without over-balancing yourself."

"Knees, sternum, and balls," she said and winked at him, making him laugh. It died on his lips.

"Been a while since you laughed, huh?" Jael asked, perceptive as ever.

"Yes."

"You want to tell me about it?"

"I'm not into confessions."

"Ha! Yeah, I wasn't either until recently." She pulled a face at him. "You do remember that you've been telling me all the stuff your memories are churning up?"

"That's different. Those happened to a…a different Mychal. What you're asking about happened to *me*." He struggled to articulate as he adjusted the angle of her batons. "Besides, you haven't told me why you were so angry at Uriel. Or how you ended up in a car park in Hungary."

"My story doesn't seem as exciting as that of the human incarnation of an archangel, who also happens to be the only demon hunter I've ever met."

"Well, I'm tired of me. I need to hear someone else's tale of misery."

"Okay," Jael replied. As they trained, she talked, telling him about being an exorcist in Melbourne, about HeosCorp, and about the shelters that were turning people into zombie demons. Mychal noticed the soft way she spoke about Alessandro, another exorcist, and how they saved each other from demons. He also began to see exactly why she was pissed off at Uriel.

"And then I ended up here with you," she said finally. "Waiting on a bunch of angels to get their shit together."

"Looks like we won't have to wait any longer," Mychal said, straightening from the crouch he'd been in. Uriel and Gabriel appeared behind Jael. She turned sharply, and Uriel caught her outstretched baton.

"Hey, glad you could show up," Jael said, and Uriel smiled down at her.

"I'm pleased you've been productive with your time," he replied, the ice melting from his eyes. Mychal pretended not to notice.

Gabriel pushed Uriel aside and offered Jael his hand. "I'm delighted to meet you properly, Jael. Uriel has spoken of you often."

"Oh yeah?" She shook Gabriel's hand. "I bet you couldn't stop his bitching."

"Well, nothing will ever stop that." Gabriel nodded to Mychal. "You're looking better. It is good to see that Uriel has managed to get you into some semblance of yourself."

"You mean *I* have," Jael said and folded her arms.

"Are you satisfied now that I didn't hurt him?" Uriel asked, glaring at Gabriel.

"I wouldn't say that I am completely undamaged, but I'm in one piece," Mychal said.

Gabriel placed a hand on Mychal's head. "Your mind seems to be catching up too. It's good enough. The rest will follow, but we must leave."

"Why? What has happened?" Jael asked.

"There have been problems in the desert. You both need to go and gather your things," Gabriel said.

33

IT TOOK MYCHAL AND me ten minutes to shove our gear into our bags and meet the archangels outside. Gabriel smiled at me, and I did my best not to blush. He had golden hair and eyes, and the way he moved, with such deadly grace, reminded me of a big cat stalking its prey. He was charming too, something Uriel never even pretended to be.

"I'm sorry I took so long," Uriel said, his hand resting on my shoulder. "How has he been?"

I shot a glance toward the cabin where Mychal was speaking with Gabriel. "Rough. Mostly sleeping. I've made sure he's been eating and all that."

"And you? Have you been taking care of yourself?" he asked, fingers brushing the tips of my hair.

"I'm a big girl, Uriel. You've never babied me before so don't start now," I said, sterner than I felt. He removed his hand from my shoulder.

"You are right. I'm sorry."

"So the desert, huh?" I said, shuffling my feet. "How are we going to get there?"

"She has a point. Unless you know how to open gates, Jael?" Mychal said as he joined us.

"Ha! Gates. Good one," I said. He looked confused. "What, seriously? You know someone who can do that?"

"I did." He looked over to Gabriel as I struggled to keep my mouth closed.

"It is impossible to create a gate to the place we are going to," Uriel replied, looping his arm around my waist. "Hold on."

"Wha—" I screamed as Uriel stepped onto a plane that no human could physically enter, an in-between space. I knew we were moving, but everything was flashing past so quickly that I shut my eyes.

I heard a chorus of a thousand voices, as if we were traveling through a cloud of prayers, words of hope, and praise. The distant singing of the angels was so beautiful that I thought my heart was going to explode.

The ground suddenly rushed up toward us as we plummeted into a free fall. I clung to Uriel with my arms and legs like a terrified cat. We hit the ground with a solid thump.

"You can open your eyes now, Jael," Uriel said, a deep chuckle rolling through him.

"You are such a bastard sometimes." I opened my eyes and saw his smiling face was close to mine. I couldn't help but smile back. "That was terrifying. Can you put me down now?"

Uriel lowered me to my unsteady feet, and I swayed. "Oh, angel express sucks."

Mychal and Gabriel appeared beside us; the demon hunter looked as nauseous as I felt.

"Where are we?" he asked. I looked around at the dry mountains and recognized them instantly from my vision.

"We are in the Duda'el…uh, the Negev," I said, earning a sharp look from Gabriel.

"How did you know that?" he asked.

"I got mad skills," I replied. The hot afternoon sun was beating down on us as I looked around and climbed up a low ridge. Beneath us was the remnants of a camp.

"What's that?" I asked.

"That's why we are here," Uriel said as he joined me. "Be on your guard."

We walked through the wreckage of broken demountable buildings and torn apart cars. I swallowed hard against the smell I was starting to know too well. I instinctively drew closer to Uriel as my intuition started screaming inside of me. When I saw the first body, I struggled not to vomit. It looked like it had been torn apart by lions.

"What did this?" I asked. My stomach dropped again when I saw the uncovered, impossibly large skeletons. A few of the victims were wearing lab coats, and laptops were scattered in broken chunks of electronics. I suddenly knew exactly whose camp we were in. "This is Nazirah's dig."

"What are you talking about?" Mychal said as he followed me. I dug around in the piles of stuff until I found what I was looking for. I held up a water bottle with a silver-and-white logo on it.

"Fucking HeosCorp! Again!" I threw the bottle to the ground as my anger rose. "They were archaeologists. What possible threat could there have been?"

"There's your answer." Gabriel pointed.

A deep, black shaft had been dug into the earth, and huge skeletons were half-exhumed around it.

"I didn't believe it could be possible," Uriel said and shook his head.

Mychal knelt down and touched the deep furrows on the sides of the hole. It looked like something had crawled out.

"Uriel?" I asked, a cold snake of fear twisting about in my gut. *What is this really about?*

"Look! There's a car up there," Mychal said. We hurried through the camp, following the Jeep's tire tracks up the rough road and on top of another small ridge.

"Jael, wait." Uriel grabbed my arm, instantly alert. "Gabriel?"

The golden angel made a hissing sound. "I feel him too."

The Jeep's sides were busted in, the doors open, and dark sprays of blood were visible on the rocky ground beside it.

Dumped beside the front tire was a dead woman. The shattered glass around her gleamed like stars. Her legs and arms had been torn to shreds and dark, coppery hair blew in dusty curls about her face. The men's shirt she was wearing was covered in blood. I recognized the sexy Lara Croft from the photos in the professor's office back in Melbourne.

"It's… Her name was Nazirah," I said. Uriel let me go, and I knelt down beside her. There was a look of agony on her face, and I brushed her eyelids closed.

Gabriel crouched beside her. "You might want to look away, Jael." He un-buttoned Nazirah's shirt, and I glimpsed the gaping wounds and the gleam of broken bones. Gabriel quickly closed the shirt again.

"What kind of monster could do something like that?" I asked.

"One who hates women because they make more humans," Gabriel replied.

"Even if the Watchers got out, why would they do this? They would be dis-orientated and—" Mychal started to say, and I looked up at him in shock.

"The Watchers are still alive?" I demanded. "I thought this was zombie de-mons."

"When I touched the edge of the pit, I saw two angels climbing out of it," Mychal said. "That's why we are here right?"

"Correct," said Uriel, and I glared at him.

"You could have said something. Look what they have done to her!"

"This wasn't done by the Watchers. This was their liberator doing damage control," said Gabriel. "He wanted to ensure that no one raised an alarm that two rampaging fallen angels were free."

"He who?" I asked. "Are you talking about one of the Watchers you impris-oned?"

"No, Hel'el did this, and I know he has killed this way before. I can feel his mark on her. He seduced her, tormented her, and then he killed her in a way that was horrifyingly unique to her sex." Gabriel pointed to the dried chunk of tissue beside the body. "That is her womb."

"Why would he do this?" I swallowed a sob. *Who is Hel'el?*

"He wanted her to pass on a message to Elyon," Gabriel explained. "He killed her this way to mock and humiliate her."

"We can't leave them all here like this. They have families. People who care for them, who will be looking for them. We need to ring the IDF…something."

"Hel'el would have put something up to prevent the humans from being found," Uriel said. "I will find the warding and destroy it. They will find them soon enough. These bodies have been out here for a few days; they would have been reported by now if there were no wards."

He unfolded his wings and launched into the sky. Mychal looked in the Jeep and found a sheet wrapped around some tools. He shook it out, and I helped him cover Nazirah's body. I crouched down beside her, unclipped her sil-ver Star of David necklace, and put it around my neck to hang with Alessandro's rosary beads.

"Why are you taking it?" Mychal asked, his tone curious but not judgmental.

I covered her face with the corner of the sheet. "As a reminder. I will get justice for this. When I find the Watchers and whoever this bastard Hel'el is, I'll make them pay."

"Hel'el is one of Lucifer's names," Mychal said beside me.

I fell backward on my butt. "What? Lucifer did this? As in *the* Lucifer?"

"Yes, he was here," Gabriel said, looking down at me. "I thought Uriel told you."

"Nope, he seriously neglected to mention I was going off to fight bloody Lucifer!" I brought my knees up to my chest and struggled to breathe through the sudden panic.

"The shield is down. We can…" Uriel appeared and knelt down beside me. "What happened?"

"I told her the truth," Gabriel said. "As you should have."

Uriel touched my shoulder gently. "Come on, Jael. We need to leave this place."

"Why didn't you tell me?" I asked.

"We had to be sure, and now we are. This changes nothing." Uriel lifted me to my feet and I leaned into his strength to calm and ground myself. "The mission is still the same."

"Fine with me," Mychal said with a growl. "Use your angel radar to find the Watchers; let's end this before they kill anyone else."

"The Watchers are cut off from *Shamayim*, what you humans know as Heaven. We can't use 'angel radar' on them," answered Gabriel.

"Then we do it the normal way. We track them and wait for the bodies to start piling up," Mychal said. "Coming, Jael?"

"Yeah," I replied, gripping one of my batons tightly. I pushed down my fear, and let anger take its place. I had seen what archangels could do to an army. *With them, we could defeat any enemy*, I reminded myself. "I want to have a word with Hel'el about how he treats ladies."

34

IT HAD BEEN A week since the remnants of the Watchers dug themselves out of their prison, and Semyaza was starting to wonder if it had been a good idea. He and Azazel had spent the first few days wandering about the desert like newborns. The burning heat of the sun on their skin held a special fascination for them, and at night they gazed up at the star-filled sky, weeping at the beauty of it all.

In the time they had ruled with their children, they were based farther north, past the Dead Sea, so it was north that they traveled. They hid from the humans in their iron chariots and flying machines. Exposed and vulnerable to the new world, they had stolen long, shapeless, dark robes and scarves to shield themselves.

They watched humans coming and going to a place until sunset. That night they explored and found a palace carved into the red rock face, but the palace had been abandoned by its rulers. From a guard, they took memories, so they could try and make sense of all that had happened. The languages had changed, and so they took them too, speaking to each other in new tongues.

From Petra, they continued to the Dead Sea. They took more memories from those they encountered. They left their victims as drooling simpletons or dead, depending on their mood.

In Jericho, Azazel pulled the arms off a man who was beating a woman in the street while other people walked by. Panicking at the thought of being exposed, Semyaza had killed the bystanders.

The grateful woman and her sister sheltered them for the night, while the city was in turmoil over the massacre. The women had offered their bodies to them, and they accepted, both relishing in the touch of another being after so long. The women whispered over and over in their gentle voices, "*Malaika, malaika...*" Their soft flesh gave the Watchers their first comfort since their escape.

Now they were in Damascus, sipping scalding black coffee in the Old Town markets. They tried to remain as inconspicuous as possible, but being around humans was becoming easier. They didn't fear them anymore. Knowledge of how the earth had changed now held the most horror for them.

"Semyaza?" Azazel was talking to him again. His fiery hair caught many stares, and now tanned from the desert, he looked even more striking.

"I'm sorry. I find it hard to concentrate with so much noise," Semyaza explained, pinching the bridge of his nose.

"Once we understand what power we still possess, we will be able to control it better," Azazel said. Semyaza sipped the scalding bitter liquid, struggling not to be overcome by the flavors and sensations on his tongue.

"I'm beginning to think Elyon was right to punish us, Azazel," he said softly. "The memories we've taken show how chaotic the world has become. Do you recall the memories of that white man at the Dead Sea? Naked women with faces painted like some terrible whore creatures."

"Imagine how I'm feeling," Azazel grumbled. "All the lands we have passed through are at war with each other. New religions have risen in our absence, and they have such cowardly ways of fighting! I taught them about weapons and warfare, but there is nothing honorable about battle now."

Semyaza's face screwed up in disgust. "This world is diseased. How are we going to find our way through this? Elyon has cut us away from Heaven, and if he saw this in mankind's future, we deserved our punishment, Azazel. We brought all of this about by teaching them. How could we ever atone for what they have done with it?"

"I don't know, brother. I spent so long being angry at Elyon that I don't know how to be anything else. Look at the horror we have seen. My anger must be nothing compared to his."

They drank their coffee, silently watching the hustle of people. The sound of children playing in the streets was something Semyaza thought he would never hear again. He thought of the children he had sired when he was so desperate to be like man. Now he couldn't think of anything more abhorrent.

Semyaza remembered the woman who made him take that final step toward coming into the light. Millions of years had passed, and he still wanted and hated Na'amah.

The angels were his only family, and now he only had Azazel. Semyaza thought of the vow they had taken with him; they were so trusting. He had led them to their destruction, and their suffering had been his fault. Now the two of them were the only angels left on the earth...

"Azazel! I think I know who can help us," Semyaza exclaimed. "What about Hel'el?"

"Hel'el! Would he even still be walking the earth?"

"Of course! We disagreed violently when he convinced Adam to give up his power, but perhaps Hel'el was right to do so... Look what man has done with all they were given! They have killed Elyon's creation."

Azazel folded his arms, considering. "I remember the power he took over all things. He would have enough to help us. He's been on the earth since creation, and he could help us understand all that has happened to turn mankind off their path."

"Do you remember how strong and magnificent he was? How Elyon loved him? He knew the mind of Elyon as well. He would be the one to ask."

"Ask him what?"

"How to get atonement, Azazel! If not atonement, then maybe he'll have some idea of how we can make this world right again. How to undo what we did."

"Your idea has merit if he'll help us. Elyon may take a long time to forgive us and let us come home, but he may be lenient if he sees that we are trying to restore order on the earth." Azazel's eyes were shining with some of his old enthusiasm. "But how are we going to find Hel'el?"

"His power was always so much more than ours," Semyaza said thoughtfully. "Perhaps all we need to do is ask."

Just then a man came and sat down at their table. He had tanned skin and fair, curly hair. His smile was open, expansive, and full of love.

"No need to summon me, brothers. I'm already here," he said.

"Hel'el?" Azazel asked, and he reached out and touched him. A hum of power burned from him, and Semyaza reached over and embraced him.

"Hel'el! Thank Elyon you found us," Semyaza said as Hel'el patted his back.

"I'm pleased to see you both again after so long," he said with a beaming smile. "I didn't think Elyon would ever let you out of that pit." Semyaza and Azazel exchanged nervous glances. "What? What's wrong?"

"Nothing, except we climbed out of the pit ourselves. It weakened enough for us to escape. I don't think it was Elyon who let us go free," Semyaza admitted.

"But that prison was made by his archangels. If you were allowed to escape, it must have been at Elyon's request."

Hel'el gestured to one of the workers, and he was brought a coffee. "Elyon's request or not, it does my heart good to see you again. I've tried to find your prison to save you, but Michael and his angels hid it from the world too completely."

"Rafael would have a hard time getting me into that pit now." Azazel fumed with old rage.

"Are you concerned that they will try to put you back?" Hel'el asked. "If they knew you were out, then I'm sure that they would have found you by now. But enough of those old bores. Tell me about your escape."

Semyaza hesitated; the coffee shop and the streets were getting fuller and noisier.

"You want privacy?" Hel'el asked. "Excellent idea."

He grabbed their hands, and the marketplace vanished. They were now beside a waterfall in the lush tropical forest. Azazel laughed approvingly. Semyaza bent to touch a spray of fern, its feathery leaves soft under his touch.

"I forgot such beauty existed," he murmured. Away from the crush of people, he could finally breathe again.

"You may tell Hel'el our story; I'm going swimming," Azazel stated as he shed his filthy clothes and dove into the clear water.

"To be that free-spirited again." Hel'el chuckled as Azazel moved through the water.

"He has suffered too much on my account."

"You have *both* suffered. Walk with me; tell me everything."

Semyaza began to speak of all that had happened since the night they had crawled out of the darkness. He spoke the fears he didn't dare speak to Azazel. He talked of his disgust with the state of mankind, and how they were tearing themselves apart.

"Honestly, Hel'el, what these men have done to the earth far exceeds what we ever did. We were punished, and yet Elyon suffers them?"

"He destroyed the earth to try and wash all trace of you from it," Hel'el said.

"What?" Semyaza said. In their prison they had felt nothing.

"He flooded it to try and rid the world of the knowledge of the Watchers and the Nephilim."

Semyaza sat down on a rock and put his head in his hands. "Still it has turned out like this. How will Azazel and I ever be able to make this right? We only wanted to *help* the humans; that's why we taught them all that we did. We took wives because we loved the women so much."

"I know," Hel'el said softly. "You must understand; there's something fundamentally rotten inside of mankind. I'm sure it's something Elyon never thought would happen when he created them, but it's true. He gave them a free will that was denied to everything else in his creation. From that free will, decay spread through their hearts and minds like ravenous worms. They start wars out of greed and a love of violence, not to protect their families or their homes. They sexually sin against children, they steal from those less fortunate, and they don't care. Their love of money and power has more value to them than feeding the hungry and the destitute."

Hel'el's expression darkened; rage filled his beautiful eyes. "Mankind is a *disease* on this planet; a festering cancer bent on their own futile destruction. They raise themselves as gods to try to rule in their perverse forms of worship. *This* is not what Elyon had in mind when he made them, and now he has left them to kill each other, because he is too sickened to even cleanse the earth once more."

Semyaza shook his head. "What can we do to stop this, Hel'el? We *must* do something. Maybe that's why Elyon released us, so we can have the chance to undo our mistakes."

"It must be for that purpose," Hel'el agreed with a sigh. "I can't think of another reason why he would release you."

"You *must* help us." Semyaza took his hand. "Please, I beg you. You know and understand this world. Azazel and I have willing hearts, but we are confused by everything around us. We don't understand what needs to be done." Hel'el hesitated, and Semyaza's grip tightened. "You were once the closest to Elyon. You understand his mind. How would we know what the right thing to do is? You would know what he wants."

"You're right. I do know," Hel'el said sadly as he placed his hand on Semyaza's shoulder. "It will be a difficult road, and I need to know that you would be willing to stay true to it no matter where it leads."

"I've already made so many mistakes. I vow that I'll do as you ask. Just *tell me* how to fix this world."

"We must do what Elyon doesn't have the heart for anymore. We must weed out this evil in the hearts of mankind and let the earth heal and start again. It's a heavy burden to place on us, but it's the only way."

Semyaza stilled, his heart racing. "What are you saying, Hel'el?"

"We must seek out the evil and kill it, Semyaza. We must kill them all."

"I agree with Hel'el. It needs to be done," Azazel said as he joined them again. "You know it's the only way, Semyaza. We've both been sickened in our spirit by what mankind has become. Elyon must have set us free for this task, because we are the only ones strong enough to carry it out."

"Listen to Azazel if you don't trust me," said Hel'el.

"I wouldn't know where to begin," Semyaza admitted. "There's only the two of us, and the weapons of this age are strong."

"You won't be alone. I'll give you my best servants to attend to you."

"Demons!" Azazel hissed in disgust.

"They were formed in the dark times and aren't as powerful as angels, but don't discount them. I've found them to be useful and loyal."

Azazel crossed his arms, becoming the general once more. "Will they obey our commands? I won't take anything into battle that doesn't perform the way I want it to."

"Following commands is all they know how to do," Hel'el said. "They will perform admirably. If they don't, kill them. It hardly matters to me."

Semyaza straightened, filled with purpose. "Where do we begin?"

35

A long time ago in Jericho

MIKHA'EL WATCHED JOSHUA, THE new leader of the Hebrews, commanding his soldiers and meeting with his priests. Three weeks ago, he had been watching a herd of goats when a demon attacked him. He had beaten it to death, caving its skull in with his shepherd's crook.

That night, Gabriel had taken him far away and told him impossible things. Now, he had his memories back and could wield a sword and spear with deadly efficiency. But with new memories came old pains; he hadn't missed Na'amah before, but now her absence was a knife wound inside of him. Joshua watched him from the corner of his eye, unsure of what to expect of him.

The first day dawned on the army standing in marching columns, ten abreast on the road toward Jericho. Mikha'el walked with Joshua behind the Ark and its priests. He knew the legends of the golden box—it still had the Ten Commandments written on the stone inside of it—and that it carried Aaron's staff. The staff was old, worn wood, just a symbol, not an artifact of power.

With his memories back, Mikha'el remembered Moses and the few times that they had spoken. Moses was a man of few words, and even those few were stuttered. His eyes had still been young and expressive when he died, burning with the words and revelations of Elyon inside of him.

Hel'el had come after those eyes had shut for the last time. He wanted the body, wanted to give it to the people to "honor properly." Mikha'el had known otherwise. If the body had been given to the people, then a temple would have been made. A monument would have been erected to the man who saved them from slavery, and who they rewarded with their insolence, their disobedience, and their complaining.

Now that Moses was dead, his worst enemies who had tried to bring him down in life would speak of his greatness, his holiness. Mikha'el filled with anger at the very thought of it. He remembered in the last few days how he had stopped Hel'el from taking the body.

The sound of shofroth jolted Mikha'el back into his body. The slips in his memory were still coming and going as they pleased. He just hoped it didn't happen when the fighting started. Mikha'el drew himself straight and walked on, the flow of memories falling behind his steps like broken pottery.

For the next six days, they marched, waited, then marched again. On the sixth evening, Joshua summoned Mikha'el to his tent.

"Tell me, is Hashem pleased so far? We are doing his will and…"

"Joshua, I'm human like you. I've no special preference in the eyes of Hashem. If anything, I'm lesser than you. We've done as Gabriel commanded, so Hashem will be pleased and our victory assured. Take heart, have faith."

"I was a young man when I left Egypt with Moses. I knew I could never hope to reach a level of holiness such as that. When he told me I was to take over as the leader, I tried to pass it on to someone else. I didn't want to lead such a wayward, ungrateful flock. Hashem has a way of giving us the courage we need for the impossible. What of you Mikha'el? Are you up to the task at hand?"

"Yes."

Joshua waited for him to say more, but when he saw none was forthcoming, he simply nodded his head.

"Very well. When the walls are breached, I want you to go and find the house of Rachav. A red cord will be tied to the door, and I want you to protect her and her family. If the men of Jericho see that we aren't going to harm her, they'll try to kill her. I won't allow her to be raped or murdered for helping us."

"You don't trust your own men to protect her?"

Joshua's voice was tired as he said, "I love my people, Mikha'el, but I'm not blind to their faults."

On the seventh day, the sun rose to the sound of shofroth and the screaming voices of the Hebrews. Great fissures split up the clay and rock walls of Jericho. The army swarmed through the city, cutting through their defenses.

Mikha'el fought beside them in the first wave. The streets of Jericho were a maze of soldiers and filled with the screams of the dying. He cut down anyone in his path with an ease that shocked him. He trained for weeks with Gabriel, but before that he had never held a sword or a spear. It took longer than anticipated, but he finally found the house with the red cord. He banged on the door and shouted, "Rachav of Jericho."

"Go away!"

"I've been sent here by Joshua of the Hebrews to protect you. I won't hurt you."

"Get away from that whore's house!" shouted an angry voice from the end of the alley. A group of six Hebrew soldiers was moving toward them.

"I was commanded to protect her," Mikha'el said firmly.

"She can't be allowed to live. Joshua's a fool to grant her sanctuary. She betrayed her people, and she'll betray us and taint our ranks." Fury and lust radiated off the man. An aura of violence clung to him like a stench, and the others followed him blindly.

"You're tainting the name of your people right now. Go from here and take the city as Joshua commanded." Mikha'el's grip tightened on his sword as they tried to circle him. "Don't do this. It won't end well for you."

A huge man rushed at Mikha'el, swinging his sword down fast and hard. Mikha'el caught the curved blade with his own and dragged the weapon from his attacker's hands. He drove the hilt of his sword up into the man's nose, smashing the bones. He couldn't see where the leader had gone with the men swarming him.

"Elyon, forgive me…" he prayed as he let his anger out and sliced his way through the soldiers. They fell under his attack, not standing a chance against him. He jumped over the broken door and searched quickly through the rooms. There was a high-pitched squeal from upstairs, and Mikha'el rushed toward the sound.

The leader was on top of a young girl, tearing at her clothes. Mikha'el dragged him off her by his hair and drove his sword through the back of his neck and out of his chest. He tossed the corpse, and his sword made a sucking sound as he pulled it out. He knelt down by the frightened girl and wrapped a blanket around her.

"I'm not here to hurt you, little one. I'm here to protect you. It's going to be all right." She nodded her head. Her brown eyes were so big they seemed to swallow the rest of her face. She came to him, and he lifted her up gently.

"Where's Mama?" she cried.

"We'll find her, don't worry." Mikha'el carried her down the stairs and over the broken furniture. In the cooking area, a woman was lying face down against the wall. Mikha'el placed the girl down and carefully rolled her mother over. As soon as his hand touched her, she swung her arm out to hit him.

"Stop! Stop!"

"My name is Mikha'el. I'm here to take you to safety. Please, stop hitting me." Mikha'el took hold of her hands to still them. Her dark hair fell back from her face. *That face...* Everything went quiet as he looked down at the bloody, frightened woman.

"Na'amah?"

"No, Rachav the whore," she said viciously. She was shivering with fear but still defiant. Mikha'el pulled the heavy red scarf from around his neck, shaking it out before wrapping it around her shoulders.

"I'll just call you Rachav; the other part doesn't matter anymore," he said, helping her stand. "Come, I'm going to get you out of here." The girl moved out from behind him.

"He saved me, Mama," she said as Rachav checked her over.

"Thank you." She looked up at him with those impossibly familiar eyes, and his chest ached.

"You're welcome. You don't have to be afraid of me, Rachav. I'll never let any harm come to you or your daughter."

"You can't promise me that. You can't watch us all the time." She stood tall and took her daughter's hand.

"I don't envy the person who would try to stop me."

Rachav's lips trembled in an almost smile. "I'm a whore, Mikha'el. I am nothing."

He shook his head. "You're the only one being spared in this place. You aren't nothing. You've been given a chance to have a new life. Come with me, Rachav. Leave this place and the past behind you." She lifted his scarf up to cover her hair.

"I don't know why, but I trust you. Lead on, Mikha'el. Where you go, I will follow."

Walking along the busy road leading to Jericho, Mychal did his best not to choke on the memories that overloaded him. He stared, stunned, as he saw the image of the old city overlaying the new.

"Mychal? What is it?" Jael asked, her small hand grabbing his elbow to steady him.

"It's nothing. I'm just a bit disorientated. My head feels like it's splitting when I remember this place. I watched the walls fall, Jael. *She* was there." Mychal rubbed the dust from his eyes.

"Aleksandra?"

"Her name was Rachav in that lifetime. She had a daughter with a smile like sunshine, and she used to twist her little fingers in my hair."

Mychal's hands curled into tight fists, and he tried to bring himself back to the present. Away from Rachav's dark eyes and their small, happy family.

The angels could travel in the blink of an eye, but they had no quick way to find the Watchers now that they were no longer connected to Heaven. Despite that, Mychal and the others tracked them easily as the Watchers had blundered their way through the Middle East. The angels simply followed the trail of human wreckage that was left in their wake.

Mychal tried to interview the Watchers' victims from Jordan to the Dead Sea, but their minds had been wiped, leaving them no better than drooling infants. Gabriel tried to restore them, but all of their thoughts, their memories, and their essence had been stripped clean. The people had been ruined by a clumsy attempt at information retrieval and the mindless violence that accompanied it.

"They're confused and scared," Uriel said with a frown. "Idiots! Thousands of years of imprisonment have taught them nothing. How arrogant to think a human life is less than their own!"

"They're heading north. What in the north was significant to them?" Mychal started to walk toward Jericho, his T-shirt brushing irritably against his damp skin. They were all dressed in black cargo pants, boots, and T-shirts. The air of military authority they gave off was enough to dissuade anyone from trying to harass or mug them.

"Semyaza built his palace in the north," Gabriel said thoughtfully. "Perhaps they are trying to find what is left of their home."

"They won't find anything. We made sure we destroyed all of it," Uriel said forcefully.

Aware of Mychal's and Jael's need to eat and sleep, they found a hotel on the outskirts of the city. It had a cold shower, and Mychal was relieved to scrub himself with soap and wash the dust out of his curly hair that had grown long after months of neglect. He relinquished the bathroom to Jael and sat down on the couch with a sigh. The reception on the TV flickered in and out, showing a news story about an attack in Damascus.

"Do you know Arabic, Uriel?" Mychal asked as he turned it up.

"Of course, I know all of Earth's languages." Uriel reached over and flicked him hard on the lips.

Mychal yelped. "What was that for?"

"Now you do too." Uriel pointed at the TV; his face was blank, but his eyes were full of mischief.

Mychal heard the Arabic, but his mind swiftly started translating. "Images are coming through…caught on a phone by a civilian…at this time the damage has been extensive. The network wishes to advise that the captured footage may be disturbing for viewers."

Hazy, chaotic images flashed across the scenes in the jumpy footage. Half of a car flying through the air. An attacker striking out at armed men, moving so fast they were no more than a blur. The red flash of hair. Another attacker bending the barrel of a tank in half before the hatch was pulled off and screaming men streamed out of it. The creature looked up, spotting the hidden spectator. The phone dropped to the ground as the man was torn apart. There had been no mistaking the look of fury, so very freshly remembered by Mychal.

"Semyaza—"

"And Azazel," Uriel muttered. "There's only one Watcher with hair that color."

"Tell Jael. I'll go and find Gabriel."

Uriel hesitated. "In a moment. She's talking to Star."

"Talking to Star isn't a priority."

"It is to Jael. She hasn't been able to contact her in weeks. You would understand if you could be bothered to keep in contact with the people who care about you."

Mychal pushed the guilt down. "They are safer without me in their lives."

"Whatever you need to tell yourself. Jael has people who love her, and she needs to reassure them that she is all right."

"We are going into a war zone. How much reassurance is she going to be able to give them?" And because Mychal was feeling vindictive, he added, "How does her boyfriend cope with all of this?"

"She doesn't have one," Uriel replied coolly. "She knows her duty."

"Yeah, I wonder why she doesn't have one. She told me you pulled her out of her last date."

"She was in an event full of demons! Of course, I had to get her out of there."

"That may be true, but you could have whisked her away. You didn't do that, did you? You appeared as a human and made sure every other male in the room knew to stay away from her."

"She deserves better." Uriel folded his arms. "She is my charge. I must protect her."

"From finding someone? It sounds like you are just selfish to me. You want to keep her to yourself even though you won't give her what she needs."

"When someone worthy of her presents himself, then perhaps I'll feel differently," Uriel said stubbornly. Mychal tried not to feel too bad for him. He knew what it was like to care too much for a human. *He doesn't see it, so stop pushing him,* a voice said in the back of his head. It sounded far too much like Aleksandra.

Uriel pushed his hands through his loose silver hair. "We need to stay the night regardless of what is happening in Damascus. You two are human, and you need to rest because when we get there, there will be a fight."

36

I WAS CLEAN FOR the first time in a week, and standing in the warm twilight breeze, looking out over the city, I almost felt normal. I pulled my phone from my pocket and called Star. I wasn't sure about time differences, but I didn't know when I would get another chance.

Star answered within three rings. "Jael! Where are you? I've been trying to call you for nearly a fortnight."

"Whoa, slow down, Starshine. I'm okay. I've been...out of range," I said, trying to hide the relief in my voice. I missed Star like crazy.

"Where are you, Jael Quinlan?" Star replied coldly.

"I am in Jericho." She wouldn't have let it go.

"Jericho as in Middle East Jericho?"

"Yep. I'm sitting in a rooftop garden watching the sunset as we speak." I tried to sound casual as I asked, "How is Meta?"

"Terrorizing Jung. He must be healing because he's up and about on his cast when he shouldn't be. He knows something's wrong, because he can't find you. I must admit, I know the feeling."

"I have two angels and a demon hunter with me. I am okay." I gave her a quick debrief on what had happened since we had last talked in Hungary. It felt like forever ago. I brushed over a lot of important details to keep her from worrying, telling her about helping Mychal recover his memory, but absolutely nothing about Nazirah being killed by the Devil. That would be a conversation for when I was home, and it was over and done with.

"How is Max?" I asked to stop her from asking too many questions.

"He's awake."

"Oh, thank God." I gripped the phone, my relief so strong I felt dizzy.

"It's going to be a while before he's back to normal. Comas mess with people. He's going to need some rehab, and his lungs will take a while to heal. He was asking for you."

"What did you tell him?"

"That you saved his life, and you are out of town at a yoga retreat to recover from the strain." Star made a noise in the back of her throat. "You know he'll only believe that for so long."

"Yeah, I know. Hopefully I'll be back soon." Even as I said it, I seriously doubted it. Wherever this mission was heading, I knew I was in it for the long haul. I looked up and saw Gabriel on the other side of the roof.

"Hey Star, I have to go."

"But Jael—"

"Listen. I'm okay, so you don't need to worry about me. Hug Meta, kiss James, and tell Max he better be up and functioning by the time I get there. I love you." I hung up before she could reply. I looked at the wallpaper on my phone of Meta and Star and tried to push down my guilt.

"They are protected, Jael. You don't need to worry about them." Gabriel came to join me. His summer-gold hair was long enough that his braid touched his butt, and he had brilliant lion eyes. Uriel could pass as a super-hot human, but I doubted that Gabriel could ever pull off the illusion. There was an air of otherworldliness about him, and despite our close proximity during the last week, I was a bit nervous talking to him.

"I still worry, you know? Friends are hard to come by when you are an exorcist." I turned my phone about in my hands. "So, what are you doing up here? Getting some peace and quiet?"

"Keeping an eye on you." Gabriel looked up at the red-and-orange sky. "And praying."

"Reporting on progress to the Big Guy?"

"Something like that. I don't know what tomorrow will bring, and it is always wise to calm your mind and heart before going into battle."

I leaned back in the faded plastic chair. "You think there will be one?"

"Most definitely. The news has picked up the Watchers in Damascus. They are tearing the place apart. Tonight, we gather our strength. Tomorrow, we find out what is happening in the city."

"You mean, Mychal and I gather our strength." I folded my arms. "Why don't you and Uriel go ahead without us?"

"It was made very clear that you both have to accompany us for it to be successful."

"That's ridiculous. Uriel is badass enough to sort them out himself." I had seen him fight. The guy could level two Watcher angels in his sleep.

Gabriel smiled. "I like the way you talk about Uriel. He's always been the most distant of all of us."

I grinned. "He's not the chattiest of creatures. I understand that."

"I know you do. You two are very well matched, despite what you may think." Gabriel smiled at me fondly. "He's different around you. Softer."

"Ha! Not that I've seen." Even as I said it, I knew it wasn't exactly true. I remembered the afternoon in the cabin when he had held me as I cried my eyes out. Not common behavior for the scariest archangel ever.

"You love him," Gabriel stated.

I shrugged, ignoring the way my stomach flipped. "He's my guardian. Despite how pissed I've been with him, I'm still glad he hasn't abandoned me altogether."

"You *love* him," Gabriel repeated. "It radiates off you and fills the room you are in and everyone in it. It pleases me to see it. Uriel is a complicated being to love."

"Are you implying what I think you are implying?" I demanded.

"And what would that be?"

Oh God, he was going to make me say the words. "That I love Uriel, or I am *in* love with him."

Gabriel tilted his head slightly. "There is a difference? Humans can be so odd. All love flows to the one source, and that is Elyon. Loving someone else is a double blessing."

"That doesn't answer my question, angel. I thought it wasn't allowed."

"It's allowed; it's love. The Watchers weren't punished because they fell in love with humans. They were punished for rejecting their duty, breaking away from Heaven, and teaching humans things they weren't ready to know."

"I suppose it's difficult to know what to do. I have hundreds of years of church doctrine telling me angels can't love, so that's hard to undo. If you are saying it's okay to love Uriel, that's going to complicate things even more," I admitted. I wondered why I was bothering to say it. Maybe I was hoping I would get the okay and stop feeling like I was committing a crime every time I thought about kissing the grumpy bastard.

The angel beside me sighed and closed his eyes, face lifted to the dying sun's rays. "You shouldn't be so uncomfortable about this conversation. Close your eyes and listen to your heart; that's where Elyon's wisdom resides, and you'll know the truth for yourself. It is amazing what you can hear if you calm your mind and just *listen*." Gabriel smiled at the sky, tilting his ear as if listening to music I knew I would never be able to hear.

I took a deep, patient breath and closed my eyes. There were the sounds of cars, mobile phones, and voices all mixing with the humming electricity in the air.

"Tell me what you hear," I whispered.

"I hear fear. I hear old names being whispered that should have long been forgotten." Gabriel's tone changed, making my eyes snap open. Every part of Gabriel was suddenly tense and alert.

"The Watchers are here in the city. We have to move."

"But you just told me they were in Damascus!"

"We still need to move. It's not where they are, but what they have left behind that concerns me now."

We hurried down the fire escape stairs, Gabriel ahead of me, alert and tense. And just like that, my peace and calm went out the freaking window.

✦

In the streets of Nahal Elisha, Mychal and Gabriel pushed their way through a crowd of people clustering about the doorway of a small house. Offerings of food and flowers lined the street, and people sat praying beside them, excited whisperings rippling over the noise of the traffic.

"It has already started," Uriel muttered beside me.

"What has?" I asked.

"The cult worship," Gabriel answered as he entered the house in front of us. The sea of women parted seamlessly for him. There was tense anticipation inside, and I tried not to gag at the smell of too much incense, flowers, food, and spice. Two women sat on cushions in the middle of a room surrounded by candles and more offerings. They were wearing silk robes and were heavily pregnant.

"Everybody, get out." Uriel's voice was barely a whisper, but instantly people were shoving me in their haste to empty the house. The pregnant women didn't say a word as Gabriel pulled his hood back and lightly touched their stomachs.

"When did this happen?" he asked gently. "How many days?"

"Days!" I whispered tersely to Mychal, who shrugged. He had about as much of a clue as to what was going on as I did.

"Five days since the holy *malaika* honored us," the first woman replied. Her face glowed, and she had a manic look in her dark eyes.

"They weren't holy," said Uriel.

Mychal took his arm. "Don't frighten them more than they already are."

"Gabriel." Uriel looked straight through Mychal at his brother. A silent message passed between them, and Gabriel nodded.

"What? What's going on?" I demanded.

"They are pregnant with Nephilim," Gabriel said as he straightened. "They can't be allowed to live." The women who had been silent started to wail and tear at their clothes, their hands moving to protect their grotesquely swollen stomachs.

"You can't do this! They are innocent. You can't just kill them for what Semyaza and Azazel have done," argued Mychal as he moved to stand in front of the women.

"Mychal, perhaps you should listen." I backed away from the women to stop them from reaching for me.

"It isn't something we enjoy doing, brother, but it needs to be done," Gabriel said.

"No! Gabriel, please see reason—"

"No, you see reason, Mychal!" Uriel snapped. "They are Nephilim. Search your memories and find them. You *know* what they will become. You know what destruction they will unleash."

"No, we don't know," Mychal said stubbornly. "The last ones could have been a product of their fathers' making. These are just infants. They aren't warriors or monsters."

He might not have been able to fully remember the Nephilim, but I sure did. I had seen them in my vision of the battle. They were hulking, violent creatures who didn't care for human life. I would never condone the murder of children, but they weren't children despite how they may look.

"These women will die if you allow them to give birth. All the mothers died," Gabriel said, "Their bodies were torn apart."

"Modern medicine could stop that from happening. If they get to the hospital in time they both may live and recover to raise the children right," replied Mychal earnestly.

"They are not like human children! They will be full-grown monsters in less than a fortnight! They will devour everything in their path, and they will rip the land to pieces to find their fathers. Then it will be two fallen Watchers, demons, and Nephilim that we will be fighting," said Uriel.

"You don't know that it will happen that way. This is a different time, the technology alone—"

"Yes, it is a different time. A time of science where they will dissect these creatures to learn about their cellular regeneration and what fuels their hideous strength and appetite," said Uriel, his voice filled with disgust. "Mankind will try to take the knowledge of their flesh and make weapons of their own. Modern medicine may save the mothers, but the rapid growth of the infants will attract the attention of doctors."

"And your solution is the sword? They are innocents, Uriel, no matter their blood."

"You don't remember what they were like, Mychal. This is a mercy to them and the humans in their path that they will destroy," said Uriel.

"I'm your commander, aren't I?" Mychal demanded. Uriel snorted, but Gabriel looked uneasy. "I am, even as a human. Then as your commander, I say that both of these women will live. If the children born are all that you say, then they will be dealt with accordingly. I will return and kill them myself."

The women gasped their relief, pawing at him. Mychal moved away from them and their worshipping hands. "For your sake, go to the hospital to have a safe birth, and get the infants out of there as soon as you can before anyone realizes how different they are. Raise them correctly and teach them to do no wrong. Otherwise, there will be no saving them from me."

Uriel's hand slammed against Mychal's chest as he tried to leave the room.

"Whatever happens now, whatever lives they destroy, it's on you," he warned.

"I know."

Uriel shook his head. "No. You don't." Mychal shoved him off and hurried to get out of the house. I went after him, doing my best to ignore the warning look in Uriel's eyes.

Outside I took great gulps of fresh air and tried to clear the incense from my nose.

"Mychal? You out here?" I moved down the street, and I spotted him leaning against the corner of the building.

"Don't you lecture me either," he said as I joined him. "They have to have the opportunity to choose their path. That's the whole point of free will, isn't it? A baby is still innocent even if it is Nephilim."

"Chill, Mychal. I just wanted to make sure you weren't alone."

"You can't agree with them, Jael. Tell me, do you have it in you to kill unborn children and their mothers?"

"I have seen them in action, so I don't have an answer for that," I admitted as honestly as I could. "You know they aren't human."

"I meant what I said. I'll kill them if they turn bad. They still deserve the chance." Mychal looked at his boots. "When you've seen as much death as I have, you tend to be hesitant to take more life. We can't be like the monsters we are fighting against."

"And you think that these women will be able to raise them alone to be good Nephilim? They will be supernatural beings, Mychal," I said gently. I didn't have an answer to give him. Both solutions were shitty.

Mychal ran a hand through his hair. "Once we have stopped Semyaza, I will return and check on them. We need to stop their fathers from making more children, from starting wars…"

I held my hand up to stop him talking as my intuition flared angrily, a coldness rushing over my skin.

"Mychal…" I said before throwing him violently out of the way. My baton came down hard on a zombie demon's head.

Mychal was on his feet in seconds, blocking a blow that was aimed at my back.

"They must've been watching the house," Mychal said.

"Oh crap." I groaned. The street began to fill with a crowd. I dropped my shields and confirmed my worst fear. There were no spirits left in the bodies, just demons.

Uriel and Gabriel emerged from the house, coming up behind the mob in a quick attack. I tried to remember my training as I flicked out my second baton. A spear shone in Mychal's hand. "Stay behind me, Jael. I'll protect you."

"And I'll watch your back."

Mychal cleaved a path through the rushing crowd. I tried my best to stay out of the reach of his spear, knocking aside the zombie demons' grabbing hands.

"Jael, to me!" Uriel shouted, cutting demons down so I could run to his side. Between Mychal and the two angels, the battle only lasted seconds. The fug of decomposing demon filled the air as the mutilated corpses of the humans they had inhabited oozed out onto the road.

"Get Jael and Mychal back to the hotel, Uriel. I'll deal with this mess," Gabriel instructed.

"Why would they attack us like this? It's bold, even for demons," Mychal said as we jogged through the streets.

"It was an ambush, they knew—*he* knew—that we would turn up," Uriel said with a growl.

"Who?" I asked.

"Hel'el. Who else?"

"Maybe he was protecting the Nephilim, making sure that they would be born," I suggested.

"Do you still think letting them live was a good idea?" Uriel asked. Mychal ignored him, but I couldn't help thinking Uriel was right.

By the time we made it back, my legs and lungs were burning. I don't know what juju Uriel used, but we were completely ignored by every person we encountered. Quite the feat considering we were smeared with chunky pieces of zombie demon.

"As the only female, I'm pulling rank to get the first shower," I declared, heading for the bathroom before either of them could argue. I put my dirty batons in the sink and stripped, carefully rolling my clothes inward to stop any bits from messing the tiles.

I turned the hot water on full blast and lathered myself over and over with the cedar-scented shower gel that the hotel provided. My hands started to shake, and I gagged violently. No matter how much time passed, I was never going to get used to zombie demons. I rubbed my ribs, feeling the ache that was still there from being tortured.

Tonight I had been focused on staying alive, but now I fought the urge to curl into a ball as the trauma of my imprisonment came rushing back with the stench of demons.

I scrubbed myself again, trying to wash away the memories more than the blood. *You are clean,* Yeshua had told me. I clung to that certainty as I did my best to push all other dark thoughts away. I turned off the shower, wrapped a towel around myself, and pulled back the black shower curtain. Uriel was sitting on top of the closed toilet seat, and I almost slipped ass-up in surprise.

"What are you doing in here?" I demanded.

Uriel seemed to struggle to formulate a sentence before saying, "I felt your fear, so I wanted to make sure you were all right. I didn't see anything, if that's what you are concerned about."

My whole body blushed. "And you couldn't wait until I finished?"

"I was worried you would…hurt yourself."

"I'm tempted to hurt *you* right now."

"Jael, don't do that," he said, as his gray-blue eyes softened. "Don't use anger to hide from my concern and push me away. You were tortured by creatures like the ones we killed tonight. You have every right to be upset."

"That doesn't mean I need you to pat my head and tell me everything will be okay," I snapped.

"Have I ever?" He let out a noise of frustration. "I know you're strong, Jael. I made sure of it. But that doesn't mean I don't care when you are hurting. This isn't a situation that a human should ever be involved in. I don't want you here."

I turned my back on him and braced myself against the sink. I felt like the air had been knocked out of me as I glared at him in the reflection of the mirror. "It's not like I had a choice either. You think this is ideal for me? Being stuck with a bunch of pissed off angels in the middle of a war zone and hunting demons? I *know* I'm the weakest of the group, and that makes me a liability—"

"You misunderstand me, as usual." Uriel stood up to loom behind me, and then he wrapped his arms around me, and leaned down to rest his chin on my shoulder. "I don't want you here, because I don't want anything happening to you, *yadid*. I don't know why I spent so many years protecting you to have Ye-shua drop you in a war zone. I'm *furious* with him because of it. You are the best of us, the most innocent. You don't deserve to see the things we are going to dis-cover in Damascus."

My heart was doing stupid things as I leaned back into his warmth, my whole body softening into his embrace. "I wouldn't be here without a reason. You should have seen me pop zombie demons with my Hand of Power recently. I was taken by surprise tonight, but you never know, my popping powers might be restored." I turned around to face him as he laughed.

"I would've liked to see it." His fingers twisted the end of my damp hair. "My Jael, full of righteous fury as she slew the demons."

"I also brought Alessandro back from the dead. I couldn't let a priest die, even if he is Catholic," I said, remembering the bullet hanging around his neck.

"You like the exorcist, don't you?" Uriel asked.

"Yeah, he's pretty rad. You know I haven't met many people like me."

"That's because there are no people like you," he said and then quickly looked away. "I'd better let you get dressed."

"That's a good idea." I gripped the towel around me. "We wouldn't want Gabriel to get the wrong idea."

Uriel rolled his eyes. "I can handle my brother's teasing."

"Yeah, he seems to think something is up, you know, with us," I said as flip-pantly as I could. I was aware of how close we were, how hard my heart was rac-ing as he gripped the sink on either side of me.

"What does that mean?"

"He said that he can feel that I love you which is super crazy." I laughed awkwardly, needing to have this conversation with him and also completely ter-rified of it.

"Why is that crazy?" Uriel said. I looked at the cracked tiles at my feet be-cause I couldn't handle looking him in the eye.

"Because you guys aren't allowed to, which means if I did, I couldn't ever do anything about it." Oh man, I was so terrible at this.

"After everything you've seen Mychal go through, do you really think that's true?" Uriel said softly. It was the tone that poked at a broken part of me that wanted to hope for impossible things that I couldn't have.

"It doesn't matter what I think. You need to get out, so I can get dressed and save the world," I replied stiffly.

"You're doing it again," Uriel said, a growl of frustration in his voice. "Stop using your anger to push me away."

"I have to get dressed. Now get out or I'm going to drop this towel, and you'll get your feathers in a bunch."

"Your threats don't frighten me, Jael Quinlan. You should know this by now," Uriel said with a smug smile.

"Fine, see if I care." I dropped my towel. I felt the second his eyes landed on my skin, and the tension in the bathroom grew as taut as a bow string.

"You still have bruises," Uriel said, his voice tight. I looked him in the eye, defiance keeping me standing straight. He had a look on his face somewhere between surprise and something...else.

"Yes, I do. Hot, aren't they?" I reached for my fresh clothes and pulled on a pair of black underwear. Uriel's hand rested on the side of my ribs where I was still a faded orange-and-brown color. Heat seeped through me, and I slowly straightened, feeling like any sudden movement would scare us both into a screaming match. *What are you doing, Jael?*

"I'm sorry," he said, but he didn't move his hand.

"They aren't your fault, Uriel. I thought we had moved past this." He used his other hand to move me, so my back was to him. He was getting a good look at every mark and scar on me. I should've moved, broken up whatever was happening, but I didn't. I stood there and tried not to turn into a quivering mess, because he was touching my skin. I almost spontaneously combusted as he traced the scars from my box cutter incident that had thrown us together and up to where my shoulders met my neck.

"I like this bit," he said, fascinated. I was about to ask why when his lips pressed softly against it, and I lost the ability to form sentences. He inhaled and his warm breath tickled against me. "I like how you smell too. I missed it when we were fighting." I was trying to think of something to say when he let me go and stepped back. "Get dressed, Jael. The world isn't going to save itself." And then he left me standing in the bathroom, half-naked and too shocked to move.

37

HEL'EL STRETCHED LIKE A well-fed cat as he watched the city burn beneath him. He sat on the walls of the Citadel of Damascus, smiling broadly as his demons and the Watchers tore the city apart around him. Hel'el was there to observe but declined to participate. He liked to watch.

Reaching into a bowl beside him, Hel'el selected a fat olive and popped it into his mouth, the tart vinegary taste mingling pleasantly with the figs and wine he had just consumed.

Semyaza had taken over the citadel to use as their personal fortress and base. Hel'el had been surprised by the Watchers' eagerness to wipe out as much of humanity as they could. He barely had to encourage them at all. Clearly, they hadn't quite forgiven the Almighty for their long imprisonment. He was chuckling to himself when he sensed something approaching. The demon had chosen a hulking human soldier as its vessel, but Hel'el would recognize it anywhere.

"What news, Belias?" he asked as he turned his eyes back to the city.

"The archangels have been sighted in Jericho. They know about the Nephilim," Belias said, its voice a low rumble.

Hel'el sighed. "It didn't take them long to sniff them out."

"They didn't kill them. The women will be readying to give birth as we speak."

"What? They let them live? They must be bigger fools than I thought, considering all they did to rid Eretz of them last time."

"A human stopped them. Tall bearing, black hair and eyes."

Hel'el fought the urge to spit. "So, they have finally recruited him. That *is* annoying."

"Who, my lord?"

"Who do you think, idiot?" Hel'el rounded on him. "Mychal the Bastard General himself." Belias flinched involuntarily. "Don't recoil from his name like a coward! He's just another human in this form. Humans are weak, impressionable, and controlled by their emotions. Mychal is the same. I thought killing the woman in Russia would have been enough to crush all purpose and meaning from him, but clearly, I must try harder."

"There was a woman with them too," said Belias.

"What woman?" Hel'el gestured him over. "Show me."

Belias took his hand, and Hel'el took the memories straight from its head. You could never trust a demon to get the facts right.

"Jael fucking Quinlan." Hel'el released Belias. "How is she involved in this? She is meant to be dead."

"I didn't know it was her," the demon grumbled. "I heard that HeosCorp in Melbourne had their operation shut down. I didn't think it was her."

"She couldn't have survived without divine intervention. Whether she's here with Mychal is irrelevant. They are both still human."

"Do you wish me to send a cohort to delay them?" Belias asked eagerly.

"Yes, send decent soldiers though; make it challenging for them. The others in Jericho would have only annoyed them."

"And the Nephilim?"

"Let them be. I'll see to their birth myself. Let them slaughter and feast and make Mychal regret ever allowing them to live. After all, humans love nothing more than their guilt. Mychal loves it most of all."

"And the exorcist?"

"The exorcist." Hel'el sneered. "She's an ignorant child scratching at the surface of her power. She'll die like the rest of them."

Belias bowed, disappearing as the flapping of great wings descended upon the walls. Azazel landed beside Hel'el, wearing cargo pants and boots stolen from a dead soldier. He had a sword in his hand and was showered with blood and dirt.

"You are looking well." Hel'el laughed. "Having fun yet?"

"I'm feeling much more myself, Hel'el. Is my forge ready yet? These bullets of the humans are starting to annoy me. I need the press of steel against me."

"I have servants constructing it in the citadel. We will need your armor soon, Azazel. They are coming."

"Who?"

"The usual favorites, Uriel and Gabriel."

Azazel's face turned as red as his hair. "I spent a millennium in that hole because of those bastards. Semyaza needs to know this. What of Michael?"

"Human."

"What did you say? How is he human?"

"Forgive me. I forget that there's much you don't know. We should wait for Semyaza; he will want to hear this."

"Hear what?" Semyaza dropped down from the sky next to them. Hel'el told them quickly of Michael's incurable bouts of humanity and the reason he was granted such a deal. Semyaza remained very still and quiet until Hel'el was finished, then a scream of animal frustration and anger poured out of him, shaking the ground beneath them. He drove a powerful fist into the stone wall, rock and rubble exploding in clouds around them.

"Calm yourself, Semyaza," Hel'el said gently. "You're overlooking one vital detail; Mychal is *human*. His flesh is soft and vulnerable, his mind and spirit susceptible and programmed for weakness. And we know what his most fatal weakness is."

"Na'amah. Why does it always come back to her? I should have killed her when I had the chance." Semyaza raved as he paced.

"I know how to weaken him, to give you and Azazel time to continue your important work. He has human limitations."

"His generals don't," Azazel said.

"They still fall under his leadership. Leave Mychal and his allies to me. They have weak spots I know how to exploit. Did you leave the bodies out in the streets as I commanded?"

"Yes, Hel'el."

"Good. I'll ensure that when they arrive, an army will meet them."

"And us?" Semyaza asked.

"You and Azazel must head north. There's a town where a cult resides, a most blasphemous place in Elyon's eyes. I want you to destroy it, and I'll join you there. There is something I need to do first."

In Jericho the night was pierced with screams. "*Malaika, Malaika,*" the two women whispered over and over. It had been hours since the strange man had saved their babies from the sword. Their bellies had become so large in the short time that they could no longer sit or move.

One cried out in agony as her ribs broke under the building pressure. Their well-wishers and worshippers had gone for the evening, and they were all alone in their suffering.

Hel'el moved invisibly around the bed. His hand rested lightly on the swollen bellies. "Come now, children. Break yourself free of these fleshy prisons." He felt life shudder under his hand as he imbued them with rage.

Hel'el drank in the dead mothers' pain as he stroked the boys' bloody heads and told them where to find their fathers. When he was satisfied, he returned to Damascus.

Hel'el walked through the desolate streets of the city, admiring how brutal the Watchers had been. They were efficient and indiscriminate. He hadn't paid them much attention when they had first roamed the earth, and perhaps, under his leadership instead of Semyaza's, the outcome would have been different.

Hel'el found a pile of dead soldiers heaped haphazardly next to the remains of a tank. He closed his eyes and lifted his hands, summoning the bodiless ones to him. Greasy gray smoke rolled about his feet before moving into the empty corpses.

Soon after his banishment, Hel'el had discovered these creatures scattered over the earth. They pledged their allegiance to him, the most beautiful and glorious of all beings. Demons were never fallen angels, though the thought of it made Hel'el smile. The angels had bodies, while demons lived without form and substance, craving the bodies of others. Over time the bodies they inhabited started to mold and change, twist and distort to accommodate the creature within.

Hel'el couldn't have cared, nor did he pity the humans who allowed themselves to be possessed. Humans spread like a plague; there was no stopping the infestation, but he was certainly going to slow it down.

The bodies of the soldiers at his feet twisted and moved as they reanimated. "Arise, my friends. Awaken your brothers. The archangels are coming, and now is your chance to destroy them," Hel'el commanded. His voice traveled throughout the streets of Damascus, and the demons rose.

Invisible to the eyes of the demons and Hel'el, tall angels in parchment-colored robes appeared on the rooftops and on street corners.

They were silent, watching and waiting.

38

IN MY DREAM, I was walking down unknown streets with Mychal by my side. People were haggling and pressing into us, market food vendors were shouting, and the heady scents of patchouli, diesel, cinnamon, and heat filled the air.

"This is weird," I whispered to Mychal. "I know I went to sleep, but this feels like a meditation, not a dream."

"There's a difference?" Mychal asked. "I feel…summoned."

I spotted a man sitting at a café table not far in front of us. He was smoking a hookah lazily and drinking steaming mint tea. The fair-haired man smiled at us, and it was like pure sunshine. There was something *familiar* about that face, and my intuition itched like crazy. He waved at us.

"Mychal, no matter how many times you are reborn you are the same rigid, uptight soldier. I knew it was you immediately," he said, offering us the empty seats at the table. "And young Jael, it's a pleasure to meet you at last."

"Is it?" I asked uncertainly. We took our seats, but I noticed Mychal was careful to make sure he was out of reach of the stranger. I tried to relax, but my hands brushed over the knife in my pocket and the closed baton in my sleeve. Whatever was going on, my unconscious mind wasn't about to leave me unarmed.

"For the amount of trouble you've caused my company and me in the past few months, I must say I expected someone more terrifying," the stranger said and offered his hand. I suddenly knew where I had seen the guy before: in the blurry shot of someone who claimed they had spotted Lucian Heosphoros, the CEO of HeosCorp, in Cyprus.

"Hey Lucian," I replied smoothly like I knew it was him all along. "I thought you'd be better looking." His tanned face was drop-dead gorgeous as it spread into a charming smile.

"Don't be fooled by his act, Jael. We know it's you, Hel'el. What do you want?" Mychal demanded, refusing to play at niceties. *Hel'el.* I looked up at the smiling man pouring me a glass of mint tea. I was about to have tea with the freaking Devil.

"It's not about what I want, Mychal. What is it that *you* want? How many of these human lives are you going to waste being Elyon's whipping boy? Have you ever gotten what you want in all of that time?"

Mychal didn't hesitate. "Yes."

"You are thinking of her. Of course," Hel'el replied in an infuriating tone.

"Say what you need to and let us get back to sleep." Mychal's voice was cold enough to make the hair on my arms rise.

"I've said it. What do you want? Do you want the girl? I'll give her back to you. You can take Aleksandra and retire in some quiet place of your choosing.

You can have all the peace and babies or whatever that you like. You know I have the power to grant it."

"In exchange for what?"

"No exchange. Just take her and go. You don't need to fight anymore, brother. Take a holiday." Mychal was quiet for a few moments, watching the crowds around us.

Don't do it, I wanted to say. I knew how much he missed her. I had been the one talking him down after every nightmare.

"My memory isn't what it was. Tell me, how many times have you offered this to me? Have I *ever* agreed?" asked Mychal.

"This is the first time I have offered it, Mychal. I see how much you are suffering this time around. We loved each other once. No matter what has happened through the eons, you are still my little brother. I don't like how Father treats you."

"Hmm, so you claim."

"It's the truth. I just want you to be happy. Lay down your sword, go and live with the woman you have loved for eternity."

"I just realized why this seems so familiar." Mychal smiled, and it wasn't pleasant. "It's the same deal you have tried to make with every human since Elyon formed them. You're mannered and unimaginative in your promises. Your only trick is to persuade people that they must trade their holiness for their happiness. Give up what Elyon wants because the path is too hard; go and retire, little human. Lay down your sword. There is *nothing* you can offer me that will make me do that."

I held my breath as the beautiful golden face in front of us slipped and distorted, revealing one broken and full of hate and rage.

"You aren't so holy anymore, Mychal. You have sin and anger in your heart, just like all of these other human cowards." Hel'el glared at me. "And you are hardly pure either, exorcist. I know the blood on your hands and the lust burning inside of you."

"True. But even with all that sin, I know that Daddy in Heaven still loves me. Can you say the same?" I replied. Mychal grinned beside me, and I figured I had scored a point.

Hel'el's laugh was cracked and bitter. "Dear misguided Mychal, you were always a favorite pet until these apes crawled out of the mud and became the apple of his eye. And then he turned around and made you one too. The cost that's demanded is so high, but I suppose Aleksandra is the one that pays for it. You decided to become human, and now her soul is forced to be reborn and murdered over and over and over again for all eternity. Did you ever ask her if it was what she wanted? Or do you just demand it of her again and again? Is that love? Think of all the times she was born and died without knowing who she was or why she was doomed."

Hel'el leaned forward, his pupils swelling to an overwhelming blackness. "Do you remember all the times I found her first, Mychal? Or do you choose to ignore those memories? Has Uriel even allowed you to remember them? She has died in the most exquisitely inventive ways. I have enjoyed hearing her scream over the years like a beloved tune."

"Enough!" Mychal said, his voice booming out, causing the glasses on the table to shatter. I felt the power surging through him, lighting up under his skin and making me shiver.

"Oh, shut up. I'm done with you anyway. But before you leave, I have a gift." Hel'el's hand sprung out and gripped Mychal's forearm tightly. "Dream and remember, little brother. Dream and remember." Mychal's huge body blinked out, leaving me all alone.

"What did you do? Where did you send him?" I demanded. My concern for the demon hunter far outweighed my fear of Hel'el.

"I need to remind him of all the damage he's caused. It might humble him." Pale green eyes zeroed in on me, and I held them. I had spent a lifetime having staring competitions with Uriel, but even then, I struggled. I didn't know if it was the dream state we were in, but Hel'el didn't feel like a demon, like the sticky presence of something evil I always felt.

"What are you doing, Jael Quinlan? You shouldn't be here, tangling with angels and demons," he said softly, his voice full of concern.

I shrugged. "I dunno. I go where I'm asked to."

"I don't want to hurt you, but I will if you choose to remain with them."

I couldn't stop the cynical laughter bubbling out of me. "It's a little late for that, or are you forgetting my stint in your HeosCorp dungeon?"

"They were only trying to scare you off. They were under orders not to kill you."

"Why? Because the Man Upstairs would have smitten you for messing with his exorcist?"

"Hardly. I've smitten plenty of his servants and suffered no consequence. You know why? Because he doesn't care about any of you. Not anymore. Trust me, I know."

"Trust the Devil? Yeah, not going to happen. You only know how to tell lies and believe me, I've heard them all."

Hel'el steepled his fingers thoughtfully. "What if I give you your heart's desire?"

"What? A never-ending packet of Tim Tams?" Oh boy, did I need to wake up from this dream.

"That's not what you want." His lips curved in an amused smile. "What about Father Alessandro? I could give him to you."

"He's not a 'thank you' hamper," I snapped.

"He is to me. If you want him to break his vows for you, I'll see it done." His smile was indulgent. "You did seem very fond of him."

"I'm fond of a lot of people."

"No, you aren't. People have hurt you too much over the years. I understand what it's like to be alone in the world." He stretched his hands out toward me. "You've had Uriel looking after you for a long time, but he's done his best to isolate you from everyone else. He's selfish that way. I can understand. He was so angry about having to be the guard dog to a dysfunctional human, all of creation felt it."

He's just trying to get a rise out you. Don't take the bait. I ground my teeth together to stop myself from giving him an earful.

"Perhaps I have it all wrong, and your heart doesn't long for the exorcist. He wouldn't be my first choice, but Uriel is—" The smile on his face vanished as I drove the blade of my knife through his hand that still rested on the table.

"That's for upsetting Mychal," I hissed, twisting the blade with my left hand. My baton came across and hit him upside the head, causing his pretty face glamour to shudder. "And that's for Nazirah, you piece of shit."

I saw his burnt and twisted smile right before I threw my spirit back into my body, waking myself up with a jolt. In the room next to me, I heard Mychal cry out in his sleep. *Oh no, what is he doing to you?* I collided with Gabriel who stood outside my room.

"It's okay, Jael," he said. "Mychal's only dreaming."

"No, he's not." I pushed my hair out of my face. "Hel'el has sent his mind off to relive Aleksandra's death through every lifetime." I went to open the door, but Gabriel rested a hand on my shoulder, holding me back.

"You can't go in there. If you are right, he might try to attack you. Wait until Uriel returns—"

I pushed his hand off my shoulder. "I can handle it. I won't touch him, but I don't want him to be alone." I opened the door and stepped into the dark room. A lamp was smashed on the floor where Mychal must have swiped at it in his sleep. He was twisted up, sweating and shaking, muttering words that sounded Spanish.

I sat down, propping my back against a wall. "It's okay, Mychal. You aren't alone." I didn't know if he heard me or not. I hoped a part of him did.

Long ago in Spain

The road from Seville was choked with carts, horses, and grieving travelers. Melchizedek and his father, Alon, did not look back. After a lifetime, the Jews had now been royally expelled from their homes.

Melchizedek had begged his father to leave months ago, to get out before there was more war, but Alon did not believe that the king and queen would allow such drastic measures. Weren't the Jews high members of Spanish society and industry? Were they not valued moneylenders, scholars, and tradesmen?

Melchizedek had believed him until the day he saw the enemy of all Spanish Jews: Father Thomas de Torquemada. By chance Melchizedek had seen him in front of the Cathedral of Saint Mary, and he also saw the demon squirming about inside of him. All of Torquemada's radical violence suddenly made sense. He had let the foul thing inside of him and let it take over.

Melchizedek wondered what the demon had promised him...but it soon became very obvious. Power. It was always power. When he had told Alon, the man's face had gone dark with unexpressed anger. He was the only one Melchizedek had told about his gift of sight.

A few weeks before Isabella and Ferdinand's edict, Melchizedek had been attacked by demons. He had thought they were supporters of Torquemada until he had seen their deformed and mutilated bodies. They ambushed him, and he sliced through them with his *espada ropera* and dagger.

It wasn't demons he was worried about now as he scanned the other travelers; it was attacks from Torquemada's supporters and the bandits who were taking advantage of the fleeing Jews. Stories had come to them of whole families slain for the wealth they had been forced to liquidize at the Crown's command.

Alon had chosen Turkey for their exile. The Sultan Bajazet welcomed the Sephardian-Sefarad as an asset to enrich his kingdom. Many other Jews they knew had fled to Portugal, but Alon was too angry from the treatment of this Catholic monarchy to suffer another, especially because it was a well-known fact that Ferdinand sought a treaty with them.

"How long would it take for them to banish us once more?" Alon said with a huff as he packed his precious scrolls into a chest.

Screams ahead drew Melchizedek from his daydreaming. He pulled the cart's reins to stop their horses. He jumped down, passing the reins to Alon.

"Stay here," he commanded. "I'm going to see what is happening."

"But Mel—"

"No, Father. Just stay; don't argue." Under normal circumstances, he would never speak to his abba so disrespectfully, but his hands were burning, just like they had when he had been attacked in the street.

Pulling out his sword, Melchizedek ran to the top of the hill. In the dip below him, a cart was burning, and bandits were attacking a small family. Melchizedek hurried to their aid, and as he took down the first attacker, he saw the demons inside of the bandits. He tried not to trip over the bodies of the fallen as he moved through the small band, cutting them down with deadly ease. One caught his arm with clawed hands, and Melchizedek sliced its fingers off with his dagger.

"Too…late…*malakhim*," the demon said, its speech garbled as it drooled blood from between its lips. Melchizedek kicked the body away from him, disgusted and furious. Looking around there was only one survivor, an old man clutching a dying girl.

"I'm sorry," Melchizedek started to say. "I tried to get to you…" He saw the face of the girl, beautiful and unmistakable even as blood pooled around her. Pain and despair flooded him as Melchizedek recognized her. He fell to his knees in her blood, taking her other hand. "I'm so sorry. I'm so sorry—"

"It's…you," she whispered as the light faded from her eyes.

Mychal woke screaming and thrashing. He could smell blood and demons mingled with the cinnamon, rose smell of the dead woman's hair.

"Easy, Mychal. Easy." Cool hands found his burning forehead, smoothing the soaked hair from his face.

"She's dead! She's dead… I couldn't save her. I can never save her." Mychal wept.

"It's not your fault," the voice said.

"It is! I should have let her live and die in peace. Not to be reborn to this fate over and over. My love kills her every time."

"Open your eyes, Mychal. Hel'el's illusions have taken hold of you."

Mychal dragged himself out of the crushing blackness and opened his blurry eyes. The figure sitting on the end of the bed was no angel. It was a man with curly brown hair and gentle eyes.

"You?" Mychal whispered as he launched backward, hitting the wall behind him. The man smiled in the darkness.

"Am I so frightening that you recoil?" he asked amused.

"I'm sorry, I did not expect…Yeshua, I'm… Forgive me," Mychal stammered, his whole body shaking. "You startled me." Jael was sitting on the floor cradled protectively in Uriel's arms, and both were fast asleep. "What happened?"

"You have let Hel'el get the better of your mind tonight."

"I know, but he was right. Aleksandra is reborn and dies because of me. I'm so selfish." Mychal hugged his knees to his chest, hiding his face in his hands.

"Loving her is not selfish. Don't you think she was asked how she felt about it before Elyon made the covenant with you? It was made only by her agreement. She believed the possibility of death to be worth the chance at life with you."

"She agreed?" Mychal lifted his head.

"Of course, she did. Hel'el twisted your mind because he knows you don't see clearly when it comes to her. It wasn't just your decision. She loves you; that transcends all."

"I keep remembering all the times I couldn't save her. Seeing my failure over and over. The pain…"

"I won't take the memories away from you, because they are a part of who you are. Your endurance shapes you into the man you must become. You didn't suffer alone. Don't you remember me there beside you in your darkest hours, just as you were there in mine?"

Mychal squeezed his head in his hands, searching the dream. And there he was, standing behind Melchizedek as he cried his rage and grief. The fog in his mind seemed to clear in that moment, and he opened his eyes.

"You were there," Mychal whispered.

"Of course, I was. I will always be there. You *know* this. You are never alone."

Mychal suddenly knew it was Yeshua who had pulled him off the bathroom floor in Budapest. His hands moved to cover his scars, ashamed he had let himself fall that deeply in despair.

"I'm sorry, I'm sorry…" Mychal gasped through the tears that were running down his face, the last few months of pain rushing to the surface. Yeshua's hands reached over to cover his.

"It's okay, Mychal. We have all known despair and pain and thought that death would be the only way out. I need you to fight this battle, and I know you have the strength. Believe in yourself, and if you can't, know that I always will."

"How can you believe in me when I'm like this? I'm so broken. There have been too many lifetimes, too much loss. I can't take it anymore. I'm a smashed vessel."

"Sometimes things need to be broken to be made new. You aren't useless or powerless, even like this. In time you will see it for yourself." He rose to his feet.

"Will I see you again?" Mychal asked. Yeshua placed a gentle hand on his head.

"Of course, you will. Be strong for those who can't. Look after Jael." And he was gone, leaving Mychal hugging himself.

"Mychal?" Gabriel came into the room, his face tight with concern. "I heard you screaming. Is it the nightmares?"

"Isn't it always?" Mychal drained the water from the glass beside his bed.

Gabriel stilled, looking at Jael and Uriel asleep, before checking the rest of the room. "Yeshua was here?"

"He woke me. Hel'el did something to me through my dreams. It triggered…the bad times. I couldn't break out of the dreams like I usually can."

"Jael told me what happened," Gabriel whispered, making sure he didn't wake the exorcist. "You must protect yourself even in sleep. You're human, and that makes you vulnerable in many ways. But then it's because you are human that you are stronger than us all."

"It certainly doesn't feel that way."

"How *does* it feel? To be human?" Gabriel asked curiously.

"What do you mean? The pain?"

"No, I'm talking about Elyon. He created humans in his image. There's a part of Elyon in every cell of your body. It allows them to wield the power of Heaven on Earth without their flesh breaking apart. Yeshua gave them back their birthright, and as a human, you are a part of that covenant. You have that power inside of you now too…so how does it feel?"

"I don't know. I have never really thought about it or explored it."

"So, Uriel was right then. Humans don't know anything about the power they can use," Gabriel said sadly.

"Maybe they aren't meant to. Knowing humans they would probably find a way to exploit it."

"Jael used it in Melbourne last month," Gabriel said softly and smiled. "It scared Uriel. He worries over her like a mother hen."

"He's still lucky to have her." They lapsed into silence for a long time, before Mychal admitted, "I miss Aleksandra. She had a way of seeing the good in everything and everyone, even me. It made me a better person to be around her. I don't trust myself to do the right things without her. I'm too angry."

"Mychal, you are still doing the right things without her. Saving the Nephilim was the right thing to do, even if it was the wrong decision. You gave them a choice with the hope they would not be like their forefathers. It was your human heart getting the better of you, even though you knew the mothers were beyond saving."

"I'm going to have to kill the Nephilim one day, aren't I?" Mychal felt sick just saying it.

"Yes. Sooner rather than later. There are rules and reasons for all things. The Nephilim are an abomination and always will be; they were born out of corruption, so it is in their very nature to corrupt. They will hunt down their fathers. I can feel Hel'el behind all of this, making them dance."

"We'll reach Damascus tomorrow. What do you think we will find there?"

Gabriel looked stricken. "The only thing Hel'el enjoys now. Death. Horrific and wasteful death."

"Sounds about right."

"You will need these." Gabriel smiled and handed him twin swords in their scabbards. "They were left for you."

Mychal took them and felt something pulse through his hands. The hilts of the swords gleamed silver and black in the murky light. "Try not to throw these away like you did the last one. Get some sleep. Tomorrow will test you."

"Every day tests me," Mychal replied as he lay back down, cradling the swords to his chest and praying he didn't dream.

39

THE GOVERNMENT AND ITS military leaders had declared Damascus a war zone. There were arguments about sending in American or UN soldiers to invade the city, but they were holding off, uncertain of what lay in front of them. One general had suggested that they drop a nuclear bomb on the city to keep the "plague" from spreading.

There were arguments from all the religious bodies because images of angels had been leaked in the early days of the siege. Some were claiming it was God's justice on the city. Muslims, Christians, and Jews alike were coming to the same conclusions—if these were angels, then they were not from God.

Satanic cults crept from their secretive crevices, claiming their time had come. There had been riots, rallies, and deaths in America. The military had tried sending in drones, but as soon as they passed the outskirts of the city, they were wrestled out of the sky. Barricades had been set up to block off all traffic trying to get into Damascus.

In the military base camp that had been established fifty kilometers away, Mychal, Gabriel, Uriel, and Jael watched on, unnoticed as men in uniforms ran drills and pulled over vehicles.

"There's no getting through that," Mychal said as he surveyed the chaos through binoculars.

"Looks like it's going to be the angel express again."

"I don't know how I feel about the term 'angel express,'" commented Uriel.

"Really? I think a flight attendant's outfit would suit you. Do you have a better idea?" Jael winked at Mychal, who grinned behind Uriel's back.

"It's the only way in," Gabriel said. "Uriel is just sensitive. The inner city is being protected; Hel'el has sealed it off to hinder us. We can break the wards once we are closer."

Without a word of warning, Gabriel grabbed Mychal by the scabbards that crisscrossed his back and launched into the air. Mychal tried not to give him the satisfaction of screaming as the wind and clouds battered him. Unlike last time, they didn't move in the in-between spaces of reality, instead they just went high and fast to stay out of the sight of the helicopters and the humans.

Mychal kept his focus on the smoking bruise of a city on the horizon and not the hard ground beneath him. The air rushed through his clothes and hair, and his fear left him, leaving only exhilaration. Then the earth was rushing toward him, and he was dropped to his feet. Gabriel kept his grip on him to make sure that Mychal's knees didn't collapse underneath him.

"You are getting better at landings," commented Gabriel.

"You are getting better at not slamming me into the ground," Mychal replied as he tightened the leather straps on his chest. He dumped his bag on the dusty road and pulled out his gun holsters. He made the straps longer and slipped them over the top of his sword scabbards, adjusting them so they wouldn't chafe under his arm. It was a heavier load to carry, but he wasn't going into battle without them.

"Where are we?" Mychal asked looking up at the old columns in front of him.

"The Temple of Jupiter. It's in the old part of the city. Uriel and Jael destroyed the wards while we were in the air. Uriel said that he could feel Hel'el near this part of the city."

"I didn't think we took that long to get here."

Gabriel smirked. "I had to make sure that your skin didn't peel off your bones."

"Enjoy your fun while I'm still human, little brother." Mychal stashed his bag inside the looted mosque and tried not to let his fury at the desecration overwhelm him.

"Hel'el doesn't care to favor one religion over another," Gabriel said sadly. "He uses whatever is in the heart and corrupts it. He doesn't wage a war against Christians, Muslims, or Jews, but against everyone and everything."

"He's a ridiculous child having a tantrum," Jael said, as she and Uriel entered the mosque.

Mychal offered her one of his handguns. "You know how to use this?"

Jael took the gun, slipped on the safety, and tucked it into her jacket. "I'm licensed back in Australia. One of my best friends is a cop. We've gone to a range more than once."

"Good. Don't hesitate to use it today." Mychal gave her an extra magazine of bullets.

"Are these silver?"

"Of course. In my experience as a hunter, silver can kill anything supernatural or otherwise."

Jael smiled. "Rad."

"Focus, Jael," Uriel said, and then gave her a grin when she stuck her tongue out at him. "Keep it up, exorcist, and see what it gets you."

They walked slowly through the streets, surveying the damage wrought by the Watchers. Houses were still burning. Cars, shops, temples, and markets decimated. Mychal could feel the anger brewing in the two angels; it bounced between them in an aura of frustration at the waste of life.

"Something is very wrong," Mychal commented.

"I thought that was obvious," Jael replied.

"It's not that, I mean… What's missing?" Mychal asked as he looked all around him. "Where are the bodies? With this much devastation, there should be bodies. They wouldn't have buried them. There is blood but nothing else."

They walked past the Mausoleum of Saladin and saw blood seeping across the ground in thick lines that looked like something had been dragged. A cold chill ran down Mychal's back, his unease growing with every cautious step they took. He tried not to think of the red that was caking his boots.

Mychal pulled a gun out as a man in parchment-colored robes appeared ahead of them. He wore no shoes; the blood in the street stained his feet and hem. His pale eyes were raised to the sky, tears streaked his face, and his lips moved in a ceaseless whisper. Mychal approached him cautiously, and he realized it wasn't a man at all; it was an angel.

"What is going on?" Mychal said as more angels in parchment-colored robes appeared around him, on the rooftops and street corners. All standing and watching.

"You can see them too, right?" Jael's eyes were wide. "They are the freakiest angels I've ever seen."

Mychal looked at the sky and saw only the dusty murk. "Gabriel?"

"Look again," Gabriel instructed.

Mychal looked up and stumbled backward. In the sky above them was an army of angels. Opposite them was a heaving, seething mass of blackness. Both armies faced each other, not moving, just watching and waiting for a command. Mychal tore his eyes away from the skies back to the silent angels.

"Do something!" he said to them. "Why do they stand here in innocent blood and do nothing?" He went to grab one, but Gabriel pulled him back.

"They are doing as commanded. They've come to bear witness," Uriel explained. "We must be getting close."

"Leave them be, Mychal. They are here to uphold us," Gabriel said and gave him a gentle push. Mychal holstered his gun and followed the blood, trying desperately to shut out the questions in his head.

"Keep close, Jael," Mychal said.

"Don't have to ask me twice." Jael already had her batons out, waiting to be jumped. Uriel followed cautiously behind her.

Minutes later Mychal stopped short, pulling out his swords. "That's where the bodies went," he muttered as adrenaline burned at the base of his neck. Surrounding the citadel was a legion of demons. They stood on the walls and in ranks in front of them.

"You'll be glad of my training now," Uriel commented as he pulled out his sword. Gabriel flicked his spear out to its full, deadly length.

"Trust Semyaza and Azazel to hide behind their armies," Gabriel said.

"It didn't help them last time." Mychal smiled at Jael who looked like she was itching for the fight as much as he was.

"Last time you weren't human," she replied.

"You weren't even there. This is going to make an interesting study for you."

"Let's just hope those blessings you put on my batons work," Jael said. She started whispering prayers under her breath, and her energy spiked. Mychal had felt that kind of energy before; she was calling down power from Heaven. He tried to shake the buzzing that hummed over his skin as the energy touched him. They had been worried about her, but seeing the white light flickering over her, he wondered if they should be more worried about whoever got in her way.

Mychal's smile widened as he turned back toward the army. On the wall, a huge man appeared and started shouting in a forgotten language. "That one is mine," he said and pointed at the hulking general with the tip of his sword.

"It's good to know some things don't change no matter what body you are in," Uriel said. "You still smile like a maniac before a fight, and you still think you can beat me to a target."

"I'll race you," Mychal said and grinned again. "Try to keep up." He didn't wait for a blast of Gabriel's shofar, the signal for an honorable battle. He ran with a shout of anger and let it overwhelm him.

The first four demons that rushed him fell in a tangled heap as he wove his way in between them, taking out arms and legs with the edge of his blades. The twin blades were made for his hands, and even though he didn't remember them, his hands did; they knew the feel of the hilts, the faint drag as they carved through flesh, armor, steel, and bone.

Mychal didn't turn to look for the others. He could feel them behind him, protecting his sides as best as they could. The screeching death cries of the demons rose up in a symphony of fury.

Mychal tried not to think that they were once people. What made them human was gone. They were puppets of Hel'el, sent to hinder them. The air rushed out of his lungs as he was hit in the chest with a wooden club. Uriel flashed past in a silver streak of swords, his assailants falling to the ground in pieces.

"Watch yourself, Mychal. They aren't interested in us; they are only focusing on you," he said as Mychal took the head off another.

"Hel'el is just upset that I turned him down again," Mychal shouted as he cut his way through.

The demons were pressing in, scrambling over the top of each other to claw at him. Mychal was pulled aside, and Uriel charged into the demons, throwing them backward with a shove of his huge shield.

"You could have led with that," Mychal said, panting.

"I would have if you hadn't charged in like a madman."

"I'm fighting a horde of demons with two archangels and an exorcist; sanity left me long ago."

Mychal threw his sword, knocking back the demon that was launching itself at Uriel's turned back. For every demon he cut down, another three rose to replace them. Mychal got a sudden idea, and Jael pulled him out of the reach of long demon claws.

"What is the matter with you! We need to get out of here!" she said as she gripped his arm.

"No, I know what we have to do. We need to get up on the wall!" Mychal replied.

"You will both be overrun," Gabriel said.

"Just do it! Trust me." Gabriel grabbed them by the arms and jumped high up onto the parapets. Inside the citadel was choked with the animated bodies of the citizens of Damascus.

"Oh, that's just perfect," said Jael.

"This is suicide! There are too many. You'll collapse before the task is done."

"Uriel flicked my mouth to make it so I could speak all languages. Can you do something to make my voice loud?" Mychal asked.

"How loud?"

"Loud enough to reach through the entire city."

"I can…but why?" Gabriel asked, confused.

"What's the point of having the ability to wield the power of Heaven on Earth if we never use it? I'd like to see what will happen if we combine it," Mychal said to Jael. She understood immediately, her eyes alight with fury and excitement.

"I'm up for it if you are," she said. Gabriel placed a bloody hand over each of their throats and heat rushed through Mychal.

"It's done," Gabriel said. "Whatever you are going to do with it, do it quickly. I'll be helping Uriel."

Mychal tried to think of the exorcism rites Vadim had used, the Latin ones he had been taught. But that had not been his way. His way was of a warrior, simple and direct.

"Would you do the honors?" Mychal asked Jael. "I've never been good at exorcisms."

"My pleasure." She took his hand and power ran up his arm, filling him even as it magnified.

Jael took a deep breath and shouted with all of her might, "In the name of Elyon, Most High God, whose authority exceeds all of the Heavens and Earth, I command you to flee back to the darkness where you came from! Go back to your master and let your filth stain this place no more!"

Mychal stumbled as the power streaked out of them. The walls trembled underneath them as her words bounced through the buildings and streets around them. The fighting stopped as the bodies collapsed like dominos, a seething pool of blackness rising out of them and into the air.

Mychal watched mesmerized as the angel army in the heavens fell upon it. Jael grabbed him by the head, pulling his face down to look at her.

"Focus on me, Mychal. Don't look at it. It's not for us to know," she shouted.

Uriel and Gabriel landed beside them. They stared at Jael in frightened awe.

"They are gone," Gabriel said softly. "Well done."

"What are we to do with all these bodies?" Jael asked sadly.

"They will be filled in a moment," Mychal said, his body and his words not his own. He turned to survey all of the fallen, the limbless, the corpses. "Get up! Shake the dust from your feet, people of Damascus!" he commanded, and his voice boomed through the city. His archangel power roared through him, bolstered by a force of supernatural blessing. He tried not to scream as he tried to contain it.

There was a great rumbling through the heavens, and a storm roared over them, splintering the sky apart with cracks of lightning. Rain started to fall, and the bodies on the ground trembled and sat up. Shouts and wails of confusion rose around them. The dismembered people watched their limbs grow back as life flooded through them.

Mychal clung to Jael, and their laughter rose over the thunder, rain, and ozone that washed the blood and dirt from them. Then Mychal pitched forward as the power sustaining him left. Gabriel caught him before he fell from the wall, and Uriel scooped Jael up in his arms, holding her close to him.

"It is done, *yadid*. It is done," he said, reassuring her.

"We need...we need to find them..." Mychal tried to speak as Gabriel took his swords from him. "The Watchers... They aren't here."

"Don't worry. We will find them," Gabriel said as he pushed the wet golden hair from his face.

Mychal's body started to shake, and through the sheen of lightning, he saw Hel'el glaring at them. Then he saw another face in the crowd. *Semyaza*. With new strength, Mychal pushed himself up.

"Stay here. Search the citadel with Uriel... I need to check something," he said to Jael.

"Mychal, you just—"

"Please, I know you are worried. Just trust me." Mychal hurried down the alley to where he had seen Semyaza. At the end of the alley, the tall Watcher stood, seething with anger.

"So, it is true," Semyaza said, snarling. "You are human."

"I am. Please, Semyaza, stop this. You know this isn't right. Hel'el is playing you both."

"You're a liar, and you always have been. Why not leave us alone? Have we not suffered enough? Haven't I?" Semyaza trembled with unexpressed emotion. "I gave up everything for her, and yet she chose you."

"This is not about Na'amah—"

"It is always about Na'amah!" Semyaza shouted. "We did all of this… Everything I convinced them to do was so that I could have her."

"She didn't make you break your vows or kill indiscriminately." Mychal shook his head. "If Aleksandra were here, you would disgust her still."

"Aleksandra? So that's the name she is going by in this life? Good. Let her see what her choices have brought her."

"She's dead. Hel'el killed her," Mychal said, his hand itching to put a bullet in Semyaza's head. He still remembered holding Na'amah's broken body after Semyaza had raped and beaten her.

"Why would Hel'el kill her? He's helping us. We'll fix our mistakes, and Elyon will welcome us back—"

"You can't possibly be this stupid, Semyaza. Whatever he has told you, this isn't what Elyon or Yeshua wants."

"Yeshua? Who is Yeshua?" Semyaza demanded, confusion flickering across his face.

"You seriously don't know?" Mychal started to explain, but before he could finish, Semyaza disappeared. "Get back here, you coward!"

Exhaustion settled on him, and Mychal started to shake. Blood thrummed in his head, and he slowly sank to his knees. Gabriel's golden eyes flashed in front of him as the blackness drove him to the ground.

"Why did you take me away from there?" Semyaza demanded of Azazel once they had landed.

"Hel'el said to leave Mychal be! He's dealing with him. Stick to the task at hand," Azazel said and pointed to the city below. "That is Ma'loula, our next target. Forget about Damascus."

Semyaza ignored him, focusing his attention in the opposite direction. He stood staring at a statue on a hill overlooking the mountain city. It was of a man, his arms outstretched as if to embrace the whole town beneath him.

A flicker of uneasiness ran through him. The town looked quiet, peaceful. It didn't strike him as a place presenting any kind of threat, but Hel'el had been clear. This town was run by a cult, one that was blasphemous beyond measure. Its occupants spread their lies to all who went there. Azazel shifted uneasily beside him, sensing his hesitation.

"What is it?" Azazel asked.

"I don't know. This man… Who is he?"

"He would be the false one that Hel'el spoke of," Azazel said, his face twisting in disgust.

"He looks familiar somehow," Semyaza replied with a frown.

"Of course, he does. We destroyed some of his idols in Damascus."

"The archangels are in Damascus still. Let's hope whatever trap Hel'el has laid for them distracts them long enough for us to complete our mission. I'm tired, Azazel. I want to be redeemed, so I can go home to Aravot. I don't fear death coming with the archangels. I fear that I won't be able to finish destroying our evil before they destroy us. They won't understand what we are trying to do."

"Now isn't the time to get melancholy, Semyaza. We have a mission and purpose that we must fulfill. Hel'el knows this world better than any other living thing. If he says this place must be destroyed, we must trust him," Azazel replied.

"I do trust him, but where was he the first time we were here? Where was his council then?"

"He was too caught up in his pain and fear to approach his brothers." Hel'el appeared beside them, beautiful and astounding in his full angelic raiment, not disguised as a poor human imitation of himself. "It has taken me a long time to stop being angry, to accept the difficult task that has been laid out before me. This town—this task—is a hard one, but we can't shrink from our duties. Mychal has more blood on his hands than all of the angels, and Elyon still gave him Na'amah and humanity—the two things you wanted most, Semyaza."

Anger swirled inside of Semyaza; Mychal had been given everything. He had obeyed and was rewarded. Now Semyaza would fix his errors, and then Elyon would reward him too.

"You are right, Hel'el. As much as I hate Mychal, he obeys no matter what the cost. Come on, Azazel. Our resolution must not waiver."

Hel'el stood at the base of the statue, watching them fly down to the town. Se-myaza was a fanatic, his favorite kind of psychopath. They were always so easy to manipulate into doing what he wanted.

"Idiots." He chuckled as fire exploded out of the buildings beneath him, and the night was filled with screams and terror.

40

I WOKE ON TOP of a strange bed in a clean hotel room. I slowly sat up, my whole body aching. I gagged when I realized I was still in my filthy clothes. *How long have I been out?* I shuffled into the small bathroom, stripped, and showered. I could have cried with joy as the hot water sluiced off the dirt and blood and the weird corpse smell of zombie demons. My right hand still tingled from when I had held on to Mychal. I'd never felt anything like that before, not even the night at HeosCorp.

Clean and dry and wrapped in one of the hotel's complimentary robes, I picked up my phone and sat down on my small balcony. I didn't know how I had gotten here or what part of the city I was in. I was learning not to worry about it too much.

I knew I should call Star, but she wasn't who I wanted at that moment. She would only tell me about Max, and I still didn't know how to deal with my guilt. She wouldn't understand what had happened on the city walls, and I would only get upset having to try to explain it to her. I opened my contacts, hesitated, swore, and then finally tapped on "A-Team." I should have checked on the time differences; I should have messaged—

"*Pronto,*" said a sleepy, masculine voice.

"Hey, it's me," I replied, feeling like an idiot.

"*Angela della Morte.*" I heard Alessandro's husky chuckle. "I was wondering if you were ever going to call me."

"I didn't know if I would be allowed to, priest. Or if you would even want to talk to me after everything that happened."

"What's wrong, Jael? You sound different. Upset. Where are you?"

"Um…Damascus?"

There was a long silence, and the rustle of blankets. I could picture him sitting up in bed in a plain monastic cell.

"What are you doing in Damascus? *How…*" He let out a long line of Italian. "Are you the reason the city was declared a war zone?"

I snorted with laughter. "More like the reason it's reopened. It's a really long story. If you need to get back to sleep, I can talk to you another time."

"Stop being ridiculous and tell me."

"Full confessional rights?" I didn't need the Vatican to send a drone to bomb me or whatever they might do if they tried to get to the rogue angels before we did.

"Of course. I'm a little offended you even had to ask."

"You'll see why." I pushed my still-wet hair from my face, took a deep breath, and told him everything. Being pulled off the roof by Yeshua himself, saving Mychal from Uriel's anger, that Mychal was the incarnation of the archangel, Nazirah's dig, Hel'el, mass exorcising a city, and—the part I was still struggling with—restoring the spirits to the zombie demons.

"Say something," I begged after I had finished. He'd been silent for over thirty minutes straight while I talked.

"I can't leave you alone for five minutes, can I?" Alessandro sighed, and I burst into relieved laughter. "Why are you laughing? You should be dead." His concern only made me laugh harder until unexpectedly, I burst into tears.

"A woman who hit Lucifer in the face with a baton shouldn't be crying," he said mockingly. "I still can't believe you did that. Can I ask what he offered you?"

"You and then Uriel." I wiped at my face and swallowed down my tears. "He's such a dick. I had no choice but to hit him for the audacity to think he could make trades about my friends."

We talked further about the exorcism, the restoration, and the angels in the parchment-colored robes. It felt good to off-load onto Alessandro, someone who would believe me no matter what, who understood. It made me miss him and selfishly wish he was with me. But another more protective side of me was happy he was on the other side of the world.

"You should have called me sooner," he said finally.

"There isn't anything you could've done. As I keep getting reminded, this is *my* mission. I could use the extra hands and a human for sanity, but I wouldn't want you caught up in this. As Max once told me, the world needs its exorcists."

"Will you be insulted if I say that I will pray for you?"

"Shit, man, get the whole League of Exorcists praying for me! I'm going to need all the help I can get to make it out of this alive."

"It does seem unusually unfair that you should be dragged into such a supernatural mess." Alessandro paused for a long moment before adding, "You know if you do survive this, you will never be the same again. You won't be able to go back to Melbourne and simply have things be as they were before."

I leaned my forehead against the wrought iron railing of the balcony. "Yeah, I know. I can't exactly worry about it now though."

"Where will you go next?"

"I'm not sure. Mychal and the others will figure out where Semyaza and Azazel went, and I'll tag along with them."

"And Uriel? Have you two made up yet?"

I glossed over the tearful argument and subsequent hugs that had happened in the cabin, Uriel's overprotective concern, and the weird tension in Jericho. There hadn't been enough time to think about it, to even attempt to process it. I couldn't shake Hel'el's mocking tone from my head either.

"We are cool. You know me; feelings aren't my forte. He's sorry, I'm sorry; we're on a mission. Things are back to normal." Except they really, really weren't.

"So you say."

As if speaking about him had summoned him, there was a tap on my door, and Uriel stuck his silver head in. He saw I was on the phone, and his expression slipped before he beckoned to me.

"Alessandro? I have to go. Um… Thank you for the confession."

"Keep it up, and I might end up converting you after all."

"Ha! You're hilarious."

"Please try to be safe, Jael. And when it is all over, if you need anything, please call me. Don't wait so long before asking for help," Alessandro said, his tone gruff.

"Won't the Church frown upon you helping me?"

"If you survive this ordeal, you will have saved the world, even though no one will know about it. But I will. And who do you think I will be more frightened of? Disapproving bishops or *Gesù Cristo* when I failed to take care of his favorite exorcist?"

"Suppose you have a point," I said with a wide smile. "Talk soon, Alessandro."

"We had better," he replied. "Go with God, *Angela della Morte.*"

"Bye," I whispered and hung up. I had a sudden mad urge to throw my phone from the balcony, but after taking a few deep breaths, I went back inside to get dressed.

41

"OH MY HEAD." MYCHAL moaned as he sat up.

"Easy. Take it slow." Uriel offered him a glass of water that he gulped down in large mouthfuls.

"What happened?"

"You don't remember? You and Jael thought it was a good idea to attempt an exorcism on an entire city mid-battle. Typical reckless humans, just jump in and hope for the best."

"We did? Did it work?" Mychal remembered the battle, standing on the walls of the citadel, and then power and static. He remembered confronting Semyaza, who was snatched right in front of him.

"It worked," said Jael as she slumped into a chair next to his bed. She looked tired and more than a little upset. She still managed a grin as she added, "Go team us."

Mychal smiled back and then winced. Even his face hurt. There was worry and sadness in Uriel's eyes when he looked at them.

"Everyone in the city is back to normal now? What is wrong?" asked Mychal.

"Gabriel and I searched the citadel. Semyaza and Azazel had been living there, but they were gone."

"What else?" asked Mychal.

"Bodies. We found pits of them. Women mostly. They had been dead for days. I don't understand why they would do such a thing."

"Maybe it is their form of birth control. It would be one way to stop more Nephilim from being born until Hel'el wants them to build an army," Jael said, her frown deepening. "I wonder why a whole city of bodies was resurrected, but the people in the pit weren't?"

"It's probably for the best," Mychal said. "Whatever they did to them isn't something you'd want to remember."

"Come on you two; you need to eat something," Uriel said as he stood.

"Are you mothering me again, Feathers?" Jael demanded.

"I wouldn't dream of it," Uriel replied. "But I've been charged to protect you. By someone I don't dare disobey."

A platter of fruit and bread was on a polished table, and Mychal all but fell on it. He couldn't ever remember being so hungry.

"Gabriel is inspecting the effects out in the streets. People don't seem to remember what happened the past week."

"That's a good thing. What about the demons in the sky and the weird angels in the parchment-colored robes?" Jael asked.

"The demons are gone," Uriel replied. "The angels are always there. They are Watchers, like Semyaza and Azazel should be."

"We'll find them and stop them," Mychal said, and for the first time, he believed it.

Jael watched him carefully before asking, "What did it feel like for you? The power that ran through you. When our hands joined… I've never felt like that before. It was like my body wanted to explode."

Mychal stopped eating, searching for the right words to explain it. "To me it felt…infinite. As if a part of me had merged with something else for a perfect moment, and it was as if my mouth, my mind, my spirit didn't belong to me anymore. I saw what needed to be done, and I did it."

"You've both been touched by the hand of God in a way that we could never understand," Uriel said solemnly. "You are both blessed."

"That power isn't something I'd want to try to hang on to," Mychal said and shivered. "It was terrifying even with its wonder. I'm happy that it worked, and the people are free, even if their city is damaged."

"It can be rebuilt; people can't," Jael said. "Alessandro was a bit jealous that his exorcism record had been beaten so badly."

"You talked to him?" Mychal asked.

"Yeah. You got a problem with that?" Her eyes flashed with challenge.

"No. It's a good thing for the other exorcists to know what's happening; it will make them more vigilant," Mychal replied, and she seemed to simmer down. He didn't know Jael all that well, but one thing he did know was to be careful around the topic of Alessandro Abbadelli and to never mention feelings and Uriel in the same sentence.

Once he had washed and put on a fresh pair of black jeans and a T-shirt, Mychal almost felt like new. His muscles ached, but he had survived the horde unscathed. Gabriel was back and arguing with Uriel.

"Is that your happy face?" Mychal asked Uriel as he joined them. Gabriel was scowling, and that was never a good sign.

"They are gone," he said. "I searched the city, but Semyaza and Azazel have disappeared entirely. Hel'el is covering their tracks."

"He is behind their release. All of it," Gabriel said and started to pace. "He's whispering in their ears. I felt his presence in the citadel. No matter what Semyaza and Azazel believe, he is the one in charge."

"What could he possibly offer them that they would listen…" Mychal started to say, but a memory itched at him. It was Na'amah telling him of how Semyaza first appeared to her. "You don't think he promised him Aleksandra? He couldn't…he doesn't have that power anymore. He made a demon take her form in Budapest to mess with me, but I knew that it wasn't her."

"Semyaza might not be so discerning. They haven't roamed the earth since that time. They wouldn't even know that Hel'el lost his power two thousand years ago," Uriel said.

"They wouldn't know Yeshua was born as a human," Gabriel added.

Mychal ran his hands through his hair in frustration. "They are following Hel'el's instructions blindly then. Who cares what he has promised them! We need to stop thinking about what Semyaza would do and start thinking about what Hel'el would do. We need to find where they are headed next."

"You need to rest. Your body needs to heal, as does Jael's," Gabriel said. "Let Uriel and I search for them."

"I'm done with resting!" Mychal snapped. "I'll live as I always have."

They sat in silence until Jael sighed loudly and turned the TV on. They had let the military into the city, and the World Health Organization was testing the water supply for poisoning. They were looking everywhere to discover the cause of the violent madness and subsequent amnesia from the past week.

A British woman was talking about the risk of the disease spreading. She talked of teams being sent to the neighboring villages, and that they had heard back from all except Ma'loula, a Christian village that was famous for still speaking Biblical Aramaic. There were fears that the unknown disease had been carried to the mountain village because of the tourists and pilgrims traveling to the area. Mychal tried not to choke on the almond he was chewing on.

"There! That's where they have gone." He pointed at the TV.

"What makes you so sure?" Jael asked.

"He's just been given two impressionable, powerful angels. He's going to point them at what he hates the most."

"I'm going to need another coffee," muttered Jael as she left the room. Uriel was looking hesitantly after her. Jael was right; he was fretting over her. After feeling her strength and the power she could command, Mychal wasn't going to be concerned for Jael ever again. God help whatever decided to mess with her.

"She's fine," Mychal said, tossing an almond at Uriel that he caught without looking.

"Give up, Mychal. He's always like that," Gabriel commented, his golden eyes dancing.

"When you are deemed fit enough to have charge over a human, maybe you will understand," muttered Uriel.

"You had better make sure she's ready for the next fight when you talk to her," Gabriel replied, but Uriel was already heading to her room.

"Good luck to any man who ever tries to marry her," Mychal commented. "They would be marrying him too."

"I pray she never feels the inclination," Gabriel said. "No other being in creation sulks like Uriel, and he would hate having to compete with another man."

"Don't forget I copped the full weight of his last sulk with my face." Mychal's smile slipped. "You don't think he's actually in love with her and is just refusing to acknowledge it?"

"I don't think it. I don't acknowledge it. I don't imagine it," Gabriel replied sharply. "And if you value your life, you won't either."

Mychal shut his mouth, but he knew from his own experience that sometimes being gruff and overprotective was a sure sign of other emotions at play.

"You ready yet?" Jael demanded, coming back in armed with her knife, handgun, and batons. Uriel followed, carrying her bag. "Come on, demon hunter. You were the one who said Ma'loula, so let's go."

42

SEMYAZA FOUGHT THE URGE to spit on a mosaic of Michael with a dragon under his feet. *Was I meant to be that dragon?* There was so much history that he and Azazel had to learn. The weeping cry of a woman brought him out of his concentration.

"I found something for you," Azazel said. He was holding a dark-haired girl by the arm. She was young and fresh, her big black eyes looking at them in awe-struck terror. Semyaza approached her, touching her face gently.

"You have nothing to fear," he said softly. She stilled under his touch, but the glint in her eyes told him that she knew he was lying. "Lock the others up in the church. I'll deal with them afterward."

Azazel nodded obediently and let the girl go. Semyaza let her run before scooping her up and carrying her into an empty house. Fear had stopped her struggling as he dropped her onto the bed.

"Why?" she asked between tears. "Why are you doing this? You are angels."

Semyaza didn't reply. He was too distracted by the brown legs that peeked out from the skirt of her blue dress.

It was watching Na'amah bathe all those centuries ago that had made him want to be a man. Her curly black hair had been piled high and tied onto the top of her head, exposing her long neck before the rest of her garments had fallen on the riverbank. He would never forget the golden light silhouetting the curves of her body. She was beautiful, and he had been overpowered by want and desire.

"We are angels," Semyaza answered as he ran his hands up her trembling thighs. "But we still have needs and wants like any other man."

He took the hem of her dress and ripped it, the fabric peeling away to reveal the soft body inside. She turned her face from him, tears and restrained sobs making her body shake invitingly. He took off his clothes while he watched her. His passion igniting at seeing naked flesh. The love of it had been his downfall.

There were times in his imprisonment that he cursed Na'amah. She caused him to go to the other Watchers. He convinced them of their right to wives because he wasn't brave enough to rebel on his own. They had finally agreed, and he went straight to the source of his desire. Semyaza had revealed himself to her, and she ran from him.

Semyaza crawled slowly on top of the girl, rubbing her softness against his skin, luxuriating in the velvety feel of it.

"Please," she begged. "Please, stop this."

"There is no stopping this. You are the spoils of war; your fate is set," he replied as he bit the curve of her breast.

"Please, please," she whispered, her eyes looking past him at something only she could perceive. "Yeshua, please stop this. Stop this."

"Praying to your false god won't save you," Semyaza said with a snarl as he pushed his way inside of her, her cries of pain exciting him as they always did.

"Save me. Save me, Yeshua. Save me," she said, her voice barely a whisper as he thrust into her harder, deeper. She tried to push him off, her nails raking his chest. He grabbed her hands and pinned them down above her head. "Yeshua, Yeshua," she said, her voice becoming louder.

"Silence!" Semyaza shouted. The constant muttering of the name was irritating him.

For a moment the girl beneath him was Na'amah crying out for Michael as he took her in all the ways he dreamt about. The way she had spoken his name, with tender familiarity. The weeping for Michael had driven Semyaza to madness, and that was when he hit her, unable to stop himself. His hands curled into fists as the woman beneath him got louder and louder. His hand rose as she screamed, "bar-Elaha! bar-Elaha!"

Semyaza threw himself backward off her as terror coursed through him.

"How *dare* you invoke that name in this place!" he said, the sweat on his body turning cold.

She curled up into a ball, hands shielding her face. "Yeshua bar-Elaha," she prayed.

"Stop it, woman. Don't you dare mix the name of your false god with the Antecedent of Time!"

The woman looked up at him from the webbing of her fingers. "But Yeshua *is* bar-Elaha, the Son of God. He was born as a man, and his name was Yeshua. It means—"

"Rescuer," Semyaza said, finishing her words, his voice painfully small. "bar-Elaha is the man in all the pictures in the churches?"

Her eyes were no longer full of fear but confusion. "Y-yes."

"But Hel'el said nothing of this," Semyaza muttered. "I don't understand. His powers…he said you were an evil cult."

"Hel'el has no power anymore. How can you not know this if you are one of the angels?" she asked.

Semyaza clutched his head to stop the sound of his heart hammering. An icon of the false god hung in the house. He ripped it off the wall and stared at it, searching for a hidden meaning.

Something moved through him, a brief flush of feeling. It was something he had almost forgotten. It was the touch of Aravot, of home, of grace. Then it disappeared as quickly as it had come, leaving a gaping hole inside of him. The picture crumbled under his grip as a scream of tortured agony was torn from him.

The people inside of the church were banging on the barred doors as Azazel calmly lit another torch. It was a sorry task, but it had to be done. He didn't suffer the deep feelings that Semyaza did, so it was best to give him something to distract him from his worries and get on with the bloody task himself.

As he turned to shove the torch into the already-flaming building, movement in a side street stopped him. A man dressed in black was coming toward him. He had swords strapped to his back and a gun in each hand. A woman was beside him, a gun on her hip and batons in her hands. Her face was a mask of righteous fury.

"Stop where you are!" Azazel commanded. They stopped, and two angels appeared in the darkness. The eyes of their leader were darker, but there was no mistaking the contempt in them...Mychal.

"Enough, Azazel. This ends now," Mychal demanded.

"It ends when the task is over," Azazel hissed.

They drew their weapons, and Azazel's bitterness and anger reared. A gut-wrenchingly familiar screech cut through the air, and his hand hesitated above the hilt of his sword.

The scream went on as the side of the building burst apart, and Semyaza streaked into the night. Cries of panic and pain were getting louder in the church as the flames took over.

Azazel tossed the torch inside. "You had better save them, Mychal, while you still can." Azazel sped into the air without looking to see if they were following.

He needed to find Semyaza and see what would be enough to scare his mighty leader.

Mychal ignored the heat in his hands as he tried to lift the heavy beam off the doors of the church.

"Out of the way," Uriel said, pulling him back. He lifted the beam lightly and chucked it aside. Gabriel and Jael pulled open the doors, and a wave of disoriented, panicked people swarmed out. Mychal went to rush into the church, but Uriel stopped him.

"Let me take care of it. I don't singe as easily as you."

Mychal helped the people coming out instead. The streets were scattered with rubble from Semyaza's break out. What had caused him to flee? Surely not their presence. He wouldn't have known they were there.

Mychal left the survivors in Jael's care and ran to the broken house. He climbed over broken doors and furniture, following the sound of sobbing. Very slowly he opened the bedroom door and saw a woman hastily wrapping a sheet around herself.

"I'm not here to hurt you," Mychal said, holding his hands up.

"Are they gone?" she asked.

"Yes, they are gone. I'm here to help. Are you hurt?" She started crying again in huge sobs. There was blood on the sheet she clung to. "It's okay. You don't have to tell me."

"He was afraid and confused," she said. "He didn't know who Yeshua was."

"No, he doesn't, and neither does the other who was with him. We will stop them from hurting anyone else, I promise."

Mychal took her outside to where Gabriel was attending to the wounded. The church still blazed on, and fear was growing that the fire would spread.

Elyon, please bring the rain. These people have suffered enough, Mychal prayed.

"Where did you disappear to?" Jael asked. Mychal pointed to the girl who was being crowded by women.

"She said Semyaza is scared."

"He should be," Uriel said as he joined them. "They are acting like animals. It's a disgrace. You would think that their time in prison would have humbled them."

"I'm not so sure it hasn't. The girl I found told me that he didn't know about Yeshua and that he mentioned Hel'el. Who knows what Semyaza and Azazel believe, or what Hel'el has even told them."

"It's still inexcusable," said Uriel.

"Agreed. Any idea where they have gone?" asked Mychal.

"If they are afraid, then there is no plan. They headed toward the Cherubim Mountains, so we'll follow in that direction," said Uriel.

"We help these people first," Mychal said as the first raindrops fell on him.

✦

Azazel found Semyaza ranting and cursing in front of a huge statue placed high in the cold mountains. He was screaming gibberish at the heavens. Azazel hesitated before approaching him. In the pit, he had thought Semyaza's mind was broken when he ranted in the same manner. Then for the last five hundred years, he had barely spoken a word. Azazel thought being out of the darkness had cured him.

"Semyaza, calm yourself," he said gently. "What's wrong? What has happened?"

Semyaza gripped him by the shoulders. "*We* are what's wrong. He should have killed us all."

"Brother, please, you aren't making any sense. What happened in the town?"

"The girl…the girl, she said…"—he clutched his head and began to pace— "she said that the man they worship is bar-Elaha. He has already become flesh. Why didn't Hel'el mention this?"

"She could've been lying! Something as important as that, Hel'el would have told us. We are trying to get redemption, not go up in opposition."

"Then why are the archangels hunting us?"

"You know Mychal would still want revenge for Na'amah, and his friends would stand behind him."

"But we don't know for sure, do we? We know nothing!" Semyaza punched a wall of rock, shattering it and making his knuckles bleed. "Hel'el! Hel'el! Come and speak with us!" The wind whipped around them, but the only response they received was silence.

"You seem very convinced about something a girl said when you were on top of her," Azazel hissed. Semyaza grabbed him roughly.

"I *felt* it, Azazel. I don't know how, but I felt grace and a connection to Aravot. And then it was gone, leaving me with this resounding nothingness inside of me. I chose this emptiness, and in doing so, I damned you all."

"*We* chose it, Semyaza. You didn't force us."

"Of course, I did! It was my lust that ignited your own. I pointed the women out to you. I encouraged you all, and I still didn't get Na'amah. This damnation was for nothing." Semyaza pushed Azazel aside and went to look again at the giant statue.

"Who are you?" he shouted before he broke down into sobs. He crumpled to his knees before it. "Who are you?"

43

MYCHAL INSISTED ON STAYING in Ma'loula for two days to ensure that Semyaza and Azazel didn't return. The archangels disguised themselves as humans in order to ease the people's fears.

"We have to keep moving, Mychal," Gabriel said on the evening of the second day. "If you don't want to find another destroyed town such as this, we must stop them while they are in the mountains."

"I know," Mychal replied as he looked out of the window of the house they had been staying in. "I thought they would come back. Semyaza is proud and bold, but he was never stupid. The knowledge of Yeshua's humanity will be a blow to him. I thought he would return to learn more."

"If Hel'el is helping them, what is to stop him from finding out from him?"

"He knows Hel'el has lied to him. He's not gullible like Azazel. Semyaza will be pissed. We may make them see sense yet."

"And then what? We can't let them go free after all they have done. If nothing else, Elyon will demand that they are put inside the earth once more," said Gabriel.

"We can't know that. I've received no commands on what to do with them. What were your original orders?" asked Mychal.

"That we must find you, awaken your memories, and find out what was happening in the Negev."

"Then we must find the Watchers and wait for further instructions. It's always bigger than us, Gabriel. Never forget that."

Gabriel's amber eyes watched him carefully. "You know, you sound more and more like your old self every day. Where is that drunken, abusive jerk we found in Budapest?"

"He's still in here, don't you worry," Mychal replied. "It's easier in a way, now that I know who I am. There is a completeness. I would dream and not remember when I woke. The emotion would be left over from it, but I didn't know where it came from. In this lifetime, I ran from it. I thought that I could ignore it, keep Aleksandra far away and safe from this destiny. All that happened was I made it harder on the both of us, and I got her killed. I couldn't protect her at all."

Gabriel sat down next to him. "I know it's pointless to tell you not to blame yourself, because you will anyway. Does it comfort you to know how much you have loved each other through the centuries? That you will see her again one day?"

Mychal shook his head. "No, I won't. I've been thinking about it since Hel'el's visit in my dream with Jael. I can't keep doing this, Gabriel. This will be the last time."

"I don't understand. Don't you love her anymore?"

Mychal grimaced. "God save me, I love her more than the breath in my body, the Heavens and the earth combined. I've loved her for thousands of years, and it has only grown in that time, not diminished. Can you not see that this is why I have to stop? It's tearing me apart. I don't care that she agreed to it. I can't keep watching her die."

Gabriel opened his mouth just as Uriel burst into the room. "Time to go. We have received word that Semyaza and Azazel have been spotted."

"Where's Jael?" Mychal asked. He saw her a few hours ago playing soccer with a group of children, laughing as they tore through the rubble-filled streets.

"She has notified Doctors Without Borders and the Church through Alessandro. She's waiting for us downstairs."

Mychal stood up, pulling his swords onto his shoulders. "Let's go."

Semyaza ranted until he grew hoarse. Azazel tried coaxing him to leave the infuriating statue, but he refused to budge until he got a sign.

"Semyaza, please," Azazel said for the hundredth time. "We need to leave. They will track us down here. We are exposed and vulnerable."

"I'm not leaving until I get some answers!" replied Semyaza. "Why hasn't Hel'el heard me call?"

"He has his own missions to carry out." Azazel tried to reason with him.

Semyaza knew when he was being ignored. Azazel hadn't felt what he felt, and now that he had been reminded of the absence of it, it left him awash with fresh madness. He had been this way for hundreds of years in the pit, and now the old wound was bleeding once more.

"Hel'el! Face me!" Semyaza shouted at the wind.

"My brother, are we enemies now?" Hel'el appeared before them, but he didn't come alone. Two tall Nephilim were with him.

"Why haven't you been answering me?" demanded Semyaza.

"I've been collecting your sons for you to ensure the humans didn't harm them," explained Hel'el, his perfect brow furrowing with concern. "What has happened?"

"You've been lying to us!"

"Lying to you?"

"I'm sorry, Hel'el," Azazel said timidly. "He is... We were in Ma'loula and..."

"And I was told that *this* man—" Semyaza waved at the statue. "This Yeshua is bar-Elaha!"

Hel'el looked from Semyaza's angry face to the statue in disbelief before starting to laugh. "Oh, I'm sorry, I didn't think you were joking for a moment there. Come now and see your sons."

The two Nephilim shuffled in between them, reaching for Semyaza in their vacant and childish way. Semyaza let out a roar of anger. He drew his sword, vaulted into the air, and took off their massive heads. Azazel cried out in horror and anguish as the bodies tumbled to the earth.

"Enough!" Semyaza bellowed. "I won't do anything more to offend Elyon. These creatures should never have been born. We have been deceived, Azazel!" His bloody sword pointed at Hel'el. His look of amusement slipped, and the gleam in his eye turned feral.

"You insult and wound me, brother. This man they worship is not who you think it is. You have been deceived but not by me."

"Why do you hate the humans so much? What did they do to deserve Elyon's wrath or your own?"

"I told you Semyaza; they are a slight against Elyon."

"They didn't appear to be doing anything that was slighting Elyon."

"You don't know the things I know, Semyaza. You have been in prison, away from the world."

"Yes, there *is* much that I don't know. I should've found out these things for myself and not blindly trusted what you had to say. You betrayed Heaven; that's why you are stuck here. You stole mankind's birthright for yourself. If you still have so much power, why do you need us to follow your orders? Why not destroy everything yourself? You don't have any power anymore, do you? You've nothing left at all, just illusions of grandeur."

"Semyaza, you've lost your mind. I shouldn't have left you alone. This world is not the one you knew, and I'm sorry it's ending this way."

"So am I—" Semyaza said before his sword fell from his hands.

"I'm sorry, brother, I'm sorry," Azazel whispered in his ear as his dagger cut deeper into Semyaza's side. "You left me no choice."

"Azazel…don't follow…him." Semyaza fell to the earth, as Azazel pulled the dagger from his body. Hel'el looked down on him, face full of scorn.

"*Now* who has no power? Let's see if Elyon will forgive you," Hel'el said, sneering. "Come, Azazel. Your army is waiting."

As he lay dying, Semyaza saw through Hel'el's glamour to the wrecked creature he now was. He tried to tell Azazel, but all that came from him was a wheezing, bloody cough. Semyaza lay his head on the ground, unable to keep it up.

Someone else stood in the distance watching him die. The grace he felt back in Ma'loula touched him gently.

"Forgive…forgive." Semyaza wept, his hand reaching out to the illusion. *I'm so sorry,* he thought as the light in his eyes faded.

Mychal gritted his teeth against the cold air rushing past him. The day was completely gone; a full moon rose to take its place. The mountains beneath him were gray in the ghostly light. They had been flying low, trying to spot a fire or any trace of Semyaza and Azazel.

"There!" Mychal shouted. Something blinked at him, the moonlight reflecting off something in a brief spark. Uriel dropped like a stone beside them, Jael screaming with mad laughter in his arms.

Gabriel muttered something that Mychal didn't catch over the roar of the wind, and they descended at a slower pace. Mychal hit the ground and managed to keep his feet.

"If you give me a heart attack and I die, you'll have no one to blame but yourself, Feathers," Jael said, chastising Uriel sharply. Uriel only smiled at her.

"Not so loud, you two," Mychal said, looking about in the darkness and waiting for his eyes to adjust.

"We are too late," whispered Gabriel behind him. Semyaza's body hung from a statue of Yeshua, arms and wings spread in a mocking mirror image.

"Cut him down," Mychal commanded. Gabriel hovered above the ropes and cut them as Uriel caught the body.

"A blade to the back," Jael said as they laid the body out. "A traitor's way to murder someone."

"Azazel finally turned on him," Mychal replied sadly. "Hel'el wouldn't have dirtied his hands and risked Azazel defecting." He closed Semyaza's open eyes with the palm of his hand. "I had more of a reason to hate Semyaza than anyone else, and even I wouldn't have wished this on him. It's not honorable."

"He had to be made accountable for what he did," Gabriel said. "He knew what Hel'el was, and he still chose to trust him."

Jael knelt down beside the body. "If we were confused and mad, maybe we would have done the same."

Mychal frowned. "Even if Azazel was the one who killed him, this arrangement of the body was the work of demons."

"How do you know?" Jael asked. "I've never seen demons act like this."

"I've seen it before when they killed my mentor Vadim in Budapest. It could be the same ones, ready to piss me off all over again," muttered Mychal. "Hel'el thinks he's being funny."

"He always does. Even Uriel has a better sense of humor," Gabriel said, trying to ease the tension.

Uriel only grunted. "We need to burn him. The humans can't find him, much less these Nephilim corpses. You have all been too preoccupied to see those." Mychal walked over to where Uriel was pointing. They had been beheaded and left to rot.

"So they joined their fathers after all," Mychal said, staring at the lives he had saved, only to have them end in violence anyway. He felt sick in his heart. "How did they get so far without being spotted?"

"Hel'el again, I imagine. I don't think he has a plan. He just wants to cause trouble and irritate us," said Uriel.

"Well, it's working," Mychal said and straightened. "These would've been good soldiers, so I think Semyaza killed them. Azazel loved his Nephilim army. He wouldn't have done this. Maybe if I'd stayed with them until their birth I could have stopped Hel'el from using them like this. I wonder if he spared the mothers." He remembered the pit of bodies of the women they had found in Damascus, and knew deep down that they would be dead. They were just two more ghosts to follow him to his grave.

Uriel made a frustrated sound in the back of his throat. "Don't think that way. You could never have saved them from their fates, Mychal."

Mychal cleared the lump of emotion from his throat. "Give me a hand, will you? We can't leave them like this."

They dragged the bodies over and laid them next to Semyaza.

"Should we say anything?" Jael asked tentatively. The angels looked at Mychal. He stared at Semyaza a long while, remembering all the things he had done, the laws he had broken, and the lives he had taken. Semyaza always believed it was because he loved Na'amah. In that way, they were linked by a bond no one else would ever understand. Semyaza had been his enemy, but now looking at his end, messy and without honor, all that Mychal felt was pity.

"I hope you found peace in death, that you never wanted in life, and that Elyon is merciful," he said finally. He looked over at the Nephilim. "I'm sorry I couldn't save you and your mothers like I wanted to."

Jael knelt down and lit the bodies with a silver lighter. They caught quickly, filling the dark with a bright light.

"Hel'el and Azazel will see this," Gabriel commented, twirling his spear around his hand absently.

"I know." Mychal looked around at the cliffs. "I can feel demons watching us. Let them report back to Hel'el. Let Azazel come with his demon army. To end it here and now would be better than letting them go out into the world again."

"What will stop them from doing that anyway?" asked Uriel.

"There's only a few of us, but we are still a threat. I'm human. It offends Hel'el to let me live. 'Yeshua's Pet' is what he has always called me. He loves killing me when I'm human. It's the only time he gets the chance to." Mychal smiled, but his companions did not. They looked grim in the flickering light of the funeral pyre.

"I don't believe using yourself as bait was a part of the plan," said Uriel. "Especially considering all the times I've had to try to keep you alive."

"There's always a plan, but I'm human, so I have free will. And I choose to draw him out."

"Even if you die?"

"I've died before. It doesn't frighten me," Mychal lied. It did frighten him. He could remember his lives and his deaths, but he could not remember the moment he died or what came after.

He had sometimes woken back in Aravot in his true form, but he never knew how much time had passed. He could never remember becoming human or angel. As a human, he was created in Elyon's image, his spirit was his own, and Elyon was a part of him. As an angel, he didn't have that, not in the same way. So what happened to his human spirit? Did it simply fuse together with his angel essence, or did it return to the source and become a part of Elyon? It was always something he wished to talk with Yeshua about, but when he was an angel, it didn't seem to matter. What happened to Aleksandra's spirit? Did it sit in some horrible stasis and wait to be reborn?

Mychal watched Semyaza's body burn quickly. There was no smoke or smell. Whatever the flame touched just ceased to be. Semyaza's noble face fell away into nothingness. Would his essence go back to Elyon or be sent to Sheol or one of the other darker places? There were prisons in the Heavens for rebellious angels. Mychal shivered; even in his true form the place filled him with dread. He looked up at the stars and they settled in to wait out the night.

44

THE NIGHT TICKED BY, and with every minute, I grew more and more restless. I was impatient at the best of times but hanging around waiting for a demon army to turn up wasn't my idea of a relaxing night. I needed to walk, even if it was just to stretch my legs. I had seen too much in the last few weeks, and my heart ached painfully whenever we stopped long enough for me to think.

I had gone about ten meters when I felt Uriel's presence following me. I hadn't been alone with him since Jericho, and I didn't know where that really left us. Maybe it was a lapse in judgment. *Probably more yours than his.* I could never manage to get my feelings straight when it came to other humans, let alone Uriel. I needed space and time, two things I hadn't had any of since Yeshua plucked me from my rooftop in Melbourne. Alessandro's words came back to me about how I wasn't ever going to fit into my old life after going through all of this. He was right, and I was already worrying about it. I tried to shove all of those thoughts down, because if I wasn't fighting to get my old life back, what would be the point to any of this?

"Jael, you know better than to wander off," said Uriel. I turned around and saw the spot of light from the fire in the distance. I'd walked a lot farther than I'd thought.

"I'm not wandering off. I needed to move. Sitting still waiting to be attacked is a dumb plan," I replied.

"Not if it works. It feels about right. Mychal doesn't want humans around to see our confrontation, and it'll be less of a liability."

"Except for me and him. As I said, it's not a great plan."

Uriel took another step toward me. "You think I'd let anything happen to you?"

"Even you can't keep me safe in the middle of a battle, Uriel. If you try it, you could get yourself hurt or killed, and I couldn't live with that." I folded my arms, so I wouldn't reach out for him.

"You are actually worried about me?" he asked, like the idea amused him.

"Of course, I'm worried about you! I love you, you big idiot! I don't want you to become demon fodder because Mychal wants to die and be with his lady love. I don't have my true love waiting in Heaven for me. I want to live!" The words exploded out of me, and I was too worked up to believe I had just said it all. *Oh, fuck it. You're about to die horribly, so your regret will be short-lived.*

"Did you just say that you loved me right before you insulted me?" Uriel asked, his silver brows furrowing.

"Yeah, I suppose I did, but God, you're frustrating sometimes," I said, pushing my hands through my hair.

"Because you are so easy and pleasant to deal with?" he demanded, and I glared at him.

"I'm human. I have an excuse to be a train wreck."

"You're more than just a human…"

"No, I'm not," I said, arguing, but he shook his head.

"To me, you are more," Uriel said, clarifying, and my heart did a stupid jumping thing I couldn't control.

"That's because I'm your charge, and you had to turn me into an exorcist," I said, trying to make sure I didn't misunderstand him.

Uriel's eyes were icy and unyielding. "No, not just because of that. Not for a long time."

"I don't understand—"

He lifted my chin. "Yes, you do, Jael. Do you love me the way you love Star or Alessandro? Or do you love me the way a woman loves a man? I need clarification from you, and Heaven help you if you lie to me about this." Despite the firmness in his tone, I knew Uriel wasn't angry, but there was a strange new intensity in his eyes that I'd never seen before. *No more running away from it now, Jael.*

"I *love* love you," I admitted slowly. "For a long time actually, but it's only recently become a problem. Especially the night of the gala when you turned up to save me. I realized then that what I was feeling wasn't platonic. I didn't think about it, didn't give it room to grow, and then everything else happened, and I haven't stopped running since. Now you know."

"Yes, now I know," Uriel whispered, his thumb stroking my cheek. Then he kissed me, just once and very gently, like he was afraid of hurting me. Heat rushed over me as I kissed him back, every part of me suddenly burning to touch him. I moved my hands to tangle in his hair and rose up on my tiptoes. His strong arms came around me, lifting me up so I could kiss him again and much more deeply. Some deep part of me suddenly felt like it was clicking into place. It was him; it was *always* him.

"I take it this means you feel the same way," I said, looking down at his harsh and beautiful face.

"Yes, I love you, Jael Quinlan," he replied with a smile that would've broken my heart if it wasn't finally whole.

I rested my forehead against his. "Good. I suppose we have to go save the world first, but we are going to talk about this after, right?"

"Yes, *yadid*. I promise," he said and then kissed me again, slow and sweet. He placed me back on my feet, and I was blushing like a dumbass teenager when I felt the tingle between my shoulder blades. My early warning system started screaming, and I looked at the shadowy mountains around us.

"Quick. They are coming!" I said and we ran.

45

"DEMONS ARE COMING," JAEL gasped as she and Uriel reappeared. "Do you feel that?"

Mychal's scars began to burn, and he unsheathed his swords. "They are here."

The demons had surrounded them in the last remaining darkness before the dawn. Azazel was dressed in magnificent black armor and stood at the head of the army. His hair was braided high in a twisting, looping mohawk that shone like molten copper in the gray morning light. The demons around them were no longer simply possessed humans. They completely took over the host bodies until the human forms were as twisted as the putrid creatures inside of them.

"That's just fucking perfect," Mychal muttered. He and Jael couldn't exorcise those demons like they had the ones in Damascus. They would have to end this the old-fashioned way. He wouldn't feel guilty about destroying them all. In fact, after the last few weeks of their wild-goose chase, he was looking forward to it.

"Morning, Azazel. Fancy meeting you out here," he called casually. "What an ugly army you have."

"I've come to destroy you. You and the other archangels have lorded over me for long enough. I'll not go back into that hole alive; that I can guarantee."

"Wake up, Azazel! You were never this stupid."

"I wouldn't be sure of that," Jael said, looking bored and unimpressed. "Stupidity is often cultivated over time, and he seems very stupid indeed."

Azazel glared at her. "I don't know what manner of human you are, but I'm going to enjoy killing you."

"You are welcome to try," Uriel replied. "After what I have seen in the last few weeks, killing a mad dog like you is going to be a mercy."

"Hel'el has tricked you, Azazel," Mychal said. "His power was lost over two thousand years ago. I was there. I saw it happen. Give up this game he has you playing."

"This is *not* a game. I'll rid the evil from this earth. The humans have taken the things we taught them and corrupted them. We did this, and only I can fix it now."

"If you sought atonement, why did you kill Semyaza?" asked Mychal. Azazel's face contorted with anger and sorrow.

"He went mad because of what you did to us! It was a mercy. He couldn't carry on."

"It was mercy perhaps, but not for Semyaza. His eyes were finally opened to the truth, and you killed him for it."

The demons shuffled restlessly in their haphazard ranks, making Mychal's trigger finger itch.

"What truth? He was ranting that this false prophet was the Son of Elyon. I know who he is; Hel'el told me everything. He was just some peasant carpenter who worked a few miracles. He had some followers who thought he was a messiah. They killed him for stirring up the people and because Rome was going to kill them all. He was just one man whose cult has lingered for far longer than it should have."

"Stop being such a fool, Azazel!" Gabriel exclaimed in frustration. "Think for yourself for once instead of letting another's ideas control your actions. Why would we be here if it wasn't the truth?"

"You're trying to interfere as you have always done. These humans don't deserve this planet. Without them, it will return to Eden, as it was before they corrupted it."

"It wasn't humans that corrupted it, and you know it. You sat and wept with the rest of us when Hel'el spun his lies," Mychal said, trying to reason with him.

"It wasn't Hel'el who chose a piece of fruit over Elyon," Azazel said with a snarl. "The humans did that."

"Well said, Azazel. Well said." Hel'el appeared beside him. He was dressed in white-and-gold armor with an elaborate insignia of a falling star emblazoned on his chest. His fine golden hair was brushed out, long and gleaming.

"Still a showy, vain bastard, aren't you?" Mychal smirked. "You look like a wedding cake."

"A freaking ugly one," Jael agreed beside him.

"Hurling insults already, are we? It's to be expected really, from filthy humans. I find the very idea of humanity repulsive—to be wrapped up in all that rotting meat. So vulnerable and breakable," Hel'el said as he looked them over. "I think this is the least impressive form you've ever had, Mychal."

"Still better looking than yours, glamour puss," retorted Jael.

Azazel might have been fooled by Hel'el's shiny appearance, but Mychal knew exactly how scarred and twisted he was underneath. He'd placed a few scars on that hide himself. "It's over Hel'el; stop this stupid game. You can't win. All you are now is *talk*. Seeing how you love the sound of your voice so much, why don't you tell Azazel the story of how you lost your power?"

"I love that story," Uriel said with an amused smile. Hel'el's ever-present sneer faltered.

"I still have power." He gestured to the demons around him. The tension in the ranks mounted, and the demons started howling.

"Ask him, Azazel!" Mychal shouted over the snarling demons. "Ask him how he lost the world and everything in it!"

Mychal was there the day the world changed, and he remembered everything.

46

Long ago in Jersusalem

A LIGHT BREEZE MOVED with a fluttering sigh of olive leaves as Michael moved from the heavenly plane to the earthly one. The light of the pilgrims' small cooking fires illuminated the night sky. They had flocked to Jerusalem for Passover, and there was a mixed tension in the air; whispers spread of Roman violence and the uproar that occurred at the Holy Temple that day.

Michael walked softly, careful to keep out of the light. He kept his hood low to shield his face and used his cloak to hide his armor. Amongst the voices of the pilgrims, there was a name whispered over and over. *Yeshua…Yeshua…Yeshua.*

People spoke of miracles, of kindness, and of Isaiah's holy prophecies. *Mashiach.* There was a man who stood up to the *kohen gadol,* the high priest Caiaphas, and others who were more interested in placating Rome than obeying God's laws and covenants. The people whispered that Yeshua was a friend of prostitutes. He saved a woman from stoning. He healed those infected with disease. He raised a man from the dead. *Yeshua…Yeshua.* Michael shut out the voices until he heard the one he was searching for.

"*Yei'aseh r'tzon'cha,*" it whispered. "Your will be done." The voice was choked with tears and fear.

Michael stopped under an olive tree and watched the man. He was on his hands and knees on the cold ground, his tears cutting trails down his dusty cheeks. He wore a long robe of plain wool, and his head was covered by a *tallit.* The leather sandals on his feet had seen many miles and were cracking at the straps. Hands roughed by heavy labor gripped the earth in despair. Michael wanted to take him far from Jerusalem.

Elyon, please… He sent the prayer and flinched as he was rebuked harshly.

"That's right. Pray and despair," a voice said mockingly. Michael's body went rigid with anger. It had been centuries since he'd heard that voice.

Hel'el, the star of the first morning, stood tall over Yeshua and was arrayed as in the days of Eden. He had been perfect from the day he was created. Hair of the finest white gold hung from his head in curls that tumbled down his back. His robe was purple silk, and he was arrayed in precious stones of carnelian, topaz, emerald, beryl, onyx, jasper, sapphire, and carbuncle all set in the purest of gold. His sandals were made of soft, white kid leather and cuffs of gold were on his wrists. Michael gripped the hilt of his sword as Hel'el circled. Yeshua prayed on, without acknowledging him.

"You have *lost*, peasant. Your time is over. My servants are going to come, and they're going to torture you in the most exquisite ways. You should've taken up my offer to join me in the desert. You're a slave to a father who does not love you; so blindly you have followed him. I was like you once, and it caused me to be cast from his presence forever. He'll do far worse to you. I was a servant, and you claim you are his son. What kind of father would abandon his own son?" Hel'el crouched down to whisper gently, kindly in Yeshua's ear. "He *is* going to abandon you, Yeshua. He already has. He has *given* you to me. Do you want to know why? Because I was his favorite first, and I always will be. Even as he cast me down, he saved me. But there's no saving you. He's not going to lift a finger. There's no hope for you, Yeshua."

"You do love to hear yourself talk, Hel'el." Michael stepped from the shadows, hand still resting on his sword. He pulled back his hood and let his black hair fall from it.

"Brother, still the soldier," Hel'el said, sneering as he rose to his full height. "Have you come to witness my victory?"

"Your victory? The battle isn't over yet, Hel'el," Michael said as he paced around Yeshua. Hel'el moved instinctively away from him, their last meeting still fresh in his mind. They had fought for the body of Moses atop Mount Nebo, and Michael had broken his perfect body in a brutal victory.

"This battle is very much over. Look at this pathetic mud creature. This is no Son of God. He has chosen poverty and let lesser men scorn him when he had the choice to rule them. Even now they ready their weapons to seize him, and he does nothing. He's no warrior. He won't even rise up off the ground and fight for himself, let alone these petty creatures he claims to love. He's not even powerful enough to see us right now. He's a false prophet like all the others."

"If he is as weak and insignificant as you claim, then why are you here? Why come to gloat over a peasant?" Michael said.

Hel'el's perfect face twisted into a snarl. "He is *nothing*. I'm here to take my revenge out on this pretender."

"He has sent many of your demons back to you, hasn't he? I suppose they are scared."

"They're lesser creatures and not very hard to scare away," Hel'el said dismissively. "This one has claimed to be something he's not. He said he would destroy me, and I'm here to witness how very wrong he was. He is nothing. A useless creation by a useless God who—"

"Enough," said Yeshua softly. He rose to his feet and looked at Hel'el, his face calm but brimming with anger. "Leave my presence, Hel'el. I'm weary of you."

"Look for me on the morrow, *Mashiach*," Hel'el said, scoffing. "I'll be there when—"

"I said go," Yeshua commanded, and Hel'el vanished. Those burning eyes of anger turned to Michael. He dropped to one knee.

"You can see us?" he asked without raising his head.

"I always see Hel'el when he comes. I expected him tonight, not you, Michael." A hand rested gently on Michael's hair, and he dared to raise his eyes. "Has Elyon changed his mind?"

"No," Michael said. "Elyon won't allow us to interfere. He has turned a deaf ear to our petitions. I have come to…bear witness. I didn't want you to think you were alone."

"So be it," Yeshua said and helped Michael to his feet. "The spirit is willing, but I'm so tired, Michael. I'm not afraid of the pain but of when I'm cut off from grace, as I know that I must be."

"If I could change this, you know that I would. I would draw my sword, and I would…"

"Shhh. No, Michael. It must be this way. They are coming," Yeshua said as angry voices echoed through the trees moving toward them. His brown eyes filled with love and sadness as they looked at him, and Michael's spirit broke inside of him. "Your presence gives me comfort and strength. Will you stay with me?"

"Until the end of all there is or ever will be," Michael promised.

Yeshua smiled softly as men swarmed the clearing. Michael watched in fury as Yehudah kissed him. Yeshua received it calmly; he knew it would happen, but it didn't make the betrayal sting less. In the squabble, a follower managed to hastily swipe off a guard's ear, leaving him screaming and clutching his head.

"Put your sword away!" Yeshua said. "If you live through the strength of your sword, you will also die by it. Do you think if that was the answer that I could not call down twelve legions of the mightiest angels to defend me? If I did, then how would the scriptures be fulfilled?"

He looked up at Michael and shook his head. It took all of Michael's strength to sheathe his sword. Yeshua knelt by the terrified, wounded man and touched his wound lightly. His ear healed instantly, whole and perfect.

The guard scrambled back from Yeshua, weeping and afraid. Yeshua's disciples had run off through the grove to hide. *Cowards.* Michael watched the guards place a bag over Yeshua's head and drag him away through the trees.

"I hope you enjoy watching what happens next," Hel'el said as he reappeared in the glade. "You know it isn't too late to change to the winning side, Michael. I could use a decent warrior to lead my demon army."

"You haven't won yet," Michael said, trying to keep the emotion out of his voice. "I wouldn't be too quick to celebrate if I were you."

"If he really were the Son, Elyon would have stepped in and saved him by now. I don't see anyone rushing to this dirty carpenter's side. Elyon is the absent, disapproving Father to this world of unloved bastards, as per usual."

"I only see one bastard here," Michael replied. "Go gloat somewhere else, or I'll beat you as I did on Mount Nebo."

"Sure, bring up Mount Nebo by all means. You can hardly think I was going to spend all my energy wrangling over the body of that stuttering old fool. Another fine example of how Elyon treats his favorites. Moses had to tolerate forty years of squabbling idiots only to die before he got rewarded for it. I only wanted his body because you were so intent on not letting me have it."

"Your memory is as selective as ever, Hel'el." Michael folded his arms to keep from hitting his perfect face. "I seem to recall great speeches of how you would raise up a great temple to honor the savior of the Hebrews with an elaborate tomb where people could come and worship."

"I was merely trying to honor him in a way that was fitting for a man who had sacrificed so much for a selfish God. I was only doing the thing Elyon refused to do, and that is to honor his children."

"If you had known anything about Moses, you would know that being honored by men meant less than the dirt on his feet. Go away, Hel'el. Your company is burdensome."

"And you're as tedious as you have always been. You are the perfect soldier, because you are too boring to have any thoughts of your own. I can't believe the whore daughter of Enoch could find you—" Michael's hand whipped out, knocking the words from Hel'el's mouth. He stumbled backward in surprise, the blood from his lip dropping on his perfect white tunic.

He smiled a bloody smile. "Oh, I forgot that she's your tender spot. Ha! It matters not. I have an execution to oversee, and as I said, you bore me." He vanished, and Michael unclenched his shaking fists. He knew Hel'el would bring up Na'amah; he always did, and yet Michael reacted every time.

It was a night that he needed to be a calm, strong presence as Yeshua underwent his great sacrifice; he could not be this trembling, furiously angry, desperate creature. He felt like every nerve in his body was stretched out and on fire. He had meant it when he had said if he could stop this night from happening, he would. *Elyon could find another way.* He recoiled at the thought. He knew this was the *only* way to save them. If not this, then Elyon would destroy it all.

It had been Yeshua's promise that had stayed Elyon's hand from destroying mankind once more. Instead of destruction, he would go himself to try to guide them back, to bring new life and new hope.

Michael knew where he would find Yeshua. Caiaphas's schemes and ego had brought this about. It was Temple coin that was chinking in Yehudah's pockets. Michael was torn between pitying the man and wanting to drive his sword through him.

Calm down, Michael, he tried to tell himself. But there would be no soothing himself in the next few days. He would be riddled with fury, but he had to be there for Yeshua and also for Miriam. She knew it would end, but she was his mother first. It would not be the Son of Elyon that she watched being murdered, but her dirty, mischievous boy who ran through the streets of Alexandria.

On the third day of his vigil at Yeshua's side, Michael felt Hel'el's presence drawing near. His hand gripped his sword as the Fallen One appeared laughing hysterically.

"Didn't I tell you, Michael?" Hel'el grinned as he leaned against Yeshua's wooden cross. "So much for all the power he was meant to have. Are you going to let me have this body, or will you fight me for it like Moses's? You don't need to worry about me building a temple for this false *Mashiach*. I'm hoping they will drag the body through the streets behind a horse—" Michael launched himself at Hel'el, the grief of the preceding days overwhelming him. He had his hands around Hel'el's neck when he heard a wheeze above him.

"Yeshua?" Michael climbed off Hel'el. As he approached to touch his master's foot, he was flung backward. Elyon would not let him comfort Yeshua even in his final moments.

Michael shuddered as he felt Elyon turn away from them, and at that moment, Michael felt what it was to be completely cut off from grace. He gasped, sinking to his knees as he caught the look of utter pain and abandonment in Yeshua's brown eyes. His lungs heaved in and out, desperate to take his final breaths.

"*Eloi!*" he shouted to the sky. "*Eloi! Lema sabachthani?*"

Hel'el approached him with a look of cold fury in his eyes. "How does it *feel* to be the one abandoned? You're experiencing but a moment of what I'm doomed to suffer for all eternity."

Michael sat on the ground, head in his hands as he watched Yeshua take one final breath, then his body went slack. The triumph on Hel'el's lips halted as a powerful tremble moved through the earth at their feet.

All of Jerusalem shook as lightning cracked overhead. Michael stood up, sword out and ready to protect Yeshua's body from whatever attack Hel'el would summon. But it was not Hel'el causing the earthquake. He wasn't laughing now, and instinctively, Michael stepped back from him.

"I don't understand—" Hel'el began to say before he started to scream. Light was ripping through him, breaking through his skin like he was burning from the inside out.

Michael felt Elyon's presence rush back through and around him. It encircled Hel'el as the power that he had stolen from Adam so long ago was pulled out of him, returning to the Source of All Things. As all of Jerusalem shook and crumbled, Michael smiled.

47

MYCHAL WATCHED AS AZAZEL hesitated, looking from Hel'el and back to them.

"Azazel, leave him now," Gabriel urged. "Put aside your hatred and join us. Save yourself from his fate."

Azazel's mouth worked as if he had swallowed something bitter, and he sprang toward Jael, ax whirling. Jael dodged the blow, shifting slightly to the right as Uriel pulled her out of the way. Hel'el's cries of laughter echoed around them, and the demons screamed and rushed toward them like a thick tide of putrid mess.

Mychal cut down the nearest three demons with his swords, stepping quickly over their corpses to try to reach Hel'el before he disappeared again. There was a shout behind him, and he ducked, narrowly escaping bone claws that reached for him. Uriel took off the creature's head in one blow.

"We have your back, Mychal," Uriel shouted over the noise. "Be careful! Hel'el wants you to follow him." Mychal shot a look behind him at Jael. She was humming with silvery light, and she calmly held out her hands to any demon who got close. The ones unlucky enough to touch her seemed to burst from the inside.

"She's fine. Focus on staying alive," Uriel commanded.

Mychal charged forward, trying not to get shoved sideways in the crush as he struggled to regain his footing on the bloody ground. The sun was rising now, and he sensed a shudder as it passed through the demons. They were creatures born in the dark, and while the light didn't harm them, they didn't like it.

Through the rotting skin and snarling mouths, Mychal caught a glimmer of white and gold, and he fought his way toward it. A massive oozing beast covered in a thousand eyes and mouths blocked his path. Mychal attacked, but the creature was faster than expected. Its sucking hands locked down on Mychal's forearms and lifted him off his feet. The hungry mouths bit deep into him and pain raced up his arms. Mychal swung, brought his legs up, and kicked the creature hard in the chest, using its slippery weight to knock it off-balance. The momentum caused the creature to drop him to the ground.

Through the stamping feet, Mychal found his dropped sword and swung out, driving it in deep as the creature fell on him. It sunk like a skewered slug, dripping a gelatinous mess on him. Thousands of eyes and mouths registered their pain and surprise as the body collapsed on him.

"Gabriel!" Mychal shouted. As he tried to budge the weight, Gabriel's golden head appeared above him. "I can't move it!"

Gabriel grimaced as he got a grip on the sticky corpse and pushed it off him. Mychal gasped as air filled his crushed lungs. At least one rib was broken, but he had no time to worry about it.

"I'm going to be smelling that on my hands for a week," Gabriel said, complaining as he wiped them on the back of Mychal's shirt. All down his front, Mychal was soaked like he had been run over by a giant snail. Gabriel started laughing.

"Shut up," Mychal said as he took his guns out of their holsters. His swords were lost in the oozing mass of eyes and mouths; he would have to dig through it and retrieve them after if the blessings on the blades didn't eat through the flesh. "I need to find Hel'el."

Through the fighting, he spotted Azazel swinging his ax in a sloppy, berserker fashion at Uriel. He was too angry to fight with precision, and Uriel was moving easily out of the way of his blows.

The demon ranks seemed to fill as quickly as they cut them down. Mychal ignored the pain that started to spread through him, giving himself wholly over to his angel side. He fought his way to Uriel to try to protect him from other attacks. Uriel's sword was knocked from his hand, the force of Azazel's blow knocking him over.

"Uriel, catch!" Mychal threw his spear as Azazel charged. Uriel caught it and braced himself behind it. Azazel's eyes went wide as he realized his error too late. His momentum carried him forward, and the sharp tip of the spear pierced through his armor and out his back. Uriel let go of the spear, and Azazel dropped to the ground.

"You should have listened to us," Uriel said sadly. "You could have stopped this from happening."

"No." Azazel spat flecks of blood. "No more…prison. Not in the dark again." His head lolled, and Uriel pulled the spear from his body.

"Mychal!" Hel'el's voice boomed around the battlefield. The demons stopped fighting, lowering their weapons. They moved out of the way, so nothing stood between Mychal and Hel'el. Hel'el had taken off his armor and stood in only his leather trousers and boots, the sword in his hand like a shard of carved obsidian.

"Come forward, little pet. Come and let us settle this."

Mychal peeled off his shirt, heavy with demon goo. Gabriel stepped forward and gave him one of his swords that he must have retrieved from under the demon remains.

"You don't have to do this," Gabriel said as Mychal took the blade. "Azazel is dead. It's over."

"No, it's not. Don't worry. I have beaten him more times than I care to remember." Mychal grinned.

"Not as a human!" said Gabriel.

"Brother," Mychal said softly. "I know you care about my well-being, but it must be this way. Every lifetime must be sealed in blood. Free will is a bitch, I know, but this is *my* life and *my* choice."

Gabriel nodded, but his eyes were full of anguish. Mychal looked at his brothers. "Make sure my body doesn't get taken by a demon. Get Jael out, no matter what happens. Don't let her be taken."

"I promise."

Mychal looked over at the blood-splattered exorcist. "Jael, look after Uriel."

"Always," she said with a smile. "Go kick some ass."

Hel'el was waiting for him, his bare skin glowing softly. Mychal wondered why he bothered with the pretense of holding his glamour. "I didn't think you would be brave enough to face me on your own."

"I didn't think you would be stupid enough to challenge me, but here we are."

"Last chance, Mychal. If you bow to me, I can give Aleksandra back to you. Or you can fight and die."

"You can't give her to me. I saw the day that you were crushed. I remember. You have nothing left but your bluff."

"As you wish. I'll kill you now, and you can go back to him. Tell him I'll never stop trying to undo this world and all that he holds precious—"

"Oh, shut up," Mychal said as he raised his sword and attacked.

Hel'el narrowly blocked him, the edge of Mychal's blade cutting his cheek. Hel'el shoved him back, returning his attack with reckless ferocity.

Mychal twisted, ducked, and sidestepped as Hel'el rained down swift blows on him, each one jarring his arms. Mychal ducked and aimed a low kick, hitting Hel'el's kneecap. He spun out of the way as Mychal brought his sword up quickly.

If it weren't for training against Uriel, he wouldn't have been able to keep up as Hel'el moved around him in a swift, deadly dance. Mychal tried to remember more of Hel'el's style from their previous battles, but he had to keep focused on the fight. Hel'el's blade nicked him in the shoulder, and he bit back a cry of pain.

"Look how the little human leaks," Hel'el said with a sneer. Mychal's vision swam, and he struggled to stay on his feet.

"You...poisoned your blade?"

"Why? Are you feeling woozy?" Hel'el swung his sword at him, and Mychal stumbled backward, blocking him and sending him to the right. The ground heaved, and Hel'el dashed past him. Pain shot through Mychal's back as his blade sliced it open. He heard Jael shouting but couldn't make out the words as he fell over onto the dusty white earth.

Hel'el's triumphant face loomed over him. "Even though you're a human, I'm disappointed. I thought you would have lasted much longer than this."

"Should've known…you would cheat," Mychal said, his chest heaving as the poison spread through him and paralysis spread from the wounds and down through his chest. "You can't…win… It's over, Hel'el."

"I'll say when it is over," Hel'el said, spitting. "I'll rise up and rule this world again. It's only a matter of time before the humans give their birthright up to me once more. You have failed again, Mychal. I hope he is disgusted with you."

Hel'el's black blade came down, driving into Mychal's chest. Mychal couldn't feel anything anymore. He could see his brothers shoving and arguing. Uriel was shouting something as he held a furious, struggling Jael back, and the demons moved in around them.

Mychal felt the blood coming from his mouth, and Hel'el's gloating, hissing laughter filled his ears. Then time stopped, and all sound vanished.

Someone was walking toward them through the frozen battlefield. Mychal's lips tried to form the name, but none would come. He was exactly how he remembered him, brown eyes burning, the sun shining behind him. He knelt down next to Mychal and placed a hand on his forehead.

"Don't be afraid, my Mychal," Yeshua said as pain and light shot through his body. Yeshua stood as heat roared through Mychal. His skin started to flake off like white ash, and his human body fell away. There was a roaring in his ears as his mind and soul came into fullness. Great wings tore out of his back and unfurled on the ground around him. Yeshua pulled Hel'el's sword out of Mychal's chest and tossed it aside.

"Now get up, Mychal! Get up!" he shouted, and time exploded back around them. Mychal surged upward, grabbed Hel'el, and tackled him to the ground.

"How?" Hel'el tried to speak as Mychal hit him hard in the face. Hel'el's fists came up, pummeling him in the ribs. Mychal rolled off him and onto his feet. Hel'el's face was bloody as he stood to face him.

"Still the fucking pet. It's the only explanation." Hel'el spat blood on the sand. "At least now you might present a challenge."

Mychal flew at him, and they tumbled together, punching and kicking in a flurry of arms and legs. Mychal picked Hel'el up by the waist of his pants and slammed him hard into the earth, the ground shaking around them from the impact.

The demons scurried and fled as Hel'el was picked up again and thrown at the great statue. He hit it hard. Mychal caught him and drove him back into the dirt.

Hel'el's glamour had fallen away now. Stretches of his white flesh were blackened and twisted from the corruption that had eaten away at him. Mychal hit him hard in the face over and over until Hel'el's defiance vanished. Mychal stood up and caught the shining spear that Uriel threw toward him.

"Do it," Hel'el said through his broken mouth. Mychal shouted and drove his spear down. Hel'el opened his swollen eyes and saw it buried in the earth a hair's breadth from his face. Mychal's trembling hands still gripped it tightly. "Why? *Do* it, you fucking coward! Just kill me!"

"I want to kill you with all that is in me," Mychal said, voice choked with emotion. "But *he* wouldn't want that."

"Please. He doesn't know what he wants. Look at all I have done, and he still allows it, allows me to live while I fuck with creation. He is weak to let me live!"

"It is love, not weakness, that stops his hand." Mychal took Hel'el's ruined face in his hands. "Do you not see it? Do you not understand why he keeps me from killing you, even at this moment? He *loves* you, Hel'el. Even though Semyaza and Azazel were deceived and led astray by you, their hearts sought atonement for what they did."

"It didn't stop them from dying!"

"No, but they died so they could go home. They are no longer angels, but they are with Elyon once more. He *endures* you because he wants you to do the same. Let your pride go, brother; apologize, atone, and then you may go home."

There was a softening in Hel'el's eyes, a deep longing and shame, but then they clouded over in rage.

"I will *never* apologize! He did this! He threw me down and made me as I am. I'm still a pawn in his great game. If you will not kill me, then get out of my way! I will *never* stop fighting to show how he lies!"

"Everything that has befallen you, Hel'el, is of your own doing. He has been trying to teach you something by letting you live. You're keeping yourself in this broken misery, far away from his grace. I pity you." Mychal let him go and stepped off him. Hel'el got to his feet angrily.

"You should've killed me. The next time you are made human, I'll find her, and I will destroy her. I will turn her into one of my servants, and you...you will have to watch as I trap her spirit. Go and tell your precious Yeshua that you were too weak to save her, you let me kill her—"

"Tell him yourself, Hel'el. He's here," Mychal said. Hel'el looked around, his face filled with fear. Yeshua was standing calmly beside Jael. He had been watching the whole time.

"I hate you!" Hel'el broke down sobbing with fury. "I *hate* you! I will hate you until the end of all things. I will hate you until Elyon finally destroys this world and whatever happens afterward."

Yeshua's face was full of sadness and pity. "I love you, Hel'el. Come home."

Hel'el stumbled backward like he had been struck; a sound of primal grief tore out of him, and he vanished.

48

I DIDN'T KNOW WHERE to look: to the freshly minted archangel in front of me or the God beside me. There was no sign of the demons except for the mess that covered the ground from when we had fought them. I felt every ache and bruise, but I was determined to keep myself upright. Now wasn't the time to swoon.

"Is it over?" I asked.

"Yes, for now," Mychal answered, his voice deeper than when he'd been a human. I'd always thought Uriel was massive, but Mychal was something else altogether.

"I'm going to be smelling like dead demons for a year," I said, looking at the bloody mess that covered my clothes. I was beginning to forget what it was like to go a whole day without getting covered in demon.

"Lots of soap, perhaps," Yeshua said, and I found myself choking on surprised laughter.

"Going to need more than soap. What now?" I asked.

"Mychal?" Yeshua turned to him. "What do you think?"

"I want to go home, wherever that is now," he said, but his face was sad.

"Home sounds perfect. I want hot water and a beer and my dog," I added. "That is if you no longer need me?" I looked up at Yeshua, half expecting to faint at any second. The last few weeks had made a visit from Yeshua seem standard. Alessandro was right; how could I ever go back to a normal life after all of this?

Even my version of normal. I needed to talk to him about Uriel, but I wasn't going to do it in the middle of a battlefield.

"You did well, Jael. I told you not to doubt your own abilities," Yeshua said. Uriel mussed my hair. "I trained her well."

"You wish." I shoved off his hand, poking him viciously even as he picked me up and enveloped me in a bear hug. "Don't make me fight you, Feathers."

"Stop calling me that, or you'll pay, little exorcist," Uriel replied, holding on to me.

"If you don't put me down, I'll lick your face!" I squirmed, poking my tongue out as he dodged me.

"Don't be gross, Jael." Uriel laughed. I wanted to kiss him just out of relief, but when I looked into his stormy eyes, I saw he felt the same and it was enough. I realized, probably too late, that the others were waiting for us. Yeshua had an affectionate smile on his face as he watched us playing around, so I figured he knew exactly how I felt about Uriel.

"Okay, okay, I'm sorry. Put me down." I wriggled until Uriel dropped me. "This has been fun, guys, but if you could send me home, I'd appreciate it." I still held his hand, trying to communicate that I was going to need him to help me get over this craziness and to not stay away from me too long. He gave my hand a gentle squeeze.

"I'll help you all get home. Are you ready, Mychal?" Yeshua asked, and the big archangel nodded. It could have been exhaustion, but I *swear* Gabriel and Yeshua were sharing a private joke on Mychal's behalf as their eyes relayed messages. I didn't have time to think about it as Yeshua took my face in his hands and pressed a kiss to my grubby forehead. "Thank you, Jael."

"No prob—" I said, and as the air and darkness rushed around me, my hand finally lost its grip on Uriel.

Gabriel stood next to Yeshua, watching the new sunrise.

"Do you think that was a good idea? Uriel is going to be mad," said Gabriel.

"He'll get over it when he realizes the benefits," Yeshua replied.

"Did you see Mychal's face? It's like he doesn't think you know what home is for him," Gabriel said, trying to hold back the bubble of laughter rising up inside of him.

EPILOGUE

I CAME TO ON the triangle rooftop of my apartment building, and surprisingly, I was demon goo free. *I knew I liked that guy for a reason.* I muttered something incoherent as I rolled onto my side, smacking into someone beside me. It was a woman. She had thick, curly, dark hair blowing around her sleeping face. She was gorgeous even while unconscious, but I had no idea who she was.

"What the—" I sat up and spotted Mychal sprawled out not far from me. I crawled over and shook him. He was human again. *How?* "Hey, dude. Wake up." He opened his black eyes, and they zeroed in on the woman.

"Do you know who she is? I just woke up and found—"

Mychal just about knocked me over as he scrambled to her side, lifting her with a gentleness I'd never seen in him before. "Aleksandra?"

Holy crap. I gaped as she opened her blue eyes and gave him a smile that was so sweet tears pricked my eyes.

"What happened? Where are we?" Aleksandra asked as he scooped her up into his lap.

"We are in Australia, I think," said Mychal, and I gave him a nod in confirmation. "I need to tell you about Katya…"

Aleksandra held him tighter. "You don't have to, Mychal. I remember. I remember *everything*. Our lives together…all of it. Tell me what happened since I died?"

"Oh my love, do I have a story to tell you."

"I can see that." Aleksandra touched his face gently. "Kiss me first?" Mychal laughed, a genuinely delighted sound I'd never heard out of him before and did as he was told.

"Come downstairs when you've finished smooching, guys," I said and stretched my aching body. I was opening the roof access door when I spotted a gleam of silver in the corner of my eye. Slumped on his side at the edge of the roof was a bulk I would know anywhere. Panic coursed through me as I ran over to him.

"Uriel? Are you okay?" I rolled him over. He was dressed in regular clothes, his silver hair loose and snarled around him. "Hey, wake up, or I'll kick your ass!" Uriel opened his stormy eyes, and I let him go with a jerk, scurrying backward before landing hard on my butt.

"Jael?" I heard Mychal behind me. "What's wrong—" He stared hard at Uriel and then burst into riotous laughter.

"Shut up, Mychal," Uriel hissed as he sat up slowly. "Don't make me teach you your place again." Uriel's face clouded with confusion as he stared at us. His expression cleared as he finally realized.

He was human.

"Oh, you'd have a much harder time of it now, little brother," Mychal said. "Looks like Yeshua has some fun in store for us to make us both human again. What do you think, Jael?"

I couldn't respond. I could barely breathe as I stared at Uriel. Maybe this was my reward for all the heartbreaking, awful shit I had gone through since the night I did Max's exorcism all those weeks ago.

"Say something," Uriel begged. His eyes locked on mine and made me feel like I was the only person on the planet. I launched off the concrete into his arms, and I kissed him.

"That explains so much," Mychal said behind me, but I didn't turn to look at him. My hands were in Uriel's beautiful silver hair, and his arms were around me. The squishy complete feeling was back.

"What are we going to do now, *yadid*?" Uriel asked, resting his forehead against mine. My head was filled with lists of calls I had to make, the loved ones I had to see, and what I was going to say to explain the three new people in my life… I told it all to shut up.

I looked up at Uriel, full of love and mad hope. "Everything."

ABOUT THE AUTHOR

Amy Kuivalainen is the bestselling author of the Magicians of Venice series (*The Immortal City, The Sea of the Dead, The King's Seal*) and the Firebird Faerie Tales (*Cry of the Firebird, Ashes of the Firebird, Rise of the Firebird*).

A Finnish-Australian writer who is obsessed with magical wardrobes, doors, auroras, and burial mounds that might offer her a way into another realm, she enjoys mashing up mythology and lore into unique retellings about monsters and magic.

Milton Keynes UK
Ingram Content Group UK Ltd.
UKHW012150270923
429475UK00004B/186

9 781643 973531